Anne Baker trained as a nurse at Birkenhead General Hospital, but after her marriage went to live first in Libya and then Nigeria. She eventually returned to her native Birkenhead where she worked as a Health Visitor for over ten years. She now lives with her husband in Merseyside. Anne Baker's other Merseyside sagas are all available from Headline and have been widely praised:

'A stirring tale of romance and passion, poverty and ambition' *Liverpool Echo*

'Highly observant writing style . . . a compelling book that you just don't want to put down' *Southport Visiter*

'A gentle tale with all the right ingredients for a heartwarming novel' *Huddersfield Daily Examiner*

'A delighful tale of love and family' *Woman's Realm*

'A truly compelling and sentimental story and rich in language and descriptive prose' *Newcastle Upon Tyne Evening Chronicle*

ECHOES ACROSS THE MERSEY

Anne Baker

headline

First published in 2000
by HEADLINE BOOK PUBLISHING
First published in paperback in 2001
by HEADLINE BOOK PUBLISHING

1

ISBN 978 0 7472 6437 8

Typeset by Palimpsest Book Production Limited,
Polmont, Stirlingshire
Printed and bound in Great Britain by
Mackays of Chatham plc, Chatham, Kent

HEADLINE PUBLISHING GROUP
A division of Hodder Headline
338 Euston Road
London NW1 3BH
www.headline.co.uk
www.hodderheadline.com

ECHOES ACROSS THE MERSEY

Chapter One

It was August Bank Holiday Monday. Maria Hoxton lay on her bed rubbing at her stomach, trying to move the ball of fear she could feel building up there. All England was frightened that war was imminent, but Maria's fear was for her eighteen-year-old daughter Sarah and their whole way of life.

She could hear Sarah in the next room humming to herself as she made drop scones in the frying pan. Wonderful scents were coming under the ill-fitting door.

Maria felt she was about to lose the contentment she'd had to fight for. Not everyone would want to keep the status quo when it meant both of them working long hours in a pickle factory, but with two wages coming in they had enough to rent two decent rooms and eat three meals a day.

Not everyone would see these rooms as comfortable, but they were the best she'd lived in for many years. They were in an old six-storey building on a busy main road. An undertaker had his office on the ground floor and the rest of the building was let out in separate rooms. There was one shared malodorous lavatory in the back yard. In the mornings, the tenants could be seen waiting their turn with pieces of newspaper in their hands. She and Sarah had to get up early to avoid that.

Maria's home was two large attics up on the top floor. Low ceilings perhaps, but nobody else came up that last flight of bare stairs. They had two dormer windows that opened

1

high above the fetid air of the yard at the back; and two more windows to the front. These overlooked the busy road, with views across the docks to the river. They had light and fresh air, and once the door was closed on the world, they had peace.

Maria valued personal peace. In this world, contentment meant more than happiness, though Sarah wouldn't accept that.

Sarah's head came round the door. The sunlight behind her lit up her blonde hair into a halo of spun gold. Probably all mothers found their daughters attractive, but Maria felt her eyes continually drawn to Sarah's face. She couldn't believe how pretty she'd grown.

'I'm making a pot of tea, Mam. Do you feel like getting up, or shall I bring it in here?'

'I'll get up. I shouldn't spend my holiday lying down.'

It was a struggle to get off the bed. Was she ill, or was this how one was meant to feel in the menopause? Or was forty-three too young for that? Maria sighed as she bent for her slippers. Today she felt ninety; it was probably just the life she'd led and the hard physical work she had to do.

She picked up her comb. Her reflection stared back at her from the spotted mirror balanced on top of the orange box. She'd covered the box with a red cloth to serve as their dressing table until she could pick up something better. Her hair was pale brown, so the grey didn't show much. In her youth she'd been much fairer, but never golden-blonde like Sarah. She patted her bun; it still felt firm. Not worth the trouble of remaking it now.

Sarah was at the living room window. The Mersey looked as blue as the Mediterranean from here, and against the deep blue sky Maria could see swirling white seagulls.

Sarah said: 'It's a shame to stay indoors today. Would you like a little walk afterwards?'

Maria didn't feel she had the energy. 'Why don't you run downstairs and see if John will go with you?'

'I thought perhaps you . . .'

At the window, Maria looked down six floors to the street. The sun didn't reach down there.

'You always do that.' Sarah turned on her. 'Look down at the pavement. As though you're expecting somebody to come looking for us.'

That stung. Sarah had teased her about the habit before, and she was near the truth. Maria was about to deny it, but there was a man studying their building. He'd been looking up at their windows.

Her voice was sharp: 'Who's that?'

They were looking down on broad shoulders and a head of light brown hair that was a mass of crinkly waves.

Sarah gave a little chirrup of joy. 'I do believe . . . It's Toby Percival.'

Maria knew she was showing the consternation she felt.

'He shouldn't come here!'

They both worked at Percival's. Toby was the owner's eldest son. As they watched, he crossed the road to the front door.

'He's not coming in? To see you?'

Sarah gulped. 'It looks like it.'

'You shouldn't let him.' Then she had another thought. 'You didn't invite him?' Sarah had the place spotless and she'd made scones.

'No, Mam! Of course not!'

That must be the truth; the surprise and the thrill of seeing him unexpectedly was clear on Sarah's face. She rushed to open the door to him as he came up the last flight of stairs.

'Come in,' she choked, hardly able to get the words out.

Maria trembled as he did so, looking round at the worn lino, cheap furniture and faded curtains. He couldn't help but notice the poverty of their home; his own would be very different.

She ought to tell him straight that she didn't want him keeping company with her daughter. That he was pushing out John Ferry, with whom Sarah would be far more likely to find happiness. Instead, Maria rushed to get another cup and saucer from their cupboard to welcome him with tea.

Toby was twenty years old, tall and well built, but his innocent baby face made him seem much younger. Maria was afraid of what he was doing to them, but like everybody else she ended up mothering him. He looked attractive and unthreatening, vulnerable even.

He was very different from his father, who had a strong-jawed, serious face and a dour expression. He ran the factory with a rod of iron and treated his employees as a class apart; they all feared him. Whereas Toby was well liked and the workers hid his failures and misdemeanours from his father.

Mr Percival would be very much against Toby having anything to do with Sarah. There could be no future for them, and Maria was afraid she'd be hurt. And worse, they needed their jobs in order to survive.

It seemed strange to see Toby sitting in their old basket chair, talking of war like everybody else.

'No longer any hope of peace, I'm afraid. Germany declared war on Russia on Saturday. Yesterday she invaded Belgium and declared war on France.'

Maria was spreading butter on Sarah's scones.

'The newspapers say there's no avoiding it,' Toby went on. 'England has issued an ultimatum to Germany and it's unlikely Germany will back down. Half Europe will be at war by eleven tonight.'

'We've had wars before.' Sarah was pouring out the tea.

Maria saw him look at her daughter with such love in his eyes. He said gently: 'This time it's different. It'll not be a skirmish in some distant part of the Empire. We'll be fighting the Kaiser and the might of Germany.'

Maria said: 'Your father's worried? For the business, I mean.'

'Yes, very. Aren't we all?'

She thought Toby wasn't the sort to worry about anything.

4

Later, when he stood up to go, he asked Sarah to walk with him to the Pier Head to catch the ferry. Then he turned to Maria to ask:

'Is that all right?'

She would have liked to say no, but working for the Percivals had trained her over the years to deny them nothing. And with such delight showing on Sarah's face at the prospect, how could she?

Yet Maria was filled with dread. She was very fearful that Sarah would be hurt by this, and that the affair might cost them their jobs and ruin everything they had.

Sarah Hoxton knew nothing would ever be the same again. It felt like walking on air to be matching her steps to Toby Percival's and holding on to his arm. She'd no sooner mentioned how disappointed she'd been that Mam hadn't felt well enough to take the trip they'd planned to New Brighton than she found herself being escorted down to the ferry.

'We can go now,' he said.

There were lots of passengers on the boat even this late in the afternoon. There was an air of expectation, of excitement, and Sarah could hear fighting talk on all sides.

'I'm dying to have a go at the Kaiser.'

'Once we get our hands on him, he'll be finished. Won't take us long.'

'He's asking for a kick up the backside.'

Sarah spent more than four magical hours with Toby, walking along the promenade in the evening sunshine, a breeze off the Irish Sea fluttering at her hair. There were people everywhere, more than usual even for a bank holiday. The coming war seemed an added source of excitement. Toby held her hand and spent more time gazing into her face than looking where he was going.

He whispered: 'I can't stop thinking about you. You're the most beautiful girl in the whole of Liverpool. I love you, Sarah.'

5

After the first delightful shock, Sarah was not surprised. Ever since she'd started working at Percival's, he'd seemed to single her out. If he wanted something special done, it was always Sarah he asked. More recently he'd been making excuses to speak to her. The other girls had teased her about him.

'He's sweet on you, Sarah,' they'd laughed.

'No, it's just his way. He's friendly with everybody, isn't he? A bit of a flirt.'

'It's you he's after. Wait till his father finds out.'

To start with Sarah had been flattered but hadn't taken Toby seriously. Why should she when she already saw her future as John Ferry's wife? She'd been thrown together with John for as long as she could remember.

He worked at Percival's too, and lived with his mother on the floor below. The other room there was occupied by a bachelor they rarely saw. Elvira Ferry, John's mother, was Mam's friend; they'd supported each other through their bad times. John was seven years older than Sarah, and she'd been proud and flattered that he was interested in her.

Mam never tired of saying: 'Your best chance of happiness lies with John. If you know which way your bread's buttered you'll marry him.'

Sarah began taking Toby seriously the day a bag of pickling onions burst as she lifted it. He'd bent to help her pick them up and his arm had accidentally brushed against hers. His touch had sent fire stabbing through her, leaving her shaking with emotions that John hadn't touched. And she'd seen the same hunger flare in Toby's smouldering eyes.

After that he'd stopped to talk to her several times a day. They had long discussions, and she felt she was getting to know him. On two occasions when her mother had been off work he'd insisted on walking her home. It had put her on edge because often she walked home with John and his mother.

She'd had no quarrel with John, but his dark eyes watched

when Toby came to speak to her. He didn't like it, she knew, but John couldn't afford to show his displeasure. Toby was the boss's son, and one day he would take over the running of the company.

But John hadn't held back to Sarah. 'You're flirting with Toby Percival.' He'd been shocked the first time he'd noticed that. 'Have you changed your mind about me?'

She'd been too unsure of Toby, too ashamed of what she was doing to John to tell him she had.

'He's no good for you, Sarah. You'll get yourself in trouble.' John's face was often full of hurt now, and that stabbed at her conscience, because she knew she'd inflicted it. And Elvira was less friendly towards her mother.

The trouble now was that her mind was filled with day-dreams about Toby, visions of what might be, and to accept Toby's attentions she'd have to reject John's. She hated the thought of telling him outright, especially after four years of what he called courtship.

The more time she spent with Toby, the more she learned about him. She and Mam had believed he must have had a very happy and comfortable life, but now she knew that wasn't so.

They walked the length of the promenade and leaned against a wall where they could look out across the Irish Sea. Sarah felt Toby's arms go round her and he pulled her close.

'I want to spend the rest of my life with you, Sarah,' he whispered. 'I love you. I want us to be married. I'd love that. How about you?'

For Sarah, that changed everything.

They stayed late in New Brighton. It grew dark, but the number of people on the promenade didn't seem to lessen. When they sailed back on the ferry to the Pier Head, a crowd was gathering there. Nobody wanted to go home without knowing whether or not Britain was at war. The clock faces on the Royal Liver Building told them it had gone ten o'clock.

'The ultimatum expires at eleven,' Toby said. 'Let's wait and see what happens.'

Sarah could feel the suspense; it sparked in the air around her. She'd had a wonderful day and she wasn't ready to go home. There was nothing she wanted more than to stay out for another hour with Toby.

'I can't,' she groaned. 'Mam will be worried stiff by now, a bag of nerves. She'll think I've been snatched by white slavers or something.'

'She knows you're with me.'

'She won't see that as safe. I'll have to go home.'

It wasn't easy to push their way through the gathering crowds. Toby clung to her arm, just as reluctant to let her go as she was to leave him. He walked her home again. In the gloom behind the front door he kissed her, leaving her to climb the stairs still feeling shaky with passion. Sarah was no longer in doubt. It was Toby she loved.

She tiptoed up towards the landing on which the Ferrys lived, not wanting to see John now, but as she came up she heard a door open. She hoped it was John's neighbour who'd come out. As she rounded a bend in the stairs she could see John framed against the light.

'Hello,' he said, and she guessed from his manner that he'd seen Toby here earlier.

She didn't think of John as a handsome man. He had straight dark hair and intense eyes, a cleft in his chin and good teeth. He was strong and made muscular by the heavy lifting he had to do at work. He had a bit of a limp that he did his best to hide, the result of an accident in boyhood. He'd jumped off a tram straight into the path of an oncoming horse and cart. The limp was more pronounced when he was tired.

What was attractive was the look of transparent honesty on his face. John didn't try to hide anything from anybody; they

8

all knew that what he said was the whole truth. He'd never let anybody down.

She thought him far too intelligent to be labouring in a pickle factory, but like his mother and hers, he thought himself fortunate to have regular work which allowed them all to have full bellies and a roof over their heads. Everybody said that one day, if he were lucky, he might be promoted to foreman. He was the steady sort who would.

But Sarah knew John was ambitious and was aiming higher than that. He talked of setting up his own business one day – a manufacturing company that would work in the way Percival's did. He'd not make pickles and chutneys; he didn't want to put himself in competition. He had an excellent recipe for a bottled sauce, the sort everybody bought to give relish to poor meat.

For months she'd felt she was being torn in two. One day she decided to cling on to John; the next she felt more drawn to Toby. It was as though she didn't know her own mind.

When she was fifteen and the Picture House had opened on Lime Street, John had started taking her there on Saturday nights. He'd been so careful, spelling out very seriously his intentions and saying he didn't want to rush her into anything she might regret.

He said he knew she was too young to tie herself down and must have time to grow up first; that he'd wait for her answer for as long as it took her to make up her mind.

John was teetotal, a huge recommendation as far as Mam was concerned. Mam had married a man who was too fond of the bottle, and so, it seemed, had Elvira. That was a shared history that drew them together. Nothing would please both mothers more than that Sarah settle down with John.

When she'd turned sixteen, Sarah had made up her mind and told him she'd be happy to marry him one day. For ages she'd wanted to do just that; she'd considered herself almost engaged to him. He'd talked of giving her a ring for her nineteenth birthday, and perhaps in another year after that they could afford to marry.

John inspired trust; she knew she'd never find a more devoted man. There couldn't be a person she admired more. He told her he was saving a little every week from his wages. He wanted money behind him for two things: to marry her and to set up his own business. He was the sort who had his life already mapped out in his head.

Sarah expected they'd be married when he'd saved enough, but saw his business ideas as a pipe dream, something to visualise for the distant future; to buoy up his spirits during long years of labouring for others. Looking at their life logically, Sarah saw it as being filled with work much as it was now. They'd have to carry on working in order to survive.

The films she saw in the Picture House showed her a life that was very different. A life where young girls could have pretty dresses and a bit of fun. It made her see her lot with John as earnest and rather dull.

She was still very fond of him. Even recently, she'd had days of doubt when she thought to marry him would be the best thing to do, and certainly the safest. It would please everybody and she needn't hurt him. Until today, when Toby had said straight out that he loved her. That altered everything.

'Hello, John.'

Even in the semi-dark she could see his face working with anxiety. It made her burn with guilt. She hated what she was about to do, but it had to be done. It was only fair; he had to know there was no longer any hope for him.

Hesitantly she said: 'I've been out with Toby.'

His jaw jerked. His chin went up. 'I know, I saw him come here. It's all off then, for me?'

'Yes.' A whisper was all she could manage.

'I was afraid it might be. I suppose I should wish you well, but it's . . . It's hard.'

Sarah cringed inwardly. He was making no fuss, letting her

go more easily than she'd expected, yet his anguish was plain to see. 'I'm sorry.'

'Wouldn't be any good,' he choked. 'Not if your heart wasn't in it.'

He was gone, closing the door quietly, leaving her in the dark. Sarah felt terrible. She'd ended all that might have been with John. He couldn't have looked more hurt if she'd stuck a knife in him. She ached for him; she'd destroyed his dreams. As she stumbled up the last flight she wiped away a tear.

But for her there was Toby. In some ways he was more of a risk, but his love was more exciting. With him she'd have fun, and a very different way of life.

Her mother was waiting up for her and was cross because she'd stayed out so late.

Maria said firmly: 'You must put Toby Percival out of your mind. It's no good thinking anything will come of it.'

'You're wrong, Mam.' Toby had sought her out at home. He'd made it very plain how he felt about her.

'He's no business to come here, raising your hopes. It will all come to nothing. Far better if you put your mind to John Ferry.'

That brought another wave of guilt. She wanted to forget John Ferry now.

'I've told John it's all over. Finished.'

'What? He's a decent, God-fearing man who'll make a good husband. He's very fond of you, Sarah.'

'I know, that made it harder. I didn't want to hurt him.'

'But you have. Must have done.'

Sarah knew she had, but she loved Toby and he offered so much more than John ever could. He could lift her out of the daily grind of working in that factory. With Toby, she'd be able to live where the air was fresh; away from these close-packed streets.

Mam said a lot more in the same vein and kept on at her half the night.

★   ★   ★

By the time Toby retraced his steps to the Pier Head, the crowd had grown. The party atmosphere had increased too, helped when the public houses began to close and put their customers out on the streets. Sailors came off the ships moored in the docks to join in.

The Liverpool City Police were there to control them, many mounted on fine horses. Buskers arrived to entertain them with accordions and mouth organs, and the crowd started to sing the popular songs of the day. The all-night tea stands were doing good business. Handcarts were arriving with more refreshments as those with entrepreneurial spirit saw a captive market.

To Toby, the air seemed charged with excitement and expectancy. The crowd was waiting for Germany's reply to the British ultimatum. How the news reached them, Toby didn't know, but shortly after the deadline, word went round that Britain was at war.

Toby saw the crowd ripple and surge, wound up now to a patriotic high. He joined in the singing of 'Land of Hope and Glory' and the National Anthem, straining to make his voice heard in the swelling crowd. His throat was sore by the time he caught the ferry home, but his head swam with patriotism.

As soon as Sarah woke the next morning, Mam started again about the terrible thing she'd done to John. She got out of bed and reached for her clothes.

'Toby says he loves me.' She knew her eyes must be shining with the joy of it.

'He can say what he likes. He'll be told to drop you. His family won't think you're a suitable match. Anyway, what's he want with the likes of you? A factory hand in heavy boots and a coarse apron? And you smell of onions.'

Sarah giggled. 'So does he.'

'Not all the time he doesn't.'

Sarah ran a comb through her thick hair. It reached halfway

to her waist and had to be twisted into a bun on top of her head and covered with a cap at work.

'He thinks I'm beautiful.'

'And so you are.' Mam's eyes were watching her with affection as well as sorrow. 'Far too beautiful, with your golden eyes and golden curls. You'll never be short of followers.'

'Toby says my eyes are amber. And my hair's blonde.'

Sarah knew there was more to the attraction than looks. She felt drawn to Toby; he'd shared with her his worries and his hopes. He'd told her about his home life, all the domestic details the workers were curious about but couldn't know; about Maurice Percival's home and how he and his family lived.

Toby's mother had died in childbirth when he was nine and his brother Edward was four. They'd adored her, but now they had a stepmother who was only nice to them when their father was within earshot. And their father was impossible to please. He always sided with his wife.

'Toby says he envies me the love and stability I have in my life.' Sarah thought his early life had left him mixed up and insecure.

'Envies you? I bet he's never gone hungry. And even if he works here in the slums, he doesn't have to live here. I envy him the chances he's had.'

'I've never gone hungry either,' Sarah retorted. 'We haven't much money but you manage it well. And the rooms are always comfortable and clean.'

It was only when Mam couldn't eat her breakfast of porridge that Sarah asked: 'How are you feeling this morning?'

'Not too bad.'

'You don't look well.'

Once her mother had been pretty, but the years had faded her looks. This morning her face was paper white.

'Perhaps you should stay home today.'

'I'll be all right.'

It didn't stop Mam carrying on. 'You gadding about with Toby Percival could get us into trouble.'

'I thought you liked him.'

'What's it matter whether I like him or not? His father won't see us as the right class. We could be sacked. That's one way he can make sure Toby sees no more of you. It scares me to think of it.'

It was time to leave for work before Sarah was quite ready. She hurried her mother through the back streets in the pale sun of early morning, feeling hampered by her long full skirts.

The streets were always busy. Trams clanked past throughout the day and for half the night. Great wagonloads of goods headed to and from the docks. They lived only a few yards from the overhead railway, and trains thundered through at regular intervals.

They could also hear the shunting in Wapping Goods Station, which was just across the road from Wapping Dock. The smuts and the steam didn't quite cover the oily smell of the river, but there were many other smells in this area of warehouses, foundries, breweries, timber yards and engine works.

Sarah neatly avoided a drunk stretched out asleep on the pavement, a stone's throw from a public house. The factory was on the next corner, a big rambling place with few windows.

Once inside, Sarah could hardly breathe. The scents of allspice and cloves, ginger and boiling malt vinegar hung like a thick haze in the air. The back room was redolent with the smell of countless onions that had been peeled there over the years; an assault on her nose to which she'd never grown accustomed.

Inside, it was dark after the morning sun. A gas lamp showed the huge mound of shallots tipped in the corner. Dimly seen figures tended the clanking machines and shouted to each other about the war that had been declared last night.

For Sarah, the thrill of knowing Toby Percival loved her eclipsed the horror of the war and the embarrassment she felt at dropping John. Now she was fully awake, she tingled all over with anticipation for the future, and her eyes were darting round seeking a glimpse of Toby.

He worked here, but he didn't have to sit by the same conveyor belt all day with a knife at the ready, watching for shallots that had missed having their brown skins removed, or needed their ends trimming. The machine that peeled them didn't do a thorough job, so two nimble-fingered women sat each side of the conveyor belt, shoulder to shoulder, their knives flying over the onions.

This had been Sarah's job all week, to watch for those onions that had been missed, to be ready to complete the job and send them on their way to the salting room.

Chapter Two

For Maurice Percival, owner of Percival's pickle factory, the day had to start with a good breakfast. His heavy build and growing paunch were evidence of his belief that nobody could work well on an empty stomach. Today, because he was plagued with worries – about Toby and about the war – he'd eaten more than usual; porridge, a bloater and now bacon and kidneys.

'I wish I knew how this war will affect the business,' he agonised to Claudia, his second wife, who was toying with a lightly boiled egg.

'Not much, I hope.'

'I need spices from India, a plentiful supply. I'm afraid if the Germans start sinking our shipping . . . If our supplies dry up, there'll be big problems.'

'Can't you get your spices from somewhere else?'

'Where else do they come from?' he barked irritably. 'They don't grow in England.'

The uncomfortable silence drove it home to him that he'd snapped too hard. Especially now Claudia was expecting again. He ought to treat her gently while she was in this condition, though to be honest, as far as he was concerned, another child would be another worry. Adam, his four-year-old son, let out a pent-up sob, shaming him further.

'All right, love.' Claudia turned to her child immediately, stroking his brown curls in a motherly fashion. He didn't like to see her lavish more attention on the boy than she did on him. 'It's all right, Adam. Papa's worried, that's all.'

'More tea,' Maurice demanded, handing over his cup. With a forced smile Claudia refilled it.

She was thirty-two, with a round plump face and fresh firm skin. Her eyes were bright blue but small in size, and if she smiled they could almost disappear into her fleshy cheeks, but she was not unattractive. She wore her pale brown plaits curled into earphones, which gave her the look of a rather prim young matron. That was how Maurice liked to think of her.

The maid came bustling in with fresh toast. Maurice always liked to finish with toast and marmalade.

'Goodness knows where Toby is this morning.' Claudia's smooth face puckered into a frown. 'Bessie, you have called him?'

'Yes, ma'am.'

'Do so again, if you please.'

Maurice sighed. That Toby was late for breakfast was a regular irritation.

Claudia's voice was a plaintive moan. 'He was late coming in last night too. I had to ask Bessie to wait up in order to lock up after him. He's wild, Maurice, and growing worse.'

Maurice had come to understand that Claudia was getting her own back. She knew how to fan the flames to make him dissatisfied with his older sons. Today it was Toby. Edward was away staying with a school friend during his holidays, but when he was home she complained just as much about his behaviour.

'They're out of control. Do just what they like. They stick together, gang up against me. Nothing I say has the slightest effect.'

It had been Claudia's idea that Edward should be sent to boarding school. Toby had gone daily to school in Birkenhead. That had proved more than adequate. Neither of them was academic.

'Separate them, that's the answer,' Claudia had said. And in an attempt to keep the peace at home and please her, he had. But once Edward was out of the way, Toby had caused twice the trouble, and since he spent most of his time in the factory, Maurice had had to deal with it himself.

Claudia had said: 'I can't believe he'll ever learn to run it properly.'

She didn't need to work on Maurice like this. He'd had more than enough of Toby this weekend. But of course he knew why she kept on at him. Claudia wanted him to see Jeffrey Masters and change his will. She wanted him to cut Toby out, and leave a share of the business to her son Adam. And damn it, he was beginning to think it would be the right thing to do. He'd had enough of Toby. The lad wasn't serious about work. His mind was never on it.

All the same, it upset Maurice to hear her going on like this. Useless to tell himself she was picking up on the complaints he'd voiced to her over past months. He could remember only the good times with his first wife, Helen. Toby had been the apple of her eye, and to complain about him now seemed somehow disloyal to her. He remembered Helen with great affection. She'd never ruffled his feathers like this.

Toby came shuffling into the dining room, looking half asleep. Maurice felt another surge of irritation.

'You sluggard. You'll not have time to eat.'

Toby poured himself a cup of tea; wary blue eyes glanced up at him.

'I'm not hungry, Father. I don't want breakfast.'

Maurice pulled himself to his feet with a jerk. He had to get away from his son. That wary glance reminded him of the row that had been grumbling on over the long weekend. He'd heard the factory hands talking, suggesting Toby was sweet on one of the girls. He'd faced him with it on Saturday and they'd both become very angry. Toby was far too involved with the workers. Last month Maurice had caught him playing poker with a whole gang of them in the dinner hour, and only last week he'd told him off for buying beer for one lad. Toby didn't understand that he'd have to stay aloof if he was to control them. He was like Peter Pan. What he needed was to grow up.

Maurice decided to take a turn round the gardens; there was still time before the ferry went, and it always soothed him. He loved the house and its river bank position at New Ferry. Out in the front garden, he was buffeted by a boisterous breeze off the river. The tide was full in and great waves were lashing against the Esplanade and spraying up lacy foam that glittered in the morning sun.

Shipping, much of it under sail, scudded busily up and down. He filled his lungs and told himself the ozone was good for him.

Maurice's father had bought this plot as soon as the pickle business he'd founded provided enough money. He'd built this bungalow in 1887 for his wife and called it Tides Reach. Maurice had lived here all his life, or all that he could remember of it. He thought of it as the Percival family home, a place of security and comfort.

It was a bungalow because that was what Mother had been used to in India. The front was faced in dun-coloured stone. On each side of the wide front door there was a massive Victorian bay window flanked by a flat one. The upper panes were of Georgian Gothic design, which no doubt had been popular at the time it was built.

The garden was terraced into three small lawns because the ground rose steeply from the shore. There were banks of rock plants and glistening white stones between the lawns, and lots of evergreen shrubs that were always tossing in the wind.

He went through the side gate to the back garden and was immediately sheltered from the wind. He enjoyed walking round his domain first thing in the morning. He was proud of his roses and his dahlias and loved the high red-brick wall that protected them and gave the house privacy. The bungalow was built in an L shape, and the back elevations were of a warm red brick that matched the wall.

He surprised Bessie's ginger cat scratching in a rose bed

20

and gave it an aggressive hiss, but it had already seen him and shot down the cellar steps to the maids' quarters. He was not fond of the animal. Any damage to his roses and he'd get somebody to wring its neck.

Some inner clock warned Maurice that time was getting on, and he went indoors to get his umbrella and bowler hat. Before he reached the dining room he could hear Toby bickering with Claudia He opened the door and looked in, meeting Toby's angry eyes.

'Let's go,' he said, and kissed Claudia on the cheek. He knew Toby had still to put on his coat and hat, but he set off anyway. Toby must catch him up. Maurice felt he was past the age when he could run to catch the ferry.

It was a very convenient journey to the factory. Today he went up the back garden and through the wrought-iron gates into New Ferry Road, to stride briskly down past the parade of shops to New Ferry Pier. It was a shorter walk along the Esplanade, but this morning, with the tide so high and the wind so blustery, he'd be in danger of getting splashed.

Toby caught him up outside the post office. 'Sorry, Father.'

'I've been thinking . . . Perhaps it was a mistake to bring you straight into the firm. You were too young. It might have been better if you'd had experience of something else. It's not too late. Accountancy would be a useful asset.'

The wild blue eyes jerked nervously to his. 'What are you saying? That you don't want me to go on working for you?'

'A break for a year or two. Give us both breathing space. You'd find accountancy useful.'

'I thought you wanted me to learn the business so I could take over . . .' Toby's eyes raked his face again. 'Eventually, I mean. When you're ready to stand down.'

'Of course that's what I want.'

Maurice sighed. He was finding it impossible to be both father and boss. He and Toby disagreed about everything. Toby had hardly started at the factory before he wanted to change everything. He said they needed new labelling,

21

new recipes and new sales outlets. He didn't know what he was talking about. Toby challenged every decision his father made; it had created a power struggle that had nothing to do with benefiting the business.

Toby had come to a stop, and his angry eyes challenged Maurice.

'It's because of Sarah Hoxton, isn't it? You want to get me out of the way, keep us apart.'

'No,' Maurice said. 'No.' But of course that was what made moving Toby imperative now.

'Nothing you say will make me change my mind about her.'

Maurice said slowly, giving each word equal emphasis: 'She won't make a suitable wife for you.' He saw Toby's chin stiffen with determination.

Walking down the pier, Maurice gave up. The wind was snatching the words out of his mouth, and he had to hold on to his hat. Once on board the ferry, he went straight to the smoking saloon to have a cigarette. He didn't feel like another fight; didn't feel like walking round on deck to get more exercise, which was what he usually did.

Maurice didn't enjoy public holidays. Yesterday he'd have preferred to be at work. Nothing pleased him more than to see hundreds of jars being filled with his excellent chutneys and pickles. To think of all his machinery lying idle made him restless.

There was, however, one thing he'd been considering for some time. He had gone to call on Benjamin Burton, a neighbour living down the Esplanade at Beechwood House, and asked for his help. It had been a pleasant afternoon, and Maurice had strolled slowly, assessing the other large houses on the Esplanade, comparing each in turn with his.

They made up a small enclave of five genuinely middle-class homes. Maurice was sure that the way New Ferry had developed over the years would have disappointed his parents. At best, the other inhabitants could only be described as lower middle class, and amongst the occupants of the five houses there was no more derogatory term than that.

Maurice was painfully aware that some applied it to Claudia and her mother, but only behind his back. They called him the Pickle King, and he didn't like that either.

Burton headed his own firm of accountants, a practice that was considered the best in Liverpool; and two of the other houses were occupied by a solicitor and a ship-owner – which sounded very grand, but his ships were old-fashioned sailing vessels now only fit for the coastal trade. Next door to Maurice, at Copstone, lived Mr Hardcastle. He was retired, but had made his money on the Cotton Exchange. Maurice knew from their snide remarks that they all considered making pickles to be rather a joke. To them it was a lower-middle-class means of earning one's bread; socially a little below their level.

But Tides Reach had much the best front gardens of the five, though he couldn't see what the other back gardens were like. Being a bungalow, it didn't look impressive, but inside he was sure it surpassed even Beechwood.

He went up the garden of Beechwood House and rang the front doorbell. It had a very handsome façade in the Georgian style, with a massive porch, but it lacked the originality of his place. The drawing room was on one side of the front door and the dining room on the other. Very ordinary.

That was one reason he'd had the conservatory and the music room built on for Helen. It evened things up that his house offered the best accommodation of the five. Particularly since it didn't show from the front. None of his neighbours thought a gentleman should display his wealth.

The maid let him in and then went upstairs to announce him to her master. Maurice hoped Burton hadn't gone to bed for a snooze. Early afternoon on Sundays and public holidays was considered the correct time for the gentlemen of the five houses to call on one another, though they usually left paying calls to their wives.

Maurice waited in the hall. Its red flock wallpaper made it rather dark, but he admired the dark oak chiffonier which had game birds hand-carved on the front. He could even see crossed guns and a pointer amongst the carved leaves.

The scent of the Burtons' lunch still hung in the air. The maids were clattering dishes in the kitchen. He didn't get noises like that in Tides Reach. Benjamin Burton came hurrying down.

'Ah, Percival. Nice to see you. Keeping well, I hope?'

He had a commanding presence. His grey eyes looked out at the world with supreme confidence. He wore a bushy moustache and neatly trimmed full beard, mostly grey now, but with a hint of the original ginger colouring.

'Come up and see my new telescope. Wonderful instrument. I tried it down here in my study but I can see so much more from upstairs.'

Maurice had followed him up. He'd been taken to what appeared to be a guest bedroom. It looked bleak; the bed wasn't made up.

When invited, he looked through the powerful telescope and spent some time studying the two training ships swinging at anchor in the Sloyne, an area of deep water almost in front of the house. He listened to Burton's discourse on them, though he'd heard it before, on his last visit.

'Once there were three. Magnificent black and white wooden sailing ships from the Napoleonic Wars. The *Akbar*, remember her? She served as a quarantine ship for the Port of Liverpool before becoming a reformatory; a corrective establishment. Here in the river for over forty years. She was towed away for dismantling in 1907. Sadly missed. And now they've changed the old *Indefatigable* for that ugly iron ship.'

'There are no more wooden ships left, Ben.'

'Just the *Conway*. The most handsome of the lot.'

24

'And that's not the original,' Maurice prompted. He wanted to indulge his neighbour in his passion for historic ships.

'No, the first *Conway* came here in the eighteen fifties but she wasn't big enough. Twice they replaced her, naming both *Conway*. This one was originally HMS *Nile*. Been here since the eighteen seventies.'

'A wonderful ship. A piece of history.'

Eventually Maurice was able to get round to the purpose of his visit.

'Take Toby on?' Ben Burton's eyes had locked on to his at that. 'To what purpose? He's going to run your business, isn't he?'

'Yes, but he needs to grow up, mature a bit. He hasn't settled. A year or two spent learning basic accounting would be a great help.'

Burton scratched his beard. 'I've two young men articled to me at present, hard-working and keen. They'll make their careers in accountancy, of course. Toby wouldn't need to sit the examinations unless he wanted to. Though I'd advise it. Would do him no harm.

'Rather than let him think less is expected of him, I suggest he enters on the same terms. We could make it an informal arrangement between friends, though no need to tell him that.'

Between friends. Maurice's shoulders straightened at that. Pickle King he might be, but Ben Burton regarded him as a friend.

'Thank you. For him it will be time well spent.'

Burton was looking through his telescope again. 'Look, there goes the *Flying Cloud*, running up to Widnes. Belongs to old Charlie Morris at West Knowe. Fine old ship.'

'So she is,' Maurice enthused, putting his eye to the instrument. 'Lovely to see her under full sail.'

Toby came into the saloon and sat down beside him. Maurice said:

'I was speaking to Benjamin Burton about you yesterday.'
Toby looked at him suspiciously.

'He's willing to take you on, to article you—'

'You mean, to be an accountant?'

'Yes, to train you.'

'But I don't want—'

'Accountancy would be very useful. Help you run the business properly. I don't think you take enough interest in the books, understand the importance—'

'How much would I earn from Mr Burton?'

'Nothing. I would be paying him a fee to take you. Burton, Wallis and Jones is a first-class—'

'No, Father.'

The finality of that took his breath away. Maurice would never have dared refuse his own father. 'I'll make you a small allowance. Anyway, you have a little income from your mother.'

'No, Father. I've been earning my own living for the last five years. I want to go on doing that. Particularly now. I told you, I want to marry Sarah Hoxton.'

'You're too young to marry anyone. I won't give my permission.'

Toby was belligerent. 'In another year I won't need it. I don't want to learn accountancy. I need—'

Maurice knew he mustn't lose his temper. His doctor had told him it wasn't good for him. Not with his high blood pressure. He said, as calmly as he could:

'Shouldn't it be a question of what I need by way of help? What the business needs?'

Toby leapt to his feet and shot out on deck without another word. Maurice groaned aloud. The lad was twenty now, high time he learned sense. Why couldn't he be more like Ben Burton's son? Gideon worked in the family business, shouldering more and more responsibility. Ben had spoken of the confidence he felt about handing everything over to him in a few years' time. Of course, Gideon was a good bit older, over thirty. All the same, Maurice wished Toby were more like him.

Maurice felt the engines cut out as the ferry glided alongside the landing stage at Pier Head. He pulled himself to his feet and groped his way out on deck. There was a crowd waiting to disembark and he couldn't see Toby amongst them. That darkened his mood even further. He set out alone. Today he felt tired even before the day's work began.

His factory was only a short walk away. On days when the weather was really bad, he could travel one stop on the overhead railway. Nothing could be more convenient. His father had organised everything very well. Everything, that is, except his death. He'd died very suddenly of heart trouble at forty-eight years of age; cut down in his prime.

Maurice had been just twenty when his father had died, and he'd had to take over the factory and run it after only four years' experience. His mother had not worked in the business for many years by then, so couldn't help much. He hadn't strayed one iota from his father's ideas, and the business had run smoothly and profitably for the last thirty years. He wasn't going to change things now because of Toby's new-fangled notions.

Toby was the same age Maurice had been when he'd taken sole charge, but Toby wasn't capable. He had an aversion to taking advice, thought he knew it all and was convinced he could fly before he'd even learned to walk. He'd never knuckle down and exercise ordinary day-to-day control over the business . . . or not yet anyway. And as for taking up with Sarah Hoxton, that really made Maurice furious. Toby had no sense.

Preoccupied with his thoughts, Maurice reached the factory in no time. The sign picked out in red and gold on the front of the building never failed to please him:

Gregory Percival and Son Ltd.
Makers of fine pickles to Liverpool,
Great Britain and the World.

The clanking of machinery told him that all was well; the day's work had started.

'Morning, sir.' Alfred Trumper, his foreman, followed him to the office as he always did for his daily instructions.

Trumper was fifty-two, exactly Maurice's own age, but he'd worked here even longer, having started at the age of twelve. He had a bushy grey beard on his chin, but his head was a bare expanse of shiny scalp, apart from a few grey wisps on a level with his ears.

Like all the workers, in the interests of hygiene, he wore a brown drill coat in the factory. Maurice thought himself very go-ahead to provide coats and caps for his workers. They were laundered on the premises and clean ones were issued each week. Percival's provided two cloakrooms, one for male workers and one for females, and both had hot running water and towels. Each also had a large notice to the effect that any employee caught wearing company overalls outside in the street would be instantly dismissed.

A routine task for Maurice was to work out exactly what would be made in the factory on each day. He liked to plan three or four weeks ahead, so that he could order the ingredients well in advance.

Always they made pickled onions. They sold more of those than of anything else, and fortunately shallots were dried and could be obtained in good condition for most of the year. It was the chutneys and mixed vegetable pickles that posed problems, because fresh fruit and vegetables were available mainly in late summer and autumn. Maurice counted himself fortunate that in a great seaport like Liverpool, vegetables from abroad were available to stretch the season, but even so, they were generally more expensive than those grown here.

Miss Potts, his clerk, had copied out what he'd planned

from the day book in her copperplate writing and left it on his desk. He sat down to peruse it to refresh his memory.

'Morning, sir.' The office boy swept in with the morning's post.

'Tea,' Maurice said, as he always did.

'Yes, sir.'

Maurice handed the sheet of paper over to Trumper. It was always like this and the routine went some way to soothe him. Recently, with having so much on his mind, he hadn't been feeling too well.

He was now fifty-two and feared he might have inherited his father's medical problems. Certainly he had his high blood pressure. He didn't want to die of apoplexy too; he wasn't ready yet. He'd already lived four years longer than his father, though. He believed in taking good care of himself, and wouldn't let himself be upset by all this. He lit another cigarette; it helped him relax.

Toby came in late, sat down at the other desk and ignored him.

It was often said that family businesses didn't go on being profitable; that in three generations they were likely to go from clogs to clogs. Maurice was beginning to think that would be the way of things for Percival's Pickles. The third Percival generation didn't seem to have the ability of their forebears.

'I've arranged for you to see Mr Burton in his office on Thursday afternoon,' he said. 'I'll come with you. We'll discuss your future sensibly. He will explain what accountancy can do for you.'

That Toby didn't deign to answer infuriated his father anew. He was still fulminating by mid morning. It made matters worse to see Toby's curly head bent silently over the ledgers on the other side of the room, his pen scratching busily. He'd never known the boy so dedicated to his work.

Maurice got up and went to his filing cabinet. He ran his fingers across the files of his employees and took two out. Sarah Hoxton had been working here for four years, ever since she'd left school. Mr Trumper reported that she was a good time-keeper and he had no complaints about her work. Maria Hoxton, age forty-three, had worked for him for over ten years, and again the foreman's reports were good. Well, Sarah had offended now. There were plenty more women out there keen to have a regular job. He paid as well as any firm in the district. He put the files back and left his office, slamming the door behind him.

He walked the factory floor every day, keeping his eyes open. He'd learned to live with the smell of onions, though today he did feel his eyes prickling. He blew his nose hard and looked round for the girl. He rarely spoke to his workers because the clanking machinery made it difficult to hear what was being said, but he knew them all by sight.

This was the one. Tall and slim, a good-looking girl. She had thick hair and a lot of it; he could tell by the way it bunched out her cap. A few yellow strands escaped to curl over her forehead. He watched her darting movements as she picked out the odd onion that needed attention; pruning the tops, taking off the occasional brown skin, wielding her knife deftly. Her fingers were stained brown; he was surprised that didn't put Toby off.

He could see her wary yellow eyes assessing him. Maurice looked away; he didn't care for the yellow eyes. Her colouring reminded him of the cat that lived in the kitchens at home. He'd told Bessie it would have to go if he ever found it in his quarters.

He was looking round for the mother. She was harder to pick out; the older women looked alike. He had to go to the packing department to find her, but he thought he had her now. Old before her time; bent, even. Maria Hoxton hadn't the strength the job needed. Her task was to take the new jars from their crates and put them on the conveyor belt that would transport them to the steam room to be sterilised. She could hardly lift the wooden crates. He could see by her flustered look that she knew he was watching her. She wasn't pulling her weight. It was high time she went.

He'd get rid of both the girl and her mother. Not immediately; he didn't want more trouble with Toby. If he sacked them now it would be obvious why he'd done it. He'd make some excuse in a few weeks' time, when all this had died down.

He'd turned to go to the salting room when he heard the scream above the rattle of the rolling conveyor belt. The woman he'd been watching was on the floor, a crate of jars tipped on top of her. Some had broken.

Within moments, a fellow worker was helping her up. Someone stopped the conveyor belt. He felt a flush of annoyance run up his cheeks; such a waste of time and money.

There was blood everywhere. The woman's hand was cut badly enough to make his stomach muscles cringe. But his father had drummed into him that to keep on good terms with his employees, he should show reasonable care for them.

'You'd better go to hospital,' he told her, 'to get it dressed properly.'

'Mam!' The yellow-haired girl came flying in to throw her arms round her mother. Her strange yellow eyes turned to him. 'She wasn't well this morning. I didn't want her to come to work.'

Toby arrived, alerted by the fact that the belt had been stopped. Everybody was clustering round, wasting the time he was paying for. The worst possible scenario for his nerves, when he wanted to reassure himself that all was well. The woman had passed out again.

'There's a cart loading up in the yard; put her on that and let the driver take her to the hospital,' he said brusquely to Toby. Then he raised his voice.

'Brush this broken glass up,' he ordered. 'Switch the belt back on. The rest of you, get back to your work.'

Everybody jumped to it except the girl.

'You!' he bellowed at Sarah. 'Do as you're told. Get back to your place.' Damn it, he didn't want shallots going to the salting room with their skins still on.

'Go on.' Toby was talking to her softly. 'I'll go with your mother, see she's all right'

That infuriated Maurice more. 'There's no need for you to go. The carter can see to her. Surely that's good enough? A cart at her disposal? You come back to your desk this instant.'

It maddened him that Toby ignored his orders. He couldn't watch him lift the woman to her feet. Somebody had fetched the carter in, and together they were half carrying her out.

'Phillips!' he bellowed, remembering the carter's name. 'Drop her at the hospital and come straight back here. I don't want you hanging round down there wasting time.'

He turned quickly on his heel and went back to his office. This would finish things for Maria Hoxton. She wouldn't be able to work for a while, and he wouldn't have her back when she was better. He needed another cup of tea and a cigarette to settle his nerves after that.

Chapter Three

Maria Hoxton was frightened, so frightened she hardly noticed the pain in her hand. That was a dull throb she could live with, though the blood was soaking through the towel somebody had wrapped loosely round it.

'Hold on, we'll soon be there.'

She could hear the panic in Toby Percival's voice. He'd disobeyed his father for her! She felt sick with fear – or had she felt sick before the accident? Certainly her head throbbed too. Mr Percival had come looking for her, and she knew why. She'd seen him watching Sarah five minutes earlier. It was because of the interest his son was showing in her.

Hadn't she been warning Sarah for weeks? The cart jolted, making the jars of pickles tinkle in the crates behind her. Maria closed her eyes as pain knifed through her.

'Sorry,' Toby said. 'Not long now.'

She knew exactly how far it was; didn't she walk this way four times a day between home and the factory? She watched Toby through half-closed eyes. She couldn't really blame Sarah; he was a good-looking lad, tall and well built. No, not a lad, he was twenty years old, a fully grown and well-developed man. But he had apple cheeks and a baby face and didn't act as though he was. He was still a boy at heart, and that scared her more, because he wouldn't realise what he was doing to Sarah.

He'd turned her head; swept her off her feet. Sarah thought he was in love with her and she with him and that they'd get married and live happily ever after. Perhaps Sarah also saw it as a way out of poverty and the daily grind in the pickle factory.

Maria winced as the cart jolted again. She couldn't see it ever happening. Maurice Percival wouldn't let it. He wouldn't want his son marrying the likes of Sarah, even though she was like the sun itself, all golden sparkle.

The carter was reining the horse in to the kerb. Maria was levering herself up on her elbow as Toby jumped down with the lithe ease of youth and turned back to help her. She almost fell into his arms and he had to steady her to keep her upright.

'We can manage,' he called to the driver. 'You go back to the yard and finish loading.'

She'd taken only two steps towards the hospital door when she doubled up in pain again, and she knew it was all Toby Percival could do to hold her upright.

'Just a few more steps,' he murmured. He was being kind to her because he loved Sarah, but even if Sarah got what she wanted – even if they ran away to Gretna Green to get married, for that was the only way in which they could – Maria was afraid he wouldn't be right for her.

Toby didn't think things through. He'd get into trouble when he got back to the factory for coming with her. Cause them trouble too, but he wouldn't see that; he lived for the moment. Fun was higher on his agenda than thrift and stability. They all knew he and his father didn't get on, that what he did in the factory could be done twice as efficiently by Charlie Trumper or John Ferry.

Toby was too young to be married. He wouldn't be able to look after Sarah; he needed a nursemaid himself, someone to run round after him. The most likely outcome wasn't marriage, though. More like he'd leave her in the lurch. Sarah hadn't lived long enough to know these things, but Maria had.

Sarah would be far better off with John. He was steady, a more mature personality. He was one of them. That was

Sarah's best route to happiness, but she was throwing it away without a second thought, turning down every advance John made.

The disinfectant smell of the hospital caught in her throat and made her cough. She'd thought the hot, spicy atmosphere of the factory had killed off her ability to smell anything else. The aroma of onions and cooking chutney she thought more pervasive than any other smell in the world. The odours were in her clothes now, in her hair, ingrained into her fingers, and no amount of washing would get rid of them.

Toby was guiding her towards a chair, and she slumped down.

'I'll wait a little while to see—'

'No, you go back.'

'Sarah will want to know . . .'

Maria's head swam. He was a caring person, she had to give him that. He had none of his father's arrogance.

She didn't know how long she waited, but at some point a nurse came and unwrapped her hand. The sight of raw flesh and blood turned her stomach. Almost before she knew it, she was vomiting on the nurse's shoes. She wanted to cry with the shame and the pain. Then she felt a cold dish held by a firm hand digging into her chin, but it was largely too late by then. The next thing she knew she was being taken somewhere where she could lie down. It was such a relief.

'Go back to work,' she told Toby when he came to her bedside. 'Your father will be angry if you don't. I'll be all right now.'

'I'll hang on a few more minutes. Wait outside. Sarah will want to know what the doctors find.'

The doctor came and the questions started. How long had she been feeling unwell?

It had been several days. She'd been having these bouts of biliousness and abdominal pain and of feeling generally unwell for several years. She ought to be used to them.

'Diarrhoea too?

'No, the reverse.'

The doctor was young and very kind, but hospitals and everything to do with them made her shake. When she was told they suspected the problem to be appendicitis, the word terrified her.

'Does that mean I'll have to have it out?' Maria could feel the sweat break out on her forehead. 'That's a dangerous operation, isn't it?'

'It's quite popular since the King had his out. The old king I mean, Edward VII. It's done quite often these days.'

Maria didn't care how popular it was; she didn't want it.

'We're not going to operate straight away. We're going to admit you for a day or two's rest. See if it settles down again first. Sometimes it does of its own accord.'

Maria relaxed. That sounded better. A day or two of rest, what more could she ask? If she felt well, she'd be able to cope. What would convince Sarah she must turn her back on Toby Percival?

They gave her something for the pain then, and she could feel herself drifting off.

Sarah's fingers were flying automatically for the onions; her mind was on her mother. Mam had looked terrible as Toby and the driver had half carried her out to the cart.

Elvira Ferry, John's mother, came to see her as soon as Mr Percival went back to the office.

'I was working near your mam.' Elvira had nervous, darting eyes. 'I think she fainted. It wasn't just an accident.'

That made Sarah feel worse. Mam hadn't been well yesterday, and though she'd made light of it this morning, it would have been better if she'd stayed in bed. They should both have known that all the bending and lifting needed to set the jars on the conveyor belt was too heavy a job for Mam when she wasn't feeling well. Sarah would have been even more worried if it hadn't been Toby who'd taken her mother to hospital.

He'd whispered to her: 'I'll see she's all right.'

She could trust Toby to do his best for them, but Mr Percival had been angry and made more so by Toby's going against his orders. It was the last thing he should have done, especially for her mother. It would only build up more trouble.

After that, it was hard to go on working as though nothing had happened. It seemed an age until dinner time came and the factory lines shut down for an hour. Usually she and Mam walked home to get something to eat. Today Sarah decided she must call at the hospital to see how she was.

But she found she didn't need to. Toby was waiting for her on the corner of Jordan Street with two meat pies.

'How's Mam?'

'Can we go to your rooms to eat these? I'll tell you on the way.'

'Of course. Is she all right?'

'I'm afraid it's not just her hand. They think she might have appendicitis.'

'Oh my goodness!'

'A surgeon examined her. She's to stay in under observation for a day or two. If her appendix doesn't settle down, he'll operate on Friday.'

'Oh dear! What about her hand?'

'Quite a bad cut. She's had eight stitches in it. I told the ward sister you'd be at work until six. She wants you to go round after that and take her night clothes in.'

'I'll put a few things together for her now. I'm afraid it'll be a long time before she can work again.'

Sarah lit the Primus to make them a cup of tea to have with the pies. She felt even more uneasy about Mam. Illness brought added expenses. Mam lived in dread of it. They both knew how easy it was to get into debt.

'I hope she's going to be all right.'

Sarah spent an anxious afternoon. The atmosphere in the

factory seemed tense. Maurice Percival spent more time than usual out on the floor, looking more dour than he normally did and finding fault with everything.

She was glad when the lines were shut down for the night and she was free to go and see her mother.

'Shall I come with you?' Toby wanted to know. He'd been hovering close to Sarah since he got back. 'They won't let you stay long, it isn't visiting time. I'll wait for you if you like.'

How could she say no to that? She wanted Toby with her. She needed somebody to lean on now Mam was sick.

Sarah saw the ward sister. She was warned Mam might still need an operation, but was told she'd had a comfortable afternoon. She was allowed to see her for a few moments. Mam was dozing as she walked up the long line of beds. Her face was grey against the white pillows; her damaged hand was in a sling. Mam always put on a good front. She seemed more worried about how the Pickle King had taken the breakage of so many jars than she did about the prognosis of her illness. The thought of several days' rest had soothed her.

Toby was waiting for Sarah outside. He took her arm to walk her home. It was hard to believe something as wonderful as this could be happening at the same time as something so awful for Mam. She tingled all over at the thought of being alone with Toby in the privacy of her home. He'd been there already in the lunch hour, but then they'd both known their time together was limited, and they'd had to eat.

'I'm hungry,' Toby said. 'Can we get fish and chips or something?'

'I made a pan of scouse yesterday. Mam won't be wanting her share.' There were scones left over too. They needn't go hungry.

Toby seemed at home in their living room. He stirred the pan of scouse as it warmed up on the Primus, while she set the table for their meal. It seemed very strange to see him in Mam's place. He congratulated her on her cooking and laughed because the pickled red cabbage was not Percival's but a rival brand.

'It's cheaper,' Sarah explained. 'That's why Mam buys it.'

Afterwards, they sat with their arms round each other, watching dusk gather over the river and the pinprick of lights come on. Sarah had known he wouldn't want to go home. She tried to persuade him, afraid his father would be furious with both of them if he didn't.

'I haven't made my peace with him yet, and I don't want to.'

'You disobeyed his orders in front of us all.'

'Don't remind me. There'd be more trouble if I went home now. Far better to give it time to fade from Father's mind. Let it blow over.'

Toby's arms tightened round her. 'I don't want to leave you. This is such a chance. Couldn't have expected this in a month of Sundays.'

He kissed her. His lips were velvety smooth against hers. 'Don't send me away and let it go to waste.'

The last thing Sarah wanted was to send him away. He was pressing his body closer, moulding it to hers. It was a delicious embrace. She forgot the outside world, forgot Mam; nothing mattered but Toby's kisses. He ended up occupying Mam's place in bed just as he had at the table.

Sarah thought of that Tuesday as a terrible day of suspense and worry about Mam, but of ecstasy and delight with Toby.

John flung himself on his bed fully clothed. It came again, the unmistakable sound of footsteps in the room above. It filled him with fury that Toby Percival dared to go up to Sarah's rooms when he knew she was alone there.

'Just shows you the sort of girl she is,' his mother had fumed. Her manner was often like this, angry and anxious at the same time. She had heavy eyebrows that went up and down as she spoke, particularly when she was cross.

'Only a hussy would take him upstairs like that when we all know her mother's in hospital.'

John was gritting his teeth. He could guess what Toby was doing with his Sarah. Percival didn't care a fig for her well-being. It knifed through John to think of what he was doing.

All evening he couldn't keep still. Half of him was listening for her call. Wondering if she needed help to get rid of Toby. He'd heard it said about the factory that Toby was one for the girls. That Sarah seemed only too willing to accept his attentions didn't help one iota.

He was like a cat on hot bricks; even thought of going up and throwing Toby out. Maria would want him to look after her daughter. Perhaps he should? His fists clenched and unclenched as he tried to make up his mind what to do.

Mam's bed was behind a curtain he'd rigged up to give her privacy, but she could hear him. She pushed her head through to look at him. She had straight iron-grey hair, cut short and pinned back off her face.

'For heaven's sake, John, lie down and go to sleep,' she said irritably.

Feeling guilty because he was keeping her awake, he went to lie down on his narrow cot bed against the far wall.

'Forget about Sarah. It's really none of your business what she does.'

John felt it was. He couldn't cut himself off from Sarah. He lay awake most of the night worrying about her.

Toby was using her. Having sex with her when John had been so careful not to get them into anything like that until they could afford to marry. It showed how little respect Toby had for her.

Sarah was so beautiful. When the wind had flattened her shabby blue dress against her slim body this morning, he'd felt such a need for her. Sometimes she had only to smile to make him feel physical desire.

He didn't doubt she'd cast the same spell on Toby, but *he'd*

40

made no effort to control himself. John felt anger rising in his throat. Toby was the sort of person who could have anything he wanted. Everything came easy to him.

John had always had a very clear idea about what he wanted from life. He'd had his future all planned out ahead of him. He'd meant to marry Sarah Hoxton and make a better life for her and his mother than they'd had up to now.

He'd known he had nobody to depend upon but himself, and known, too, how Percival's Pickles had been started by Toby's grandparents. He thought he might do much the same; make money from a recipe for brown sauce which his grandmother used to make.

His problem had always been how to set about it. He couldn't afford to rent premises like those in which he worked, but he'd need something similar. For years he'd been turning the idea over in his head. He knew what he needed; the real stumbling blocks were the money to set up the operation, and the knowledge of how to sell what he made.

He'd done his best to get Toby to talk about how he sold the pickles. He'd listened avidly to all he said, asked leading questions, tried to pick up all the guidance he could. If the Percivals could do it, so could he.

He'd talked it over with his mother countless times, and she was as keen as he was. It seemed the only way would be to start small, just as the Percivals had, by making a few bottles at home and trying to sell them. The problem was, they lived in one room. Ate and slept and did everything in it. They had a fire on which they managed to do their cooking, but it was only a bedroom grate over which John had rigged a trivet on which to set a kettle or a pan. They really needed more space and a proper stove if they were to make more than half a dozen bottles at a time.

Two years ago, in an effort to make some progress, he'd summoned up the courage to talk to Maurice Percival about his recipe for brown sauce. After all, sauces were very much the same sort of thing as pickles and chutneys. He'd hoped Mr Percival would agree to make it and allow him a fraction of the profit, or at the very least pay him a few pounds for using the recipe until he could set up on his own.

Maurice Percival had looked at him over the top of his horn-rimmed spectacles.

'Use your recipe for brown sauce? For a few years? You've got a sauce all right.' He'd laughed unpleasantly at his own pun.

John had told himself not to get rattled. 'I've brought a sample for you. I'd be glad if you'd try it and let me know what you think.'

Mr Percival had picked the bottle up and held it to the light. Unscrewed the top and sniffed suspiciously at the contents.

'There's a dozen firms making brown sauce already.'

'Mine is a little different, sir. Its taste is excellent.'

Maurice Percival's arrogant eyes met his. 'There's more to making sauce than a good taste. To be commercial, you have to think about what it would cost to make. It'd need bottles instead of the jars we use for everything else.'

'You use several different types of jars, sir.'

'I prefer my products to fit into the jars we already use. We'd need more storage space for bottles, different crates; it would be an added complication and increase the costs.

'Anyway, if I wanted to make brown sauce, I'd use a recipe of my own. I'd try out a few and see which was the easiest and cheapest with the best taste. I wouldn't need yours. My taste and nose tell me all I need to know about the ingredients in brown sauce.'

John felt he hadn't explained his proposition adequately. 'With all due respect, my sauce is different. Darker than you'd expect, and not so thick.'

'Yes, Lea and Perrins, but we can't copy their—'

'Nothing like Lea and Perrins in taste, I promise you.'

Now the boss was pointing it out, he could see it had been

rather cheeky of him to suggest Percival's contract to use his recipe.

'Why would I want to build up a following for your sauce? What good would that do my business? It's not on, lad. Nothing like that is on, not even if your sauce makes gristle taste like best rump. Off you go, and take your sauce with you.'

He'd taken that disappointment as he'd taken hundreds before it. Perhaps he was naïve, but he'd had to try. He knew now that the only way to make money from his recipe was to go into business for himself. To get Maurice Percival to go in with him had been a pipe dream from the word go.

His plan for a better life had had a setback, but it hadn't changed his goals. He'd go on saving a little each week, and when he had enough, he'd marry Sarah and they'd make the sauce together.

All that had changed when Sarah had rejected him; that had really sent him reeling. Her big amber eyes had blinked up at him nervously, telling him she wanted to be honest, but oh, how hurtful it had been. The truth had been stark. She didn't want him any more. Toby had lured her away. For John that knocked the bottom out of everything. He felt he'd lost his way; he'd set his heart on Sarah.

He'd half known it was coming, but would not let himself believe it until he heard it from her lips.

'What's the matter?' Mam had demanded last night. 'What's making you look so down in the mouth?'

When he told her, Mam was angry.

'If Sarah can do this to you, she's not worth worrying about.' But he knew she was disappointed too. She'd liked Sarah, and Maria was her closest friend. 'Better to find out before you marry her rather than later.'

But John could see nothing good in it. Losing Sarah filled him with despair; it was more than he could take. He couldn't see his future at all without her and it was sending him completely off the rails.

All the talk at work was of war. He'd listened to Charlie Trumper holding forth about enlisting and all the excitement and fun he was going to have. The foreman's son had quite set his mind on going to fight. John thought it would be the best way out for him too. He could get right away. He needn't see what Sarah and Toby were doing.

'Enlist because of her?' Mam had blazed at him. 'What about me? You're going to leave me to fend for myself?'

For once, he hadn't stopped to think of his mother. He knew she relied on him. She told him often enough that he'd been a rock of support to her since he was nine, and she didn't know what she'd have done without him.

'You'll manage,' he said roughly. He could think of nothing but his own loss.

'Don't be such a fool.' She'd never raised her voice in anger to him like this before. Her eyebrows were going up and down every few seconds, her dark eyes flashing wild rage. The habit had caused deep parallel wrinkles across her forehead.

'It's that Toby Percival. He's been making eyes at her for months. I blame him as well as her.'

So did John.

'Don't join up. No need for that. You'll get yourself killed.'

What did it matter if he was, if he couldn't have Sarah?

John hadn't been able to show his anger to her and had bottled it up, but now his mother's reaction fuelled his resentment against Toby.

Chapter Four

By eleven o'clock that night, Maurice was shaking with rage. As the clocks began to strike, he got up to stamp round the house bolting the doors before going to bed. If Toby couldn't get home at a reasonable hour, he wasn't going to get in at all.

But what really enraged him was knowing that Toby probably had no intention of coming home. Hadn't Maurice been generous enough to send the Hoxton woman to hospital? That must mean Toby's yellow-haired wench would have the free run of the hovel they lived in. Of course Toby wouldn't come home. He'd be having a fine time. Maurice couldn't get to sleep when he went to bed for thinking about his eldest son.

An hour later, he was doubled up with indigestion. It was probably worry, combined with the gammon he'd eaten at dinner. It had been too fatty.

He woke Claudia and sent her to get some bicarbonate of soda and heat a beaker of milk for him. Even that didn't help much, and he spent a most uncomfortable night. When he finally got off, he must have slept heavily.

Next morning, he felt heavy-eyed and jaded. It was a real effort to get out of bed, and for once he didn't feel like going to work.

He went, of course – it was his duty to go – but he was later than usual.

That morning, Sarah woke up in Toby's arms.

'You're wonderful.' He was smiling down at her. 'Don't let's go to work today. We could stay here . . .'

'I've got to go to work.' She was struggling out of his embrace. She didn't manage it for ten more delicious minutes.

She knew when she threw off the bedclothes that she should feel heavy with shame. She'd committed a terrible sin by allowing Toby to stay the night with her while her mother was away.

'Nobody must know,' she told him as she dressed. 'Particularly not the Ferrys.'

John would be the last man to do what Toby had. He'd be shocked if he knew. She rushed round making a pot of tea and setting out bread and marmalade on the table for their breakfast.

Her plan was that Toby would go off to work a few moments before she set out herself and creep quietly across the landing below. But Toby couldn't be rushed this morning.

'You're beautiful, Sarah. Do you know? You've made me so happy. Last night was wonderful.'

'It was,' she laughed at him. 'But this morning won't be if we don't get a move on.' She found it easier to set out at the usual time and leave Toby to turn the key in her door and leave when he was ready.

As she clattered down the bare stairs on her way to work, Elvira Ferry slammed her door and followed her down. Sarah wasn't finding her company so pleasant since she'd broken things off with John, but since they knew exactly how many minutes it took to walk to the factory, they often met up. This morning, Elvira was alone.

'Where's John?' Sarah asked. She'd never known him miss a day's work.

'You might well ask.' There was pent-up fury in Elvira's voice. They were out in the street before Sarah saw that her face was blotchy with tears. Her heavy eyebrows were working hard.

'Is he sick or something?'

She knew John rarely was. And even if he didn't feel well,

he would, like the rest of them, turn up for work and hope to feel better as the day went on. They all knew that if they didn't turn up, they wouldn't be paid.

'Not sick the way you mean. It's all your fault. I blame you.'

'What's happened?'

'He's not coming to work this morning. He's made up his mind to enlist. He's got this thing in his head about going to fight.'

Sarah's heart sank. 'That's nothing to do with me. Lots of men are joining up. I've seen it in the newspapers. It's war fever.'

'War fever or not, he'd never have thought of it if it hadn't been for you. You turned him down after three years of courtship and he can't wait to get away. Can't wait to get away from Percival's either. We know you had Toby Percival up there with you last night. How d'you think my John feels about that?'

Sarah gasped and came to a stop. She could feel herself blushing. Elvira went on:

'We could hear him walking round. Makes more noise than you and your mother. I suppose you thought we wouldn't know?'

Sarah covered her face with her hands. 'Don't say anything at work. Please!'

'I suppose he's still up there in your room, lying low till the coast's clear?'

Sarah was moving again; she put on a spurt.

'I'll be on my own when John goes. He'd never have done such a thing if it hadn't been for you. He'd set his heart on marrying you. It was cruel to turn him down like that.

'It scares me stiff to think of it. He won't listen to reason. My John out there fighting; he could be killed. If it isn't your fault, what's put such an idea in his head?'

Sarah was glad to reach the factory, where she could escape

Elvira's tongue. As she put on her brown overall and pushed her hair under one of the ugly caps they all had to wear, she was fighting with her conscience.

Elvira was right: of course it was her fault. She'd seen the agony on John's face. How would she live with herself if he was killed? The world no longer seemed a safe place.

When Maurice reached the office that morning, Toby was already at his desk with his ledgers open before him, but he looked very drowsy.

'It's clear,' Maurice said coldly, 'you didn't waste much time in sleep last night.'

Toby ignored him. Maurice released his own ire by expounding on the dangers of venereal disease.

'The pox is rampant in the slums, as well as the clap.'

Toby had the nerve to give him that so-innocent look and say: 'How would you know, Father?'

'And don't forget, syphilis is incurable once you catch it. You're bound to if you carry on like this.'

That certainly got to him. He was staring at his father in disgust. It made Maurice feel he'd been a little coarse.

Toby said: 'There's no point in discussing this. It's not getting us anywhere.' He turned a page of his ledger and lifted his pen.

Maurice felt he'd lost the argument. 'I hope you'll be over this sulkiness and act like a reasonable being when we go to see Ben Burton tomorrow afternoon.'

His son give a snort that sounded negative.

Maurice jerked to his feet and swept out into the factory, feeling livid. He couldn't take any more from Toby. He stamped round, hardly knowing what he was doing. The yellow-haired girl, the one he blamed for much of this trouble, was perkier than usual.

'I want to thank you, sir, for supplying a cart to take my mother to hospital. And men to help her. She couldn't have managed on her own. They think it's appendicitis.'

That confirmed his suspicions about where Toby had spent the night. At least the girl knew when to show gratitude for what he'd done.

He stayed out of his office for much of the morning, watching the flow of raw ingredients being turned into the finished product and then packed into gleaming jars.

How he admired what his own father had achieved. How much more able were the older generation; how much more willing to work hard.

His father had been born Gregor Mauritzi Kucharski in the Ukraine, and had come to Liverpool as a penniless immigrant at eighteen years of age. As a child, Maurice had loved to hear him talk about the hard times he'd endured when he'd first arrived here. He'd had a succession of poorly paid jobs in factories and foundries, and shared a room with another immigrant in an airless Liverpool court.

Gregor had had big ideas; he was determined to make his fortune, but he found himself trapped in poverty. The long hours he had to work meant he had no energy to do anything else, and he had to work to pay his rent and eat. He'd hated working indoors all through the hours of daylight, and felt trapped.

This had made him apply for a job as a gardener in a private household. He didn't expect to earn any more, but it allowed him to stay in the fresh air all day in the pleasant district of Princes Park.

His employer, Major Arnold Stanhope, had recently retired from the Indian Army and returned to Liverpool. His daughter Felicity had been brought up in India and was now keeping house for her father, her mother having succumbed to the evil climate of Bangalore.

Across the roses Gregor was tending, he'd been able to smell the curries Felicity cooked for her father; the chutneys and sauces and pickles she made to accompany them. Maurice knew his father had worshipped Felicity from afar for several years before he'd dared to speak more than a few words to her.

Felicity had had to cope with something of a domestic crisis when her housemaid ran off with the gardener from next door, a married man. On the spur of the moment, Gregor had stepped into the kitchen to help with the heavier chores. He'd loved working close to her, watching her move deftly about her domain. That was when he first tasted her cooking, and he thought her spicy food and unusual chutneys were absolutely wonderful.

When her father died unexpectedly a month or so later, Felicity had been very shaken and upset. She hadn't made close friends in Liverpool and she turned to Gregor for help with the funeral.

He'd had no idea how to go about it, but he very soon found out. There was nothing he wouldn't do for her. Felicity was even more distressed when she discovered her father's pension had died with him, leaving her with very little to live on. Gregor ached to put his arms round her to comfort her. She was nine years older than he was, and at thirty-six had expected to remain a spinster.

He found the confidence to propose to her and caused her many months of indecision. He thought that she was afraid of being on her own in a part of the world she didn't know well, and that marriage was more a question of gaining a supportive companion than of falling in love. He told her he had enough love for both of them.

Gregor had occupied the months trying to decide on a name that sounded thoroughly English. Felicity had anglicised his name to Gregory; the rest she couldn't pronounce. He'd smiled when he told Maurice:

'I couldn't expect a nicely brought-up lady like your mother to answer to the name of Mrs Kucharski, could I?'

Gregor had changed his name by deed poll to Percival, and become more English in his ways than the English themselves.

From the first, he'd had his ideas about how they could earn a living. He knew that as an employee, he could not earn enough to keep Felicity in the comfort to which she was accustomed. All she had ever done was to keep house, and that with the help of a large staff in Bangalore and a general maid in Princes Park. Cooking had been almost a hobby.

He suggested they try to market her chutneys and sauces as well as English pickled onions. There was the huge advantage that Felicity could start up the business in the kitchen in Princes Park.

She bought some handsome glass jars, and together they designed attractive labels and had them printed professionally. Gregory said they must aim for the top end of the market. He went round Liverpool seeking orders from shops who supplied the carriage trade.

Within a month or two, when the initial orders were renewed and in some cases increased, they knew their pickles were a success, but the neighbours were beginning to complain about the smell and about such a business being carried on in a residential district.

Felicity had said: 'The kitchens here are too small anyway.'

It meant they had to move from the pleasant house with a garden in Princes Park to a hovel in a back street near to the Coburg Dock and the Southern Hospital, where Maurice had been born.

The premises they first moved to had been built as a billiard hall and had living accommodation above, but they were in a very run-down area.

'Your mother was very brave,' his father had told him.

She'd said: 'I don't go out much. I can't if I'm going to cook all day, so what does the district matter?'

His father hadn't minced his words.

'It's a slum. Your friends will say I shouldn't have brought you here.'

She'd smiled sadly. 'My father's friends, not mine. We can find somewhere better as soon as we get the business on its feet.'

'I promise you we will,' Gregory had said. 'Just as soon as it's possible. We'll have a fine house one day.'

The pickles sold well and the business expanded quickly. Within two years it was outgrowing the billiard hall. By the following summer, the strong smell of pickles was permeating the new district, and the heat from the stoves rising into their rooms above was very trying. People who lived near by started to call Gregory the Pickle King, and his premises Little India.

He knew the time had come to move the factory and find a more suitable home for his family. He wanted to keep the staff they were building up, so could not move the factory far. He and Felicity spent their Sundays looking for alternative accommodation, and it wasn't long before they came across a vast warehouse on nearby Jordan Street. It was empty at the time, and just what they were looking for. There was space to work; space to store both the ingredients they would use and some of the finished product.

Maurice's father had bought these premises thirty years ago and set up the assembly line using rollers to make mass production possible. He'd brought the great cauldrons from the billiard hall, but he'd also bought the latest machines and equipment, most of which were still in daily use today. They'd changed from coal-burning stoves to gas, but that was just about the only change Maurice had had to make.

He stood lost in thought, watching his jars of Madras chutney roll past on the line. This was one of his mother's original recipes, sharp on the tongue with lemons, and hot too with mustard seed, celery seed and dill. The full jars were being lifted off and packed into wooden crates for transport to the shops.

When Maurice returned to the office, having had a meal at Radley's Refreshment Rooms, Toby was already at his desk taking out his ledgers, as though he couldn't wait to get down to work.

Maurice stood in front of Toby's desk.

'Come home to your own bed tonight,' he ordered. 'I'm not putting up with this sort of thing.'

Toby ignored him and started to write. For Maurice, nothing could have been more infuriating. Toby's behaviour over the last few days had really rankled. He couldn't hold back any longer.

'You made me look a fool in front of the workers yesterday. I told you to do one thing and you did the opposite.' That had really infuriated him.

'I took Mrs Hoxton to hospital.' Toby's boyish blue eyes were more confrontational than usual.

'Yes, against my direct orders.' Maurice was still seething.

'She needed help, Father.'

'I told Phillips to take her on the cart. That was perfectly adequate.'

'She was ill.'

'Appendicitis, so I hear. That was no reason to waste the rest of the morning. I take it you were hanging round the hospital to find that out?'

'I sent Phillips back with the cart.'

'So I saw.' He added, with a touch of sarcasm: 'You didn't feel the need to keep it waiting in case she needed to be driven home?'

Maurice saw his son's lips tighten. 'It was an accident in the workplace. The company ought to pay her compensation.'

'What nonsense!' The nerve of that! 'The woman was ill, that's what caused the accident. She should have had the sense to stay home.'

'They're worried about paying the hospital bill, Father. They've both worked here for years, mother and daughter, and—'

'It's not our problem. Not if it's appendicitis. She's not strong enough for the work here, it's proved that. I'll not have her back when she's better.'

He knew that had really set Toby off. His face had gone crimson. 'You don't realise what the job means to—'

'If she'd been anyone else, you wouldn't care. I can't believe you've got involved with a girl like that. A working girl from the slums. I don't know what you see in her. Drop her, before this goes any further.'

'I love her, Father. I'm not going to drop her. I think any decent employer would pay wages for—'

'This factory has to earn a profit,' he'd had to point out. 'That's the whole point of running it. It's not our job to provide alms and succour the poor.'

Toby knew he couldn't spend another minute anywhere near his father. He couldn't sit in the same room as him; not even pass the afternoon in the same building. Father was always so worked up, so full of anger, so outrageous in what he said. Ten minutes in his company caused Toby to fume too. He had to get away from him for a few hours at least.

Toby took his case of samples from the cupboard. One part of his job, which he enjoyed very much, was to seek new outlets for their products. He visited shops all over the district and persuaded them to stock Percival's Pickles. He reckoned he was good at doing that. Their sales were rising steadily. It had been entirely his idea to get his pickles aboard the many ships that docked in Liverpool. They weren't fancy enough to grace the tables of the trans-Atlantic passenger liners, but the sailors loved them. He now delivered to four big shipping companies.

'I'm going out,' he announced to his father.

'Tuesdays and Thursdays are your days for selling.'

'That isn't written in stone. Change of plan; I'm going now.'

He strode briskly along the dock road, swinging the case as though it weighed only ounces. He had to work off some of his rage against his father.

Maurice was a hard man, a very hard man to work for,

54

never pleased with anything he did. Rather the reverse, in fact. Whatever Toby suggested, it was vetoed because Grandfather hadn't done it.

Father was always telling him how he'd taken over the running of the business when he was twenty, and pointing out that now Toby was twenty and a grown man he should be capable of doing more. Yet he was allowed no responsibilities of any sort. It was do this, do that, and no, I don't want you to meddle and change things.

Father oversaw everything, including the marketing. He'd given Toby a book in which he'd organised which district of the city he was to work in on each day. He thought Toby should make six visits each time he went out selling. Damn it, some visits took much longer than others. Even Father couldn't alter that.

And he'd been horribly rude about Sarah and ordered him to drop her. No thought for Toby's feelings or hers. But on top of everything else, in his high-handed way, he'd suddenly decided to turn Toby into an accountant. He hadn't thought to ask if he'd like to do it. Well, accountancy was out. Toby was having none of that.

It was a sunny afternoon with a blustery wind off the river. Toby turned up Paradise Street and saw flags fluttering from almost every building. The faint strains of a Souza march were being carried on the wind. Gradually he realised the band was coming closer. His step lengthened unconsciously as he began to march in time. He could hear the cheering crowd too.

He felt better, although he'd come out without his book of directions and had no particular plans in his head. There were posters everywhere; he'd heard all about the huge recruitment drive to get men into uniform. Kitchener's Army, they called it. England needed them. Ahead of him, he could see the military band crossing from Lord Street into Chapel Street. He quickened his step. It was a fine sight; the horses groomed to perfection, the soldiers in their bright uniforms, the sun glinting on their brass instruments, and all stepping out in such a jaunty fashion to the stirring tune.

Traffic was having to pull to the kerb to let them pass. Women on the pavements waved and shouted encouragement. The crowd was cheering; everybody seemed to welcome the war.

The Kaiser had five armies all sweeping through Belgium and France and heading for the Channel ports. The Belgians were fighting hard and were holding the line against the first and second German armies. The French and the British were trying to halt the rest of the Kaiser's force as it advanced in a spearhead towards Paris.

This was going to be a rapid, mobile modern war; everybody, even Kitchener, said it would be over before Christmas.

The band had lured a mass of youths to follow it; small boys and dogs marched behind them. Toby joined them, his spirits uplifted, and marched up Ranleigh Street, where a crowd was already pressing around one of the shops. It had been an empty shop, Toby thought, last time he'd been up here. Now there was a clutch of flags flying over the door, and two soldiers in full dress uniform standing one each side. The imposing figure of a regimental sergeant major with waxed moustaches presided over proceedings.

Toby understood now: this was the new recruiting office. A notice told him they were recruiting for the King's Own Regiment, Liverpool's own. A crowd of youths jostled to enlist, pressing to get in, and a long line snaked down the pavement. More were joining it by the minute. Toby felt the heady lure of enlistment fever himself.

All round him, eager voices were discussing it:

'It'll be a lark.'

'We'll have a go at the Kaiser. He's asking for it.'

'Get me out of this awful job.'

'Stop shoving in. We've been waiting here all morning.'

'Wish they'd get a move on. At this rate, the war'll be over before we're sworn in.'

'See a bit of the world, why not?'

'We don't want to miss it. Mightn't get another chance like this.'

Toby could feel the tremendous excitement and enthusiasm all round him. How could he not be moved?

At that moment he recognised John Ferry at the head of the line. Toby saw him as a familiar face, and in his excitement forgot about his association with Sarah.

'Trumper told me you were about to do it.' He slapped John on the back. 'It'll be a jolly good show. You'll have a bit of fun.'

'More fun than if I stay home.' It shocked Toby to see John Ferry looking so fierce. 'You've ruined everything there for me. I'll be glad to get away from you. At least you're not likely to enlist.'

'I don't know . . .'

John's hostile eyes raked him. 'You knew Sarah Hoxton was spoken for. It didn't stop you taking her. It's easy for men like you to dazzle a young girl, turn her head. I can't bear to watch you hurt her. Staying all night with her behind her mother's back!'

Toby knew Sarah had been very upset that they knew. She was afraid it would soon be all round the factory. He'd felt so sure they'd been quiet.

'Ruining her reputation.' Toby could see the other's fists clenching. 'No decent man will look at her now you've played around with her.'

'Hang on a minute!' Toby couldn't believe his ears. None of the workers spoke out of turn at the factory. He'd thought John deferential. 'I love Sarah and she loves me. She won't need—'

'Don't make me sick. If you hurt her, I'll do for you, I'm promising you that.'

Toby was taken aback at John's outburst. 'I won't hurt her. It's the last thing—'

'You've done it already. Why can't you see that?'

'Next,' bellowed the sergeant. 'Come on, lad.'

'I want to get away from all you Percivals. You won't be following me in here. The likes of you don't have the guts to fight for your country. You're featherbedded here, so why should you bother?' With that John Ferry passed through the door of the recruiting centre.

'You in this line?' a voice asked behind Toby.

'Er, no . . .' Toby backed away, barely able to control his anger. How dare John Ferry suggest he hadn't the guts to fight?

Did it take guts? A few jolly marches behind a band, and a great battle or two to knock the Kaiser on the head. It sounded a damn sight more attractive than learning to be an accountant. Father was determined to put him out of his present job and article him to his friend at Burton, Wallis and Jones. Father wouldn't listen when he told him he didn't want that.

Toby was afraid nothing would turn him into an accountant, not in a month of Sundays; he didn't have it in him. He was used to the stink and rattle of the factory floor. He didn't want to wear a smart suit and sit in a handsome office.

Damn it, he wasn't going to do it; he'd rather enlist. What a laugh he'd have, explaining to Father why his plans would come to nought. But he didn't want to find himself fighting alongside John Ferry. The mood John was in today, Toby could be in more danger from a bayonet in his back than an enemy bullet. Anyway, he belonged the other side of the water. The Cheshire Regiment would be more his line than the King's Own.

There was a table set out on the pavement with leaflets on it. Toby pushed through the crowd towards it and took one. It looked very interesting. Far better to go with the boys than spend the rest of his life jumping round to Father's orders.

Despite the unexpected brush with John Ferry, Toby was still buoyed up by his afternoon out, though he hadn't made a single call. His mind had been on other things. It had been a jolly good band and it had done him good to go out, even though he'd have to fake a couple of entries in the book, to side-step the row Father would otherwise start.

Chapter Five

Toby felt very close to Sarah. Each day in the dinner break he went with her to the hospital to enquire about Maria. She was told her mother was having less pain and feeling better for the rest.

Sarah had been worried about the hospital bill, and he'd persuaded her to see the almoner. He'd gone with her and waited while she did. That had set her mind at rest. They'd have to pay something, but she considered the amount affordable.

She seemed to inhabit a very different world from his. A simpler world, with very few personal belongings, but it was a more caring one. He couldn't get enough of it.

He was filled with admiration for her. Sarah was strong, both physically and mentally. The women in his family did little but organise the household, while Sarah worked a long, hard day and still had the energy to shop and cook and to enjoy the little leisure she had.

He thought the two rooms she shared with her mother a triumph considering their circumstances. They were kept spotlessly clean despite the grime of the street below. He could even say he found them reasonably comfortable, though they'd be more so if they'd had running water and didn't have to carry up all their coal.

Sarah ran down the stairs at precisely twenty-three minutes past seven, so she could arrive at the factory before seven thirty. As she did each morning now, she left Toby to drink a second cup of tea and lock up.

She met John Ferry coming out of his room below. This morning she rounded on him.

'You didn't have to join up like that. I don't know what's getting into you men. Rushing off in droves to the recruitment centres. Your mother's blaming me. You'd better tell her it wasn't my idea.'

His dark eyes turned on her full of abject misery. 'It doesn't matter.'

'Of course it matters.'

'I mean I'm not going. The army's rejected me. Not fit for active service. My ankle . . .'

'Your limp?' Sarah laughed with relief. 'Thank goodness for that. You'll be staying on at Percival's then?'

'I wrote out my notice. Mam gave it to Mr Trumper yesterday.'

'I shouldn't worry. With so many going, they'll be glad to keep you on.'

Elvira came out and turned the key in the door with savage intensity.

'I don't know how you can laugh like that, Sarah.' She headed down the stairs at breakneck pace. 'I still blame you for this mess.'

'What mess?' Sarah asked John.

He looked downcast. 'I've spoken out of turn. I said things to Toby Percival . . . told him a few home truths. He might not want me to go on working for them.'

She said: 'He won't hold it against you. He's not that sort.'

'I think I said too much. Things I wouldn't have dared say otherwise. I thought I was leaving, you see.'

Their fellow workers were all round John the moment they went through the door of the factory.

'When are you going?'

'If I'd enlisted, you'd not see me here. Not likely.'

'Wish my wife would let me go.'

When Mr Trumper came out of the cloakroom, John said:

'They won't take me. I've got a dicky ankle. No good for route marches and that.'

Sarah heard the yard door swing open. Toby was amongst those who came in just as John was saying:

'I'd like to stay on working here. Keep my job. If that's all right?'

'Course you can, lad. More than glad to have you. You know that.' Trumper was fastening up his drill coat over his waistcoat and collarless shirt. 'We all are, aren't we, Master Toby? The army won't have John Ferry. They don't know a good lad when they see one.'

Sarah saw John and Toby eyeing each other up.

'You've been rejected?'

'Medical grounds.' After a pause John added: 'Very sorry about what I said yesterday. Should never have opened my mouth.' He explained about his ankle.

Toby looked unusually cold. 'Strong on guts, eh? But weak on ankles.'

'That's about it. I'm sorry. You'll not put me out?'

Sarah saw Toby relax; he slapped John on the back and laughed.

'Course not. You do a good job for us, and anyway, we're going to be short-handed the way things are going.'

John started work. He told himself he ought to feel relief that Toby had allowed him to go on working with so little fuss, but Toby filled him with resentment; John couldn't stomach that he'd lured Sarah from him. He was filled with rancour, though he'd always thought of himself as a person who didn't bear a grudge.

His job was to help in the stockroom. He was hoping that when the stock controller retired next year, he'd get his job. With this in mind, he was doing as much as he was allowed towards keeping a running record of the various types of pickle in stock. It was quite complicated, as most of their products needed to be kept a few weeks to mature.

In the mean time, he sorted and stacked the cases which were freshly made each day and helped to load the carts with those going out to be sold.

He'd made himself apologise to Toby, though it had stuck in his throat. He couldn't afford to make an enemy of him if he wanted to keep his job. Nowhere else would be so convenient; the factory was close to their room and his mother worked here too.

It had never occurred to John that the army might reject him on medical grounds. That had incensed him further, made him feel he was no good for anything. Mam had been mollified, though. As they walked home together at dinner time, she'd said:

'Luck was on our side for once. Rejected on medical grounds, a strong man like you? I find that hard to believe. At least I won't be left to fend for myself.'

'I didn't expect Toby to forgive . . . Not like that. Generous of him, I suppose.'

Elvira's anxious eyes went up and down the street in case there was anyone near enough to overhear.

'Nothing generous about the Percivals. Rotters, both of them. The old man's as hard as nails, and we know what Toby gets up to. It suits them to keep you on. You do a good job for them. I never thought I'd be glad of what your dad did to you, but I am. It means you'll be staying with me.'

He and Mam had made up a story about his ankle being injured in a road accident. The truth was that John had tried to intervene between his parents when his father, in a drunken rage, had attacked his mother. Dad had gone for him instead. He'd been only nine and no match for his strength.

John had relived it a hundred times in nightmares. The thud as he'd been thrown to the floor, knocking the breath out of his body. His father, wearing hob-nailed boots, had stood on his bare ankle. The searing pain had made him scream, but his father had laughed and jumped on him, breaking several bones.

Mam didn't want people to know the sort of father he'd had, though drunkenness was common in the district where they lived.

She'd said sadly: 'No decent person would believe a father would do such a thing. Maim his own son.' John hadn't been able to walk on it for a year.

'Your dad was half crazed by drink. Never knew when he'd had enough and wouldn't leave it alone. He'd do anything when the drink was in him.'

That evening, they were getting tea on the table when they heard Toby going upstairs again with Sarah. John wanted to put his hands over his ears.

His mother said: 'There's a lot of rotten people in the world. They don't understand what they're doing to you.'

For Maurice, it was making matters worse that Toby was deliberately flouting his orders and not coming home at night. He knew he was still running round after the yellow-eyed girl and her mother; it could only lead to further trouble. He was afraid Toby was going to make a fool of himself. It would be a disaster if he married her.

Maurice went to bed early feeling exhausted. Mercifully, he slept. Thursday came; he knew he was facing another difficult day. It was the day he had arranged for Toby to see Benjamin Burton in his Liverpool office.

At breakfast, he complained to Claudia about Toby's behaviour. It didn't help when she said:

'It's a relief not to have him sulking at the table every meal time. This way there's no arguments.'

'That's not the point,' he flared angrily.

He'd been in the office for fifteen minutes when Toby came to his desk yawning, looking as though he'd had a wakeful night.

'Two thirty this afternoon,' Maurice reminded him. 'I'll come in with you, but I'll not stay. If we leave here around two, we won't have to hurry.'

He wanted to take Toby in, not only to make sure he got there but to show family solidarity. Also he wanted to see Burton's office; by all accounts it was quite grand.

Toby gave him a baleful glance. His silence, his refusal to say anything that wasn't strictly to do with the work of the moment was winding Maurice up tighter and tighter, just as he wound his clocks on Saturday nights.

Maurice knew this was the right thing to do. He'd reached the stage when he could no longer hold his tongue, and to say anything to Toby while they both felt such alienation would only make matters worse. Toby needed to spend the working day somewhere else. A year or two spent apart would alter their relationship, hopefully put it back on a better footing.

He must think of bringing Edward in. He'd already paid his school fees for next term, so perhaps after Christmas would be the best time. He needed somebody here to help him.

Claudia was fuelling the flames, as always. She wanted him to alter his will. To give Adam a share of the business was what she was saying openly, but beneath that reasonable front, he knew she wanted him to cut Toby out and put Adam in.

He'd telephoned for an appointment to see his solicitor later this afternoon. His office was close to Burton's. He could leave Toby to discuss details and pop in to see Jeffrey Masters.

He should do something for Adam. He was a noisy, boisterous child – Claudia didn't give him enough discipline – but it was only right he should leave him a share of the business. God knows, he couldn't grow up with less business sense than Toby, and might just have more.

Maurice hadn't quite made up his mind what to leave Toby in his will. He didn't deserve anything; Maurice would like to cut him out, but no, he shouldn't do that. As a little boy, Toby had been his pride and joy. A third share perhaps, instead of half?

All the same, Toby was taking no interest in the business.

Why should Maurice bend over backwards for him? He had hoped for and expected so much from Toby, and had been disappointed time and time again. He wanted to give up on him but knew he couldn't. Toby was still his son, his first-born. Once he'd felt such love for him, been so proud. Now, it would serve the boy right if he were thrown out on his neck.

Maurice felt he was being pushed over the edge, and it wasn't just Toby. The war was on everybody's mind. There was talk of the Germans blockading British ports, and nobody seemed to realise how serious that could be for a business like his.

A wave of nationalism was sweeping the country as a huge recruitment campaign got under way. The newspapers were full of it; there were posters going up everywhere with a picture of Kitchener pointing his finger. 'Your Country Needs You' was the message they were driving home. Flags were flying from every building and brass bands were playing in the streets. The atmosphere was more that of a carnival than a war. Already, half a dozen of his best workers had answered the call. This morning, he'd had to put a notice on the gate saying he had vacancies, but it was unlikely to bring in young men.

Lunch time came. Maurice usually went down the street to Mr Radley's Refreshment Rooms for a hot meal. It did him good to get out of the office and take a walk, but understandably, with all this trouble, he wasn't feeling well and his indigestion was bothering him more. He ordered steak and kidney pie, but couldn't eat it when it came.

Back in the office, Maurice looked at the clock. Toby had been at his desk first thing this morning, but when Maurice had wanted him to clarify the address of a new customer at ten o'clock he'd been unable to find him. Now he had something new to worry about.

When Maurice had first suggested it, Toby had said he wasn't prepared to be articled to Benjamin Burton, and since then he'd clammed up completely. But although Toby said no to almost everything suggested to him, eventually he was persuaded to do it. It was his way of kicking back. Maurice had had no doubts that he'd knuckle down when the time came.

Now, as Maurice looked anxiously at the office clock, he felt another rush of fury. It shocked him that Toby dared to treat him like this. If he wasn't back within the next fifteen minutes he'd have to phone Benjamin and ask him to postpone the meeting until another day. That was what he'd say: postpone, not cancel, though cancelling was what it would amount to. He couldn't ask Burton to give him a second chance.

Maurice could feel sweat breaking out on his forehead; he could feel himself boiling up with reproach and anger. He'd never treated his own father in this way. How ungrateful could a son be? Toby had been offered a good living, and eventually would own part of a successful business, built up by his grandfather. That ought to give him some feeling for family, but Toby didn't feel bound by any rules; he was above them. He did what he wanted to do, whatever gave him pleasure at the moment; and conversely, he refused to do anything that didn't.

The quarter of an hour was up. Maurice couldn't delay any longer; already he'd left it much later than good manners required. He cursed Toby as he lifted his telephone.

Benjamin sounded shirty at the other end, as well he might. To be articled to Burton, Wallis and Jones was a highly sought-after position which, if completed satisfactorily, guaranteed a well-paid career in the future. Benjamin had been doing them both a favour.

Maurice sank back in his chair feeling defeated. Toby could do what he damn well liked. He needn't expect anything more from him. He'd cut him right out of his will after this, leave the business between Edward and Adam. He'd tried hard with Toby. Far too hard.

Maurice pulled himself up in his chair. Was that Toby he could hear outside? Yes, that was his laugh; he sounded good-humoured, even excited. That he'd come back at this late hour made Maurice burn with anger again. If he thought they were going to rush off to Dale Street to see Burton now, he'd have to think again. The office door burst open.

'Hello, Father. I'm back.'

He must know he'd gone too far this time. 'It's too late,' Maurice said with irritable force. 'No good changing your mind now. I've rung Burton and cancelled our meeting.'

'Good!'

He couldn't believe it. This was Toby at his most insolent. Clearly, he hadn't relented and decided to fall in with his father's wishes. That added a further boost to Maurice's anger.

'You're right about one thing.' Toby's eyes challenged his. 'We can't go on like this. We're making each other's life a misery.'

'You've managed to work that out? So what are you going to do?'

'I've already done it. I've signed up.'

Maurice didn't take in what he meant at first. 'Signed up for what?'

'Joined the army. Had my medical, passed A1. Been sworn in and everything. England needs me even if you don't.' Toby's wide smile mocked him. 'Isn't that a good way of getting away from you?'

For Maurice, it was as though something had exploded within him. He was shaking. The office and Toby's face swam before his eyes.

'You fool! You bloody stupid fool.'

Toby wasn't smiling now. 'I'm ordered to report for basic training at nine o'clock on Monday morning.'

'Next Monday? Good God! Don't you ever stop to think anything through? There'll be no going back on this. No way out.'

69

'I know that.'

'The war could last for years. Don't you care what happens to this business?'

'You brought me up to care. According to you, the whole point of my life is to learn to run Percival's Pickles.'

'How can you run it if you aren't here?'

'You wanted to sign me up to do accounts. What's the difference?'

'You would have learned a useful skill. It would have helped you run the business. If you'd stuck it for only a year, it would still have been useful to you. Firing a gun won't help with anything else. How damn foolish . . . You got carried away like the rest of them. You're like lemmings!'

Maurice took a shuddering breath and tried to think. The silence lengthened. 'You've gone in as a private?'

'Yes.' There was something sheepish about Toby now.

'You might have had a commission if you'd gone about it the right way. You're in too much of a hurry.'

Maurice wanted to weep at the stupidity of it. His head was throbbing and he felt sick. There was a spinning kaleidoscope of lights behind Toby's face.

'For how long? How long have you signed up for?'

'For three years or until the end of the war.'

'Good God!'

'It'll be over before Christmas, Father. Kitchener says it'll all be over quickly. I didn't want to miss the fun.'

'Fun!' Maurice covered his eyes with his hands to stop the flickering lights, but they were still there. 'I hope you find it fun. Let me tell you, you're going to regret this. I didn't realise what a bloody fool you were. You could get yourself killed, you stupid ass.'

Toby returned with venom: 'I suppose you hope I will?'

Maurice slumped forward against his desk, supporting his head on his hands.

'Get out of here and leave me in peace.' His indigestion

was worse; it was hardening to a pain that stabbed at him, taking his breath away.

Toby could be killed! This could be the end of him. Oh God, he was his son after all.

Toby wanted to scream that he was at his wits' end too; that Father had driven him to this. The afternoon had been an emotional drain. Elation was what he'd felt as he'd stood in the long queue of men waiting to join up. If a factory lad like John Ferry could do it, so could he.

The wait of two hours until his turn came to approach the desk flew past. He handed in the forms he'd filled out. That was followed by another wait for his medical exam. The time was filled with the good-humoured banter from others who hoped to join up. They passed round printed cards setting out the terms and conditions for a fighting man. The pay was to be a shilling a day.

'That'll buy five pints of beer.'

'Six in the Lord Nelson.'

'Never; it says sixpence a week is deducted for laundry.'

'And you'll have to buy your own blanco and shoe polish,' the sergeant told them.

But nobody was put off; the atmosphere had been terrific.

'I can swear you in now,' the sergeant had told Toby once he was pronounced fit and well. Taking a Bible in his right hand, Toby had repeated the oath after him. The solemnity of that, of knowing he was needed to defend his King and country in this time of need, made him feel a hero.

Coming face to face with Father again had been like being doused with cold water. Never had Maurice called him a bloody fool to his face before, and suddenly what had seemed clever and a load of fun now looked foolish.

Toby told himself that thousands were joining up. Like them, he'd done it for his country. He slammed out of the office and on to the factory floor. He had never felt in such a fever as this. Dad had accused him of being wild, but this was the first time he'd truly felt wild.

Even though he was about to leave, he felt he had duties here he must see to. One line was making pickled cabbage today. The hard red cabbages first had to have their outer leaves stripped by hand and some of the stalk removed before the machine chopped them up. Pickling cabbage was more popular with the workers than pickling onions, but they didn't make all that much of it.

From a distance, he watched Sarah Hoxton working like a robot. She understood him, the only person who did. He wanted to feel the comfort of her arms round him. He wanted to bury his face in her lovely fair hair. She could make his distress melt away, but he couldn't take her away from her job. If his father came out and caught him with her in working hours, he'd do what he'd threatened and sack her. She and her mother were relying on her wages now.

Today, even Sarah couldn't stop him fuming. He couldn't settle to anything; he was striding from the great vats where the piccalilli was cooking, to the machine chopping red cabbage, to the salting room, and back again. But what did it matter? In three more days he'd be in the army. Father would have to get on with this by himself.

'Mr Toby, Mr Toby, come quick.' Miss Potts, the office clerk, was rushing towards him. Her face was grey.

'What's the matter?'

'Come quick, come quick. I was taking his tea in.' The woman was plucking at his sleeve, hardly coherent.

'Tea for my father?' Toby followed her back to the office.

Father was slumped across his desk. Half the contents of the tea cup were in its saucer. Three Marie biscuits were on the floor and crunched under his feet as he went closer.

Eunice Potts was breathing heavily behind him. 'I think he's dead.'

Chapter Six

Toby couldn't take it in. He couldn't think straight. He put out his hand to touch his father; his skin was clammy and cold. How long since he'd left him? Half an hour? An hour?

'Oh God!' It didn't matter how long; Father was dead. What was he to do now?

'Get Sarah Hoxton. Ask her to come in here.'

Miss Potts' frightened eyes stared at him. 'Now, in here?'

Toby went to his own desk and slumped down. He was sweating under the burden of guilt. His father had died because he'd joined the army to get away from him, and because of the awful rows they were having. With another jolt, Toby remembered that he was supposed to report to the camp in three days' time. That made his neck crawl with horror. He felt he was drowning in a sea of remorse and grief. This had turned into a truly terrible afternoon. He was shaking so much he almost missed the soft tap on the door.

'Sarah? Come in.' Her head came slowly round the door. She gave an explosive gasp when she caught sight of his father.

'Come in and close the door,' he implored.

She came creeping towards him, keeping her back to the wall and as far away from Father as she could, never taking her eyes from him. Toby moistened his lips.

'He died at his desk.' He could hardly get the words out. 'What have I done?'

'Done? Do – you mean what must you *do*?'

His teeth had begun to chatter. 'Yes, yes.'

'A doctor. That's it, get a doctor here. I'll go and fetch one from the hospital.'

'No! I want you to stay here. With me.' He needed her. 'Send Trumper.' Toby saw the foreman as the next most reliable person.

Sarah stared at him, her amber eyes full of doubt. 'I can't tell him what to do. He's the foreman. Mr Trumper won't go for me.'

'Tell him Father's been taken ill. That I'm asking him. Tell him to hurry.'

After one more frightened glance at his father, she fled.

Toby tried to pull himself together; he would have to deal with this. Sarah came back, bringing a cup of tea for him.

'Drink this,' she said. 'It'll make you feel better. Trumper's gone.'

He gulped at the tea; he hadn't realised just how dry his mouth had become. It helped a little.

'You'll be running the company now.' He knew Sarah was trying to reassure him. 'You'll have a free hand with all those ideas you have.'

'No!'

She was frowning. 'You'll have to; no one else can.'

'I know that, but I've done a terrible thing. I enlisted this morning. I'm to be Private Tobias Percival, of some new service battalion, I've forgotten the number. It's the Cheshire Regiment.'

'Joined the army?' The shock on her face showed that she saw it as a catastrophe too.

'Yes, signed up for it. Been sworn in, everything. But this changes things. I can't go now. I won't be able to. I'm needed here.'

'You didn't say . . . You didn't tell me you were going to.' Sarah's eyes were wide with shock. 'Whatever made you do it?'

'John Ferry said I hadn't the guts.'

'Just that!'

'Oh no, it's everything. Father wanted me out of here, and all the lads are going off to fight. They'll have a good time. I didn't want to miss out.'

'What about me?' He'd hurt her feelings, he could see that. 'I thought . . . you'd want to stay with me. You said . . .'

'I do, Sarah. I'd do anything to stay here now.'

'Then hadn't you better let them know what's happened?'

His eyes went to the telephone on the wall behind Father's desk.

'Now?'

'The sooner the better.'

He'd been given a copy of the paper he'd signed, and now he drew it from his pocket. There was an address on it, and a telephone number. It seemed all wrong to make such a call with Father still there at his desk. He unhooked the phone and asked the operator for the number.

When he was put through he couldn't explain himself properly. He was tongue-tied, all mixed up with nerves.

'I signed up this lunch time,' he said. 'But I won't be able to report as directed.'

A long pause while all he could hear was sheets of paper being flicked over as they checked. Then a voice thundered at him that it wasn't an option, he couldn't change his mind. He'd signed up and that was that. He was in the army now.

'My father's just died.'

He tried to explain about having to run the business on which the whole family depended for a living. 'We employ fifty-two people.'

There was another long-drawn-out silence. Toby's hopes soared, then the voice said: 'If you bring your father's death certificate in, you'll be granted compassionate leave to attend the funeral and settle his affairs. Bring the papers you were given with you. You'll be given another date to report to barracks.'

Toby was stunned. It was hard to believe, but Father had

been right: it seemed there was no way out for him now. What would happen to the business?

He was putting the phone back on its hook when Mr Trumper ushered the doctor in.

'He's dead. There's nothing I can do. You did realise?' Sympathetic eyes searched Toby's face.

Toby felt dazed. Without mentioning the arguments, he tried to explain what had happened.

The doctor looked very little older than Toby was himself, and yet he seemed competent and professional as he went about his duties. It sapped Toby's self-esteem further.

'You mustn't blame yourself. Because it was sudden, there'll have to be a post-mortem to decide the cause of death. Most likely it's a heart attack or a stroke. I'll arrange for the body to be taken to the morgue.' The doctor paused at the door. 'I can't issue a death certificate yet.'

Toby was left with Sarah.

'Now what?' It was the fate of the business that was overwhelming him.

She said: 'Hadn't you better let your family know? Your brother and your stepmother.'

He felt drained. 'Yes, I must.' He had no energy. 'You'd better let everybody know here.'

'Shall I stop the lines? As a mark of respect?'

He heaved a sigh. 'Do what you think best.'

'And what about tomorrow? Will the factory work as usual?'

'I suppose so. Father would have a fit if he thought they were all having a paid holiday.'

Toby groaned. He'd have to devise some way in which the business could run. He'd have to appoint a new manager. He couldn't afford to close the place down now.

Sarah hesitated. 'I'd better say you'll close for his funeral, then?'

'I suppose so.'

He was asking himself over and over who could possibly run

76

the business. Mr Trumper, the foreman? It was hammering at Toby now that he'd done a very foolish thing by signing up. If only he hadn't, things would be very different.

It was a relief when two porters came to the office with a covered handcart to wheel his father's body away.

'Sir, would you remove his personal effects first? His valuables, his watch.'

Toby unthreaded the gold chain from across his father's waistcoat and withdrew the half-hunter from his pocket. It felt like desecration to open his jacket and push his fingers into his inside pocket to take the wallet with its purse heavy with sovereigns. There was his fountain pen – Father had been fond of that – and his big silver cigarette case of which he'd been even fonder.

Toby opened it. Only three cigarettes left. Father filled it with his favourite Senior Service every morning before leaving home. How many times had Toby watched him do that? Father's key ring, matches and handkerchief. He always wore gold cuff links and collar studs. The cuff links were easy to remove; the back collar stud almost impossible. He'd leave that. He backed away, feeling a little sick.

'He's wearing a ring, sir.'

Father had always worn the heavy gold signet ring on his little finger. It had Grandfather's initials inscribed on it, because once it had belonged to him. Perhaps Adam would like it as a keepsake when he grew up? Toby swallowed the lump in his throat as he tried to pull it off. How could he have shown so much ill feeling for his own father?

The ring was too tight and wouldn't come over Father's knuckle. One of the porters had to take it off for him. To see Father leaving his office for the last time like this brought pain Toby hadn't anticipated. If only they hadn't parted on such bad terms. If only he'd told Father that he did admire the way he'd held the business together all these years and that he wanted so much to do the same.

Toby rested for a few moments on the edge of his father's

chair. The office looked different from this unfamiliar angle. The work, the atmosphere, everything would be different from now on. He ought to stay here and run it; he was angry with himself for what he'd done, because now he couldn't imagine what the future would bring. The euphoria he'd felt this morning seemed in another, earlier age.

He began to sweep the papers Father had been working on into the top drawer of his desk. He'd been working out the wages that were due to be paid tomorrow. He'd made out the cheque and even signed it. The chequebooks and ledgers had to go in the safe; Father had been fanatical about keeping everything locked up. Toby put his father's large key ring in his pocket, then bent down and took a large used envelope from the waste-paper basket to pack Father's personal belongings in. He could hardly bear to look at them.

There were so many things he should be doing. They pressed down on him. He had to let everybody know. Edward . . .

His brother was staying near Bristol with a school friend and his family. Toby didn't even know their name. Father would know, of course; he'd have a note of it somewhere. He unlocked Father's desk drawer again and looked for the notebook in which he kept telephone numbers and addresses. There were half a dozen notebooks. Father always wrote everything down. Toby found what he was looking for. As luck would have it, he was able to talk to his brother straight away.

'How awful! What are we going to do? I'll come home,' Edward choked. 'Tonight. I was coming back on Monday anyway.'

He was more upset than Toby had expected. Over the last few years Edward had had rows with Father too, and he didn't get on with their stepmother. That was why he'd been sent away to school.

'Shall I meet your train?'

'I don't know the times. No, I'll get a taxi or something. You'll have to run the business now, won't you?'

That made Toby feel worse. He sat with his head in his hands for a long time. In Edward's place, he knew he'd find this easier to accept. Edward hadn't caused Father's death and brought this on them all. He was far enough away not to feel involved. He hadn't done a stupid thing like volunteering to go and fight a war; something that could cause an insurmountable problem.

But it might be all right. His circumstances had changed totally in the few hours since he'd signed. It wasn't as though he was really in the army. He'd go down and talk to them in a day or two, when he'd got Father's death certificate. They'd surely let him off to run a family business? They'd have to. Hadn't he heard somewhere that it was possible to buy one's way out? He'd be able to fix it. In the mean time, he mustn't dwell on it too much.

The telephone started to ring; the bell jangled his nerves. Somebody wanting to speak to Father? No need to panic; it would be a business call, and he was in charge now.

He took the receiver from the wall. 'Hello,' he said. 'Percival's Pickles.'

'Jeffrey Masters here.'

It took Toby a moment to place the name. Yes, his father's solicitor. He tried to explain what had happened; Masters would have to know anyway. He could feel the shock at the other end of the line.

'I'm so sorry. Do accept my condolences. I've known your father for years, admired him. I rang because he made an appointment to see me this afternoon. It was so unlike him not to keep it; he was always on time. I thought I ought to find out.'

Toby felt the hairs on the back of his neck stand up. Father had said nothing to him about seeing his solicitor.

'What did he want to see you for? Do you know?'

'He said he wanted to draw up a new will.'

Toby felt as though the breath had been knocked out of his body. 'A new will?' His mouth was parched again.

'I'm afraid he's left it too late.' Masters sounded quite dazed. 'I am sorry.'

Toby roused himself. 'What do I have to do? There must be things . . . I can't think.'

'Erm . . . There are registration formalities. Registration of the death, I mean. And the funeral to arrange, of course. I have a will here; I drew it up for your father some years ago. In the absence of a more recent one, it remains valid. I'll apply for probate in due course.'

When he put the phone down, Toby collapsed on his chair. His heart was still racing. Father had been about to change his will. He'd been close to cutting him out. Father had thought he'd never be able to run this business, thought him incapable. Toby believed he'd been within an inch of losing the inheritance he'd been brought up to expect.

Sarah came back and said she'd closed down the factory lines and sent everybody home an hour early, except those working on the piccalilli.

'It was ready to put in the jars,' she said. It needed to be done straight away, while it was still hot. 'The jars were hot too, so I told them to get it done and seal the lids down before they go.'

Toby felt at a loss. 'Thank you. I don't think I'd have coped on my own.'

'Course you would.'

'There's still Stepmother. I wish I didn't have to go home and face her.' He pushed his curls back from his forehead, agonised at the thought.

Father had not thought a telephone necessary at home. Grandfather had managed without, and Father didn't think he needed one either.

Sarah said: 'You've had a terrible shock. Come to my rooms for a while. Mr Trumper says he'll lock up here.'

* * *

Sarah felt she'd been knocked sideways. Mr Percival had been such a force. If she hadn't seen it with her own eyes, she'd not believe he could die like that at his desk, so suddenly and all by himself. Even more shocking was that Toby had enlisted without saying a word to her.

She'd heard that one or two of the factory lads had done it without telling their mothers, but for Toby it was different. He'd said he loved her and wanted to spend the rest of his life with her. He'd said he wanted them to share everything, and she'd believed him.

For the first time she wondered if she'd been mistaken about Toby. It had shocked her too to find him going to pieces. More than anything else she wanted to help him, but she didn't know how she could. She'd been working here for four years, during which time nothing much had changed, and now . . .

'Who's going to run the business?' Toby kept asking, as though there was an answer she could give him.

She'd done the right thing by bringing him here to her home. The colour was coming back into his round baby cheeks, but he looked vulnerable, like a lad who'd lost his way.

When she realised he'd had no lunch because he'd been at the recruiting centre, she heated them each a bowl of soup that she'd prepared for their supper.

His innocent troubled eyes looked into hers.

'I'll have to go home and tell my stepmother. She'll be expecting Father at the usual time. Come with me, Sarah.'

That made her heart jolt. She'd never have dared go there if Mr Percival were still alive. She was curious about Toby's home. Curious about the stepmother he didn't like. She wanted to go with him, but it seemed very daring.

'Say you will.'

'Then you'll come back here with me?' He'd stayed with her since Mam had gone into hospital. It had been three days of anxiety and joy, of anguish, horror and sensuous passion. A shocking, enchanting two nights of delight. Now, soon, he'd have to go away.

'If you'll let me.'

'You know I want you here.' Goodness knows what Mam would say when she found out. Sarah felt heavy with foreboding about that too.

She changed her dress and put on her best fawn hat and coat. She didn't look really smart even now. She'd bought the coat second-hand, but it was of good quality and there was still plenty of wear in it.

To Sarah, the other side of the river had seemed a long way from work. But now she couldn't believe how quick and pleasant the journey was. Just a short walk out of the mean streets to the Pier Head. Then the ferry boat ride, which was a real treat.

'That's where I live.' He pointed from the rail of the boat as it turned to come alongside New Ferry Pier. 'See the terrace of red-brick villas, then the five big houses beyond? I live in the bungalow on the end.'

'Right there on the river bank?' She hadn't known that.

'It looks great now the tide's in, but there's a huge stretch of brown mud when it's out.'

Set in its large garden, with the evening sun playing on the soft dun-coloured stone, she thought his home looked beautiful.

'It's grand.'

It seemed a different country here. So many trees, and gardens filled with flowers and grass. There wasn't a blade to be seen on her side of the water.

Toby pulled her hand on to his arm and they walked up the Pier and into New Ferry Road. Everything seemed cleaner and brighter on this side. He took her through tall wrought-iron gates into his back garden. It was so big, and there were so many roses; its magnificence took her breath away.

Sarah could see that the low house was L-shaped and seemed to be built of red brick.

'I thought it was stone.'

'It's faced with stone on the front.'

'It doesn't seem the same house.'

There were eight large sash windows facing her, each made up of small panes, with the top row being of a Georgian gothic design. The main path led to the back door and to steps leading down to the cellars, but Toby led her to the other wing and opened the door to a conservatory full of the warm scent of flowers. As soon as she stepped inside she could hear a piano tinkling.

'Stepmother's in the music room,' he whispered.

Sarah took a deep breath and followed him in. A music room? She'd never seen anything like this before. Here, two neo-Georgian sash windows stretched from floor to ceiling, filling the room with the last of the evening sun. At the grand piano, a small boy was practising scales under the tutelage of his mother. Claudia straightened up as soon as she saw Toby.

'You've decided to come home, then? Where've you been these last few nights? You've really upset your father.' Only then did she catch sight of Sarah. 'And who's this you've brought with you?'

'This is Sarah.'

'I've heard of you.' Claudia's manner was not welcoming.

The small boy shot across the room and threw himself at Toby, making him gasp. 'Play snap with me, Toby. A game of snap.'

'Not now.' He smoothed back the child's thick brown hair.

'This is Adam.' He smiled at Sarah. 'My little half-brother.' He gave him a hug and a little push back towards his mother.

'I'm afraid I have bad news for you, Stepmother.'

'All your news is bad news.' She slammed the lid of the piano and stood up.

Sarah thought her tall but overweight. She was wearing a

very handsome grey silk dress with cream lace at the throat, and her light brown hair was plaited in intricate stylish coils. Her plump face was somewhat peevish, but as yet it had no permanent lines.

'Has your father not come home with you?'

'No,' Toby said. 'And he won't be coming. Not ever again.'

She burst out impatiently: 'Don't play silly games—'

'He died at his desk this afternoon. That's what I've come to tell you.'

Sarah gasped at the bald way in which he delivered the news. It was easy to see there was no love lost here. She watched Claudia's mouth open in shock; there was incredulity and disbelief in her eyes.

'He slumped over and died there quite alone. I was out in the factory, working.'

Sarah saw Claudia sway and went over to her.

'Sit down for a minute,' she said, backing the older woman against the piano stool. 'I'm afraid this must be a dreadful shock for you.'

'What's the matter?' the child demanded. 'Has something happened to Papa?' His mother pulled him on to her knee and buried her face in his hair.

'It was a shock for me too,' Toby told her. 'I'm not over it now. I go cold when I think about it; it was so sudden.' His tone softened. 'Do you want us to go? Leave you to rest?'

His stepmother's head came up. Her eyes were glazed with tears. 'Wait a minute. I have to know . . .'

Sarah said, as gently as she could: 'He's been taken to the morgue of the Southern Hospital. They'll be doing a post-mortem tomorrow to find the cause of death.'

Toby said: 'Heart attack, they think, or possibly a stroke. It's in the family, isn't it? My grandfather dropped dead like this.

'Oh.' He dragged the brown envelope from his pocket. 'I've brought you his personal belongings.'

84

He tipped the contents out on top of the piano. Claudia stared at them, horrified, then felt for her husband's ring.

Toby said: 'I've told Ed. He's coming straight home.'

His stepmother's face was white and set as she turned viciously on him.

'I suppose you're glad? Now you'll have a free hand to put all your hare-brained schemes in hand. I expect you'll drive the business into the ground in next to no time.'

They all heard the tap on the door. The second's silence was heavy. Then a housemaid put her head round.

'Yes, Bessie?'

'Dinner's ready, ma'am.'

Bessie had come as a nursery maid when Toby and Edward were small. Now she was well past middle age, with a staid motherly face and grey hair showing under her frilly cap. Her back was still ramrod straight under her black dress.

Claudia covered her face with her hands, but her voice sounded more normal. 'Is it that time already?'

'It's seven thirty, ma'am, but the master isn't home yet. Shall we hold dinner back till he gets here?'

Toby stirred. 'He won't be coming home, Bessie. He died at his desk this afternoon.'

Sarah saw Bessie's eyes widen with shock; heard her gasp of horror too.

'You'd better tell Ena.'

'Yes, sir.

'I'm not hungry, I don't want dinner.' Claudia's eyes went to Toby. 'Do you want to eat?'

'Pity to waste it; we might as well. Sarah?'

She nodded; she was always hungry.

Claudia seemed to remember her duties. 'Save something for Edward; he's coming later,' she told Bessie. 'I'll have a tray in my room. Just a little soup, please.'

Chapter Seven

Claudia hugged her young son to her. Maurice was dead! Now that she was over the first shock, relief was flooding through her. She'd been absolutely tormented about what she should do; worried he might find out. She set Adam down on the carpet and got slowly to her feet.

'Come along, it's time you were in bed.'

'Not tired.' He jumped up and down to prove it. 'Not yet, Mama.'

'Yes, it's late.'

She took him by the hand and led him to his room. Adam was always reluctant to go to bed, especially on these warm summer evenings, but it was one of Maurice's rules. She must have the boy ready to settle down for the night by the time he arrived home. The usual routine was that they kissed him good night together and then went straight to the dining room for dinner. Maurice liked to have her undivided attention when he was at home.

'Has something happened to Papa?' Adam's big eyes were searching her face. She sat down on his bed, pulled him on to her knee and explained as simply as she could.

Adam didn't seem upset. He saw little of his father, except on Sundays, and then Maurice wanted to read quietly or go to church. He'd considered it his duty to play with his son, but only for ten minutes or so at any one time; he couldn't stand much of Adam's boisterous company. Adam looked on his father as something of an ogre.

Claudia's mind was racing. She'd had to hide her first feelings of relief from Toby. Nobody must ever know about the problem she'd had to face. For months she'd been terrified that Maurice might find out about Gideon. Here she was, three months gone with another child, with no way of knowing which of them was the father.

Maurice had been very surprised when she'd told him she was expecting, and in no way pleased at the prospect of another child in the family. She'd told herself over and over that even if it was Gideon's, no one else need know. Except that at the back of her mind was this dread that the child might have a noticeable likeness to him. Red hair ran in the Burton family.

Now it didn't matter. Maurice would never find out. That opened up the future for her, without her having to go ahead with the frightening things she'd planned. Just to dwell on what she'd meant to do gave her the shakes, but now she was free. Free of Maurice and free to marry again.

She went to the bathroom to run a bath for Adam, leaving him to take his clothes off. When she went back to fetch him, he'd become distracted by his toy soldiers set out in battle lines on his chest of drawers. She had to undress him herself.

But why did Maurice have to die now? She'd managed to persuade him to change his will, and he'd died before he'd had a chance to do it. Frustration was tearing her apart. He'd got his timing so wrong. Just another few days . . . She needed to be a rich widow if she was to get what she wanted from life.

Maurice had not been the ideal husband, not even a good one; and definitely not a good father either. He'd always been too wrapped up in his business. Pickles and chutneys had been the beginning and end of everything for him. He'd been obsessed with them. And pickles were not something she could discuss with pride on social occasions. Not that there had been many social occasions.

Maurice was twenty years older than her. After a day's work at the factory, all he'd wanted was a good meal. Then he'd settle down for the evening with a newspaper or a book in his armchair. He'd wanted early nights because he had to get up early. Sunday was the only day he didn't go to work.

Just occasionally he'd ask her to play the piano for him and they'd go along to the music room. But the room had been built for his first wife, Helen, and the piano had belonged to his mother. He'd let her know that both had played better than she did, even though she'd learned all manner of difficult pieces by Liszt to please him. Her own taste ran more to the sort of songs Marie Lloyd sang.

Claudia thought she had quite a good voice herself, but Maurice never wanted to hear her sing. He was too steeped in family traditions. Neither Helen nor his mother had sung, and he wanted nothing new.

'Come on, Adam. Clean your teeth.'

Claudia knew putting him to bed was taking twice the time it usually did, but it soothed her to linger here with her child. The evening sun had gone now, but the tide was still in and it was a balmy evening. She let down the heavy window sash. The river air would do Adam good, and the gentle lapping of waves on the beach below would surely lull him to sleep. It no longer mattered how much time she took to settle him for the night; the days of having to rush to eat huge meals with his father were over.

Maurice had wanted everything done his way, both in the factory and at home. As an only son, he'd inherited everything his parents had built up. After his demise, he'd envisaged that Toby and Edward would run the business together.

'What about Adam?' Claudia had asked.

It seemed Maurice had seen him earning his living elsewhere. 'As a solicitor, perhaps, or an accountant. Unless he can set up some other business for himself.'

'But that isn't fair.'

'On present showing, the factory won't provide a living for three families,' he'd said.

When Toby started working for him, Maurice had found

him so difficult that he'd begun to question the wisdom of these plans. Claudia had never got on with Toby. Not since Maurice had brought her here as a bride after a week's honeymoon in London.

Toby had been almost fifteen at the time, big for his age and well advanced in puberty. His baby-blue eyes had followed her round the room with scarcely veiled hostility.

On her first night at Tides Reach he'd made what he called an apple-pie bed for her. As if she wasn't embarrassed enough about going to bed with their father. Maurice, of course, had shut himself in his study to enjoy a glass or two of brandy before retiring, and hardly noticed that both boys were hanging about the hall in their dressing gowns, giggling and scuffling long after they should have been asleep.

It had taken her a long time to get ready for bed – she was, after all, a new bride – but when she'd tried to get into it, she'd found the bottom sheet had been folded back halfway to look like the top one. She'd been upset; it had seemed a spiteful trick and had made her feel unwelcome in the house. She'd pulled on her négligé and run to find Maurice to shed a few emotional tears on his shoulder.

He'd been furious with Toby and sent him to summon Bessie from her bed to remake theirs properly. Toby had had to come to their room too, to show Bessie where he'd hidden their top sheet and retrieve it from under the bed. He'd been giggling all the time but nobody else had thought it funny. It was just the sort of senseless joke he enjoyed.

'New boys at school have apple-pie beds made for them,' he'd told Claudia.

'How would you know that?' his father had thundered. 'You've never been away to school.'

'From books. I've read about it.'

'What utter nonsense. I should burn all those books before Edward reads them.'

'He has, ages ago.'

'Then I hope he has more sense than you.'

Toby had played lots of similar tricks that hadn't come from books. He acquired a device that made a disgustingly rude noise when anybody sat on it. He was adept at putting it under the cushions on chairs where Claudia sat. All that sort of thing appealed to him.

She'd started out on the wrong foot with Toby and gone on to despise him. He'd upset his father time and time again. Tonight he'd upset her.

'I want a story,' Adam pleaded as she tucked him in. '"Hansel and Gretel".'

Tonight she hadn't the patience. She wanted to lie down and rest.

'I'll get Bessie to tell you a story.'

'No, where's my storybook?' He was struggling to get out of bed for it. 'Read to me,' he insisted. 'Bessie can't read.'

Claudia opened the book. Her head was heavy with all the problems Maurice's death would bring, but it was a treat to linger here.

'Just one story, then you must go to sleep.'

Adam was a beautiful child; he knew how to get round her. She started: 'Once upon a time . . .'

Reading such a simple text didn't stop her thinking. She was afraid Maurice hadn't left Adam a fair share of his estate. Afraid too that he hadn't remembered his responsibilities towards her.

'I never forget my responsibilities, Claudia,' he'd said when she'd asked him. But he hadn't spelled out exactly what he was going to leave her. She'd had to be so careful not to upset him by showing an interest in what would happen after his death. It was only the fact that she was pregnant again that made talking about it possible. With such an age gap between them, it was only sensible to assume she'd be left a widow, particularly as the men in his family seemed to die young. But she hadn't expected it to happen when she was only thirty-two.

She'd hinted to Maurice that he should cut Toby out of

his will. Maurice wasn't so rich that there would be plenty to go round so large a family. He hadn't wanted to, but she'd thought he was coming round to the idea.

She felt herself flush with anger. Why did Maurice have to die like this? She'd put all her plans in place, but he'd died too soon and thrown them all out.

She was afraid that now Maurice's estate would pass largely to Toby. He would have full control of the business. She certainly couldn't see him working at it as his father had. Toby hadn't the staying power, and his father hadn't thought he had the acumen to do it either.

Edward was only fifteen, too young to do much for the next few years; and anyway, he hadn't started to work at the factory except for an odd day or two in his school holidays.

Claudia came to the end of the story and closed the book. She kissed Adam and settled him down to sleep, then tiptoed out and went to her own bedroom. She stood gazing out of the window, feeling half dazed.

Maurice had treated her as a plaything, though she'd wanted to be his equal. She had more energy than he'd had and an equally good brain, though he didn't believe her capable of anything but housekeeping and playing the piano.

She'd tried to talk to him about his business, understand what it was all about. She'd asked to see over it and he'd taken her there and explained it all to her. He brought the books home and often left them here, and Claudia had studied them closely. She thought she understood how the accounts were made up and what the balance sheet showed.

Now she was afraid she'd have to take a more active interest if she wanted to ensure comfort in her own old age. And she might have a fight on her hands if her children were to have a rightful share of their father's estate.

Sarah felt Toby's hand on her arm, leading her away.

'I'll take your coat.'

He hung it in a cloakroom, then showed her where she could wash her hands and left her. Her face looked flushed in the mirror.

The house seemed vast, and it wasn't that easy to find the dining room. That was big too; so was the table, a huge expanse of freshly ironed white damask. Toby pulled out a chair for her.

'You'd better have Claudia's place. I'll have Father's. After all, I'm head of the family now.'

The array of china and cutlery set before her seemed prodigious, and yet Toby had been pleased to stay in their two attic rooms and seemed at home there. Oh, how the other half lived! Surely even at Buckingham Palace dinner couldn't be served with more style than this?

They had soup, a great tureen of it put on the table for them. At home, Sarah knew it would have been been the main part of the meal.

She said: 'You weren't very kind to your stepmother.'

'She's never kind to me. Or to Ed.' Toby was tight-lipped.

'But to tell her so baldly . . . She was upset.'

'She upsets me. Goes out of her way to do it. You've heard about wicked stepmothers?'

'They don't all have to be wicked, do they?'

'This one is.'

'I don't suppose it was easy to take your mother's place.'

'She didn't try. She married Father for what she could get out of him; more money and a better standard of living. I'm sure of that.'

Sarah found it hard to imagine such difficult relationships within a family.

'This soup is delicious.' She spooned up the last drop. 'Does she mind you calling her Stepmother? To her face, I mean? It sounds a bit . . .'

'Derisory? It's meant to.' Toby smiled wryly. 'When she moved in, Father told us in his high-handed way that we were to call her Mother. Ed burst into tears, it stuck in my throat too. We hadn't had time to get over . . .

'We agreed between us and told him Stepmother was as near as we could get. He pleaded, said she was our new mother and would treat us as her own children; said Stepmother sounded distant. But it stuck, and since that's what she is there was nothing either of them could do about it.'

'Didn't she resent it?'

'She did. That made us all the more determined to stick to it. She resents everything about me and Ed. Always has. It was our way of getting our own back.'

A joint of roast beef arrived which Toby carved inexpertly after a great show of sharpening the knife. It was unbelievable that he took all this for granted. Didn't even seem to value it.

'Do you remember your mother?'

'Very well. She was fair-haired and frail-looking. Things were much better in those days. We were a real family.'

'How old were you when she died?'

'Nine. She became an invalid in the last months of her life and spent much of her time in bed. She moved out of the room she shared with Father and into one at the front of the house where she could see the river and the shipping and the ever-changing tide. I wanted that room; it's been mine since she died.

'Is this enough for you?' A plate piled high with beef was placed in front of her.

'Thank you. Lovely. Tell me more about her.'

'I remember one long-ago Mothering Sunday. It must have been her last. I'd been wondering what I might get her as a present.

'Flowers, my father suggested. "You can pick her a nice bunch from the garden."

'But I knew there was always a vase in my mother's room

filled with fresh flowers from the garden. For her, there could be nothing special in a bunch of flowers.

'Bessie had taken me and Ed for a walk, and was buying stamps for Mama while we were out. While Bessie was in the post office, I looked in the shop window next to it, and a long string of beads caught my eye.

'I dragged Bessie to see them and she said they were made of varnished wood. Just a long string, no catch or anything like that.

'I asked her if she thought Mama would like them.'

'"I'd like them," Bessie smiled. "They look very smart."

'That was enough for me. I wanted to buy them for Mama, a present for Mothering Sunday. They cost sixpence. I had to borrow three-halfpence from Bessie to pay for them since I had only fourpence-halfpenny. I carried them home wrapped in a piece of tissue paper, feeling very proud.

'Ena gave me a little box to put them in, and more paper to wrap that up. Mama was delighted with them. She said so over and over, and she wore them in bed over her frilly nightdress.'

Sarah felt half mesmerised by his soft voice. 'It must have been awful for you when she died.'

'Yes, it wasn't long after . . . Cancer it was, though I really didn't understand why she had died, because she kept saying she felt better when she wore my beads, and she wished she could stay with me and Ed.

'Afterwards, when it was all over, Father took me into her bedroom to see her in her coffin. The beads she'd worn continuously over the last weeks were in a little heap on her nightstand. I took them as a keepsake.

'I used to play with them a lot, put them round my own neck and sometimes round Ed's. I always had them under my pillow at night. They helped me to think of Mama; to keep a clear picture of her frail face in my mind.

'When Claudia came – that was years later, I was fifteen by then – she said: "What nonsense, a big boy like you

95

wanting beads." By that time, I was keeping them looped over a framed photograph of Mama. Claudia said they were cheap and nasty.

'While I was at school one day, she cleared them out with a lot of other things that had belonged to my mother. The clothes in her wardrobe and the bottles of lavender water and eau-de-Cologne.

'I've never been able to forgive her for that.'

Sarah thought it a sad little story. The last thing a stepmother should have done.

'You didn't tell her you'd joined the army,' she said.

He smiled. 'Perhaps I won't have to. I mean, Father's death . . . that changes everything.'

Sarah shook her head. She and Mam knew they had to accept the consequences of what they did, but Toby believed he could make everything bend to his will.

'If I have to go to war, she'll find out soon enough. It'll make her day, won't it?'

Sarah didn't know when she'd eaten so well before. After a big dinner she'd had two helpings of damson pie with cream. It had tasted fabulous. She was trying to memorise all the details to tell Mam. The starched napkins were folded into the shape of water lilies. There was one place opposite, undisturbed. The sideboard was set with decanters of port and sherry, and a huge cheese covered with muslin weighed down with coloured beads. She thought that rather smelly.

When Bessie brought in the coffee pot, it was clear she was upset.

'What's going to happen to us, Mr Toby?' She brought out a handkerchief to dab at her eyes. 'What with the war and now this. Will Mrs Percival keep the house on?'

'Bessie, I can't tell you what the future will hold. I wish I could.'

'Shall I serve cheese and biscuits before the coffee?'

'No thanks. Sarah?' She shook her head; she couldn't eat another crumb.

'Father always finished with Stilton and port.'

'You eat like this every night?'

'Of course.'

Bessie was setting out dainty coffee cups on the table.

'Bessie, there have been two generations of Percivals living at Tides Reach, and I think there'll be a third. We aren't all going to rush off. You and Ena will still be needed.'

Sarah noticed he was kinder to Bessie than he'd been to his stepmother.

'Thank you. Will there be anything else?'

'Not for us, but Ed will be here later.'

When the door closed behind her, Toby said: 'Bessie's right to worry about the future. I need to find out all I can. If you've finished your coffee, let's go.'

She followed him along the passage and he threw open a door. 'This was my father's study.'

There were several bookcases, one easy chair and a lingering aroma of cigarette smoke. Toby sat down at the large mahogany desk that took up most of the floor space and from which it was possible to see out of the window and across the back garden. He'd taken his father's key ring from his pocket before he realised the desk wasn't locked. He opened and closed some of the lower drawers.

'No, it won't be in here; he'd lock that away very securely.'

'Lock what?'

'His will. He's bound to have a copy somewhere. He kept telling me he was leaving the business to me and Edward and we must learn to run it. He was paranoid about my learning to do everything exactly as it has always been done. But what about the rest of the family? He must have left something to Claudia and Adam. I'd like to know exactly . . .

'He was very keen on locking everything up at the office; he's bound to have the copy of his will under lock and key. Wouldn't want any of us poking our noses in too soon.'

Sarah felt ignorant about wills. Only the wealthy needed

those. Toby was on his feet prowling round the cupboards, of which there were several. He was tugging at the doors.

'All locked,' he grunted. 'Just as I thought. I hardly ever come in here and it wouldn't have done to show too much interest in his will. He wouldn't have told me if I'd asked. None of my business, he'd have said.'

Toby fitted a key into one of the locks.

'Ah, this looks promising.'

Inside the cupboard was a metal strong box. He was searching the key ring for the key to fit it. Seconds later the lid was up and he was riffling through the documents inside. He looked up and smiled at her.

'Here we are. Father's will.' He went back to sit at the desk to read it.

Sarah was tired. It had been a long day. The comfort and grandeur of Toby's home dazzled and bemused her. She sank down in the armchair. How Mam would love to see this.

When she looked up, Toby was beaming at her, his eyes dancing with joy.

'It's all here in black and white,' he chortled. 'The business is left jointly to me and Edward. Claudia is to be paid four hundred a year from the profits and have the right to live in Tides Reach for her lifetime.'

As he laughed outright and clapped his hands, Sarah could see the door opening behind him and Claudia coming in.

Toby's voice was full of triumph. 'She'll be furious. Not a ha'p'orth of capital.'

Claudia was scowling. 'Here you are. Edward's arrived. I've just given him money to pay off his taxi.' Her eyes fastened suspiciously on Toby. 'Who's going to be furious?'

The next moment she was whirling towards him.

'Where did you get that? Is it your father's will?' She snatched at it and took it to the window to read.

'You won't like it, Stepmother.' Toby's voice mocked her. 'You aren't mentioned until the codicil at the end. Father makes provision for you in that and states that he doesn't wish to have this will revoked by his marriage to you.'

There was a commotion in the hall. Toby opened the door. 'Hello, Ed, we're in here.'

He came in and Toby introduced them.

'Hello, Sarah.' Edward came to shake her hand. Sarah studied him as he stood close to his brother.

He wasn't much like Toby to look at, though he had his brother's friendly manner. He was far more like their father. He had Maurice's strong chin, and there was a sober maturity about his face. His hair was quite a lot darker than Toby's; his skin too. Sarah knew he was only fifteen and had thought of him as just a lad. Seeing them now side by side, she'd never have believed he was so much younger.

Claudia turned from the window, her face crimson; angry tears glistened on her cheeks.

'It's not enough! Adam is his son too, and there'll be another child at the end of January. He's not made reasonable provision for us. His first family shouldn't get all his assets. You no longer need his support; we do. I shall see his solicitor and ask for proper provision to be made for us. Four hundred a year is not enough to keep me and two children.'

'He says you're to be allowed to live here for the rest of your life.'

'He's left me this house?'

'Not exactly. He sees this as the home of the Percivals. You can live here, but so can we.'

'That's no good.'

'You don't want me and Ed here, then?'

'Don't be silly, I didn't say that. But it won't be mine?'

'No; when you die I shall have it to myself.' Toby smirked. 'No, that's not quite right. Edward has the same right, so I shall have to wait for his demise too.'

Sarah could see Claudia shaking with determination.

'It's not good enough. I need a home of my own and I want a share of the business for my children. I don't want to rely on you running it, Toby, because I don't believe you can.'

'Of course I can.'

'Your father didn't think so. He kept complaining about you, kept saying you weren't shaping up and had no sense. How long will it be before there isn't even four hundred pounds' profit? I could end up with nothing if I rely on you.'

Edward put in stiffly: 'Who do you suggest runs the business then?'

'I shall take an interest.'

'Now you're being silly!' Toby was half laughing at her. 'What do you know about pickles? You've been cushioned here in comfort all these years. You'd hate the factory.'

'I'm going to start work,' Edward said with determination. 'I'm not going back to school.'

'You're too young to do anything,' Claudia snapped. 'Of course you must go back.'

'Toby started at fifteen.'

'He was no good at lessons.'

'You're trying to make out I'm no good at anything,' Toby complained.

Sarah closed her eyes and sank back in the chair. She couldn't join in – this was none of her business – but apart from Toby she was the only one with any experience of how the factory worked. She reckoned she could do it as well as any of the family.

Edward said: 'I'll help Toby. I'll soon learn what's needed.'

'You'll not get away with this,' Claudia snarled at them.

'Father wanted to hand the business on to me and Edward. He wanted us to run it.'

'I'll have the will changed.'

Edward said: 'That's a bit strong. Surely it's up to Father to decide?'

'Your father added this codicil the week before we were married. He's had another son since then, and there'll soon be a fourth child. He knew he hadn't made enough provision; we talked about it. He promised me he'd change his will. He made an appointment with Jeffrey Masters to do it, but I think . . . I think he died too soon.' Claudia's face crumpled, and she mopped at her eyes with a lace handkerchief.

'But surely that makes this will valid,' Edward pointed out, with a glance at his brother.

'I can get it changed. I know what I'm talking about.' She gave another gasp of distress and hurried to the door.

'You'll come back here tomorrow?' she asked Toby. 'I need to know what's happening.'

'I might,' he retorted.

That made her slam the door in temper.

Sarah watched the brothers in the lengthening silence. Then Edward asked: 'Can she? Can she get it changed?'

'I don't know. We'll have to ask Masters.'

'She just wants to take what's ours. Grab all she can.'

Toby said softly: 'Father would have changed it if he'd lived. She was right about that. Mr Masters rang the office. He was expecting Father this afternoon. I think he was going to cut me out.'

'What about me?' Edward's eyes were filled with foreboding.

'I don't know.'

'You don't really know anything. Well, I'm glad he didn't have time to change things. I don't like Stepmother.'

Chapter Eight

Sarah was trying to keep up with Toby as he strode round the house throwing open doors. He hardly gave her time to take anything in. The row with Claudia had left him in a tempestuous mood. When Edward went off to the kitchen to get something to eat, he'd leapt to his feet.

'I'll show you round the place; you said you wanted to see it.'

Sarah had been full of curiosity, and what she'd seen so far had whetted it.

'The plans were drawn up to suit my grandmother's taste. Although it was built in Victorian times, much of it is in the Georgian style. This is the drawing room.'

Sarah let her eyes travel round. A big square room with a window overlooking the river. Bessie was closing off the evening sky with shutters that opened in the traditional Georgian manner from the panelling surrounding the window. The back wall was of matching linenfold panelling.

Toby was speaking fast. 'This can be folded back too, to double the size of the room for entertaining. Not that we ever do any. You're the first visitor here in months. Probably years.'

To Sarah, that would seem to make the room the size of a church hall, and it was furnished with such grand taste. She could see on each side of the panelled divide matching fireplaces of Victorian tile set in oak surrounds.

'Father liked a fire even on summer evenings.'

There was one lit in the front half; the other grate was filled with flowers. Glass doors opened into a conservatory at the far end.

'My mother loved to grow carnations and those big pompom chrysanthemums in here. Now it's all left to the gardener.'

Sarah had never seen such banks of flowers. She could see now that the conservatory separated the music room from the living quarters.

But it was the bathroom that really opened her eyes. A huge bath on Queen Anne legs and a magnificent washbowl. How easy it would be to keep clean here. In another tiny room next to it was the second lavatory she'd seen in this house. Two indoor lavatories for one family! That was luxury. Neither was anything like the one in the yard back home. They didn't smell at all, and there were blue willow-pattern pictures in the bowl of this one, and a heavy mahogany seat. It was all terribly impressive.

He took her round some of the bedrooms then; she couldn't compare them with the attic she and Mam shared. They finished up in Toby's room, which overlooked the river. He was calmer now.

'Let's stay here tonight. I can do what I like now. I earn part of the income that supports this house.'

'Oh, no! You said you'd come back with me.' Sarah had had enough grandeur for one day. 'I'd never be able to relax here; there's too many people.'

Stay in Toby's bedroom? She'd die of embarrassment. She could just imagine Bessie coming in with morning tea and seeing her there in Toby's arms.

He smiled. 'If that's what you want.'

It was late, but not yet quite dark; a lovely evening. To Sarah's eyes, the nearer they got to her home, the scruffier everything seemed. As they passed a public house near the docks, they heard singing.

'On a Thursday night?' Toby raised his eyebrows.

'Sailors, home from the sea. It'll be twice as loud tomorrow night and on Saturday.'

There were drunks on the streets, one lying across the

pavement. She was glad when they reached the building in which she lived.

Once inside, the stairs seemed very dark, and she took Toby's hand to guide him up. She'd come this way so often, the darkness was no problem. The smell from the yard seemed stronger than usual. There was a light on the landing one floor below hers. Sarah's heart sank.

'Be very quiet,' she cautioned. 'Don't forget John Ferry and his mother live here.'

'They know already. They've had their say about us.'

'All the same . . .'

Sarah knew she couldn't have timed things worse. As they came round the bend in the stairs, she could see John crossing the landing. He paused as they climbed towards him.

The look he gave her spoke volumes. She could see by the way he was eyeing Toby that he was hurt and shocked. He now knew she was bringing him here night after night. No doubt he'd listen for every move they made. Imagining what they were doing.

John collected himself enough to ask: 'How's your mother, Sarah?'

'Better.' She told him as little as she could without appearing rude. She wanted to pass but he was leaning against the stair rail, blocking her way.

'If there's anything we can do to help, we'll be glad to. Give her our good wishes.'

Sarah couldn't wait to get Toby inside her own rooms and shut the door behind them. He leaned back against it and breathed:

'Oh God! I thought he was going to stop me coming up.'

'He couldn't.'

'He hates me for this; for loving you. He's only being civil because he wants to keep his job. He was very rude to me the other day, but I let it pass, so he has to too.'

'I wish he didn't live so close,' Sarah breathed. 'Mam's going to hear about it. He'll think it's his duty to tell her.'

She knew Mam would disapprove even more than John did. She'd be upset at how far things had progressed between her and Toby.

Toby threw himself into Mam's basket chair and started to talk.

'I can hardly take it all in. What it means.'

He looked like a schoolboy, with his flushed rounded cheeks and overbright eyes. Sarah could see nothing but trouble ahead for him, but he seemed suddenly light-hearted.

'I started in the business at fifteen.'

'I was there too,' she said gently. Even then she'd felt his eyes watching her. It had made her nervous, thinking he found her slow with the work or not pulling her weight.

He gave a little laugh. 'I was terribly keen to master everything it entailed. I was proud that my grandfather had started it up. I was a Percival and would be the third generation to carry it on. I was determined to build it up, develop it, so by the time I was handing it on to my own son, it would be twice the size it is now.'

She set about making a cup of tea for them.

'Dad poured cold water on all my ideas. He couldn't see that we needed new labels – still do. Don't they look old-fashioned? They're unchanged since Queen Victoria's day.'

Sarah knew he'd lost his pleasure in working in the business long ago. She'd heard this several times over.

He had his arms clasped round his legs, his heels up on the seat of the basket chair.

'Although Dad's death was a dreadful shock – I'm burning with guilt because I helped bring it about – don't you see, it'll open doors for me?

'Suddenly everything's wide open, I can take charge of the company and put my ideas in force. It needs a young man's hand at the helm.'

Sarah was shocked; he seemed to be discounting a lot of complications.

'But you've enlisted,' she said, pressing a cup of tea into

his hand. He'd told nobody but her, and at times like this he seemed to be pretending he hadn't done it. 'You mightn't be able to do anything.'

His good humour burst like a bubble. It was only then that his worries came pouring out, and Sarah realised what an impact his father's death was having on him.

Edward took his bag to his bedroom and started to unpack. Father's death was changing everything. He couldn't believe Toby had dared to bring a girlfriend here. Yet he'd never seen him so stressed and restless. Stepmother too, was agitated and had barely bothered to say hello to Edward. Not that she'd ever shown him any affection unless Father had been watching. He shouldn't expect it now her audience had gone.

Bessie came to the door with a smile on her face; ramrod-straight in her black housemaid's dress, with frilly apron and cap.

'Such sad news to bring you home, ducks. Upsetting for all of us.'

Her plump arms went round him in a welcoming hug. He kissed her soft cheek.

'Your poor father. A terrible thing to happen, the last thing we expected. You never know when your last minute is coming.'

'You're still here, Bessie; that's something.'

'Your father was younger than me, d'you know that?' Her eyes looked into his, deeply anxious.

Bessie had come to Tides Reach as a nursemaid when Toby was a baby and had stayed on to look after Edward and then to care for their mother when she became ill. She was a motherly sort of person; indeed, she had been more of a mother to him than Claudia had.

'Are you hungry?' She laughed. 'Silly question, you always are. Come to the kitchen. Ena's saved something for you.'

Ena was Bessie's cousin and about the same age. They'd been brought up together and were more like sisters. The kitchen was always warm and welcoming. Ena gave him a hug too.

'Lovely to have you back, laddie. Whatever the circumstances.'

Her white cap had slipped backwards and showed more grey hair than usual. Edward felt he had more in common with these two elderly spinsters than he had with Father and Stepmother. They'd shown him more affection. Shown Toby more too. He beamed across the scrubbed table at them.

'I'm glad you're both still here. Wouldn't seem like home without you.'

'I've saved you some roast beef. Sit yourself down, I'll have to fry up the potatoes for you.'

'You know I like them better fried up.'

He was hungry and finished off the damson tart and cream greedily. It was always like this: his family busy with their own affairs, leaving him on his own. When he'd finished his supper, he mooned round the house, going slowly from room to room, taking in the old familiar things. He loved it all.

It had been a shock to hear about Father; gone so suddenly without a chance to say goodbye. But he was glad to be home. He'd never wanted to leave here.

It was a lovely evening and dusk had fallen. He went out into the front garden. The full tide was splashing up over the railings of the Esplanade, sucking and crashing back. He could smell the Mersey, all tar and ships; there was nothing like it anywhere else in the world.

But without Father, everything would have to change. The prospect scared him a little. He wouldn't go back to school if he could help it. School had been all right, but it wasn't where he'd choose to spend his days. He'd be needed to work in the business now. He'd have to help Toby.

Claudia went to the bedroom she'd shared with Maurice and lay down on top of the bed. Her eyes prickled and burned with the tears that had kept filling them. She dabbed at them with a saturated handkerchief, then threw it on the floor in disgust.

She hadn't expected to feel so emotional when Maurice died. It was shock at the suddenness; shock, and anger and frustration that he'd chosen such an inconvenient moment to go.

She'd been laying careful plans over the last three months, ever since she'd found herself pregnant. The first thing had been to get him to change his will. Everything had hinged on that.

Once she'd managed that, she could perhaps deal with Maurice by adding arsenic to a jar of his own chutney and dishing it up for dinner with the curry he loved so much. The strong flavours should surely be enough to hide the taste.

At a time when all the family except the maids were out, and they were busy in the kitchen, she'd gone looking for arsenic in the garden shed. She knew Maurice had bought some a little time back, to deal with the moles that were causing hillocks to erupt in his precious rose beds and ruining their root structure. He'd been pleased at its rapid effect on the moles, and she thought there could be some left over.

How long ago had he bought it? Claudia reckoned it up carefully: about three years. She'd been concerned that Maurice would remember that it was there. But they'd had a new gardener since then, because old Zachary had become ill and retired, only to die shortly afterwards. She'd counted herself lucky there.

The shelves in the shed had been covered with dust and crammed with oddments, but she'd found what she was looking for. She'd had to prise the lid off the rusting tin and open the half-used packet inside. She'd stared with awe at the steely-grey crystalline substance that was reputed to be extremely poisonous to animals and humans.

She'd forced the lid back on. Deliberated about leaving it there or taking it indoors. She'd left it; pushed it to the back of an old cupboard, where it wouldn't be seen. There were dozens of half-used tins containing poisons to see off garden pests, and other remedies for plant diseases. She crowded them over and in front of the arsenic.

What she hadn't decided was whether to give him regular small doses or one large one. She'd been trying to find out how big a dose it would need to kill him. It didn't tell you that on the packet, and it wasn't something she could ask about.

Of course it was a great relief that now she didn't have to do it. It would have taken great courage on her part, because of the risks involved. She didn't want to be caught and charged with murder. It gave her little frissons of horror just to think about that. She was glad he'd died without help from her, but he'd died too soon. Damn Maurice!

She rolled off the bed to get a clean handkerchief from the drawer in her dressing table. Catching sight of herself in the mirror made her wince. Her eyes, glittery with tears, were red and puffy. They looked smaller and beadier than usual, and her whole face was blotchy. A good job Gideon couldn't see her like this; it was a long time since she'd looked so awful.

Of course she felt grief, but it was trepidation for the future that was making her shake like this. How many times had Gideon told her he wished they could be married? It had seemed an impossible dream, but now everything looked as though it was going to come about without any effort on her part.

Claudia had only to think of Gideon to feel a flutter of excitement. He'd make a dashing husband. He was one year younger than she was, full of energy and keen to sample every enjoyment life could offer. He was not all thrift and work, like Maurice had been. Gideon was a professional man, an accountant, and he'd inherit a good business from his own father; a business she could talk about with pride.

But she'd need money of her own too. She never wanted to be dependent on a man again, having to ask for money for every little thing. Without Maurice, her life was going to change, and she was determined it would change for the better.

She hadn't been happy in her marriage. No husband should expect a second wife to move into the first wife's bed and accept things exactly as they were throughout the home. The furniture had been frightful – heavy, bulbous Victorian stuff – and much of it still was.

'My parents' choice, not Helen's.' Maurice had been offended when she'd put it to him.

She'd insisted on making over the bedroom, with new paint and curtains. Maurice had been more malleable in the early days of their marriage.

She'd said: 'And I want some new bedroom furniture, something that's halfway decent.'

Her own father had been an antique dealer and she recognised good-class furniture when she saw it. She'd chosen a beautiful George III mahogany-fitted toilet table on square tapering legs. She knew Maurice had been horrified at the price, but he'd been impressed by her knowledge of antiques.

His knowledge was of pickles; hers was much more middle class, though he'd looked down on her origins.

'Get what you can while you can,' her mother had advised, and she had. She'd loved the Regency satinwood work table by her bed the moment she'd seen it in the shop. It was fully fitted out with needles, thread, a silver thimble and silver scissors, and it was lined prettily with pink satin. She didn't sew at all, but she knew it would be easily saleable should she need money. The huge fitted wardrobe she hated. It had been here when she'd arrived, with some of Helen's clothes still inside.

It was Mama who'd talked her into marrying Maurice in the first place. Money and possessions were always Mama's first thought. She was in the habit of saying:

'Without money, you can do nothing in this life.'

That reminded Claudia that as yet her mother wouldn't know of Maurice's death. Honoria Digby lived in rooms in the red-brick terrace just a few hundred yards down the Esplanade. Claudia would need an ally here, someone of her own now Toby and Edward were ranged against her. Since she could hardly ask Gideon to come up so soon after her husband's death, it would have to be Mama.

Claudia scribbled a note at the davenport she'd persuaded Maurice to buy for his own use and install in his dressing room. She asked her mother to come immediately and stay the night. To have it delivered, she had to go to the kitchen in search of Ena. Maurice had been against putting a bell pull in his bedroom.

'I don't want serving girls coming in here,' he'd said when she suggested it. He wouldn't even allow morning tea. The gong was beaten outside their door when it was time to get up.

She found Edward eating at the kitchen table with the servants. Chatting to them too. She didn't approve of that.

'Ena,' she put the note on the table in front of her plate, 'I want you to deliver this to my mother straight away. You'd better wait and help her carry her things up. I've asked her to come and spend the night.'

Mama was turned fifty, and after a life of indulgence, no work and little exercise, she'd need help to walk up here now it was almost dark.

Claudia turned to Bessie: 'Make sure the guest room is ready to receive her, and we'll need a tray of tea when she arrives.'

She went to the small sitting room she called her boudoir to wait impatiently for Mama's coming. It was almost an hour before she heard Ena bringing her up the hall. She leapt to her feet to draw her mother in. They spent several days each week together in here, though of course Mama was always gone by the time Maurice came home from work.

'My poor child.' Mrs Digby threw her arms round her daughter. 'What a terrible shock for you.'

112

'Awful. Let Ena take your coat.'

Honoria Digby removed her hat and went to the mirror over the mantelpiece to pat her hair into place. She prided herself on her hair. Pale brown like Claudia's, with hardly any grey in it. She wore it in a dressy style with curls piled on top of her head and a Queen Alexandra fringe. She dressed as well as funds allowed and was particularly fond of burgundy satin. Tonight, her long-sleeved, high-necked blouse was of that material.

It was only later, when Claudia had poured the tea and cut the cake and they had the sitting room door firmly shut, that Honoria said, in derogatory tones: 'So the Pickle King is dead. Didn't I say he was unlikely to make old bones?'

She was surprised to see Claudia looking so grief-stricken. Her eyes were red and puffy and her face blotched and tear-stained. She was feeling for her handkerchief again.

'Such an upset for you. A difficult time.' Honoria drew out her own handkerchief to show sympathy. The cool night air was inclined to make her eyes water. She dabbed at them, then stood up to look in the mirror.

She was shorter and plumper than her daughter, with the same small eyes that with age had become hooded. Her nose, though, was much bigger than Claudia's; she'd never been pleased with that. Some might say it was rather beaky. She patted at it and deplored the broken veins over her cheeks. Surely they couldn't be getting worse?

'I am upset, Mama. Toby's found a copy of a will.' She was waving it at Honoria, telling her all about it. 'It's enough to upset anyone.'

Honoria understood now. She took the will and studied it.

'Why didn't you know about this? If Toby could find it, surely you . . .' She flung it away from her.

'I suspected but I didn't know. Maurice kept it locked away and the keys were always in his pocket. If this is all I'm going to get, it was hardly worth marrying him.'

113

'Silly girl! You didn't handle him properly. He was easily the most eligible man we knew.'

Honoria had done all she could to bring the match about. Wasn't it every mother's duty to see her daughter settled comfortably in life? She knew better than anybody else how important that was.

'We were very poor after your father was made bankrupt,' she said. 'I wanted you lifted out of that.'

Mr Digby had owned two shops: one in central Liverpool, the other in Birkenhead. Beautiful shops filled with high-class antiques and silver. Shops that attracted the carriage trade.

Honoria had thought herself made for life. She'd been brought up in India and had grown used to being waited on. She told everybody her father had been a colonel in the Indian Army, but that wasn't true. His rank had been that of sergeant. Life had been very hard when he had been killed in a native uprising and she and her mother had had to come back to England and survive on his pension. Honoria had hated the poor rooms in back streets, the lack of warm, smart clothes to face the cold weather and the shortage of good food. Most of all, she hated having no help with the housework.

The only obvious way out of poverty was to acquire a rich husband, so Honoria had made out her background was more genteel than it was. Easy enough when they'd lived on a different continent.

She'd made the acquaintance of Robert Digby in his shop and had thought herself very fortunate to marry him. He'd settled her and her mother into a fine six-bedroomed house in Rock Park, where they'd lived in high style. But the elegance of his shops had misled her into believing his business earned more than it did.

Its collapse had ruined Robert's health as well as that of her mother, and at the age of thirty-eight Honoria had found herself left with a daughter of eleven years to educate and care for.

Neither of them would forget the many more years of

penny-pinching that followed. Honoria knew only too well what back-street life was like, and to avoid it she had rented, at very little extra, two rooms in a house in New Ferry Terrace with views of the river from both. She and Claudia – named after her grandfather, Sergeant Claud Egbert Howarth – had taken their exercise up and down the Esplanade on warm summer afternoons, passing very slowly in front of the five large houses at the far end, always ready to wish the occupants a good afternoon should they be within earshot in their front gardens.

Honoria had stopped regularly to pass the time of day with Mrs Burton of Beechwood House, who was a keen gardener. One day, Mrs Burton's daughter Elizabeth had taken Claudia indoors to see her new doll's house, and had kept her so long that Honoria had been invited inside to retrieve her.

Occasionally after that Claudia had been asked round to play with Elizabeth. From that beginning, Honoria had built up an acquaintance with several of the ladies who lived along the Esplanade, including Helen Percival of Tides Reach. When Helen had died a few years later, Honoria had attended her funeral and offered Mr Percival her sincere and deeply felt condolences.

Honoria had pursued Maurice patiently for some years, with a view to marrying again herself. He was in trade, and this time round she'd have preferred a professional man. Not a very nice trade either. Pickles were unmentionable in polite society; they made ladies wrinkle their noses, or worse, titter with mirth. But Maurice Percival was making the money she craved, and Tides Reach was a vast improvement on two rented rooms in New Ferry Terrace.

Having learned that Maurice's grandmother had lived in India, Honoria recounted anecdotes of the time she'd spent there, and this served to give them a basis for conversation.

Mr Percival, whose mind was always on his business, asked her about chutneys. Up until that moment, Honoria had not been particularly fond of chutney, but that didn't stop her expressing a delight in them and looking out several recipes for him that she'd never tried.

His only other interest seemed to be his roses. Honoria bought a book and learned all she could about them, so that she was able to show an interest and offer informed advice.

It was many years before she gave up hope. She was growing older and stouter and began to feel she didn't want to be bothered with another husband and all that marriage entailed. Claudia by that time was in her mid twenties, and it didn't look as though she was going to achieve a suitable husband by her own efforts.

Claudia had been a great worry to Honoria. From the age of sixteen she'd attracted quite the wrong sort of men. The first had been a youth who delivered telegrams for the post office; another had been a labourer in the local brickworks. Honoria had had to talk very seriously to her daughter about the life she was likely to lead with men like that. She'd get herself trapped in total poverty.

She'd urged Claudia to aim higher, try to better herself, but even though she'd chaperoned her as closely as any mother could, Claudia had continued to make the same mistake. She'd been quite headstrong about men.

There had been a torrid affair with a bank clerk. Claudia had made light of her mother's objections, saying he'd be a bank manager one day. She'd wanted to marry him, but just in time, he was found to be defrauding the bank. He already had a criminal record, too. It was after that débâcle that Honoria began to propel Claudia towards Maurice Percival.

To have her daughter married to the Pickle King had suited her very well. It not only settled her worries about the company Claudia was keeping, but it gave her ready access to Tides Reach. She spent a lot of her time at the house, often eating lunch there on weekdays. Claudia had asked her not to come when Maurice would be at home; he didn't care for company, which was rather a pity because it meant Honoria had to stay at home over the weekends.

She now adopted a snobbish attitude towards the pickle factory in order to raise Claudia's opinion of her own worth, but she was not above accepting free samples of his pickles, as well as other luxuries from the Tides Reach kitchen.

Honoria Digby bit into a second slice of sponge cake. Claudia was still tearful, but her daughter's distress didn't spoil her appetite.

'Don't upset yourself. Marrying Maurice was the best choice at the time. The only choice.'

'Mama, he died too soon. That's why I'm upset.'

'You should have acted more quickly. I kept urging you to keep on at him.'

'You don't realise how difficult he could be. I did my best. Another month and it would have been all right. Just another month.'

'You've had six years to do it and you've complained the time seemed long. You should have stood up to him more.'

'You said it would set me up for life if I married Maurice,' Claudia sobbed.

'It would have done if you'd kept your wits about you and got on with things.'

'He isn't leaving me enough.'

'It still might be all right. I'm almost sure . . . almost certain that whatever the will says, you're entitled by law to have proper provision from his estate.'

Honoria poured herself another cup of tea. 'We'll go and see the solicitor in the morning. Get it straightened out before things go any further.'

Chapter Nine

Even with her mother under the same roof, Claudia spent a restless night tossing and turning in the unaccustomed space of the double bed. Mama had reawakened old memories, making her mind race with them.

Claudia was well aware that at the time of their marriage, Maurice had looked down on her social position. She and Mama had fallen on hard times, the family of a shopkeeper who had gone bankrupt. Only she knew that her father had adored Honoria and had given in to her every whim. His bankruptcy had been hastened, Claudia suspected, by her mother's profligate spending.

Her father, by then a broken man, had died young. The poverty of his family had perhaps not been so obvious to those around them, because Mama would spend on what showed; not on fuel, warm underclothes or enough food. She had no control at all over her money and never had enough to cover essentials. What she had went on smart clothes, particularly hats. She also liked sherry and flowers.

Claudia had had to learn to look after the family purse or they'd have starved. She'd had to fight to pay the rent of their rooms and buy enough food not to feel permanently hungry. She'd never loved Maurice – he was almost old enough to be her father – but she'd been prepared to marry him to improve her standard of living. Mama had wanted it and persuaded her, because it improved her standard of living too.

One of Claudia's problems had been that from the beginning, Maurice had suspected that she'd married him for his money. Therefore he was not as generous as he otherwise might have been. He always seemed to be watching for any sign of overspending, or any desire on her part to buy expensive objects.

Mama was always urging her to ask him for luxuries – jewellery, furs, fine clothes and such-like – so she'd felt pressure from both sides. She'd had to play her cards close to her chest. Maurice had plenty of money, but she must not be seen to want too much of it. To ease her mother's poverty, she gave her money regularly from the housekeeping.

Last night she and Mama had been late going to bed, and the gong was sounding outside her bedroom door before she was ready for it. Claudia got up straight away, without fuss, as Maurice had trained her. Her first job was to wake Adam and see that he washed and dressed properly. When she took him to the dining room for breakfast, she found nobody else there.

There was a place set for Maurice as usual, with his newspaper beside it. She had to point out the mistake to Bessie, who was contrite and hastened to remove the place setting.

'In future, I'll have morning tea in bed,' Claudia told her. 'Perhaps you'd better take some to my mother now.'

Last night Claudia had not been thinking of her duties as hostess. She was well aware that Mama paid her landlady to provide her with morning tea before she left her bed every morning. She put a bowl of porridge in front of Adam.

Mama came to the breakfast table before Bessie had time to deliver a tea tray to her room, and started laying the law down in a very dogmatic manner.

'Claudia, you must stand up for yourself now. Know your rights and go after them. We must see the solicitor without delay. It must take precedence over everything else.'

'This morning, Mama. As soon as we have Adam ready for school.'

'Don't want to go to school,' Adam giggled. 'Want to go out with you.'

His grandmother was severe. 'Certainly not. You'll go to school like a good boy and learn all you can.'

Adam had recently started at the kindergarten in Osborne House School in Rock Park. The maids took turns to walk him there in the morning and collect him again before lunch. It had been her mother's suggestion that he should start. Claudia knew that her mother, like Maurice, only enjoyed Adam's company for short periods.

'I'll be a good boy, Grandma, if—'

'Definitely not, Adam. We can't even think of it this morning. Can't do with any extra trouble if we are to get everything done.

'Make a list, Claudia. We'll both need mourning for the funeral. You'll have to get your mourning cards printed. Embossed and pierced, I think, and you'd better order your mourning stationery while we're in town.'

It was a pleasant morning, and under different circumstances Claudia would have enjoyed the ferry trip. Today she felt too keyed up to appreciate the salty sea breeze. She knew how important this interview with Maurice's solicitor was for her future.

'Don't hold back your tears,' her mother advised as a taxi took them up Dale Street. 'Let him see how distressed you are.'

Claudia certainly felt very distressed; her eyes were heavy and burning again. Though they'd made no appointment, they were received with great civility and provided with tea while Mr Masters made haste to free himself from another client.

Soon they were ushered to a large office overlooking the busy thoroughfare. Files tied with pink ribbons were stacked everywhere, some even piled up on the floor.

Mr Masters had very little hair. He was near retirement age and rather bent. He shook Claudia's hand.

'My heartfelt condolences, Mrs Percival. So very sudden.'

121

Claudia put the copy of the will on his desk and explained why she'd come.

'My husband was about to make a new will . . .'

'Yes, he was due to see me. He made an appointment to come yesterday. Such a shock to hear he'd died that afternoon.'

'My daughter is expecting another child,' Mrs Digby was quick to put in. 'It was for that reason her husband was about to change his will. He wanted to make better provision for her.'

'Yes, I understand that, but it leaves this as his valid will. I've looked through it, and I agree that what seemed reasonable at the time of his marriage—'

'No longer is,' Mrs Digby said firmly. 'Not in her present circumstances. Penury is what it would mean for her and her children.'

'Well, er . . . yes.' Masters' brow screwed up in thought. 'I was about to suggest that we apply to the courts to have more provision made. Is that what you'd like me to do?'

'Yes,' Claudia gulped. 'Please do.'

'Such a sad time for you, my dear.' His rheumy eyes came to rest on her. 'Another child . . . a son would make a difference too. I think it would be wise to wait until your child is born. That means, I'm afraid, that it could be some time before your husband's estate is settled. You have a little money of your own?'

'No.'

'Entirely dependent on your husband?'

'Totally.' The flowers on Mrs Digby's large hat shook in vehement confirmation.

Mr Masters looked grave and pursed his lips as he turned back to Claudia.

'Your husband had children by a previous marriage, did he not?'

She nodded.

'Children not yet entirely independent of his support?'

'Toby is.' Claudia's mother answered for her again. 'He's twenty years old and has been working in the family business. Edward is fifteen and determined to leave school and work there too.'

Claudia could see dust mites dancing in the shaft of sunlight that lit up the room and put a shine on Jeffrey Masters' bald head.

'Mr Percival has appointed me executor and trustee. I'll need a copy of his death certificate and a list of his assets at the time of his death: insurance policies, bank books, share certificates and such-like. I must warn you that all his accounts will be frozen until probate is granted.'

'My daughter won't be able to draw on them? For personal expenses?'

'Not unless they are held in joint names.'

'That could be awkward.' Mrs Digby's flowers danced in consternation.

'For some people it can be. The business must continue to trade, of course. Ask Toby to come in and see me; I'll need to talk to him about it.'

Claudia shivered. It seemed her days of comfort were at an end.

'Rest assured, my dear, I'll do my best to hasten matters.' Mr Masters shook her hand when they stood up to leave. 'I'll endeavour to see that fairness prevails in the settlement of your husband's estate.'

Claudia was glad to get out of his office. Once on the pavement again, her mother said:

'Now we must cheer you up.' She steered Claudia round all the big department stores. They visited Hendersons, Bunnies, Owen Owen's and Lewis's to compare the goods on offer. They bought an outfit each in deepest black for the funeral, a selection of jet jewellery and a quantity of black-edged handkerchiefs.

They rested then in the Ladies' Lounge in George Henry

Lee's, and afterwards had an extravagant lunch in the restaurant there. On the way out, Honoria saw a black hat that she preferred to the one she'd bought earlier and had to have that too.

Claudia was almost too tired to visit the printer, but her mother insisted. On the way home she said: 'You may need to make economies now, Claudia. The best thing would be for me to give up my rooms and move into Tides Reach with you. That would save a little, and I'd be able to look after you.'

Sarah was glad to find Toby calmer by the next morning.

In fact he was quiet and subdued as they walked to work. She thought the atmosphere in the factory had changed too. Maurice Percival had ruled with a rod of iron and had been a stickler for time-keeping. Now everybody seemed more relaxed, though the lines were running and work had started just as early.

Sarah set about her job of making sure every onion carried to the salting room was perfectly skinned and without blemish, but she noticed that Mr Trumper was spending more time than usual in the office with Toby. At mid morning Edward arrived, and she saw nothing more of Toby until the lines were shut down at dinner time.

'I'll walk down to the hospital with you as usual,' he told Sarah. They'd been calling each day in the dinner break to ask after her mother.

'If the autopsy's been done we should be able to collect Father's death certificate as well. Hang on a minute, Ed's coming too.'

Sarah was bothered. 'I'll need to get something for us to eat.' She hadn't enough food left in the house to feed all three of them.

'I've told Ed I'll take him to the Refreshment Rooms. He's a big eater. Come with us.'

Sarah was told by the ward sister that her mother had been seen by the surgeon that morning and could go home. Her appendix had settled down and they'd decided to leave things as they were.

'Bring her clothes in and you can take her home straight away.'

Sarah was relieved. She knew her mother would be delighted, but Toby would not be able to spend any more nights with her. She went running downstairs, and found him and Edward waiting for her.

'Good news for you,' Toby said when she told him. He was trying to smile but she knew he realised the position too. He showed her his father's death certificate.

'It was what the doctor thought. It says here coronary occlusion, but that's just the official way of saying Father died of a heart attack.

'We'll be able to see to the funeral arrangements now. After that . . .' He waved the document at her. 'There's something else . . . We won't be in this afternoon.'

She understood. He was going down to the recruiting office to see if he could get his enlistment cancelled. He hadn't told anybody else about that yet. Everybody assumed he'd be taking his father's place and running the business.

She said: 'Thank you, but I won't come to the Refreshment Rooms. I'd better get home – for Mam's clothes.'

'Call back at the factory. I'll leave word with Trumper that you're to have the use of the first cart that comes into the yard. Your mother won't be able to walk home.'

'Sister thought she'd be all right.'

'She's been in bed for days. Better if she rides this first time.'

'Thank you.'

'Take your time. Make your mother comfortable before you come back to work.'

To Sarah, it seemed no time at all since she'd been clinging to her mother's skirts and looking to her for everything. Now her mother seemed infinitely weaker, and Sarah was looking after her. Mam had been tired by the time she'd climbed all those stairs, though the carter had half carried her up the last flight.

'Rest on the bed till I come back,' Sarah told her. She'd made her a cup of tea and gone back to work. She felt she had to; looking at the way Mam was now, she might be the only bread-winner for some time.

The Ferrys, mother and son, both asked after Mam, as did many others at the factory. The routine work went on just as it always had. The lines flowed at the same pace, nobody slacked off, although it was the first time there had been no member of the Percival family to oversee what went on.

When work was over for the day, Sarah didn't go straight home; instead she went to the shops to buy a bit of fish for their suppers and some meat to make a stew for tomorrow. Mam was up and sitting bolt upright in her basket chair when she got in.

'Elvira's been up to see me,' she said. Sarah knew what that meant. 'She told me Toby Percival's been staying here with you. All through the night. Every night that I've been in hospital. I'm shocked, Sarah. I've been shaking ever since. What if you've made a baby? What's that lad going to do about it if you have?'

Sarah busied herself getting the meal ready. There was nothing she could say that would quieten her mother's fears.

'He's nothing but an overgrown child himself.'

'I love Toby, Mam. I told you. It's shaken him up, his father dying like this.'

She retorted irritably: 'He's the sort that needs shaking up.'

'Mam, that's not fair.'

'Nothing's fair in this life.' Maria took a deep, shuddering breath. 'It shook me too, to get your note. About Mr Percival.'

Sarah had not been allowed in to see Mam earlier, but she'd scribbled a few lines and given them to Sister when she'd called to ask after her. That was news that affected them all.

'I know you think everything's changed now, but to let Toby stay here was madness. What'll they think at work? To let him stay all night, allow him to . . .'

Maria burst into tears. 'I'm afraid for you. You could pay a terrible price.'

'I won't, Mam. Toby wouldn't do anything to hurt me.'

'He's turned your head.'

With the fish cooked and the bread cut, her mother went over the old ground.

'John Ferry would have been far better for you. He's got his head on straight. He's been keen on you for years, taking you out—'

'That was before I realised Toby was serious.'

'John was always serious. You'll learn, lass. John's worth ten of Toby Percival. You had it right the first time, but he won't want you now. Not now he knows Toby Percival's been spending whole nights up here with you. I wish you hadn't done that. John's steady and he doesn't drink.'

'Toby doesn't drink much either. That's all you think of – doesn't drink.'

She saw the pain on her mother's face. Saw her lean back in her chair and close her eyes. 'A teetotaller is so much safer.'

'Because Toby has an occasional drink it doesn't mean he's anything like Dad.'

Mam straightened up and said with pent-up feeling: 'How much drunkenness do you see around here? It's everywhere, every day. Women too, so drunk they can hardly stand. Spending their wages on drink when it should be spent on food and boots for their children.

'We manage on what we earn, don't we? It's because we don't spend anything on drink. I married a man who drank and I know what I'm talking about.'

Sarah had heard her story many times. 'Toby's different. That couldn't happen to him.'

'It could. I thought I was doing well for myself when I married your father. He was a good-looking fellow and he was a librarian. Nicely spoken, good manners and well educated. He had more brains than your Toby, I can tell you. And as much charm. And we weren't poor. Not to start with.'

Sarah's memories of her father were fading, but it was hard to equate them with Mam's. She saw him with three days' growth of scratchy stubble on his chin and breath that smelled of alcohol. Occasionally he'd pulled her on to his knee in a show of rough affection, but more often a swipe from his large callused hand would spin her across their room.

Mam's cheeks were scarlet and her eyes blazed. 'We started married life in a nice house in Walton. We had a bathroom and every comfort. I didn't have to go to work. He didn't think I should have to. I even had a girl to help in the house. Can you imagine me with a servant?'

'Mam . . .'

'It was the drink; he couldn't leave it alone even then. Gin was what he liked.' She laughed, but there was no mirth in it. 'It's supposed to be mother's ruin, isn't it? I can tell you that it doesn't do fathers any good either. He promised a thousand times to give it up, but he couldn't. He used to hide bottles of it all over the house and go upstairs for a drink every so often. He thought I didn't know he was drinking. He used to buy a bottle to take to work because he couldn't get through the day without it.'

'I know, Mam, but—'

'His good manners were the first thing to go. He was only too ready to put his fists up when he'd got drink in his belly. He lost his job when he picked a fight with an old man in the library. Laid him out flat on the floor, he did. They had to send for an ambulance. All the old man did was to ask for that day's newspapers, which your dad had forgotten to set out in the reading room.'

The silence lasted so long, Sarah thought Mam's outburst was over. Then she started again, more calmly.

'I had to get a job then. It wasn't easy – you were a baby. We moved house. We were always moving house because we couldn't pay the rent, or your father had had a fight with the landlord or the neighbours. Each move we made was to a worse place than the last. It wasn't long before we were living in a single room. The last one was just off Scotland Road.

'It wasn't as though Harold didn't work. He kept getting jobs even after he was dismissed from the library service, but each job he got required less of him than the last, and the pay was less. He got to the stage when he'd do anything to earn a few shillings, and as soon as he had money in his hand he spent it on drink. He ended up doing odd jobs about the market.'

'You had a terrible life, Mam. He wasn't much of a husband.'

'Wasn't much of a father either. I had to take any job I could get in order to feed us. And moving house made jobs difficult to keep. I couldn't afford to spend time and money on bus fares; I needed something close by because of you.

'But he wouldn't let me spend the money I earned on food and rent. He was always wanting it for drink, and that caused terrible rows. He'd go berserk when I said no. And I *had* to say no.'

Sarah remembered cowering behind the furniture when he came home. She'd been scared of him. She knew her father had thought nothing of using his fists on her mother when he was drunk. She remembered it happening several times.

Mam looked woebegone. 'Harold put me in hospital once with broken ribs and terrible weals on my back, not to mention a black eye.'

Sarah had been six years old at the time. She remembered being terrified by her mother's screams and the sight of her being treated so brutally. She'd run to the next room, but the family there had already heard the shouts and the abuse and had sent one of their boys for the policeman on the corner.

When the policeman came to their room, her father used

the poker he'd been beating Maria with to assault him. He'd been arrested and hauled before the magistrates, who gave him twenty-eight days in jail to cool off. With her mother in hospital, that had left Sarah alone in their single room, but the woman in the next room had taken pity on her. She'd given her food she could ill spare from her own family of six, and her eldest, a girl of thirteen, had slept in Sarah's room with her. A younger daughter who was still at school had taken Sarah there with her every day.

When Mam had been discharged from hospital, she'd found a different room and a new job, and she and Sarah had left for good before her father was released.

'I couldn't stand it any more. He was dragging both of us down. You weren't getting enough to eat.'

'Mam, you couldn't stay with a man who was beating you with a poker.'

'I was terrified he'd turn on you.'

Sarah stopped to think for a moment. 'Are you afraid he'll find us? Is that why you're always looking behind you?'

Mam mopped at her eyes. 'Wouldn't you in my place? I'd tried to leave him before but he found me because he knew where I worked. That time he moved into our new room with us and I couldn't stop him. I didn't make that mistake again.

'Harold didn't want us to leave him. When he was sober he was pathetic and promised to turn over a new leaf. I cooked and cleaned for him. I provided what little comfort we had, as well as some of the money he spent on drink.'

'What happened to him?'

'I don't know. I've never been back. I was afraid I hadn't gone far enough away and that he'd find us. I used to have nightmares in which he did. He's probably drunk himself to death by now.'

'You married the wrong man.'

'That's why I'm afraid you'll do the same. Marriage is a lottery.'

Sarah smiled. 'With Toby, I'd feel I was winning the prize.'

'I thought Harold was wonderful. I loved him. I knew he drank a little, but I didn't think it mattered. I believed in him, I trusted him. Oh yes, and I did what you've just done. I let him do everything he wanted before we were married. I was led astray in the way Toby Percival's leading you.'

That sobered Sarah up. Mam felt so strongly about this. She let out a long pent-up breath.

'What do we know about Toby? He's the sort that'll be off like a will-o'-the-wisp after another girl next month.'

Sarah protested: 'No, you don't know him, Mam. He wants to marry me, he loves me.'

'They all say that.'

'Toby means it, I'm sure.' Her mother had had a terrible life. She'd never been able to rely on anyone.

'You'd be fine with John. Toby's a toff with his head in the air. He'll not look after you.'

Sarah couldn't believe he'd ever abandon her; but hadn't he enlisted without a thought for her? She shivered.

Mam's eyes implored her. 'With both of us working, I'd put all my troubles behind me, but I'm not as strong as I was and my strength is failing. I'm terrified you'll upset the apple cart with this affair with Toby. If you haven't already.'

Nothing seemed real to Toby. He felt he'd wake up soon and find all this was a nightmare. He'd been ordered to report for basic army training on Monday morning. It was Friday lunch time now; he hadn't much time to sort this out. On top of that there were a thousand things he had to do, and Ed was sticking to him like gum.

He didn't want to tell anybody he'd enlisted because he thought there was still a good chance he could get out of it. Hadn't he seen hordes of men queuing for hours, desperate for the chance to sign up? And the newspapers were full of stories about there being so many that recruiting offices had to close early to complete the paperwork. Those still waiting were being told to come back the next day.

He couldn't have foreseen his father's sudden death; that changed absolutely everything for him. He couldn't leave the business now.

He'd telephoned for an appointment with a firm of undertakers in Birkenhead, chosen because of the proximity of their premises to the recruiting office. He took Edward there.

'Shouldn't Stepmother be with us?' Edward asked. 'She'll want to choose . . . Bound to.'

Good point, Toby thought; but if they went home to get her, it would make him late getting to the recruiting office. He solved that problem by merely booking the firm to bury Father on Tuesday afternoon. Then he sent Ed home on the tram with brochures and other details that Claudia would want to settle herself.

The streets were even more full of flags and posters urging men to sign up. When he arrived at the recruiting office there was the same buzz of excitement and even longer lines of eager men. Toby had heard the lads at the factory talking; they all had enlistment fever. Six had already signed up and were regarded as heroes.

Despite his appointment, they were so busy he had to wait. It was more tedious this time. The cheery welcome meted out by the sergeant major in charge changed completely when he explained what he wanted and showed him his father's death certificate. He was taken to a small room at the back where those waiting to enlist would not hear.

'An extra week granted on compassionate grounds,' he was told, and his papers were stamped with an adjusted date.

Toby felt panic rising in his throat. That wouldn't do. He tried to explain about the family business; that he was the only person who could run it now.

The sergeant major was standing tall, shoulders back, face severe. 'You volunteered. You've been sworn in, accepted into the ranks of the British Army. You took the King's shilling. Changing your mind isn't an option now.'

Toby knew this was his last chance, and there was frenzy in his voice.

'Can I buy myself out? I believe that's possible.'

'No, it isn't,' the sergeant major thundered. 'Not in your circumstances. Haven't you heard, the country's at war? You're needed. You've got a week to sort yourself out.'

'I need longer; the business . . .'

'If you don't turn up on this date,' his thumb jabbed down on Toby's papers, 'military police will come and get you. You've given us your address.'

Toby found himself outside in the street feeling as though he'd been kicked in the stomach. He could hardly breathe. What had he done?

He rode home on the tram, his head in a whirl, unable to think straight. He felt defeated, without hope. He knew there was no way out for him now. He'd have to fight for his country when fighting for the business seemed suddenly much more important. Father had been right: he hadn't given the army enough thought.

He'd let Father down again, let the whole family down this time. After five years of working in the business, he was the one best fitted to run it. He'd have loved to increase the profits and prove Father's opinion of him wrong, but now the work Father had done, as well as what Toby had done himself, would have to be continued by somebody else. And there was nobody else who could do it. The company was going to be left without a manager. Toby was appalled.

He was going to have to tell the family what he'd done, and that was going to need a bit of courage too.

He wanted Sarah – he'd never needed her more – but her mother was home and he couldn't stay there any more. He'd have to leave Sarah. Why hadn't the thought of that stopped him enlisting?

He went on down to the New Ferry Hotel for a glass of

beer and stayed long enough to have three pints. When he arrived home, Bessie was just taking the soup tureen into the dining room. He followed her in.

Edward and Claudia were there, and Claudia's mother was having dinner with them.

Mrs Digby snapped: 'Why didn't you tell us you were going to the undertaker?'

'We couldn't do anything until we had the death certificate,' Toby didn't care for Mrs Digby, 'and we only got that at lunch time. Ed's given you the details?'

'We should have gone with you. Taking it all on yourself . . .'

'I don't care what you arrange for the funeral. Do what you like.'

Mrs Digby was drawing herself up. 'That's not the right attitude for a son. You must—'

'You might as well all know now,' Toby interrupted. 'I've enlisted. I'm in the army from a week on Monday. You can do what you like about everything.'

That got to them; they were all staring at him in stunned silence.

Edward's face crumpled in alarm. 'What did you do that for?'

'Who's going to run the business?' There was alarm on Claudia's plump face. 'Your father said you'd be useless. It's just as he predicted. Worse; you won't even be here. But then, knowing what you're like, perhaps it's just as well.'

It made Toby fret more to know it suited his stepmother to have him out of the way.

She said: 'It looks as though it will be up to me after all.'

'It won't,' Edward said fiercely. 'The business has nothing to do with you.'

Chapter Ten

On the morning of the funeral, Claudia pulled on her new black dress. It hadn't been easy to get mourning that was attractive, but she reckoned she hadn't done too badly. She'd refused crêpe and had gone for a mixture of wool and silk, making the excuse that once the cold weather came she'd need the warmth.

Mama had told her: 'Parramatta's the thing. That'll keep you warm.'

The assistant had agreed and brought out ugly gowns of matt-black parramatta, and Claudia had refused those too.

Her mother had been a little shocked. 'Whatever will the neighbours think? For a husband, you should wear full mourning for a year and a day. You shouldn't wear that silk mixture until next year.'

'I'm going to.' Claudia was determined about that. 'You're so old-fashioned. All that went out with Queen Victoria.'

The hat she'd chosen was a flattering little bonnet. She'd bought thick black veiling to cover her face, but she didn't intend to wear it except for the funeral itself. It would be as well to hide her face today; a fluttering handkerchief would denote tears and grief. She shivered, partly from excitement. She'd felt this inner turmoil since Maurice had died.

Today she would see Gideon again. He'd be at the funeral. She'd found his calling card amongst many on the silver salver she kept in the hall. His parents had each sent a card too. Mrs Burton had written on hers: 'Heartfelt condolences.'

Claudia held her At Home on the second Friday in the

month, and usually most of the ladies living along the Esplanade called between two and four in the afternoon to gossip and take tea with her. Not those living in New Ferry Terrace, of course, apart from Mama; only those from the big houses.

Last Friday had been her At Home. Fortunately, Bessie had thought to go along the Esplanade with the news of Maurice's death, so nobody had come. The cards had been delivered by servants; Claudia received two letters of sympathy too.

For the last five years she'd bought schoolmarmish clothes to wear when Maurice was with her, dresses with high necks and long sleeves. She'd kept her more daring and exciting clothes to wear during the day while he was at work.

She'd first made Gideon's acquaintance on his mother's At Home day. She'd been walking down the Esplanade towards Beechwood House, wearing an emerald-green dress and hat of which Maurice would have disapproved, as Gideon had been hurrying home from the ferry. They'd met at his garden gate.

'It's Mrs Percival, isn't it?' He'd doffed his hat, clearly unsure.

She knew exactly who he was. 'Yes, I'm calling on your mother. It's her At Home.'

'Oh dear!'

'It is the first Wednesday in the month, isn't it?'

'Yes, I'd forgotten. Mother doesn't like me creeping round the house when she's entertaining.'

Claudia had been daring. She'd thought him handsome, with his gingery hair and probing eyes. 'Why don't you join the ladies, then? We'd all like that.'

He laughed. 'They aren't all like you.'

The air had been heavy with drizzle. He'd made haste to open the front door with his key and usher her inside. At Beechwood House the hall was vast, with a gracious staircase winding up from it. The grandfather clock was striking the hour.

He'd taken her umbrella, shaken it on the step and slid it into the umbrella stand. Alongside was an immense Victorian chiffonier, carved with dead game birds. Claudia thought it hideous. On top stood an unopened jar of crystallised ginger in syrup. He picked it up and smiled at her.

'Do you like ginger?'

Gideon Burton was a ladies' man, with ready charm and a waxed moustache in a somewhat darker red than his hair. He was a bit of a dandy and given to rather garish waistcoats.

'When it's covered in chocolate.' She'd never tasted it crystallised in syrup. It didn't occur to Maurice to buy it in that form, though she knew he ordered root ginger in large amounts to add to his chutneys.

'I have a passion for ginger in any form.' Gideon paused at the drawing room door.

'I'd better ring for Kate to take you in. There'd be no escape if I ventured closer.'

By the time Claudia had dropped her card on Mrs Burton's oval salver, the maid was waiting to show her in and Gideon was striding up the stairs, two at a time.

Claudia was in the habit of taking a stroll along the Esplanade when the weather was warm and sunny, and on the following Saturday afternoon she took several turns past Beechwood House. When she saw Gideon bounding down the steps of his front garden to join her, she felt her pulse race.

'Hello, Mrs Percival. I trust you have no objection to my joining you? We aren't strangers, after all.'

'I'd be delighted.'

'I've been reminded that you used to come to play with my sister Elizabeth when you were children.'

'You've been discussing me.' She smiled.

'Not really; that was volunteered when I mentioned to Mama that I'd met you on the step the other day.'

'I remember you very well.' Claudia put on her coquettish smile. She flattered herself she could respond to people in a way that pleased them. 'You broke Elizabeth's favourite doll and tormented all her friends. You weren't fond of girls then.'

He laughed. 'I am now, and I treat them very well.' All the time his eyes wouldn't leave hers.

They'd spent more than an hour leaning over the railings of the Esplanade deep in conversation as the tide crept nearer.

Claudia had been watching the ferry boats coming and going from New Ferry Pier. She'd known it was time for Maurice to come home. When she saw his stiff upright figure striding along the pier, with his bowler hat and walking stick, she'd said:

'I shall have to go now.'

'I'll look out for you tomorrow.'

'No; on Sundays my husband likes to have my company. During the evenings too. Every evening.' She was edging back towards Tides Reach.

He'd smiled. 'We must do this again. I could manage Thursday afternoon or next Saturday?'

Claudia had been tingling as she rushed to her bedroom and changed into a prim high-necked dress of navy silk that Maurice liked. She'd barely managed it before he was coming up the hall, calling to Bessie to make afternoon tea.

After that her friendship with Gideon had grown and deepened. She met him in town once or twice a week, and she spent more time than she should dreaming about him. He'd become very important to her.

Adam pulled at her skirt, bringing her thoughts back to the present. He looked very sweet today. Her mother had managed to find a little black suit for him to wear to the funeral. In church he was in a playful mood, playing peekaboo with her veil. He kept lifting it to peep underneath and gurgling with laughter, it wasn't the right moment for games like that.

The church was full. Toby had hastened to let their suppliers and customers know, and of course there were the workers from the factory, all of whom had been given a holiday with pay. Claudia didn't approve of that, but Toby had insisted. Once he was out of the way, she'd soon show them who was boss. Edward was white-faced today; he'd not throw his weight about like Toby. She wouldn't let him.

It was a dreary occasion, but she wasn't going to be miserable, even if Maurice had got the timing wrong. He was gone, that episode in her life was over, and she wasn't sorry. Everybody looked very serious but nobody wept for him. Gideon was sitting behind her, she knew without turning round; she'd heard him clear his throat.

At last the service was over and they all trooped out into the churchyard. There was such a finality about seeing Maurice's coffin being lowered into the grave and dropping a handful of soil on top of it. He'd not be able to give her any more trouble.

Then everybody, even mild acquaintances, was pressing her hand and murmuring: 'Your husband will be sadly missed.'

She responded over and over: 'Do please come to the house and take refreshment.'

At last Gideon's long, tapering fingers were squeezing hers, and his intense dark eyes burned down: 'What a shock for you. A shock for us all.'

His touch thrilled her in a way Maurice's never had. He made her feel alive and on the brink of something wonderful. She wondered how long it would be before they could be married. Of course, she'd be in mourning for a year, so it couldn't be very soon. His parents were of the old school and sticklers for convention; they might insist on eighteen months. But as time went on, it could stop being the hole-in-the-corner affair it had been up till now. She could meet him openly. She was free.

Over the last few years they'd met to have lunch quite often, but she'd had to meet him in the outskirts of Liverpool. After lunch they usually went to a high-class private hotel in Crosby called the Portland. Gideon was friendly with the manager, who allowed them the use of a room there for a few hours, though it was not that sort of hotel at all. Claudia wasn't ashamed of being seen there, except that it wouldn't do at all for Maurice Percival's wife to be recognised having lunch with Gideon Burton.

Out at Crosby, Claudia had felt safe enough. Maurice was a man of habit and usually had his lunch in eating houses close to the factory. Occasionally he might take one of his acquaintances or customers to lunch, and then he'd go into the centre of Liverpool.

When the funeral car had delivered her and the family back to Tides Reach, Claudia prepared to receive her guests. She took off her coat and the ugly veil but kept on her little black bonnet. She was very conscious of having Gideon in her own double drawing room. She could hear his deep voice above the rest, but she dared not show too much interest in him yet. Instead she talked to each of her neighbours and many of Maurice's dull connections.

From time to time she met his warm glances across the room, and at last deemed it would not be out of order to approach him.

'Such lovely roses you have,' he said, looking at them through the window. 'They put ours to shame.'

'Roses were Maurice's passion. He loved them.'

Gideon's voice dropped. 'Are you all right for next Thursday?'

'Yes.' She'd have to get rid of Mama without arousing her suspicions. She'd managed to keep her affair with Gideon from her mother for almost three years; it would be better to go on doing so for another few months.

'As usual then?'

'Yes.' She could see Bessie approaching them with the decanters.

'A little more sherry, Mr Burton?' He smiled at her over Bessie's head as his glass was refilled.

'A visit to the races perhaps,' he said as soon as she'd moved on. 'Cheer you up.'

Claudia felt a warm glow of anticipation. She'd have a few inches trimmed from her long hair and wear it piled up on her head in a more fetching style. She'd be glad to be rid of these plaits wound into earphones that Maurice had liked so much. She wanted to be finished with all that.

Toby had a sinking feeling in his stomach all through the funeral. He'd wanted Sarah beside him. He'd persuaded her to come over for the service, but since a goodly number of their employees had turned out, in suits of greenish-black, nobody thought her presence unusual.

He kept turning round, his eyes seeking her out across the church. He hated the thought of leaving her. After years of searching for a soul mate, someone with whom he wanted to share his life, he'd found her but now would have to leave her. What had he been thinking about? Whatever had driven him to enlist? This was where he wanted to be, where he ought to be to run the business.

Sarah refused to come to the house with him when the service was over.

'A funeral tea is a family matter,' she'd insisted, 'and I'd be the only one from the works.'

Now, standing around with a glass of sherry in his hand, in the double drawing room opened up for once, he craved her presence. He needed her to lean on.

Jeffrey Masters came up to him. 'Could I take you and Edward aside, somewhere quiet? There are problems with your father's will. I'd like to explain.'

Toby ushered them both to his father's study and sat Mr Masters down at the desk. The solicitor cleared his throat.

'You've seen a copy of your father's will? Then you'll agree that he hasn't made reasonable provision for his second family?'

Edward was prepared to fight his stepmother on this. 'How can you say that? Surely he can leave his business to anyone he likes?'

'Only within reason. Your stepmother and her child have been wholly maintained by him during his lifetime. They are entitled to expect the same provision from his estate.

'I know he meant to change his will; he even made an appointment to see me. I'll have to put this will before a court to have it altered.'

'But what about us?' Edward wanted to know.

'The effect will be similar to your father having died intestate. As the will stands, the business was to be divided between you two. It will probably now have to be divided into three to give Adam the same share.

'However, probate won't be settled and the estate distributed until your father's fourth child is born. If it should be another son, then the business will be quartered, to provide for him.

'If the child is a daughter, then an income of two hundred pounds a year would be deemed sufficient. And a greater income will be settled on your stepmother; that goes without saying. So it's important that in the mean time the company continues to trade.'

'Of course.' Toby caught his brother's eye. 'We'll see to that.'

'How fortunate that your father took you into the business at an early age, Toby. You have the experience now to run it.'

'Yes, sir.' Toby was reluctant to explain yet again why that wouldn't be possible. Particularly not to Mr Masters, who'd known the family for so long. He'd been Toby's grandfather's solicitor before he was Father's.

'I shall need the books. All the ledgers and bank books relating to the business. Bring them in to my office as soon as possible. I have to assess its worth for probate.'

'Oh!'

'Toby, are you entitled to sign cheques on behalf of the business? Did your father arrange that?'

Toby pushed his crinkly hair back from his forehead. He was reluctant to say more but knew he had to: 'Yes, but only for amounts up to ten pounds. Father countersigned for larger sums.'

'Then you'll have a problem. Somebody else will have to countersign now.'

Toby knew he'd have to tell him he'd enlisted. When he did, the look on the solicitor's face confirmed what he'd expected. Masters thought him a stupid fool too.

'I'm shocked! Who then is to run this business?'

'I'll be doing it,' Edward said, but there was a brave note to his voice. Everybody knew that was impossible.

'Well, I certainly can't allow Edward to sign cheques on behalf of the business. I'd be lacking in my responsibilities as executor if I did. I shall have to countersign, unless . . . What about your stepmother?'

'No,' Edward said. 'Your office is quite near. It would be easier to slip to you than to come home.'

'This worries me. I should put a manager in. Do you know of anyone, Toby?'

He shook his head.

'Perhaps we should advertise? But there's so little time.'

'We'll manage,' Edward said, straight-lipped.

Mr Masters sat back in his chair, frowning heavily.

'The business is a valuable asset. You mustn't allow it to slip through your fingers. You're both minors; you could say it's my duty to see you don't. Very worrying.'

The funeral guests had departed, leaving the family feeling flat. Edward was restless and at a loose end. On a whim he let himself out through the front door and went down the garden.

He'd expected big changes to follow Father's death but it looked as though they were going to be more far-reaching than anything he'd anticipated. It was one shock after another.

The funeral had really churned him up, and with what Mr Masters had said and Toby enlisting as well, it looked as though he'd be left with the impossible task of coping with the business. And there was Stepmother to cope with too. He was afraid it would be beyond him. His ordered world was falling apart.

He let himself out on to the Esplanade. Tides Reach was the last house; high railings blocked off the end. Below was a small beach known as Fisherman's Cove. Yellow sand with a grassy bank and a steep path up to the road.

He turned and strolled away from that. When he came home from school, it always felt like stepping back in time. This was his childhood territory. He went past Copstone, another bungalow; smaller than Tides Reach, but with the same Victorian bay windows.

He was drawing level now with a pair of massive semi-detached houses faced with handsome grey stone. These had their front doors at the side. Across the front, each had three Georgian-type sash windows that came down to the ground, similar to those in their music room at home. They were called West Knowe and East Knowe. His friend Charlie Dowling lived in East Knowe, and he'd been sent away to boarding school too.

After that came Beechwood House, where the Burtons lived. Benjamin Burton was Father's friend. Gideon Burton had been a boyhood enemy.

Then came the terrace of smaller houses built of shiny red brick. He'd had friends who'd lived here, Willie Lowther in particular. In those far-off days, they'd all attended a small dame school in Rock Ferry.

Edward paused to lean on the low handrails of the Esplanade. It had been a good place to grow up. He and the other boys had played on the shore and scaled this wall with such ease. It had been one place where he could evade Bessie when it was time for bed. He'd never seen a woman climb up or down the wall, and not many grown men could do it either.

There was a fringe of yellow sand below, a yard or two of pebbles and then came the Mersey mud. How many times had he taken a jam jar down there and collected the crabs that lived under the big stones?

He and Willie Lowther used to race them on the garden paths. They had to be matched for size, and most were not much bigger than his thumbnail. When they found crabs that could move fast, they'd keep them overnight in their bedrooms, so they could race them again the next day.

Willie said the crabs would be very comfortable if they put a handful of sand, a few pebbles and a little river water in the jars and then added a generous piece of seaweed on top.

Once Edward's crabs had got out. In the middle of the night he'd heard funny scratching noises on his lino as they'd scampered round. Bessie had not been pleased.

'I don't want crabs loose in any room I have to clean, no thank you. They don't like being here and they'll die without food and water. How d'you know they eat seaweed? Catch them. Collect them all up and take them back to the shore, this minute.'

That had proved easier to say than do. He and Bessie had had to move the wardrobe and the chest of drawers before they were all caught.

'Don't you dare bring another crab into this house, young man,' she'd ordered.

Edward looked at the row of yachts moored out in the river where there was permanent deep water. He could just pick out the one that belonged to Gideon Burton. Gideon also owned a small dinghy to row himself ashore when the tide was in. That was easy to see, moored now in front of his house, marooned high and dry on its side in the mud.

When they were younger, Edward and his friends had loved playing in the mud. Stepmother forbade it and was cross if she saw him coming home covered in it. Charlie Dowling hadn't much liked walking across the mud in his bare feet, though he never wanted to be left behind. He was heavier than either Edward or Willie, and sank deeper.

'I'm sinking up to my knees,' he'd yelled after them one day when they were walking out to low water. 'Wait for me.'

They had. 'The mud looks awful over there.' Charlie pointed. 'It's sinking sand, not safe to wade through. We could get sucked right down in that part. Just think of it, being swallowed up in that terrible muck.'

The mud could be seen in great gullies and mounds, where the currents of the receding tide had churned it up. It changed in colour from rich chocolate to a dark greyish-brown, and that made it look ominous.

'I wish I had waders like the yachtsmen,' Charlie said.

'It's all right if you follow us,' Willie assured him.

Later that same afternoon, when the tide had come in and begun to lap round Gideon Burton's dinghy, they'd climbed in and tried to fish, paying lines over the side into eight inches or so of swirling tide. Gideon Burton had come rushing out in his waders, splashing out to them, shouting at them to leave his property alone.

They'd abandoned his dinghy in a hurry, leaping over the side, but only Charlie escaped. Gideon had caught Edward and Willie, banged their heads together and given them a right telling-off, forbidding them to go near his property ever again. He'd snapped the cane on Willie's new shrimping net with his bare hands. They'd retired hurt, with Willie breathing threats of revenge.

The next afternoon, when they thought Gideon would be out at work, they'd smeared mud thickly all over the white hull of his dinghy. In the sun, it was soon drying into a hard coating, but Gideon came home early and saw them from the pier as he came off the ferry. They scattered, of course, and he couldn't give chase in his city clothes.

But he knew who they were and he went round to their

various homes later on that evening to complain to their parents. He'd stored up trouble for them there. Then he'd given them scrubbing brushes and buckets and told them to clean all the mud off, and stood over them until they had. Then he'd banged their heads together again for good measure.

Willie and Charlie had declared war on Gideon Burton for that.

'We'll get even with him,' Willie said. 'If I have to knock a hole through his boat.'

'Don't touch his boat again,' Edward breathed in horror. 'He'll know it's us.'

'What else can we do? What would hurt him most?'

'The garden?'

'Belongs to his mother and father, not him. Besides, I've never seen him in it. Not at the front.'

Charlie said: 'We'll just watch him for a while. Let him forget this first. If we put our minds to it, some way of giving him a dig will come up.'

A few days later, Willie had said: 'I saw him at the Pier Head in Liverpool with your stepmother.'

Edward had shrugged it off. 'Probably just happened to catch the same boat home.'

'No, I saw them walking towards me. She was holding on to his arm and they were talking, you know sort of engrossed in each other. I think she's two-timing your dad.'

'This is big,' Charlie crowed. 'This will really give us a chance to put the boot in.'

At first, Edward hadn't believed it. He thought Willie was imagining things, but he started to watch his stepmother. She often went out while Father was at work, spending most of the day in town, but was always back before he and Toby returned. She never wanted to talk about where she'd been. She brushed Edward away when he asked.

He talked it over with Toby. 'If Father knew she was going out with Gideon Burton, he'd be shocked. If they're having an affair he'd divorce her and we'd be rid of both her and Mrs Digby.'

Toby shook his head. 'Are you sure about all this?'

'Almost.'

'I'd be two hundred per cent sure before you say anything to Father. Stepmother will be livid. If you're wrong . . .'

'But if we're right, what could be better? And it would bring disgrace on Gideon Burton. That would really please Willie Lowther too.'

Chapter Eleven

On those same long-ago holidays from the dame school, Edward had been kicking a football around with his friends outside the ferry buildings when Claudia came off the ferry. It was a Thursday afternoon, and they'd been playing there in the hope that they would see her. They were nudging each other.

'Watch for Gideon Burton; he's probably not far behind.'

Stepmother's plump face was working with displeasure.

'I don't like to see you hanging around here,' she told him. 'Come home with me, Edward.'

'Do I have to? I'd like to play longer with Willie.'

He knew why she wanted to take him home. It was so he wouldn't see Gideon Burton following five minutes behind her.

'Come along now.'

Obediently, he fell into step with her. 'Where've you been?'

'Shopping in Liverpool.'

'But you haven't bought anything.'

She was carrying nothing but her lizard handbag and her umbrella. The slight pause was telling.

'Yes I have. I bought a dress but had to leave it in the shop to have the hem turned up.'

Edward looked up at her plump and handsome face. Her beady eyes were staring straight ahead. Was Stepmother good at off-the-cuff fibs? It sounded just the sort of thing Willie Lowther could come out with. Something that sounded like the truth but wasn't.

'What colour?'

Her voice was sharper. 'What d'you mean?'

'What colour is your new dress?'

'Blue. Why the sudden interest in my clothes?'

Edward ignored that. 'Why didn't you take Mrs Digby with you? She loves to go shopping.'

'Sometimes I like to go alone.'

He turned round to see if he could spot Gideon Burton anywhere along the pier. Most of the passengers from the ferry had gone now. There were two men fishing off the side. A man with a dog was talking to them. Not Burton. It was only five in the afternoon; perhaps he'd gone back to his office.

'But to have lunch alone too? You caught the eleven thirty ferry.' That made her swing round to look at him. Her eyes were sharp with suspicion.

'I met a friend in town, a lady I used to go to school with.'

Edward thought that was another porker. He reckoned she must have had lunch with Gideon Burton. Willie said Thursday was their regular day. He turned round to check the pier one last time and almost laughed aloud. There was no mistaking the tall, well-built figure in a bowler hat, striding out with his mackintosh over his arm. That was him all right.

Edward paused long enough to see Gideon Burton head up New Ferry Road towards the back gate of Beechwood House. He smiled with pleasure. He'd caught her out, he was sure of it now.

'Come along, Edward.' Stepmother sounded irritable. 'What are you staring at?'

'That man fishing from the pier. He's just caught something.' Two could play at her game.

He couldn't wait to tell his brother. As soon as Toby came home from work, Edward went to his bedroom and sprawled on his bed.

'Father would throw Stepmother out if he knew.'

Toby was tired. 'He wouldn't believe you.'

'But it's true. Surely he'd want a divorce? And that's what we want to happen. If Father divorced Claudia, we'd get rid of her and that dreadful Mrs Digby. She's here almost every day.

'And if everybody knows what Gideon Burton gets up to, his reputation will come down a peg at the same time. Two birds with one stone.'

'Move over.' Toby threw himself across the bed too. 'Father's been on at me all day. Given me a terrible time. He won't believe you, and even if it is true, I don't think he'd do anything. Divorce is a big step.'

'But surely . . .'

'I keep trying to tell him things. Things which need doing at the factory. Nothing's changed there since Grandfather's day. But he can't see it. You can't tell him anything. Wouldn't believe anything bad about Stepmother.

'He'd say: "You're too old for fairy stories now, Edward."'

A little later that same night, when they'd gathered in the dining room for dinner, Father had fixed Edward with a steely glare.

'What have you been doing today?'

'Playing.'

'Hanging about the ferry buildings,' Claudia said. 'With that Willie Lowther.'

Neither she nor Father approved of Willie Lowther. He lived in the terrace, so they didn't think he was quite the right class, but even worse, his father was a bookmaker. Father didn't approve of betting either.

'I played with Charlie Dowling too.'

Charlie was thought suitable because his father was a solicitor in Liverpool. Junior, though; he didn't have a practice of his own. Not yet.

'In his garden. We played cricket, the three of us. Well,

it means one can bat, one bowl and the other has to be wicketkeeper. Then we had a swim in the river and walked miles up past the brickfields to Bromborough Dock.'

'He's running wild.' Claudia attacked her lamb chop viciously. 'Willie Lowther's a little devil. Not at all suitable. I've heard him swear.'

Father's dark eyes had fixed on Edward. 'Not at all the sort of boy you should mix with.'

'Boarding school is the answer, Maurice. I think it would suit Edward very well.'

Toby turned on them hotly. 'Don't send him away. The school I went to was fine. I want Edward to stay here with me. We want to be together. That's what you want, isn't it, Ed?'

'I like it here. I don't want to go away.'

'It's for his own good, Toby.'

'But I'll miss him.'

Father said: 'We'll think seriously about boarding school for you, Edward. Find a good one where you'll be happy.'

Edward knew then that meant Father's mind was made up.

'Charlie Dowling's going to board at Osborne House in September.'

'Osborne House? We could do better than that for you.'

Edward knew they wanted to separate him from Charlie too. Stepmother's eyes glistened at him from across the table. He knew she was responsible for this. She was arranging for him to be sent away because she knew he was watching her and Gideon Burton. She wanted him far away, where he couldn't make trouble for her.

He went to Toby's room when they were both supposed to be asleep. He was down in the dumps because he was being sent to boarding school.

'You asked for it,' Toby sighed. 'You let Stepmother know you were watching her. Taking too much interest in what she was doing.'

'I saw him, I tell you. Gideon Burton came over on the same boat.'

'That's exactly why she doesn't want you around as you grow older – why you're off to boarding school. Probably thinks you're not old enough yet to put two and two together. Wouldn't be, if it wasn't for that Willie Lowther,' Toby grinned. 'Stepmother's won this round.'

Edward shook his head. 'Shall I say something to Father?'

'Not unless you want trouble. Stepmother will hate you.'

'I think she does already. Right, it's up to you now. You'll have to keep an eye on her.'

'I have to go to work with Father, Ed. What chance do I have to watch Stepmother?'

'Willie Lowther's keeping watch. Mostly she walks past his house when she goes anywhere. Give her enough rope and she'll hang herself.'

Arrangements had been put in hand to find a boarding school for him. It was yet another reason for Edward's vendetta against Claudia. The idea of Father divorcing her pleased him. He couldn't get it out of his mind. He talked to Toby about it several times.

'Charlie Dowling knows all about it. His dad's a solicitor who specialises in divorce. Charlie says that for Father to get one, we'd have to have proof. Photographs are what we need.'

'Photographs of them together?'

'Yes, going into a hotel. That sort of thing.'

Edward could see Toby was ready to brush him off again.

'How are we going to get those? Even supposing they go to a hotel?'

'Follow them.'

'They'd see you.'

'Charlie says some husbands hire private detectives to follow their wives. When they're suspicious.'

'Father isn't suspicious.'

'Well, he should be. Do you want them to divorce or not?'

'Of course I do. It's a lovely idea, but I can't do much when I'm pinned down at work, can I? Anyway, how do we get a camera?'

'I shall ask for one for my next birthday. Father sometimes asks us what we want.'

'You'll manage to convey what you want, Ed, whether he asks you or not.'

'I'll try for a camera, then.'

'You'll be off at this boarding school before your birthday.'

'I know, that's the worst part.'

'Stepmother's going to win.'

Now, all these years later, Edward was ready to concede that Stepmother had won. When he'd gone away to school he'd lost interest in what she was doing. He'd never got that camera either. Anyway, what did it matter now that Father had died?

On second thoughts, it mattered a lot. If Father had known, they might not have had Stepmother on their backs now, wanting Father's will changed and threatening to take over the business.

Edward turned round and surveyed the terrace of shiny red-brick houses. He'd call and see his old friend Willie Lowther. He'd be here; there had never been any likelihood of Willie going off to boarding school.

Mrs Lowther opened the front door, anxiously wiping her hands on her apron. She was welcoming.

'So sorry to hear about your father, Edward.' Strong scents of frying food billowed up the hall round her.

'You want our Willie?' She called up the stairs. 'Here's Edward Percival to see you.'

Willie's stockinged feet scampered down. He seemed inches taller than when Edward had last seen him; tall and

154

scrawny-thin. A beaming smile split his face and he thumped Edward on the shoulder, delighted to see him again. He took him up to his bedroom, as untidy as always. Edward sat on the unmade bed. Nothing had changed in this house.

'I've just remembered.' Willie was suddenly serious. 'Your father's died. I'm very sorry.'

'That's why I'm home. I'm not going back to school.'

'I've just started working for my father, learning to be a bookmaker.'

'I'm starting work too.'

'Poor old Charlie Dowling; he'll be staying at school until he's eighteen.'

They started to talk about the old days. It cheered Edward, lifted him away from the funeral and the uncertainties of the future.

'Remember how we used to watch your stepmother? I still see her quite often. D'you know what? I think her affair with Gideon Burton's still going on. I saw them together the other day in Simpson's Café on the landing stage. Having tea and cakes as bold as brass. Yes, it's still going on all right.'

'But it doesn't matter now,' Edward said. 'With Father dying like this, she can have tea with who she likes.'

'And so can Gideon Burton. We never did get even with him.'

Edward thought, as he walked home, that it seemed Claudia won all the time.

Toby had a restless night. He had no idea how Percival's Pickles could be run in his absence. His mind went blank every time he thought about it. How could Ed, at the age of fifteen, manage the company without ever having worked in it? He was landing his brother in a mess that could ruin the work of three generations of his family. And leave them all without income.

When Bessie called him in the morning, he felt he couldn't get out of bed, though he knew it was very important that he went over to the factory to sort something out. If it hadn't been for Edward banging back his bedroom door and opening the curtains, he didn't think he'd have made it at all. It all seemed hopeless; he felt really down and depressed.

At the last minute, Edward reminded him about the ledgers he'd seen in Father's study, and Toby ran back to get them. They'd need them; they showed this year's figures. Ed was cross with him, and who could blame him? They bickered all the way there and were late.

Ed said: 'You'll have to show me everything, teach me what to do.'

Toby knew it wasn't possible. Not in the few days they had left. It helped a little to find the factory functioning as it always did, with Sarah in her usual place in the line.

It came to him then that she'd been working here for four years and must have learned a lot about the business. He found another girl to take her place in the line.

'We need you in here,' he said, leading her to the office. 'You've got to look after things for me. Help Edward. You know more than he does.'

Sarah looked round the office cautiously; she'd been inside only once before. Old Mr Percival hadn't encouraged the factory girls to enter what he considered his personal space.

'We're in a hole,' Edward told her. 'Toby's done a very silly thing.'

Sarah knew how serious it was. She tried to smile at Toby. 'I know what he's done.'

'I think we should sell the business,' Edward said. 'Now, before it begins to run down.'

Toby looked rueful. 'I've thought of that too, but could we do it quickly? And with the war, it's not the best time. Nobody's thinking of making pickles.'

'Mam and I talked about it last night.' Sarah was frowning. 'About what you could do. The best way to go about it.'

'Go on.' There was just a hint of Toby's little-boy smile.

'There are two people . . . Mr Trumper virtually runs the factory anyway; he's been foreman for years. And Miss Potts runs the office.'

Toby was looking at her with respect. 'You're right. Miss Potts taught me most of what I know about the accounts.'

'Mam thinks if you gave them new titles, like office manager and—'

'Production manager?'

'Yes, because that's what they really are. And perhaps a small increase in pay. They've worked here all their lives; they'll do their very best for you.'

Toby was thinking. 'There's a lot of things they won't know about. Jobs that Father did and that I did.'

'You'll have to divide those between the rest of us and hope we'll learn enough to do them in the few days left. You'll be able to come back, won't you? To check that everything's all right? Over the first weeks anyway.'

'I expect so.' They looked at each other in the silence that followed.

'So what are those jobs?' Edward wanted to know.

Toby was frowning. 'Let me see . . .'

Sarah prompted: 'Who ordered all the things we use? The onions and vinegar and all that.'

'Father did. Whatever you do, don't fall down on that. If you run out of ingredients, production would have to stop and all profit would be gone. Even when the conveyor belts are turned off, the workers would have to be paid.'

Sarah saw Toby look at his brother. Edward's hands were half covering his face. 'It's a big responsibility,' he muttered.

Sarah could feel her stomach muscles tightening. It was a job that had to be done. She had to help Toby.

'I think I could do it,' she said slowly. 'If you show me the records of what's been bought in the past and from where.'

She could see the gratitude in his blue eyes.

'It's only like shopping on a large scale, isn't it?' she smiled.

Toby got the files out and spread them across the desk in front of her. She pored over them.

'This tells us exactly what was used last month . . .'

'Every month,' Toby said. 'It's all there.'

'I'm sure I could do it. I'll keep an eye on the stocks and make sure we aren't running short.'

'Father was going to double the order for spices. He was afraid they'd soon be in short supply. Because of the war.'

'I'll do that.'

Toby's baby face was full of uncertainty. 'It's quite complicated, because it's all tied up with what we manufacture; what sort of pickle and chutney we're going to make. And that depends on what orders we have to fulfil and what's in season. Father liked to work that out weeks in advance.'

'So it's all been done for the next month or two?'

'Yes, but you must start thinking about what you'll be making in the weeks after that.'

'Perhaps if we all sat down together and worked it out . . . Could Mr Trumper help?'

'He'll know what's been made in the past. How it was all done.'

Sarah swallowed hard. It sounded terribly complicated. 'What else did your father do?'

'He kept the books and made up the wages. But Miss Potts helped with that. Probably did most of the work.'

'Let's get her in,' Sarah said, jumping to her feet to do so. Miss Potts had worked in the adjoining office for over thirty years. 'Let's talk to her.'

Eunice Potts was stout, with thick grey hair done up in a large bun. She wore tortoiseshell spectacles and swinging serge skirts that covered her button boots.

'Yes,' she said. 'I do the book-keeping and make up the wages every week. Under your father's supervision, of course.'

Toby asked: 'Could you do it without supervision? From

anybody? What I'm asking is, do you feel you could manage it on your own?'

'Ye-es. But Mr Percival did a lot and he checked everything. I think I could do what he did, yes, but it would be a lot to manage.'

'We'd increase your salary. Make it commensurate with the increase in responsibility. Would you do it?'

Her face screwed. 'It would take me more time . . . There'd be more to do.'

'You'd need help?'

Her face cleared. 'Yes.'

'Another clerk?'

'That's it. Somebody to help me with the books. Jimmy can't do it.' Jimmy was the office boy.

'Could you do that?' Toby asked his brother. Edward pulled a face. 'Father showed you the books. Explained them.'

'Yes, but . . . They're so complicated. I don't understand . . .'

'There's Mam,' Sarah suggested. 'She was trained as a post office clerk when she was young. I'm sure she could get back into the way of it.'

'Your mam?' Toby groaned. 'Oh God! This is awful. Even if she could . . . Is she well enough?'

'She's getting better, pottering about our rooms. The job she had before was heavy; she can't go on lifting crates about much longer. She needs a sit-down job. She's well enough to come here and talk about it, to see if she thinks she could do it.'

'This afternoon?' For the first time she saw a glimmer of hope on Toby's face. 'If she could.'

'I'll bring her back after dinner.'

Edward said: 'So what did you do, Toby?'

'I went out looking for orders. Sought out shops, ship's chandlers and places like that to stock our products. Who's going to do that?'

'Do we have to have somebody straight away?' Sarah asked, looking at the books. 'There seem to be plenty of outlets. You must have been good at it.'

'I liked doing it. Yes, somebody will have to keep working at it. Markets can be lost as well as gained.'

Edward said, 'What about me?'

'You're too young. We can hardly send out a lad of fifteen, even if you do look older. Nobody will take you seriously. You'd have to talk to customers about the different lines we make; prices and discounts and when we can deliver, that sort of thing.'

'What can I do then?' Edward asked plaintively. 'I want to help. I've got to do something.'

'Mam and I talked about that too,' Sarah told him. 'You need to spend a few months with each of us in turn, learning what we do. Coming in straight from school, you couldn't take on responsibility for any part of it. Not straight away. It'll all seem very strange to you at first.'

'That's true,' Toby said. 'Very sensible. You need to learn all you can, Ed. As fast as you can, so you can take over the running of it.'

'I'd like that.' Edward looked relieved.

Sarah said: 'How about starting on the factory floor with Mr Trumper in the mornings? Afternoons with Miss Potts learning about the books. They both know what they're doing. The rest of us are going to be feeling our way at first.'

'Good idea.' Toby was enthusiastic. 'A sort of training programme. From the bottom up, so when you do take over as manager, you'll know exactly how the company works.'

'Don't worry, we'll start unloading jobs on you as soon as you understand what has to be done.'

Edward smiled. 'I want to be useful. Pull my weight.'

'Right,' Toby said. 'That's settled then. But who's going to manage the company now?'

'We'll all have to pull together,' Sarah said. 'We'll all have a say in how it's run. We'll sit in here a couple of times each week and talk things through, make sure we're doing the right things. Feel our way and support each other.'

'That should do it.' Toby smiled with relief. 'Team management. But hang on, what about the marketing? We haven't decided that yet.'

Miss Potts said: 'What about Mr Trumper's son, Charlie? Mr Percival thought he'd make foreman one day.'

'I've heard he's going off to fight,' Sarah said. 'Would have done by now if his mother hadn't been dead against it. We could end up very short-handed here. Choose an older man, Toby. Somebody who'll stay.'

'I don't know . . .'

'I do,' Sarah said, then stopped to think. All her instincts were to hold John Ferry at arm's-length. Since she'd dropped him, their relationship had been prickly. Could they work together after what had happened? He'd been stroppy to Toby. Much easier to keep him loading their carts and checking things in the stock room.

'Who then?' Toby wanted to know.

She swallowed hard. He was the best man available. It wouldn't be fair to stop him having this chance.

'What about John Ferry? He's capable of more than labouring. He's reliable and sensible and takes everything seriously. He's been turned down by the army and I think he'd jump at the chance of a better job.'

Toby wrinkled his nose. 'Have my reservations about him.'

So had she. 'Did he upset you too much the other day?'

Toby smiled properly for the first time that morning. 'I'd be daft if I held that against him now. No, it's . . .'

It was only later, when Miss Potts had gone back to her desk and Edward had been dispatched to stop the lines for the dinner break, that she found out why Toby was bothered about John Ferry.

'I'll be leaving you here together. If he's doing the selling you'll have to liaise closely. He'll bring in the orders; you have to order the supplies to make them. I'll be leaving the coast clear for him. I'm afraid you'll get together again and forget all about me.'

'Toby! Of course I won't! Not after . . . It's you I love. You don't have to worry about that.'

'You're a gem, Sarah. What would I do without you? Will you put it to him? See what he says?'

'I'd rather you did that.'

'He doesn't like me.'

'Together, then. I can't do it by myself.'

'Why not? You know him well enough.'

'And he knows me. I've been peeling onions for the last four years. He won't see how things have changed.'

'He soon will. Shall I see if I can catch him now, before he knocks off for dinner? Let's get things organised.'

Chapter Twelve

Sarah sat at Maurice Percival's desk, waiting with trepidation. There was an eagerness about Toby as he brought John in; he wanted everything settled. Once John caught sight of her sitting at the desk, he was hanging back, plainly reluctant. Toby's baby cheeks were like red apples; John's were equally flushed, but he looked uncomfortable.

'I don't understand,' John said, looking from her to Toby. 'What sort of a job do you want me to do?'

'Have a seat.' Toby waved him to a chair, and tried to explain how the work was being redistributed.

'Toby's enlisted,' Sarah said, since he'd not mentioned that.

'You've enlisted? What made you do that?'

'You thought I hadn't the guts. You wanted to get away from me. Well, I'm the one that's going.'

'Leaving? Who's going to run this company?'

The door opened and Edward came in.

'Edward is, with help from everybody else. What d'you say? Are you up to marketing our products?'

'Marketing? I know nothing about that.' John looked amazed. 'Wouldn't know where to begin.'

Toby was opening ledgers in front of him. 'I think you would; you were always asking questions. I thought you were interested in selling.'

'Yes, I am.'

'I'll have a few days to explain everything to you. It's a question of going round our customers and getting more orders. I'm afraid you'll have to find your own way round from the address book.'

'I know Liverpool pretty well.'

'That's a start. I go further afield. Chester and Manchester. I'm sure you could get good business if you went further still. I wanted Father to get a full-time salesman.'

Edward interrupted: 'Aren't we going for dinner, Toby?'

John was frowning. 'I don't know. I don't know whether I'd be any good at it. I don't want to lose business for you. Can I have an hour to think about it?'

'Yes. We'd all better have our dinner.'

Sarah found herself walking home with John.

'I still don't understand,' he said. 'Whose idea was this?'

'Toby's.'

It had been drizzling all morning. It was blowing in her face now as they strode out quickly.

'He wouldn't want me.'

'He does; we think you're the best person to do it.'

'He could advertise for a proper salesman.'

'That takes time. Toby's leaving in a few days.'

'I can't believe he's enlisted. What made him do that?'

'You did; he told you. You said he hadn't the guts for it. He wanted to prove you wrong.'

John pulled at her arm and made her stop. 'Are you saying it's my fault? That I drove him to it?'

'Don't be so touchy. It's one of several reasons. And Toby didn't know his father was going to die like that, did he? He thought the army would be more fun than working here.'

'Oh God! What a mess.'

'You'll take this job?'

'Was it your idea? To offer it to me?'

'Toby's too. Everything's changing overnight. Mr Percival gone, Toby going. Trumper and Miss Potts are going to take more responsibility; so am I. So you're not the only one. Toby thinks it better to promote the people he had. He knows us; he thinks we've already shown loyalty.'

'It sounds a complicated job.'

'John! You once told me you only needed a chance to show

what you could do; that you'd be as good as anyone and better than most. Toby's giving you that chance.'

'Toby?' They were climbing the stairs to their rooms. 'I thought Toby Percival had robbed me of everything.'

John Ferry let himself into the room he shared with his mother and listened to Sarah's footfall as she went on up the bare stairs. He'd thought Sarah and Toby had turned against him, but it seemed they hadn't. Not altogether. What they'd done had aroused such raw feelings of hostility in him, such bitterness; he was dumbfounded that they seemed to think it need change nothing. Now they were giving him the chance he'd craved.

His mother had gone to the shops to buy food. John set about the household chores, laying the fire ready for evening, bringing up coal and water from the yard below and setting the kettle on the Primus to boil.

He was twenty-five years old, much older than Toby. He'd prided himself on being more sensible, yet he was filled with both hatred and envy. Toby had been born with a silver spoon in his mouth and seemed to have no idea how fortunate he was. He had no appreciation of class or social hierarchy either.

Toby was popular with the workers in the factory. He larked about with them and treated them as friends. He'd played cards with them in the dinner break, and poker too, mostly for matches. He'd brought in a dartboard and set it up in the loading shed outside for them to play on.

He'd been particularly friendly with those near his own age. He'd taken Charlie Trumper for a glass of beer one dinner time and had an almighty row with his father as a result. They'd heard the boss shouting angrily in his office, forbidding Toby to take the lads drinking in the middle of the working day. Forbidding him to make friends of them.

Now Toby took the lads for a drink only on Friday nights after work was finished. Mostly it was Charlie and Fred

Blaney, though when they'd been on better terms he'd asked John to go with them. John hadn't wanted to.

'I'm teetotal,' he'd said. 'I don't drink.'

'Come and try it. It's good fun.'

'No thanks.'

'A couple of pints won't hurt you.'

'I don't want to.' John didn't find it easy to refuse. Toby could be good company. One day he'd run the business that employed John, but still John couldn't drink with him. He knew he had a hang-up about alcohol.

As a child, he'd seen what it could do to people. His own father, normally a gentle giant of a man, had attacked his mother and deliberately jumped on John's ankle in hob-nail boots in a drunken frenzy.

John had been recovering from that in hospital when his father had come to his bedside.

'I'm sorry, lad, terribly sorry.' He'd wept, full of remorse, a broken man. 'I didn't know what I was doing. Honest, son, I wouldn't hurt you for the world.'

Even today, as a grown man, the thought of drinking ale frightened John as it frightened his mother. She'd be horrified if he so much as let half a pint of ale pass down his throat. She'd feel he was on the same slippery slope that had finished his father.

Dad had been a docker. It was hard work that left him hot and thirsty and tired at the end of the day.

'Everybody takes a glass or two,' John remembered him saying. 'We sweat so much we need it. We earn so little there isn't much comfort at home. For men like us, where else is there to go but the pub?'

John had learned early in life that his dad had an alcohol problem he couldn't control. He'd tried very hard, but alcohol had defeated him. Mam had pleaded with him to leave it alone, and he did for weeks on end, but eventually he'd go on another bender.

His mother had found it easier to get work than his father.

166

She'd always worked, but when Dad was on a drinking spree he took the money that she'd put aside for rent and coal. Intoxication brought terrible family rows, and often his father was violent.

He was a binge drinker, and a binge could last for more than a week. He'd come home rolling drunk with empty pockets, knowing he'd let his wife and family down. Then he'd lash out at Elvira. John had grown up ready to protect his mother from him. He'd grown up fast; he'd had to. The love he'd had for his father turned to contempt.

He'd pleaded with his mother to leave Mick Ferry, but she wouldn't.

'It's not easy for your dad,' she'd told him. 'A docker's life is hard. Sometimes he hangs around all day and doesn't get any work, and that makes him depressed. He thinks he has an empty existence. All his mates go for a drink and they persuade him to go with them. What else is there for him? It's what he enjoys. He'd drink himself to death if he didn't have us. We're all he's got to live for. It's just that he doesn't see it that way when he's drunk.'

John had thought his mother something of a saint, because she'd had more than her share of black eyes. He'd heard her threaten:

'If you ever hurt our John again, if you so much as lay another finger on him, we'll be off. You mark my words. I'm promising you that.'

Mam was tiny, hardly five feet tall, but she knew how to stand up to a six-foot man. Dad hadn't laid a finger on him since, though he'd come very near it when John had pushed himself between them to protect his mother.

But when his father was on a drinking binge, John and his mother had gone to bed hungry.

When Dad sobered up, Mam would start on him. She'd tell him over and over that booze was making them poor. They desperately needed the money he spent on ale to put food on their plates.

167

John had been eleven when, long after midnight, a policeman had come knocking on their door. He told them Mick Ferry had been killed in a pub brawl with a sailor who had drawn a knife on him.

John had gone to work at twelve years of age, telling Mr Percival he was fourteen. He'd earned only eight shillings to start with, but it was eight shillings they could rely on.

He felt he had good reason for his hang-up about drink. He intended to remain teetotal.

The following days seemed hectic to Sarah as she tried to familiarise herself with the work she'd taken on. Toby hardly had time to talk to her, as the others demanded his attention.

John in particular needed a lot of help. 'I've often wondered how our pickles got into the shops, but I'm still vague about the details.'

Toby told him all he could and handed over the records his father had made him keep: the book showing the calls he'd made and the rounds he'd worked. John saw that as very valuable.

'It's important to keep thinking about new sales outlets. I want you to find new customers for us,' Toby told him. 'As well as keeping the old ones happy.'

The factory usually closed for the weekend at one o'clock on Saturday, but this week Mr Trumper, Miss Potts, Edward, John and Sarah and her mother returned for a last session in the afternoon.

'How are we going to cope with your stepmother?' Sarah wanted to know. 'She says she's coming here to take over.'

Toby sighed. He felt time was running out; that a feeling of desperation was creeping in.

'She won't be able to. She can't just come in and take over. She's never worked here, she knows nothing about what goes on.'

'She says she's going to try,' Edward said gloomily. 'She's

just waiting until you've gone. She'll come in here asking questions and start telling us what we must do.'

'She'll have to find out what the routine is first.'

'We can't not tell her. Not if she asks questions.' Eunice Potts was frowning.

'Tell her too much.' Toby grinned. 'That's the way to do it. Blind her with science, all of you. Keep feeding her facts, down to minute details. Give her far too much to take in at once. Then if she asks again about the same thing, just say, it's as I explained yesterday, or whenever. Nobody can take it all in at once. Hopefully that will take Claudia down a peg, sap her confidence.'

'She's got plenty of that,' Edward sighed.

'She'll pretend she knows more than you, but that's impossible. You've learned a lot in the last day or so.

'Don't let her talk you into altering anything. Say I want all decisions discussed between you six. You mustn't be too deferential to her. Ed knows how to cope with her.'

On Sunday, Sarah spent all day alone with Toby, despite her mother's protests. Most of it in the factory, which seemed very different with none of the machinery running. That morning, he sat at his father's desk, his head in his hands.

'I wish I didn't have to go. I'm dreading it. Scared too. I shall be worried stiff about this place. My father and my grandfather worked so hard to build it up and now it's all hanging by a thread.

'I'll be the black sheep of the family if things don't work out.' He gave a wry laugh. 'I'm the black sheep already for doing this. How could I have been such a fool?'

Sarah felt she'd done her best to help him thrash out a workable plan of action. She was still trying to seem upbeat and optimistic, but really she felt empty, drained at the thought of being parted from him. She was full of foreboding too.

'Edward and me, all of us, we'll do our best to keep things going.'

'I've no one to blame but myself. I did it of my own free will. I've shot myself in the foot, haven't I?'

Sarah spent a lot of that last day in his arms, but she wasn't comfortable in the office. Mr Percival still seemed close; the atmosphere was still heavy with his cigarette smoke.

Toby's leave-taking was desperate as well as passionate. 'I don't know when I'll be able to see you again,' he said.

Toby had studied his recruitment papers so many times, he could reel off all the information they contained. He was to report to Bebington Show Ground, where he was to join a newly raised service battalion of the Cheshire Regiment.

The Cheshires had already been mobilised and were fighting in France. There were so many new recuits, they were using tented accommodation as sleeping quarters, and the weather, which had been pleasantly fine, suddenly became wet. Toby was allocated to a bell-tent in which he was to sleep with eleven other men. Black mould was already beginning to grow on the inside of the canvas. The dining quarters were in a leaking temporary hut.

His fellow volunteers were in such high good humour they might have been enjoying their summer holidays. They were still burning in a fever of patriotism. Their high spirits depressed him.

His first morning was taken up standing in line to draw his kit. His uniform was of very rough material and made him itch; the boots were heavy and didn't fit properly.

That afternoon, they turned out in the rain to learn to march. Toby felt he had two left feet. The new experiences left him feeling confused and useless.

By Thursday, Claudia had managed to persuade her mother to go back to her rooms along the terrace.

'Only right that you should go home and pay your rent,' she told her. 'And you must want to make sure your belongings are still there safe and sound.'

Claudia didn't want her every movement watched. She gave her mother a couple of slices of ham to take home for her lunch. That should keep her there.

Mama seemed reluctant to go. When she overheard Claudia telling Ena they'd have what remained of yesterday's cold mutton for dinner, she said:

'Will there be enough? I know Toby's gone, but there'll still be three of us, as well as Adam.'

That was Mama's way of telling her she didn't expect to be put out of her comfortable new home for more than a few hours.

It wouldn't be easy to slip out to see Gideon if Mama were always here. Perhaps she should just tell her now. No point in worrying herself about what Mama thought. Probably she'd approve. She hadn't been that fond of Maurice after all.

Claudia decided she'd do whatever was easiest. She'd see how things turned out. In the meantime, she put her mind to more immediate problems. She didn't want to wear full mourning when she went out with Gideon. Pale colours suited her better than black, and the recently bereaved didn't go racing at Haydock Park and to lunch in hotels. His parents would consider that the height of bad taste.

The weather had changed. It was a grey morning, but with a cutting cold wind. Claudia didn't mind, because that gave her an excuse to wear a mackintosh. Hers was silver-grey and would look well over her black dress and little black bonnet. She would brighten it up with a multicoloured scarf, which could be pushed in her pocket when she got back on the ferry. Nobody she knew need see her wear it.

She had to have a bit of fun. Soon she'd look too pregnant to be seen out and about. Much better to take advantage of Gideon's invitations while she could.

Edward felt lost in the factory without his brother to lean on. He returned to Tides Reach every evening of that first week feeling as though he'd been mangled. Working for a

171

living was not the treat he'd expected it to be. It was hard for them all without Toby. The hours of concentration were long. In retrospect, school was both pleasanter and easier, but he couldn't go back.

He was going to be the Percival who kept the business on track. He was relying on Eunice Potts and Alfred Trumper to lead the way right now, but he was determined to take command as soon as he could.

At dinner on Thursday evening, he was surprised to find Mrs Digby sitting down to the meal with them.

'I thought you said you were going back to your room?' He didn't miss the look she gave her daughter.

'Claudia needs help.' Mrs Digby had a haughty voice. 'I don't like leaving her here on her own. She's got so much to cope with; the house and everything.'

Edward couldn't see why his stepmother should find it difficult. She surely must be used to running the house, and there need be less formality about everything now Father had gone. He was the fusspot who'd wanted everything to be just so.

Mrs Digby went on: 'Would it be better if I stayed for good, Claudia? I could have my things brought up tomorrow and dispense with my room down there in the terrace.'

Edward was taken aback. Then he noticed Claudia had straightened up in her chair. She wasn't welcoming such a move either.

'You'll find Adam too much for you, Mother. Better if you kept a place of your own.'

'But I'm needed here, and it would save the cost of the rent.'

'You'll not be needed here permanently. I'm sure you need your privacy.' Claudia was frosty.

Edward was left in no doubt that Claudia needed her own privacy. He relaxed. That would suit him too.

'Is everything all right at the factory?'

Having rebuffed her mother, Claudia was aroused and in a

fighting mood. She questioned Edward closely about progress at the factory, particularly about the cost of running it and the amount of money it brought in. By that time of the day he was too tired to think clearly.

'You say it's still working, but it depends on how many jars you've been able to fill. Will you be making as much as your father did?'

'We're aiming to do that,' he confirmed. 'Mr Trumper says it's possible, and he must know.'

'I think you should go over,' Mrs Digby told her daughter. 'You mustn't expect much from a young lad like Edward. It's in your interests to go. Maurice felt he was needed there; he never missed a day.'

Edward was alarmed. 'What can Stepmother do? Everything continues to turn over, like I told you.'

'Just turning over won't do. The business must thrive. I'll come over with Claudia. Give my support too.'

'Really, there's nothing either of you can do,' Edward told them as firmly as he knew how. 'We have everything under control.' He swallowed hard; he hoped they had. As they left the table, he heard Mrs Digby say:

'We should see for ourselves what's going on, Claudia. We'll go over tomorrow morning. You must look after your money while you can.'

Chapter Thirteen

Claudia continued to feel that her life was divided into two separate parts. She loved the wonderful days out with Gideon, but there was still the debris of her life with Maurice from which she couldn't escape.

The feeling that she was being done down wouldn't go away. Maurice had not treated her fairly in his will, and if she didn't watch it, Toby and Edward would do the same. Edward was increasingly hostile.

Mama was of the same opinion, and decided that they should go to see what was happening in the factory. In fact, she felt so strongly, she'd have had Claudia there before Maurice was cold in his grave if she'd had her way.

There'd been so much more expense recently, with the funeral and everything else, that Claudia's housekeeping allowance was quite gone. The need for more money was beginning to niggle.

Claudia dressed rapidly the next morning, feeling tense with determination. Yesterday she'd had a wonderful day out with Gideon; today she and Mama would go to the factory.

She knew it wasn't a suitable place for a lady, but she had to go to make a stand for her own rights. She'd been once before, when she was first married and had wanted to see the place where Maurice spent most of his waking hours. He'd spoken of little else and she thought seeing it would help her understand better what went on. The attraction then, as now, was the money it earned.

What she'd seen had horrified her. However much she needed to ensure her income, she didn't think she could work there as Maurice had, day in and day out. What she wanted was to have some control over the income it generated, and to do that she needed to know more about what went on there.

Mama had sown doubts in her mind about the business earning much less now that Maurice and Toby were gone. Edward was such a child, he'd not know how to control anything. Maurice had kept a strict eye on his workers; he hadn't trusted them not to rob him if they had a chance. Claudia knew she'd have to make her presence felt.

'You're up early,' Edward said to her mother at breakfast. Usually Mama had her breakfast in bed before getting up.

'We're coming over to the factory with you,' she said. 'We told you last night.'

He didn't seem happy with that. 'I can't wait for you; I'll have to go. I'll let everybody know you're coming to look round.'

'Not look round exactly,' Claudia tried to tell him. 'We're coming to work. To lend a hand.'

'Oh!' That seemed to upset him more. He leapt up from the table without drinking his second cup of tea. Claudia had the feeling they wouldn't be welcomed.

Mama had already started to nag: 'You know what it's like to have no money. You must look after the business before Edward ruins it.'

And there was Adam to think of. She had to look after his interests too. She sent him off to school with Bessie and got herself ready. Mama took the best part of an hour to dress herself in her black silk gown with black velvet cape and matching hat.

Claudia always enjoyed a trip on the ferry, and this morning it was pleasant on deck, but Mama insisted on taking her to the saloon only to complain about the oily smell from the engines. The only other place was the forward smoking saloon, but the air was blue with pipe and cigarette smoke, and anyway, ladies didn't go there.

They had to take a taxi from the Pier Head. It was years since she'd been to the factory, and that day she'd taken little notice of the direction in which they'd walked. It was in a very poor part of the city, that had registered; there were barefooted children swarming everywhere. To find her way to it was beyond her now, but anyway, Mama wouldn't want to walk.

She could smell the place as she got out of the taxi. It made her gag even though she'd thought she was over her morning sickness.

It was a vast building, coated with grime like all the others round it, and gloomy inside despite the bright morning. It was a few moments before Claudia could see anything. It had once been a warehouse with windows in the roof, but these were now coated with smuts and grime, and very little light filtered through. Gas jets flared all day.

The clanking of machinery and the shouts of the workers trying to make themselves heard above it made her cover her ears with her hands. There was an overpowering smell of onions and spices. Mama had her handkerchief to her nose within seconds and was gathering her skirts close to her ankles.

Claudia caught the eye of one of the workers. 'The office, please.' She had to raise her voice. 'Direct me to the office.'

The old woman led her across a huge expanse of floor, past a row of boiling cauldrons that sent out a wall of heat. No need to ask what was in them; the most pungent smell of chutney choked the atmosphere. It was an evil place.

Mama caught hold of her arm and mouthed: 'Purgatory itself.'

Another, younger figure came out of the gloom and shouted at her: 'This way.'

Moments later they were in the relative quiet of the office. Maurice's mackintosh still hung on a peg behind the door and the place reeked of his cigarettes. It brought a vision of him before Claudia's eyes, telling her it was no place for her, that she shouldn't have come. When the girl who had shown them in turned, Claudia recognised the curling yellow tendrils of hair escaping round her cap, and knew she was Toby's girlfriend.

She said: 'You've come to look round, Mrs Percival. See what the business is like?'

'We've come to make sure the business continues to run properly,' Claudia retorted.

She pulled out Maurice's chair and seated herself at his desk. 'I'll start by looking at the books.'

Her mother was groping towards the other desk and slumped into the chair.

'A glass of water, if you please.'

When the girl ran to get it, Claudia said:

'This is no place for you, Mama. You're having one of your turns before you start.'

'My smelling salts, dear. Quickly, in my bag.'

Claudia didn't feel too much sympathy for her mother; she'd insisted on coming. Claudia had been glad enough of her company on the way, but Mama would be no earthly use to her if she was going to faint.

When the girl returned with the glass of water, Edward was with her, as well as some other people. There were too many of them packed into the office now, Claudia could hardly breathe, and it took ten minutes to revive Mama.

'Perhaps you'd better tell me who all these people are,' Claudia said testily to Edward. 'Before you bring me the books.'

Edward started to introduce them:

'This is Miss Potts, our office manager, and Mr Ferry, our salesman.' He was making out they had a good team. 'And Mr Trumper, our production manager.'

Claudia recognised that name. He was Maurice's foreman. Production manager indeed!

'And you know Sarah.' The girl's yellow eyes made Claudia shiver. They were cat's eyes.

'The books,' Claudia demanded. 'All the ledgers in which you keep records. I shall manage this business until Edward is old enough.'

She'd made them jump to it. They were hastily opening them in front of her.

'You'd better explain all this to me.'

'Miss Potts is best equipped to do that,' Sarah said, and before Claudia knew what was happening, the clerk was pointing out figures and letting forth a torrent of information.

'We'll leave you to it,' Sarah told her. 'We need to get on with our work.'

Claudia did her best to concentrate on what she was being told. It was all far more complicated than she'd supposed. Pages were being turned back and forth and she was finding the commentary almost incomprehensible, but she picked up one fact she didn't like. She jabbed her finger at the figures.

'This week's order for stores – it's vastly increased. Almost twice what my husband spent. Who is responsible for this?'

'I'll get Sarah for you, ma'am. She's seeing to ordering the supplies.'

'Sarah! What does a girl like that know about it? Get her back in here. I need to sort this out.'

Claudia looked across the office to where her mother was slumped against the desk opposite, still sniffing at her salts.

'Honestly, Mama, what does it have to do with that girl? Pushing herself forward like this.'

Sarah came back; Edward and Trumper were with her. Claudia was shaking with indignation.

'Is this your doing, Sarah?' She swivelled the ledgers round and pointed out the figures. 'Did you take it upon yourself to order all this stuff?'

'Yes,' Sarah agreed. 'It was decided that I should take charge of the ordering.'

Claudia let fly. 'There's far too much money gone out of

the company accounts. My husband wouldn't agree to this. He was always very careful. I don't like the look of this at all. Ordering supplies for the factory is an important job.'

'Very important.' Sarah's amber eyes looked straight into hers.

'I shall have to take it over. You can't spend like this.'

Mr Trumper said: 'It's because of the war. You explain, Sarah.'

'This is what Toby wanted us to do. Order more than usual, especially spices. He thinks the Germans could intercept our shipping, then they could be in short supply.'

'And prices are likely to go up,' Edward said. 'Because of the war.'

Claudia began to think she'd made a mistake. It seemed they'd given the ordering more thought than she had. Perhaps she'd been wrong to jump on the girl, but there was something about her that made her hackles rise.

Sarah was going on: 'We all sat down and gave very careful consideration to what we should order. We have space to store more than we usually buy. We doubled our order for jars and for certain spices, though we have to be careful with spices because they lose their strength if we keep them too long. We thought it the logical thing to do; it wasn't just a whim.'

Edward said seriously, 'We took everything into consideration, such as which things are likely to become scarce. Toby thinks all prices will go up with the war, so we expect to gain in the long run.'

Claudia ran her fingers round the neck of her blouse. Was she making a fool of herself?

Sarah went on calmly: 'It's right to take these decisions now. Careful thought has been given to everything we're doing. You must believe that. It's what Toby wants.'

Edward said: 'Everything's under control, Stepmother. You mustn't worry yourself.'

Claudia swallowed hard. It was painfully obvious that they

knew more about the running of this place than she did. She wouldn't be able to do it.

'I understand quite a lot about the books,' she said defensively. She knew which figures denoted the profit.

'You'd like to work here? Help a little?' the yellow eyes were playing with hers, but Sarah seemed sincere.

'Yes,' Mrs Digby said, her voice a trifle hollow. 'Claudia would certainly like to help. Do you have a job for her?'

The foreman spoke. 'We're short-handed as it happens. So many of the lads . . . With this war, they're rushing like lemmings to join up. We've just taken on two more girls this morning, but I'm looking for more.'

Claudia had her misgivings. 'What would I have to do?'

'Shall I show you?'

She balked at going back to that inferno. 'Can't you explain?'

'We need more checkers.'

Claudia thought checking didn't sound too bad.

'You can sit down to do it. We have a machine that peels the shallots but we need girls to check that they're peeled clean. Sometimes the tops need to be trimmed more and the odd bit of brown skin gets left on. Then they're dropped back on the line to be taken on.'

Claudia was affronted. 'I couldn't do that!'

Trumper said in a reassuring tone: 'You'll soon learn how. It only takes a day or two to quicken up so you don't miss any.'

'I've done it off and on for years,' Sarah said. 'It's not a bad job, but I preferred cooking the chutney.'

'No!' She wasn't going anywhere near those onions or the cauldrons. Were they laughing at her? Surely they didn't think for one moment she'd do anything like that?

'In the office,' Mrs Digby choked. 'Factory work wouldn't suit Claudia. She's good with money. She could help with the accounts.' She fixed her stare on Miss Potts.

'Well . . .'

'We've just found Miss Potts a new accounts assistant,' Edward told them.

'That's the sort of job Claudia could do. She could take the new assistant's place. She has an interest in the amount of money the company makes; she'll be able to keep a check on the finances. Yes, that would do, wouldn't it, dear?'

'I'm afraid not, Mrs Digby.' Claudia could see Edward drawing himself up. 'The accounts are very important. Miss Potts needs an experienced clerk – the company does. Stepmother would not be able to manage that job.'

Claudia gasped. Never before had Edward told her what she could or could not manage. She was used to laying down the law to him.

'Toby organised everything before he went. This was what he thought was needed.' Sarah was being painfully polite.

'Perhaps Claudia could help, in addition to your new clerk,' Mrs Digby said.

Claudia found herself being led to an adjoining smaller office, where the desks were jammed tightly together. She was introduced to two clerks, whose names she couldn't remember. Her head was swimming; this was awful. Anger rose in her throat. She hated this place and blamed Maurice for putting her in this position. She didn't want to come here every day and cope with the basic accounting. That would be too much of a burden.

The morning seemed endless. Miss Potts and Mrs Hoxton were adding up figures and getting on with the work. She knew they didn't want her or her mother here. She could feel the antagonism. Miss Potts gave them both little jobs, but Claudia didn't understand fully why she was doing them, and the woman didn't explain properly. She felt useless; her mother certainly was. Soon Mama was asleep with her chin on her chest in the only comfortable chair in the room.

When the whistle sounded and the rattling lines came to a halt, the office staff stood up.

'Dinner time,' Miss Potts said. 'One hour.'

Claudia was all for going home.

'Show some backbone,' her mother told her. 'We're in the office. Didn't I have to fight to get you in here? They'd have had you peeling onions if I hadn't come. Let's get something to eat. Think of the baby; you must eat, you'll feel better if you do. Where did Maurice have his lunch?'

Claudia tried to think. 'He spoke of Radley's Refreshment Rooms, and a pub called Old Harry's.'

'We can't go to a public house. Ask the whereabouts of the Refreshment Rooms.'

Mrs Hoxton found a barefoot street urchin to guide them and they set off. Claudia didn't feel it was safe for unaccompanied ladies to walk on these streets. Mama was clinging on to her, her fingers biting into Claudia's wrist.

Maurice had described this to her as a poor area. Claudia had never seen or imagined such squalor. The buildings were half derelict. The breeze was blowing dust-covered litter up the pavement. There were children in rags, dirty and unwashed, and women not much better. A drunken man followed them, begging for money until their urchin guide turned and swore at him.

The Refreshment Rooms were near and looked little better from the outside. The menu was chalked on two blackboards, and each time the door opened, savoury smells came out. Claudia gave their urchin twopence.

'A penny would have been more than enough,' Mama shot at her. 'You've no sense.'

Inside, the air was hazy with smoke. The clientele were entirely male. Mamma used her gloves to fan her face. 'Find us a quiet corner,' she demanded of the waiter.

The food was exactly what Maurice would have enjoyed. Steak and kidney pie, boiled beef and carrots. Claudia had no appetite at all and could hardly eat the finnan haddock with mashed potatoes she ordered. Mama consumed her gammon and parsley sauce with gusto.

*　　*　　*

It was Friday afternoon, and Edward was helping Miss Potts and Mrs Hoxton to make up the wages. This was a job he could understand and cope with.

'Looks as though your stepmother isn't coming back,' Miss Potts said, looking at the clock.

'Thank goodness,' he said. 'She just gets in the way. And as for Mrs Digby . . .'

They'd spent the morning working out exactly what each worker had earned and estimating what the cash requirements would be for the business during the coming week. That had been totalled up and the cheque made out. Edward had then set out with Miss Potts. He wanted to show her where Mr Masters' office was and introduce her to him. This cheque needed his countersignature, and in future there'd be others. On the way back they called in at the bank to cash it, and Edward carried back the big leather bag full of coins.

Edward was helping to count and set out little heaps of coins across the table when Claudia and her mother returned to the office. His spirits sank.

'Now then,' Claudia said brightly. 'What can I do to help?'

'We're making up the wages,' Edward said. Mrs Hoxton was cross-checking each heap before screwing it in paper with a name written on it.

'Shall I check the bank books? Make sure you've withdrawn the right amount?' Claudia asked.

Edward tried not to show he was affronted. He didn't want to give her a chance to fight him.

'We did that this morning and Mr Masters has checked it. You can give a hand here if you want to.' It was easy to involve extra workers in this.

He could see from her face that Stepmother thought it somewhat beneath her, but she came to do it. Mrs Digby removed herself to Father's desk to read a newspaper.

'Envelopes would be better than these screws of paper.' Claudia was making heavy weather of it. 'It would be easier to see the names afterwards.'

'We know, but they cost more,' Miss Potts told her.

'We have to keep costs as low as possible just now,' Edward added. He was hammering that home. It would be what Stepmother wanted to hear.

'It's worked out exactly.' Eunice Potts was smiling at him. 'Always a relief when it does, because we know we've counted out the wages right. If we're a few pence out, it can take ages finding out who's being paid the wrong amount. There's one pound, two shillings for the stamp book and petty cash.' She rattled the coins into the metal box and shut it back into a drawer in her desk.

At four o'clock another table was set across the office door and a large notice propped on it: 'CHECK YOUR WAGES IMMEDIATELY. MISTAKES CANNOT BE RECTIFIED LATER.'

As the workers started to file past, Edward watched them closely. He knew very few of them yet, but soon he would. He wanted to feel at home in this strange world. Mrs Hoxton called out the names and Miss Potts handed over their screw, while he tried to memorise the name with the face. He'd taken charge of the register which all had to sign. Those who signed with a cross – and there were several – had to be countersigned by a witness. His stepmother was seeing to that, though he could just as easily have done it himself.

He didn't want Claudia and her mother here. Miss Potts had enough to do explaining things to him. This was the first time she'd made up and paid the wages without any supervision. She needed to keep her wits about her too and could do without the distraction of visitors. Stepmother and Mrs Digby were just an extra burden for those who were doing the work. But he didn't think they'd come regularly; it surprised him that they'd stuck it out for the whole day.

The long line of workers came to an end.

'Just us in here now.' Miss Potts was signing for her own screw.

'Your turn.' She pushed Edward's screw to him.

He'd agreed with Toby that he should be paid half of his brother's wage for the first six months, then three quarters for the rest of his first year. By then he hoped to be on top of the work and be worth more.

Mrs Hoxton signed and took hers. Miss Potts was checking the register.

'Would you mind signing for your money, Mrs Percival?' Edward saw her put her finger on the entry and push the register in front of his stepmother. 'It's to keep the records straight.'

'Me?' Claudia's beady eyes were eager. 'I hoped I'd be paid for today, though I haven't done a lot.'

'Not for today. It's your allowance from the firm.'

Edward heard Miss Potts' tone change. There was an agonised note in her voice and she was clutching at the bow round the neck of her blouse.

'Where's it gone?'

There was only one screw left on the table. Edward picked it up.

'This is John Ferry's.'

'He's gone out,' Maria Hoxton said. 'Shall I give it to his mother and get her to sign for it?'

'Where's the other one gone?' Miss Potts asked.

'It was there,' Maria said. 'I saw it.'

Edward said distractedly: 'Yes, get Elvira to sign for John's money.' When Maria had gone, he turned to his stepmother.

'You've picked it up? Your housekeeping money and allowance. It's what Father gave you every week.'

'I'm to have that just the same?'

'Of course.'

He saw her tongue go round her lips. 'Mr Masters said Maurice's bank accounts would be frozen. You know, until after probate was granted. I thought . . .'

'His personal account, yes, but not the business accounts; it has to go on trading. Mr Masters authorised me to add your

186

allowances to the wages bill. Since the company has to pay you an allowance he thought there was no point in letting it mount up until after probate has been granted.'

'Oh! I didn't understand that.'

'We have to live and the house bills have to be paid. He said Father would have wanted it this way.'

'Good!' She was smiling with relief. 'Five pounds as usual?'

'Yes, five for housekeeping, plus your personal allowance of thirty shillings.'

'That's my dress allowance, though I have to meet most of Adam's needs from it.'

'Any money still owing to you at the end of the year will be paid then.'

'The four hundred a year?'

'Yes.'

'Maurice paid the servants at the end of the month and saw to the coal bill and—'

'You've already taken it?' Edward asked again. 'The six pounds ten shillings? It was on the table; I counted it out myself.'

Her eyes were wide. The silence dragged out.

'No.'

The colour was draining from Miss Potts' face. 'What's happened to it?' she whispered.

Edward went cold with horror as they looked at each other. 'Surely no one could have taken it?'

Toby had said the staff were friendly and honest. Edward had never heard the slightest whisper of dishonesty.

The little table had been across the door. Nobody had come into the office from the time the money had been counted out until it had been paid over. He felt panicky.

'We all saw it.' Miss Potts looked white enough to faint. 'Who wrote her name on the paper?' It seemed nobody remembered doing that.

'It's been gone for some time then,' Edward said slowly. 'Since before four o'clock, when we started to pay out. But nobody's been in this office all afternoon; just the three of us and . . .'

He went through the adjoining door to his father's office. Mrs Digby had lowered her newspaper to the desk. He knew from her face that it must be her. Apart from Claudia, she was the only other person who'd had the opportunity. He could feel the heat running up his cheeks. Oh God! How could he possibly accuse her of theft?

He took a deep breath. 'Did you take some money from our table?'

He had to make himself look her in the eye. 'Six guineas and two florins?' Her heavy-lidded eyes slid away from his.

'You did, didn't you?' He knew his voice was heavy with suspicion. Accusing, almost.

'Mama!' Even Stepmother seemed to accept her guilt.

He had enough presence of mind to shut the door between the two offices, keeping Claudia with him. He didn't want Miss Potts to witness this.

Somewhat sheepishly, Mrs Digby produced the coins from her pocket.

'What did you do that for? You had us all worried stiff. I almost accused . . .' Edward was angry. He was tired too with the continual effort to concentrate. The unaccustomed length of the working day and the newness of the work had taken an emotional toll.

'You come here saying you want to help and then cause all this bother. That's stealing.'

A purplish tinge ran up Mrs Digby's heavy jowls. 'Stealing? Of course it isn't. I'm no thief. I took a little for Claudia. She is desperately worried about money. The company is to pay her four hundred pounds a year. I'm just helping her to keep going.'

Edward was appalled. 'Mrs Digby, what do you think Miss Potts and I have been doing all day? This is a business; all monies have to be accounted for and checked carefully. You can't just take the money you see. We went about it properly;

188

discussed with Mr Masters how best to pay Stepmother's allowance. That money you took was meant for her.'

'Then I haven't stolen anything! It stands to reason!'

'We missed the money. We were all upset and thought it had been stolen. You must have heard us. You knew we were worried about it and you kept your head down in here and said nothing.'

'Well, I'm sorry, young man. I have to look after my own too.'

'Don't come here tomorrow, Mrs Digby. Or any other day. I don't want you on these premises ever again. You're an embarrassment to me and a distraction to everybody. I'll not allow you inside this works if you come. You're barred.'

'You've no need to turn nasty about it,' she started to bluster. 'I was only taking what was Claudia's. Trying to help. What's wrong with that?'

'I've told you.'

'Come, Claudia, I'm too old to work here, and your condition makes it unsuitable for you. It's a hateful place.'

Edward turned. Claudia's face was scarlet with embarrassment.

'I'd be grateful, Stepmother, if you would stay at home too. As you can see, you will not lose your allowance. I shall bring it home to you.'

'It isn't just my allowance.' Claudia was not one to give up easily. 'I feel I need to keep abreast of what's happening here. I won't come to work here – I don't think I'd fit in – but I shall continue to visit from time to time. To look at the books. Make sure all is well.'

'That's quite unnecessary. I'll tell you all you need to know over dinner any evening.'

Having said that, Edward felt more of a man. He'd done what Toby had told him to do, and he hoped he'd seen Stepmother off for good.

Chapter Fourteen

Claudia felt the heat rush into her cheeks. Never had she expected to be so insulted by Edward.

She snarled at him: 'If your father were alive you wouldn't dare speak to me like this.'

'If Father were alive, I'm sure there'd be no need.'

'Come along, Mama, no point in staying where we aren't wanted.'

She went striding through the awful factory with her head held high and her back very straight. Once in the fresher air outside, she took a deep breath and headed back towards the Pier Head.

'What a stupid thing to do,' she stormed at her mother. 'To steal like that.'

'How can it be stealing if it was yours anyway? Slow down, can't you?' Her mother was breathing heavily. 'Claudia, we need a taxi. I can't walk all that way.'

'You'll have to, unless we can pick one up.'

'Slow down, I beg you. What has got into you?'

'You made us look such fools.'

'You didn't help yourself. Here's a cab.'

Claudia clucked with impatience. 'We're nearly there. It's hardly worth it now.'

'Of course it is.

'For heaven's sake, Mama.' Claudia had to help her up into the old growler. Horse cabs were not easy to get into. It smelt inside of horse sweat and lamp oil.

'You're in a very bad mood, Claudia, I must say.'

'After what you just did, you can't say it isn't your fault.'

'It's not just today. You're being quite nasty to me. Reject-
ing me.'

'No, never that.'

'You don't want me to move into Tides Reach with you. If
that isn't rejection, what is? I've always done my very best to
further your interests. I looked after you for years. Now you
have a good home, which I helped you achieve, you want to
push me out.'

'It's not that . . .' But Claudia was afraid it must look that
way. Her mother might act like a bumbling fool at times, but
she'd been a staunch ally in the past.

'The house is so big you'd hardly notice I was there. And
now you're free of Maurice, I should have thought you'd be
glad of some adult company. Somebody to take your side
against Edward and Toby. They're very selfish boys.'

'Don't I know it. Of course I want you with me, Mama.
I'm not trying to push you out.'

'But you are.'

'The thing is, I'd like to marry again.'

'It's a bit early for that.'

'I know.' Claudia realised her tone was testy again.

'It's that Burton fellow, isn't it?'

She was taken aback. 'How did you know?'

'Aren't I denied my lunch at Tides Reach every time you
go to meet him? I'm not blind, you know.'

Claudia was full of misgivings. If Mama knew, perhaps
others had worked it out too.

'I had to stop Maurice finding out. That wouldn't have
done at all.'

'I'd have been the last person to tell him, Claudia.'

'Bessie would have thought it odd for you to lunch there
without me. How did you find out?'

'I guessed you were meeting somebody. I could see you
from my rooms, rushing out to catch the ferry. Then coming
back just before Maurice . . . What else was I supposed
to think?'

'That armchair you have right in the window!'

'I like to see something of the world, even if I don't go out much. I've seen you come back off the ferry with Burton, but you don't walk up the Esplanade together. One of you always goes the back way. Besides, if you were going shopping, you would have asked me to go with you.'

Claudia was astounded. 'How long have you known?'

'It was only when I saw you at the funeral, so carefully avoiding Burton, that I was sure it was him.'

'Oh, goodness! I hope nobody else saw . . .'

'I don't suppose they did. Nobody else knows you as well as I do.' Honoria tossed her head. 'It's a love match this time, eh?'

Claudia relaxed. What harm was there in Mama knowing now? 'Yes, a love match.' She smiled radiantly. 'It's easier now I don't have to worry about Maurice finding out. Of course you must come and live at Tides Reach for the time being. Though I'll want Gideon there when we marry.'

'Oh!' Mama looked quite upset. 'It's gone that far?'

'It can't go that far until I'm decently out of mourning. His family wouldn't like it.'

'No. At least you've the sense to marry into a family with a little money.'

'We've done very well for ourselves, all things considered.'

'Yes, you'll get your allowance from Percival's Pickles as Maurice laid down. But you must make every effort to get everything else you can from them now, before you move on to better things with the Burtons.'

'I'm glad I won't have to work there for it.'

'It's not a suitable place for a lady, Claudia. Let those who are used to peeling onions get on with it.'

Mama was right, Claudia mused. She didn't want to return to that dreadful place and work with those awful people. Trumper had been very rude to her, quite uncouth, but in particular, she didn't like Toby's girlfriend.

*   *   *

For Sarah, the first weeks without Toby seemed chaotic. Percival's Pickles seemed to be drifting without anybody at the helm. Edward, Mam and John were, like her, all struggling with the unknown and fearful that they wouldn't manage the work they'd taken on.

Twice each week they sat down together and talked about what they were doing. Sometimes one could help another.

'I miss having Toby to turn to,' John said. 'Sarah, you must know more about selling than I do. Toby must have talked about what he was doing. Did he ever mention Hardman's?'

'He did, I think, but I'll ask him directly, since I'm writing. That's the best thing. What exactly do you want to know?'

Toby was able to sort out problems for them all in those early days.

'I didn't think it would be like this,' Edward told them. 'I don't like the place much. The smell is terrible, it catches in my throat. Takes a bit of getting used to.'

He was dividing his time between accompanying Mr Trumper round the factory and collating figures with Miss Potts and Maria as they kept the account books up to date.

'I thought it was hell on earth when I first came,' Maria said. 'But now it doesn't seem too bad. I think I might even enjoy the accounts once I understand what I'm supposed to be doing.'

Sarah knew that like the rest of them her mother lacked confidence in her ability to do what was needed. As they were passing the school in Norfolk Street, she noticed a poster advertising night classes and drew her mother's attention to it. Amongst other things, there were lessons in double-entry book-keeping. They went in that evening and Mam signed up straight away.

'I used to do it when I was a girl and worked for the post office,' she said. 'But I've forgotten in all the years since.'

'You just need to be refreshed,' Sarah told her.

When Edward heard of the classes, he decided to go with her. Sarah felt she ought to sign up too because she didn't understand how the accounting was done. She told Toby when she wrote to him, and he instructed her to pay the night-school fees from the company accounts.

She read part of his letter out to the others. He'd written: 'It's vital you all understood how the accounting system works and that you keep accurate figures.'

'Like Father did,' Edward added.

'I count myself very fortunate to have the records he kept,' Sarah told him. 'He was meticulous. When it comes to ordering the ingredients we're going to use, I can see exactly what was ordered this time last year, where the goods came from and how much they cost. It makes all the difference.'

'It's a big responsibility,' Trumper told her. 'Ordering the supplies.'

'You're a great help to me.'

Sarah spent a lot of her working day in the store room where the ingredients were kept. She needed to make herself familiar with what was stored there and in what amounts. Some of the spices she'd never heard of.

When she first noticed that the inventory showed a far larger amount of dried green chilli peppers than she could locate on the shelves, she wasn't unduly bothered. She assumed she just couldn't find them. A long search produced no result.

She and Mam spent almost a whole Sunday tidying up the store room and checking the inventory against the stock. She was sure now that the chilli peppers were not there.

In her next letter she told Toby of the discrepancy. He suggested she check with Trumper as to what he'd used over the last six months. 'Most likely,' he wrote, 'they've been used up and the amount taken from the store hasn't been subtracted from the stock book. Order more straight away.'

When Sarah discussed it with Trumper, he scratched his beard.

'Couldn't have used all that amount. Them dried chilli peppers blow your head off. A little goes a long way.'

Together they checked through the records of what had been made.

'Nothing to account for a load like that,' he said. 'They were in a sack in the far corner. I remember it well. We had enough to last us for weeks. I'm going up now, for today's supplies. I'll look for that sack. A thing like that, it shouldn't be hard to find.'

It was Trumper's responsibility to withdraw from the stock room what would be needed for the day's production. His accounting for everything he took was reliable. He knew his way round the stock better than anybody else. Hardly any of the others went up there. But he failed to find the dried green chilli peppers.

'Could somebody have taken them?' Sarah asked.

Trumper shook his head. 'Who'd want chilli peppers? They add nothing to food but fire.'

When the new supply arrived, the incident went from Sarah's mind.

Edward felt he'd been taken under Alfred Trumper's wing, and the old man was doing his best to pass on the knowledge he had. But then so were Eunice Potts, Sarah and Mrs Hoxton and even John. They seemed to be melding together as a team.

Edward felt he was learning a lot about the business but even more about the people who were now running it. After the first few weeks, he realised the place was growing on him, and he began to understand something of the fascination it had had for his father.

'As I see it,' Edward told them at one of their meetings, 'my father ran the company like a dictator. Now there are six of us and it's more a democracy. We're pooling our ideas; talking them over, considering them carefully.'

They all agreed that the atmosphere in the factory was loosening up.

John said: 'The girls out there are working harder. They've got more enthusiasm.'

'Smiling more,' Edward added. 'They seem to have more energy.'

'They all think things are better now,' Sarah said.

Edward hoped they were right. Father had drummed one fact about business into his head: it had to make a profit. Whether they could do that remained to be seen.

'This is a lot more interesting than skinning the onions and boiling up vinegar and spices,' Sarah said as the meeting was breaking up.

'Doing the accounts is a bit nerve-racking,' her mother laughed. 'All the money coming in and going out. But yes, it's much more interesting. I still feel spent when it's time to go home, but I'm not physically exhausted.'

'Nerve-racking for us all,' John agreed. 'I feel such a weight of responsibility.'

Edward said, 'I wonder how Toby's getting on.'

Sarah frowned. She honestly didn't know. Toby was writing long letters to her every day – letters which told her how much he loved her; letters answering her questions about running the business, making further suggestions – but there was never a word about how he was faring or what was happening to him. She couldn't imagine what army life was like.

He wrote:

I feel I've caused such havoc. The morning I was leaving to come here, Stepmother burst into tears and sobbed: 'You caused your father's death. He worried himself silly over you.'

You know I felt responsible for it anyway; that she had to say so was like driving nails into me. She just kept going on at me:

'If you're going to skip off like this, who is going to look after the business? Somebody's got to do it. It can't be left to run itself. It's our only means of livelihood. I shall have to keep an eye on it. Edward's

197

far too young. It's unreasonable to expect him to take over straight away.'

Toby told Sarah he missed her and wished he could be with her to cope with the business. He sounded homesick. She thought his letters showed a determination to make the best of things, but there was tension too, as though he hated what was going on. He gave no clue as to what that might be. That evening, Sarah wrote to him.

I've got to know what's happening to you. You're trying to shut me out. It's as though you've stepped into a void. I can't imagine how things are for you. It's not fair and I hate it. It's almost as though I've lost you.

How are you finding life as one of Kitchener's volunteers? Is it as exciting as everybody said it would be? I need to know every detail, about what you do and what you eat and how you feel. I want to know about your friends, what you talk about, the things you like and the things you don't like. Everything.

Toby felt angry and frustrated. He longed to be back with Sarah. He wrote to her every day and looked forward to her replies as the only comfort he had. He'd told her to let Percival's Pickles pay for the postage; he desperately needed to know what was going on. She'd told him that Claudia and Mrs Digby had come to the office and caused havoc on pay day. That made him boil up anew. They wouldn't have done that had he been there. But Sarah said Edward had dealt with them firmly.

Toby found rifle drill and bayonet practice no more to his liking than marching. The soggy parade ground was turning into a sea of mud. He was only a short distance from his home, and at the weekends he longed to go there for a hot bath and a dry bed and to find out from Edward how the business fared. Instead, for the first four weeks, they were all ordered to remain in camp.

As the weeks went on, he marched and countermarched, paraded and drilled. It was drummed into them all that the point of the iron discipline and relentless drilling was to train them to respond to orders instantly, without conscious thought. Not to do so in an emergency could result in death or injury to themselves or their comrades.

Toby had plenty of time to dwell on this. He didn't think he was psychologically suited to blind obedience. He'd had a bad time at school and earned a reputation for disobedience. With hindsight, he felt he might have got on better with his father if he'd done what he'd asked without question. He didn't feel he'd fit in any better here.

Now he truly understood what a fool he'd been to join the army. He felt he might just as well have joined the Boy's Brigade for all the good it was doing the country to have him here.

For Sarah there was something unreal about her new life at the factory. It took a lot more effort on her part to do what was expected of her now. She had to keep searching through the files for information she needed and checking that she hadn't forgotten anything vital.

All the time, she could sense Maurice Percival's antagonistic presence close by; watching her.

Every lunch time when she went home she found a letter from Toby waiting for her. He used thick, expensive notepaper and a fountain pen.

Today she read:

My darling Sarah,

I miss you terribly. I hate being here, parted from you and everything that's important to me. However, only two more weekends to get through (and all the days in between) and after that we will be allowed to leave camp when off duty. So the Sunday after next, I shall be able to come over to see you. I'm living for that. It's the only thing that keeps me going.

I'm definitely not suited to army life. What I'm required to do seems pointless and I attract the ire of every officer and non-commissioned officer who comes in contact with me. Nothing I do pleases them, however hard I try. Either I'm not quick enough or I'm not doing it right.

'Jump to it,' they all shout at me. 'Jump to it, Percival.'

Sergeant Cooper is particularly vicious; he's always driving me, hassling me. His attitude seems to tell me that Kitchener's volunteers are the lowest form of life. I resent that; I've been brought up to think of myself as equal to the best.

I've always treated our workers as I would like to be treated myself; with friendly politeness. And I've never had the slightest trouble from any of them. Except perhaps John Ferry, and we all know what caused that.

I think I was popular with our workers. If they picked up on a mistake I'd made, they put things right and never mentioned it to Father.

Goodness knows what made me believe myself unhappy at home. Things could get fraught between me and Father, and Stepmother kept everything on the boil, but I'm beginning to think I was comfortably cushioned there.

To wake me, Bessie always brought a cup of tea to my bedside, and though Father complained all the time of my tardiness in getting to the breakfast table, I took no notice. I'm just one of those people who's slow to wake up and start the day.

But here, the army doesn't allow anybody a gentle start. I'm forced to be up and washed and dressed in an instant. Often I still feel half asleep when I'm out on parade.

And the needless trouble that overtakes me . . . At home, Bessie took my shoes from my room and brought them back clean and polished. Now I have to polish my own, and Sergeant Cooper makes it clear at the top of his voice that he doesn't think I do an adequate job. A fellow volunteer in the same tent by the name of Clement Blake had to show me how to apply spit as well as polish and really work it in. It takes much time and effort and it's all wasted when we have to go on a ten-mile route march in the rain.

Every evening, as soon as the evening meal had been eaten and cleared away, Sarah sat down to answer Toby's letter. She brought stationery and a stamp from the office and posted her letter in the box on St James Street.

Then she went to the bed she shared with her mother. She yearned to have Toby beside her; he was always in her thoughts. It brought a sadness and an ache. If only he were here now, running the factory, it would be wonderful. Fun even. It would make everything so easy for them all, but she dared drop no hint of that in her letters. To do so would only make Toby feel worse. He knew well enough that he'd caused a virtual disaster.

She was pleased that he was telling her all about life in the army now, though he was making no secret about hating it.

What made matters much worse was news of fierce fighting in France with a heavy loss of life. The Kaiser's armies had been stopped by the British and the French in the Battle of the Marne as they'd tried to sweep in a great spearhead towards Paris. The Belgians had held the line at Ypres when the Germans had tried to break out there. On all fronts the flat countryside provided little cover for fighting, so both sides dug down and built machine-gun posts and had become locked in bloody warfare, with a front line that hardly moved more than a mile or two either way.

Sarah knew Toby would more than likely be sent there; it was what he was being trained for. She was dreading the time when he would.

Chapter Fifteen

September 1914

Toby could stand it no longer. It was as though he was a prisoner in the camp. He felt he'd wasted his first Sundays here. He'd had to attend church parade and then they were marched off to a service, but after that his time was his own until the next morning, but he was not allowed to leave the camp. He could have gone to see Sarah and Edward. Always at the back of his mind was the worry about how the business was faring without him.

By the third Sunday, he'd made up his mind. He'd slip out and go over to Liverpool. He thought he'd be unlikely to be missed. It really was necessary for him to go. It would set his mind at rest if he knew all was well.

He was keyed up for it, all set to go, when on Sunday morning he found he'd been put on the list for guard duty that night. It seemed the man originally posted had reported sick. Toby couldn't believe his bad luck that he'd been chosen to replace him.

He went on church parade feeling a searing disappointment. Then he decided he'd go just the same. He had until eight o'clock before he had to present himself.

He still had the civilian clothes he'd worn when he came here. He changed into them, and with help from Clemmo Blake managed to cross the camp and get out without being seen.

He had such a sense of freedom as he walked down to Bebington station to catch a train. He was returning to the world he knew. He went straight over to Liverpool and to Sarah's home.

She wasn't expecting him; he'd not said anything about this in his letters in case it proved impossible to do. The look on her face when she opened the door and saw him standing there was worth a lot. She shrieked with joy and threw herself into his arms before dragging him over the threshold. Even Maria seemed pleased to see him.

'Wonderful!' Sarah's eyes wouldn't leave his and she was beaming with delight. They gave him a sandwich and a cup of tea.

'We all went back to the office yesterday afternoon, to try to sort out what we're supposed to be doing . . . It takes time to work things out. We'll be all right once we've got the hang of it.'

He wanted to have Sarah to himself, take her out somewhere, but he had to satisfy himself about the business. Too much rested on that.

Sarah insisted on going downstairs to fetch John Ferry up.

'He wants to talk to you about the orders. He's been out trying to get more business and there are things he needs to ask you.'

Toby told himself it was what he'd come to do. John brought up the familiar book and showed him what he'd done since Toby had been away.

'I think I'm going to like the job,' he said. 'Once I get a clear picture of what I'm supposed to be doing. Do you think I could try and get the armed forces to take our pickles?'

Toby was pleased with the progress John had made. He was taking his responsibilities seriously. Sarah and Maria took him down to the factory after that. They both had queries he settled quickly. He even enjoyed being there. The noxious smells now seemed homely. Everything was exactly as it always had been. Another supply of shallots had been delivered, enough to keep the line working for two more weeks. The war seemed to have had little effect here so far.

Toby felt better about the business, but time was flying; it was already after six.

'I want to call in at Tides Reach. There's still time. I'd like to see Edward.'

Sarah went over on the ferry with him. It was a chilly evening and they hovered close to the iron grille that ventilated the engine room. Warm air billowed out smelling of hot oil. Toby looked down at the working engine and the men in overalls tending it. This was a part of his past life and he missed it too.

When the boat tied up at New Ferry Pier, Sarah said: 'I'll go straight back on this boat.'

He held tightly to her hand and wouldn't let her. He couldn't bear to part from her a second before he had to.

He persuaded her to go home with him, and of course it all took much more time than he'd thought it would. Bessie wanted to hug him, Ena made them something to eat, and Edward had countless questions.

'I'll come again next Sunday if I can.' Toby kissed Sarah goodbye just inside his own back garden. He hated to see her walking down to the ferry while he had to go in the opposite direction up to the Toll Bar to catch a bus.

Waiting at the bus stop, he began to feel panicky. He'd forgotten there were many fewer buses on Sunday evenings. It wasn't all that far to the camp; he could walk it with ease, but his watch told him it was almost twenty minutes to eight. He was afraid he was going to be late.

He had to change into his uniform and go on parade. From there, he'd be marched down to the gates to relieve the present guard at eight o'clock on the dot.

He decided he could wait no longer and set off at a jog. A motor bus came almost immediately. He ran to the next stop and jumped on it, but by then he knew it wouldn't get him there in time.

He wished now he'd let Sarah return by the same ferry and that he had not called in at Tides Reach at all. That way he'd have been back in good time. It wasn't as though he'd helped Edward with a particular problem.

There were two guards on the main gate as usual when the bus bowled past, and he was afraid one of them should have been him. Impossible now to hope his absence had not been noticed. He got back into camp without being seen, but Sergeant Cooper had stationed a watch outside his tent. As soon as he tried to get in to change into his uniform, he was arrested and marched off to the guard house.

The next morning, with considerable formality, Sergeant Cooper marched him before the senior officer of his unit. Toby stood up ramrod straight and threw salutes as he'd been taught.

He listened with sinking heart as Sergeant Cooper brayed out the crimes he'd committed. He was charged with disobeying orders, leaving camp without permission and evading guard duty.

'These are very serious charges,' he was told. 'You're lucky not to be charged with desertion. What d'you have to say for yourself?'

'I didn't desert; I came back.'

He was warned that his manner was flippant and could get him into further trouble.

'You disobeyed orders and left camp. The army considers that to be desertion. You do realise that in certain circumstances desertion can carry the death penalty?'

Toby was shocked. 'Yes, sir,' he said. But he hadn't. Death penalty? That sounded Draconian for skipping out of camp for a few hours. He tried to explain why he'd had to go out.

'Our business is very important to me and my family, and I went in my rest-and-relaxation time.'

'On this occasion I'll accept there are mitigating circumstances,' he was told. 'You've served for only three weeks. Nevertheless, you wilfully disobeyed an order given by a superior officer in the execution of his duty.' Toby was sentenced to forty days of Field Punishment No. 1.

He had no idea what that meant, but back in the guard room Sergeant Cooper made haste to explain it to him. He was to be kept busy with continual labouring duties and might be restrained in fetters or handcuffs. In addition he could be attached to a post or wheel as a humiliation.

Toby's hard labour started immediately. He was to dig new latrine trenches at one end of the sports ground. He was kept at it for ten hours a day, much longer than his fellow workers. He was allowed no meals, nothing but bread and water.

In addition, he was spread-eagled across a gunwheel, tied to it at wrists and ankles with rope, and kept like that in the pouring rain for two hours at a time. He found it very uncomfortable, but made himself look at it as a rest after all the digging.

Sergeant Cooper did his best to mortify him. His unit was made to file past to witness what would happen to them if they disobeyed orders. Toby hated it and didn't know how he was to get through forty days of this.

As it happened, his friend Clemmo had a cousin on guard duty who turned a blind eye, allowing mess tins of hot food left over from dinner in the officers' mess to be smuggled in to him. Toby gobbled everything down gratefully. He'd felt empty and light-headed on bread and water alone.

After three days, he was marched in front of the Adjutant to be told his sentence had been suspended and he was to return to his unit and proceed with his training.

Toby was glad to be finished with the hard labour, but reckoned the whole thing was a farce. He'd been sentenced to forty days to put the fear of God into him, but it had never been their intention to let him serve more than three. No man could work like that for forty days on bread and water. He'd not be fit to fight afterwards. Toby had lost weight as it was.

He wrote and told Sarah what had happened, and said

he wouldn't be coming again until the army allowed the privilege. As they were confined to camp only for the first four weeks, he would be free to come and see her a week on Sunday. He was looking forward to that very much.

Sarah too was looking forward to that Sunday. The thought of being with Toby again made her spirits soar. But on the Friday before he was due to come, she received a letter that changed all that.

Terrible, terrible news. I'm feeling hounded. Yesterday, Sergeant Cooper found fault with the way I laid out my kit for inspection.

'Jump to it, Private Percival. And clean your boots again. They won't do like that.'

This morning, he put me on a charge for being unshaven on parade. I was marched before the Commanding Officer and he's confined me to camp for a week.

I'm sick with disappointment. Nobody needs to get out of this place more than I do. I was late crawling out of my bed and hadn't time to shave. Quite often I don't first thing; I haven't much of a beard and there's always such a crush in the ablutions tents. I didn't think Sergeant Cooper would notice; I've done this before and he hasn't.

Clemmo laughs and says I've got the complexion of a girl and he's very envious. I think I must have skipped shaving for more than one day for anyone to notice.

It's been a bad day all round. Sergeant Cooper found fault with the way we did our drill and we were all kept out on the parade ground in the rain standing to attention for what seemed hours.

He's picking on me, victimising me, and it's driving me spare. I can feel my hackles rise and my fingers tighten into a fist as soon as the man comes near me.

But I know I have to take everything the Sergeant meters out. In the army, there's no answering back.

Sarah couldn't hide her disappointment. A tear rolled down her cheek as she lit the Primus to make tea for herself and Mam.

'Just the sort of daft thing Toby would do,' Mam retorted when she told her. 'Why can't he get up and shave like everyone else? He thinks all rules and regulations are made to control others, and that he's above all that.'

'It's only for another week.' Sarah made herself look on the bright side. 'We all need to talk to him. There's things he could sort out.'

Later that week, though, Sarah had more disappointing news.

Sunday was another black day here. I thought of you and wanted so much to be with you. I don't think I'll ever settle to this. All day, I couldn't throw off my worries about the business. I know you're all struggling with jobs I could have done with ease if I were there. Be sure to check on the orders John Ferry's bringing in. The factory must make the varieties needed to fulfil them.

Sarah, darling, I miss you so much. I have worse news and hardly know how to tell you. On parade this morning, Sergeant Cooper deemed me to be improperly dressed. For that crime, my punishment has been doubled. I'm to be gated for an additional week. When will I ever get out of this place?

Sarah was kept so busy and her mind was so filled with work that it came as something of a shock to find her own body was not behaving as it usually did.

She had been feeling sick in the mornings. Once she'd actually been sick. It was impossible to hide it from her mother. Mam had shown sympathy and put it down to the fatty pork they'd had for supper, but Sarah was frightened. She was very much afraid her symptoms were caused by something altogether different.

She would have liked to consult her mother about it, but didn't dare. She couldn't, not yet. Mam would fly at her; she had spelled out the risks Sarah had run.

'Letting Toby Percival spend all night here with you . . . Oh, I know what he wanted. You could have a baby. He'll be off like a rocket at the first sign. Don't be so silly as to think he'll marry you. He won't. What does he think he's doing? You should take more care of yourself.'

'You didn't take care of yourself,' Sarah had retorted. That had shut Mam up.

Sarah hadn't worried about it up until now. There had been too many other things on her mind. But apart from being sick, there were other signs that made her think the future looked ominous. If she were married, of course, it would be different.

To start with she hadn't thought Toby would desert her, but listening to Mam saying with such certainty that he would worried her. She could be right.

If only Toby were here, she could unburden herself to him and talk through what they should do. She wanted quite desperately to know if he was willing to marry her. But now he was in the army, it wouldn't be easy for him to do that. And he could be killed. Every newspaper she picked up these days carried lists of names inside a black border. At night, lying awake in bed, Sarah could feel herself crawling with dread.

There was only one thing she could do: she must write and tell Toby of her fears.

Toby took his turn at guard duty on the main gate. He was one of the pair of private soldiers detailed to stand one in front of each gatepost. Clemmo Blake was the other.

A temporary gatehouse had been erected just inside the gates from where a corporal supervised them. It was a fine moonlit night. Toby could see clearly for some distance up and down the suburban road, which since darkness had fallen had been virtually deserted. He knew there was no danger of any sort, and saw standing outside during the night as another pointless exercise.

He found it very tedious. Clemmo was near but they were not allowed to pass the time in talk. From time to time he stamped his feet to keep his circulation going, and could hear Clemmo doing the same. On the hour, a buzzer sounded in the gatehouse. As instructed, they marched back and forth three times as though wound up by clockwork, and ended up changing places.

After that they had another hour to stand on watch. All was silent except for an occasional shuffle or cough, or the telephone ringing in the gatehouse. Although the night was mild, there was a sharp wind, and standing still made him cold. He saw Clemmo draw back slightly against his gatepost. Toby did the same. Here he was in the shadows and out of the wind. He moved another inch until he could settle his back against the posts that eased his discomfort a little and allowed him to relax.

The next thing Toby knew, Sergeant Cooper was yelling at him.

'Wake up, you lazy good-for-nothing bastard! Wake up.'

Toby felt his rifle slide though his cold fingers to clatter to the ground. All the antagonism he felt rushed to his fists when he saw Sergeant Cooper's red face gloating over him.

'Move yourself. Jump to it.'

As he'd been trained to do, Toby jumped to it without a second thought, but he was still half dazed and he cannoned into his sergeant with such force it sent Cooper staggering backwards. To see his adversary caught off balance made Toby jump closer and bring his fists up. He wanted to give him the right hook to the chin he so richly deserved. He was

211

itching to get his own back for all the indignities he'd suffered at Cooper's hands.

It didn't happen. Sergeant Cooper stumbled into the corporal from the gatehouse who was with him, and that prevented him falling. Clemmo Blake had come closer too, and Toby felt him clutch at his arm and hang on to swing him round; that prevented his fist making contact.

Toby stood back, breathing heavily. Sergeant Cooper was standing in front of him, legs apart, swaying slightly.

'That was a stupid thing to do.' His face leered into Toby's. 'Raising your fists to me. Asleep at your post. You're in big trouble now. You've done it this time.'

Once again Toby found himself being led away to the guard room under close arrest. He was glad to lie down on the bed. It was hard, but more comfortable than his tented quarters. He slept solidly for as long as he was allowed to.

As before, he was marched in front of his commanding officer to be charged, this time with sleeping at his post and threatening and striking a senior officer.

'Court martial,' the CO barked at Toby. It was fixed for the following day.

Back in the guard room, Toby was very worried. He was visited by an officer who introduced himself as Lieutenant Nelson.

Nelson said: 'A court martial is like a civilian court of law. You'll be asked whether you're guilty or not guilty. You should plead not guilty to both charges.

'Every prisoner is allowed a friend to speak in his defence. I'll put your defence to the court for you, if you wish.'

Toby felt like a common criminal. His problems seemed to be multiplying.

'These are two very serious charges. Were you asleep?'

'I suppose I could have dozed off, but I certainly didn't strike Sergeant Cooper. I didn't strike anybody.' He'd have loved to do it, but he hadn't. Clemmo had stopped him.

'You're getting a bad name for yourself. You've got a

suspended sentence now. You won't be dealt with so leniently again. You need to keep your head down after this and stay out of trouble.'

At ten o'clock the next morning, Toby was marched to the dining room in the officers' mess. The scent of fried bacon betrayed the fact that breakfast had been recently served, but there had been some hasty improvising to fit the room for holding a court martial. A row of very senior officers faced him.

Toby had almost convinced himself that the case would be dismissed. They were really just playing at soldiers. Practising, for when they went to war. And what had he done but doze off for an instant at three in the morning?

The battalion adjutant acted as prosecutor. Toby thought he made the case for the prosecution sound dire. A major transgression of duty. He found the whole process intimidating.

When questioned, he said: 'I was startled by Sergeant Cooper and that made me drop my rifle and jump to attention.

'It was dark at the time. Sergeant Cooper came to stand closer to me than he would have done if he'd been able to see me.' Although he did have a habit of standing very close and putting his face to within an inch of his victim's. 'I couldn't see him, and somehow when I came to attention we collided, and that's how Sergeant Cooper was knocked off balance.'

Lieutenant Nelson spoke at length about Toby's good character and his brief period of service. He called Private Blake to give evidence.

Clemmo confirmed that it had been a dark night; that the moon had been hidden by clouds at the time. He said he'd been unable to see Toby from where he stood on guard but he'd heard him stamp his feet and cough less than five minutes earlier.

He'd moved closer when he heard the commotion to see if he could help. He'd not seen Toby hit anybody and had heard nothing to suggest that he had.

Toby was taken back to the guard room without being told of the outcome. Lieutenant Nelson had advised him that if he was found not guilty, he'd be told immediately. The fact that he hadn't been told anything led him to believe he'd been found guilty.

He felt very low. It could be ages before he was allowed out of camp. Then he remembered that his sentence had been suspended last time. It was reasonable to hope that the same thing would happen again.

He had to wait another twenty-four hours before he was called back in front of the Adjutant.

'You've been found guilty of sleeping at your post,' he was told. 'You were on watch and nobody should be able to approach you unseen.

'I can't stress too strongly the importance of keeping yourself alert whilst you are on guard. If you do not, the safety of the battalion is put in jeopardy. Had this occurred in France, you could have been sentenced to death.'

Toby's knees were suddenly as soft as sponges. There'd been absolutely no danger to anybody. If there had been, his own fear and the adrenalin running through him would have kept him on his toes, as they were now. He was being threatened with the death sentence again! He felt himself sway. It was outrageous; they seemed to have no grasp on reality.

'You have been found not guilty on the second charge, of striking a senior officer, but guilty of using threatening behaviour towards him.

'On this occasion, bearing in mind the short time you have served, you are sentenced to one year's imprisonment with hard labour.'

Toby gasped. A full year!

'You will serve this in a military detention centre.'

He felt pulverised as he was marched back to the guard room. A year's imprisonment! And not to be allowed out to see Sarah in all that time? He couldn't believe it. Within ten minutes he had been marched outside again to commence his hard labour. He was to fill his waiting time digging trenches in which the volunteers could be taught the skills needed to survive in the battlefield.

At one o'clock, he was marched back to a lonely meal of soup and bread in the guard room. With the meal came two letters from Sarah that had accumulated since he'd been put under arrest. He fell on them, quite certain that he'd find her news soothing. The first one he opened floored him. She'd written:

Dearest Toby,

I have news which I'm sure will shock you. I have to tell you that I'm almost certain now that I'm going to have a baby. I've suspected it for the last month, but you have so many worries of your own, I didn't want to add to them. I put off telling you, hoping that perhaps I was wrong and it was just my imagination.

But I'm as certain now as I can be. Mam will be furious with me when she finds out. What can I do?

He couldn't read any more. He pushed her letters into his pocket. Neither could he eat his lunch, though he'd been famished moments before.

He wanted to marry Sarah. It was his duty to do so now. It would have been no problem if he could go home to her. What must she be going through? He pulled her letter out to look at the date; this one had been written several days ago. She'd be worried stiff by now because he hadn't answered.

Toby felt sick every time he thought of what he'd done. He was beginning to think he was a walking disaster.

He asked if he might have pen and paper and send a letter. Permission was refused, and he had to return to trench-digging. When he returned in the late evening to another meal of soup, he ached all over and had blisters on his hands.

Lieutenant Nelson came to see him, and Toby was able to ask him if he'd be given permission to write letters during his year of imprisonment. It seemed that two a month were allowed, so Toby told him why he needed to write to Sarah so urgently.

Some of his personal belongings were brought to the guard room for him; they included his fountain pen and stationery. He'd had plenty of time to think about what he wanted to tell Sarah, and he began to write immediately.

We must get married just as soon as we can. It is my dearest wish as well as my duty now. I'm not quite sure how and when I'll be able to manage it, but we shall be married before I go to France. I promise you that, insofar as it is in my ability.

Not in church, I'm afraid, Sarah. If the banns were called in my parish, Stepmother would find out what I intended; she and her mother are churchgoers. I'm not yet twenty-one and a free agent and she'd stop me marrying you if she could. I shall just add a year to my age. There are at least four volunteers here with me who have done just that to join the army, and they've got away with it. One is only fifteen.

I assume your mother will give you permission to marry; under the circumstances, I'm sure she will. We'll be married in the Liverpool register office, that's our best bet. We'll need a special licence, which I believe is available from the registrar.

I just wish I could get out of here and apply for it. Can you do that? If not, send me the address and I'll write for it. Or, when I can give my jailers the slip, I could apply in person on the way back to you.

It'll be legal when it's done. That's the main thing.

Toby felt desperate. If he were removed to a military prison, he'd have less chance of getting out. Probably none at all.

And he'd no idea where in the country the military prisons were. He couldn't let Sarah know just how difficult this might be. Even if he did get the opportunity to slip off, he'd be given an even longer sentence in the detention centre when he came back.

But he was going to do it if he could. He had to, for Sarah's sake.

Chapter Sixteen

October 1914

Toby received a long letter from Sarah by return. He could almost feel her relief.

> I'm so thrilled that you want us to be married as soon as possible. Mam is too, and is more than willing to give her permission, though I haven't told her yet about the baby. Haven't dared, I know it'll worry her. Marriage can't come too quickly for me.
>
> There is a problem. I've been down to the register office but I couldn't get a special licence, because there is a charge of twenty pounds and Mam and I don't have such a sum between us. Neither do I think Mr Masters will feel this is a reasonable charge for the business to meet.

Toby felt his own problems were much more acute. As yet he couldn't see any way of getting out to marry Sarah.

He wrote back at great length because he was afraid he might not be allowed to do so again for some time. His personal chequebook had come with his stationery. He made out a cheque to the registrar and enclosed it together with a personal cheque to Sarah, saying:

> It seems terrible to ask you to buy your own wedding ring, but I know of no other way to get one. Buy

yourself a new outfit too. You must look your best on your wedding day.

Toby knew he had to wait until he heard that preparations were in place and Sarah was ready. He spent every moment he had assessing what would be the best moment in the day to make a break for freedom. Very soon he decided there wasn't a good moment.

He was under close arrest; there was no way he'd be able to walk out of the guard room. And he was under observation all the time he had to dig. He couldn't see how he could get away. He considered asking Clemmo for help but was afraid he'd get him into trouble too. He'd made no progress when he received another letter from Sarah telling him that all the arrangements were in place.

The following morning, Toby had had his breakfast and was expecting to be marched out for another day's digging when the guard told him he was to go in front of the Adjutant again. As he marched out, Toby was stiff with dread. He expected now to be told he'd be setting off within the hour for a military prison on the other side of the country.

Instead, he was told his sentence had been suspended. He was to be ready by ten o'clock to move with his unit to Inkerman Barracks near Woking. They would all learn how to use a rifle on the firing ranges at nearby Bisley.

As he had feared, he was being moved much further away from Sarah and the factory, and because of his sentence, he hadn't been allowed the forty-eight hours' leave that the others had had. At least, though, he was no longer under close arrest. As he walked across to his tent, Toby felt relieved and appalled by turns.

Inside, it was almost impossible to move; everybody else was packing too. He was welcomed back warmly. He had his back slapped and was told he was a lucky fellow to have his sentence suspended like this. Many hands were helping him put his kit and belongings together. Everybody wanted to know what it felt like to be under close arrest. Toby had no time to say very much, no time to think out any plan. Foremost in his mind was the need to slip away unseen; he was watching all the time for half a chance.

They all paraded and stood to attention, and when the band formed and started to play, they fell in behind to march to the station. Toby knew he hadn't much time left. He felt poised for flight and was still watching for the right opportunity, but they were surrounded by officers, mostly on horseback, who had nothing to do but keep an eye on the ranks.

They filed up on to the station platform, where the train was waiting to take them south. They were being checked aboard, eight to each carriage. Like all his unit, Toby was in uniform and carried his rifle and full kit bag. He sat wedged in his seat, seeing his chances melting away. The carriages further up the train were still being filled and the platform was thronged with military personnel. The band continued to play in the distance.

He heard the swoosh as another train thundered into the station on the up line, heading in to Rock Ferry. It stopped, and suddenly his heart was pounding. He knew this was the only chance he was likely to get.

'I'm going, lads,' he announced. 'Don't let on; I don't want to get caught.'

He opened the door on the far side of the carriage, grabbed his kit and dropped four feet down to the line. The jolt shook him, but he was up and running to get behind the other train, afraid he could easily be seen as he scrambled alone across the line. Carrying full kit slowed him down, but now he'd reached the opposite platform and it shelved gently upwards.

There was no outcry, no order to stand still. He felt safer though there were fewer people here. He boarded the other train and a moment later it started with a jerk. He kept his head down and away from the window until they were well out of the station.

The train was slowing down for Rock Ferry before he'd got his breath back. He changed to the Liverpool underground line, half expecting every moment to feel a tap on his shoulder. From a seat on the Liverpool train he dared at last to look about him. There were other service personnel, lots of them. Toby was sweating; he tried to relax. He'd done it, he'd really deserted this time, but there had been no other way. He loved Sarah and he had obligations to her now.

Sarah was in the office, writing to suppliers and filling out orders for the raw materials the factory would need a couple of months hence. Toby had wanted to get a typewriter, but his father had been against such innovations. For Sarah, though, it made it easier that correspondence was still done in longhand in copying ink. Before the letters were posted, the office boy duplicated them in a damp-leafed book which also indexed them for reference purposes.

Sarah took comfort in using the desk that had once been Toby's. She'd had to tell her mother about the coming baby; it had proved impossible to hide her morning sickness. Mam had given her a real dressing-down. Sarah could understand why. Mam was frightened for her. She'd said a lot that wasn't complimentary about Toby. She didn't think he'd ever get round to marriage.

Sarah had shown her his letters, shown her the special licence he'd asked her to get. Mam still didn't think it would ever happen, and that prospect was making Sarah more and more anxious as the days went by.

'He'll be sent to France and get killed, that's what's likely to happen to him.' Mam was fraught about it.

Sarah straightened up in her chair. Above the clatter of machinery from the factory lines, she heard what sounded like a joyous whoop and raised voices. The next moment the office door burst open and Toby was bounding across the room to her. Sarah was laughing aloud as he swept her into his arms. Within moments her cheeks were wet with tears, but they were tears of joy and relief and utter gladness to see him again.

'I've come so we can be married,' he told her.

Mam and then Edward came in and were both slapping him on the back and telling him how pleased they were to see him.

'I've had to slip away to do this.' Toby grimaced at them. Sarah knew exactly what that meant. 'I had to, didn't I? I couldn't leave you in the lurch. But we must get married as soon as we can.'

'You're afraid you'll be caught and taken back?' Maria wanted to know.

He knew that, as a matter of course, details of deserters were circulated to both the military and civil police, sometimes with photographs.

'It could happen. Sarah, could you ring the registrar's office and see if we can be married this afternoon? Better if I keep my head down. If you have to tell them my address, give this one and don't mention the army.'

Sarah felt a bag of nerves as she unhooked the phone and waited for the operator to answer. She could see new lines of tension on Toby's face as he watched her. How strange it was to be talking to strangers about her own wedding.

'Four o'clock this afternoon? Yes, thank you, that will be excellent.'

'I'd like to go to your rooms and change,' Toby said. 'I'll feel better if I could get out of this uniform.'

Edward said: 'I'll stop the lines; it's dinner time.'

Sarah could feel the excitement growing inside her. Mam made sandwiches for the four of them with the cold beef that had been meant for their dinner tonight. Sarah changed into the wedding finery she'd bought for herself, a wool costume in mustard-yellow tweed.

Toby couldn't get out of his uniform quick enough. He hid his kit bag and rifle under their bed.

His sports jacket and flannels were all he had.

'Not exactly a wedding outfit,' he smiled. 'But I feel safer in them. Have you got a suitcase, Sarah? An overnight bag?'

'No.'

'We'll book into a hotel. Might as well have a bit of a honeymoon if we can.'

'I might be able to borrow a carpet bag for you,' Maria said. 'Elvira Ferry has one, I think. They'll be home now for the dinner break.'

By the time Sarah had put her overnight things together, Mam was back with a carpet bag to pack them in.

'What are we going to do until four o'clock?' Mam wanted to know.

'Sarah and I have a lot to do,' Toby told her. 'Can you and Edward meet us there?'

'We'll need two witnesses,' Sarah said. 'Edward isn't old enough. Could you bring somebody else?'

'Who?'

'Anybody. Old Trumper if you like.'

Sarah found herself holding on to Toby's arm as they strode into town. He swung the carpet bag as though its weight was of no consequence.

'We're going to book into the Adelphi,' he said.

'The Midland Adelphi? I've heard it's very grand. Won't it be too . . . ?'

'It'll be the safest place for me. They won't be searching for a private soldier there.'

Sarah couldn't believe the grandeur: the liveried doorman, the grand reception hall and the palatial bedroom which was assigned to them. Toby hugged her again as soon as the door closed behind them, but after a few moment he put her away from him.

'There are things I must see to urgently. Important things.'

Sarah shivered. 'You're afraid you'll be caught. Taken back before . . .'

'It could happen, but not this quickly. I want to see Jeffrey Masters, the solicitor. I've never made a will, but I think I must now. If Father's death taught me one thing, it was the importance of having a will. Look how upset Stepmother is because Father didn't make proper provision for her. If anything happens to me, I don't want you and our child to be in difficulties.'

If anything happens to me . . . His words made Sarah shiver again.

'It won't, of course. But I have to do it just in case.'

She couldn't believe the ease with which he ushered her into a large office suite in Dale Street, the main business area of Liverpool. Nor the welcome they were given there. They were soon in an inner sanctum and Toby was introducing her to Jeffrey Masters as the girl he would be marrying that afternoon.

'I want you to draw up a will for me,' he told the solicitor. 'I want to leave everything I own to Sarah.'

'Very sensible.'

'How long will it take you to do that?'

'I usually allow three days.'

'I'm in the army as you know, Mr Masters. I only have forty-eight hours. If I came back tomorrow morning, could you have it ready for me to sign?'

'It's a very simple will, Toby. I think under the circumstances I can have it drawn up by eleven tomorrow.'

Mr Masters kept them for a while to talk about the business, but time was going on and they had to take a taxi to the register office. Mam, Edward and Miss Potts were already waiting for them.

There were formalities that had to be attended to, then they were taken to a small room. It was panelled in wood and furnished elegantly with a large desk and a few chairs upholstered in red velvet. There were several vases of flowers. Sarah felt nervous. She told herself not to be silly; far more reason to be nervous if this *wasn't* happening to her.

She stood by Toby's side. There was a short homily on the sanctity of marriage, then she was being asked:

'Do you take this man to be your wedded husband, to live together . . . ?'

Toby's voice shook with emotion as he took his vows. It seemed no time at all before the ring she'd chosen herself was on the third finger of her left hand and they were signing the register as man and wife. It was over. Sarah was given her marriage lines.

Once outside on the pavement, Edward was pointing out a photography shop and suggesting they had their pictures taken. After that Toby invited them back to the Adelphi. Eunice Potts said she ought to go home now, because she wasn't family, and anyway she'd have worn her best hat if she'd known she was going to a wedding and then on to the Adelphi Hotel.

'We're none of us very smart, except Sarah,' Toby laughed. He felt triumphant; he'd succeeded in what he'd set out to do.

'Come along, a glass of champagne to drink our health. Just for an hour.'

'Champagne? That's what the toffs drink. I've never tasted it,' Miss Potts said. 'Perhaps I shouldn't miss this chance.'

'I haven't tasted it either,' Mam smiled. 'Nor has Sarah.'

'Nor me,' Edward grinned. 'And I don't think Toby has.'

'Father didn't believe in frills, but it is our wedding day. We're all going to try it.'

Glasses were raised and they drank to the future. It turned into a merry party. Sarah watched the bubbles spinning up the glasses and found all this hard to believe. It seemed like a fairy tale. Miss Potts left after two glasses but Toby insisted Mam and Edward stay to have dinner with them. A dinner such as Sarah had never had before. It all seemed very grand and expensive.

Afterwards they went outside to see Edward and Maria

into a taxi. Edward was going to be dropped at the Pier Head to catch the ferry home; Mam would go on alone to her rooms.

As she went up the grand staircase with Toby, Sarah told herself she'd been right to trust him. She felt very much in love and very lucky to have him. Today she had everything she could wish for.

She watched him undress. He was broad-chested, handsome.

'What are those tags round your neck?'

'All serving soldiers have to wear them. Identity tags.'

'Why are there two?' Sarah looked at them. One was red and one green. They showed his name, religion and number.

'I asked that myself. It's in case I'm killed,' he shrugged. 'One goes to records and one remains to identify the body.'

Sarah froze. It brought home to her that she might not have Toby for long.

At breakfast the next morning, Toby started talking about money.

'Now that you're my wife, I should support you, but the army pays me only a shilling a day, but it would also pay you an allowance of seven shillings a week if I were to allot half my wages to you.'

Sarah knew from the files at the office that he had been paid three hundred a year by his father. 'You'll do that?'

'It would leave me only three and six a week to pay for my washing and buy blanco and shoe polish. I use a lot of that. Stamps too and razor blades.'

'You should, between us we'd gain an extra three shillings and sixpence a week. That's the rent of a room.'

'Is that what you and your mother pay?'

'No, our rent's five shillings and sixpence because we've got the two big rooms.'

'You ought to have somewhere better.'

'It's the best we've ever had.'

'With a baby coming, you need—'

'We'll be fine until the war's over.'

Sarah couldn't stop her eyes going round the restaurant. The dark-suited waiters were pouring from coffee pots with a serviette over one arm with which to catch drips. She'd never tasted coffee before. She ordered kedgeree from the menu because she'd never even heard of that.

She said, aghast: 'Breakfast here costs two shillings each! How can you afford all this on a shilling a day?'

'My mother left me and Edward some shares in her will and that brings me in a little income. About two hundred a year.'

'That's . . . riches.' Sarah worked out in an instant that it was almost four pounds a week. 'You could live on that.'

'Not three of us. As soon as the bank opens at ten, we're going in. I'm going to change my account. I want it in our joint names now. Then I'll know you won't starve, whatever happens.'

Sarah had always known he didn't get the value from money that she and Mam did. He'd never had to.

'Father would have paid me an allowance had I agreed to be articled to his accountant friend. But if he'd lived a bit longer, I think he might have cut me out of his will. As things stand I shall be given either one third or one quarter of the business. You'll get my share if the worst happens.'

'Don't talk like that. Nothing may happen.'

'It could, and I have to consider the consequences of what I do. If I'd been thinking this way with Father, we'd not be in this position now. I've got to work things through. Father kept telling me I didn't do that, and I'm afraid events have proved him right. I'm determined to do better this time round.

'As my wife, you could draw an allowance from the business.'

'I have my wages, Toby. I won't need more. Mam and I can manage.'

'Your wages should be increased. You're both doing much more now. We saw to it for Miss Potts and Trumper, but I forgot all about you. I'm sure everybody would agree.'

Sarah thought they'd had a busy morning, going to the bank to put his private account into their joint names and then back to his solicitor's office for Toby to sign his will.

'You're being very thoughtful for me, very generous.'

'Practical for once,' he said. 'It wasn't easy to get away; I might not be able to do this again.'

He took her back to the Adelphi for lunch, although she suggested they buy some food and take it to her home. He shook his head and smiled. 'We aren't going to have much opportunity to live it up. Not for a long time. We're on our honeymoon now, so we should try to enjoy ourselves.'

To Sarah, it seemed the height of extravagance.

'We'll go to the factory this afternoon. I'll feel happier about things there if I know everything's running as it should.'

Sarah led Toby towards the office, wanting to show him how well they were managing. When she flung open the door, she saw Toby's stepmother sitting at his father's desk poring over ledgers. She looked up, alarmed.

'Hello, Stepmother,' Toby said.

'You shouldn't be here!'

'Edward would say the same to you,' Sarah told her. She didn't like Claudia coming; she was afraid of what she might do.

Claudia looked at them disdainfully. 'I came to see if you were here, Toby. The military police are looking for you. They came to the house yesterday. I thought you must be up to something.'

'What did you tell them?'

'What could I tell them? I didn't know where you were.'

Sarah shivered. She could see the lines of strain on Toby's

face again. He was used to having fun, a carefree life, and now trouble was building up.

He lifted Sarah's left hand to show her ring. 'I came home to marry Sarah. She's my legal wife; you'll be pleased to know the family's growing.'

Claudia looked anything but pleased. 'You can't get married without permission. You're not of age.'

'I've managed it, Stepmother, believe me. The army taught me how. There's hundreds of underage boys enlisting in it. I just added a year to my age.'

'But that can't be legal.'

'It's perfectly legal. Sarah and I are as much married as you and Father were. I would like her to live at Tides Reach too.'

There was no mistaking Claudia's fury. Her plump cheeks flushed scarlet. 'That's quite impossible. There isn't room.'

'I've talked it over with Edward. We think more room could be made. The house could be split in two.'

'No! Absolutely not. I won't stand for it. Why should I?'

'It's the Percival family home and Sarah is now as much a Percival as you are.'

'I have a child; soon there'll be two. They are the coming generation of Percivals . . .'

Toby said with a slow smile: 'Don't be surprised, you might find Sarah has a child too.'

Sarah was shocked at the glance of pure hatred Claudia gave her.

'I might have known!' The scarlet in her cheeks deepened to angry crimson. 'You've got her pregnant! It's a good job your father isn't here to see this. He'd be very upset. You've gone too far this time.'

Claudia was so upset at Toby's news that she left for home straight away. She was fuming and set out as briskly as she could now that her pregnancy was more advanced. From her point of view, nothing could be worse. She wasn't the only Mrs Percival any more.

They had both stood in front of her, smiling calmly, not one whit ashamed of what they'd done. If anything, Toby was proud that he'd managed to get home to marry the girl. Claudia knew that for her it was a disaster, and she could see no way round it.

On top of that, Toby had had the nerve to suggest that Sarah Hoxton come to live at Tides Reach! Maurice would turn in his grave if he knew.

She had her own plans for the house. She wanted Gideon Burton to come and live with her when they were married, and how could she do that if the Hoxtons came? That girl, with her yellow cats' eyes, might even bring her mother with her, filling the house with factory riffraff.

Claudia had been trying to work out how she could get Edward to leave. When she married, she could push Mama back to her old rooms – she'd forbidden her to give them up. She'd like to push Edward out too, but in any event he'd have to go and fight before much longer. She didn't want anyone else to live there, except of course Adam and the new baby. A newly married couple needed a place of their own. They'd be family enough.

She leaned against the rails of the ferry boat and focused her gaze across the muddy water of the Mersey to where she could see the elegant front of Tides Reach nestling amongst the trees.

Once again Toby was trying to get the better of her. She certainly wasn't going to open her doors to the Hoxtons. By the time the ferry had tied up to the end of the pier, she'd changed her mind about going home. She went straight back to town. She'd go to see Jeffrey Masters, let him know what Toby was trying to do and get him to put a stop to it.

She had to take a cab up to his office in Dale Street, but there she was given a comfortable chair in which to rest while she waited for the client he had with him to go.

Her anger didn't leave her. When she was shown into Mr Masters' office, the words of explanation tumbled out so fast she knew she sounded incoherent.

'You mustn't fret yourself, my dear.' The old man patted her hand. 'I do understand your dismay and I'll do what I can, you can be sure of that.'

He got out Maurice's will to show her. 'The problem is in the way your husband worded his original codicil. He insisted on it. He saw Tides Reach as a family home for the Percivals. You have the right to live there for your lifetime, but so has Toby, and so has Edward. He wanted you all to live there. The freehold rests with . . . yes, it will be Toby's. It's a little unusual to bequeath a house in this fashion. More frequently, the wife is given the entire use of a family home for her lifetime and only then does it revert to another family member.'

'You said you'd go to court to get this will overturned.'

'Yes, because Maurice hadn't made adequate provision for you.'

'Can't you get the part about the house changed too?'

'That's a different matter altogether. Neither of Mr Percival's two sons by his previous marriage has reached their majority. It could be argued that they need a roof over their heads too. I think he wanted you all to live happily together.'

Claudia felt she was being wound tighter. Maurice had not been fair to her. She said sarcastically: 'I doubt that's possible.'

Mr Masters was being sympathetic, but what good did sympathy do?'

'Then what Toby has suggested – to divide the house – might be the best plan. I seem to remember that it's a big house. There'd be room for you all that way.'

Claudia was shaking with rage when she got up to leave. When she reached home and told her mother what had happened, Mama said:

'It's your own fault, Claudia. I spent years nagging you

to get Maurice to sort his will out. You wouldn't listen to me. You thought you had all the time in the world. I'm very sorry this has come to pass, I don't want to share this comfortable house with anyone else, but it's no good letting fly at me. It's not my fault.'

Sarah was very happy to have Toby back with her. Relieved too to be married and with her future secure. They kept their room at the Adelphi on, and in the evenings they enjoyed the entertainment that Liverpool could offer. They sampled the theatres and cinemas and ate in different restaurants.

'We need a bit of fun.' Toby smiled down at her. 'Something good to look back on.'

They were spending most of the daylight hours in the factory, Toby said he wanted to make sure they could manage to run it without him. Mam and Edward, Sarah and John Ferry, together with Miss Potts and Mr Trumper, had had a few weeks to settle to their new jobs. Now that Toby was back they were all clearer about what they knew and what they still needed to know.

Toby also went again to Dale Street to discuss factory business with Mr Masters, who agreed that Sarah and her mother should be given an increase in their wages.

At the end of the third day, Toby said: 'I feel satisfied that all is well now, both for you and at the factory. I won't worry so much when I'm back in camp.'

'You're going back?'

'I have to sometime. Better if I do before I'm caught. We'll have another day or two to ourselves first.'

He took her round the big shops in Liverpool and bought her many gifts: a new dress and a leather handbag from Hendersons; a hat and some gloves from the Bon Marche. In Bunnies, he helped her choose baby clothes. The next day they took the train to Southport, but it was cold and wet. In the morning he bought her a pair of fine leather shoes. They ate lunch at the Prince of Wales Hotel and then went to the cinema.

'I'll have to go back,' he worried.

'It's been the perfect honeymoon,' Sarah assured him. It would have been if she hadn't had to worry about what would happen to him when he got back. 'You'll be in terrible trouble for this.'

'Yes, but I've been let off twice. I'll be let off again, don't you fret yourself.'

Sarah was of the opinion that that wasn't likely. Surely this time punishment would be deemed essential. She kept quiet. Whatever Toby said, he must be worried stiff. She didn't want to add to that.

On what he'd decided must be their last night, Sarah clung to him. She wanted to plead with him to stay one more day, but she knew it wouldn't alter anything. In the end he'd have to go.

They got up late and had a leisurely breakfast. Then he took Sarah to her rooms with all her new possessions. He changed back into his uniform, collected his rifle from under the bed and went down to the factory to say goodbye to Edward.

Sarah walked to the Pier Head with him. She hadn't intended to go further, but she couldn't bear to part from him and accompanied him on the tram to Lime Street Station.

She stood beside him and heard him buy his ticket to Woking. He had twenty minutes to wait for the London train. He bought a platform ticket for her.

'I'll have to ask where the camp is when I get there,' he worried.

'I can't bear to think of the trouble you'll be in.'

'It's been worth it. My mind's at rest now. I know everything's all right here.'

She clung to him. This parting was tearing her in two. At last he had to board the train. He let the glass down in the

234

door so he could go on talking to her, though they'd long since passed the stage when they had anything to say. All that was left was the final wrench of parting. Toby waved from the train until the line turned and she couldn't see him any more.

Chapter Seventeen

Toby sank down on the seat feeling that nothing mattered any more. He'd spent the last week keeping a sharp eye out for the military police and on one occasion pulling Sarah quickly into a shop when he'd seen two policemen coming towards them. Now he didn't care if he was picked up.

When he arrived in Woking, he took a taxi to the camp and gave himself up to the guard on the gate. He found himself under close arrest. He knew he could expect to be marched before his commanding officer in the morning, and that he'd be charged with desertion and court-martialled.

He asked for help from Lieutenant Nelson again. Nelson came to see him in the guard room:

'Each time you get into trouble it makes it harder to defend what you do. Desertion is the worst of crimes.'

Toby explained why he'd deserted.

'I got my girlfriend into trouble. I had to go home and marry her. I was doing the decent thing for her.'

'In the army you have to ask for permission to marry. You can't just go and do it.'

'But I did.'

'How did you manage that in one week? You'd have had to have a special licence.'

'Yes, I got it all arranged beforehand. It was no good asking for a few days off, was it? I had to do it. I couldn't let my girlfriend down.'

'You couldn't afford a special licence.'

'I had to have it whatever it cost.' Toby had asked for a second copy of the marriage lines for just this reason. He

237

brought the document out of his breast pocket for Nelson to see.

The lieutenant gave a little hiccup of surprise.

'Well, you had your reason and you've brought proof. But you disobeyed orders by not asking for permission first.'

'Would I have been given permission? Been allowed to do it quickly?'

Nelson tried to hide his smile. 'Perhaps not; you'd just had a sentence of a year's imprisonment suspended. I don't know whether it's better to forget your reasons . . .'

His voice was weary. 'You've now got two suspended sentences, one from a court martial. Deserters can be sentenced to death.'

'But surely not if they desert in England?'

'It can happen even if it is in England. You seem a reasonable lad; I can't understand why you don't keep out of trouble.'

In due course, Toby was found guilty of desertion. He was relieved to hear that his sentence was not to be the death penalty but two years' detention with hard labour.

Afterwards, when he'd been returned to the guard room, Lieutenant Nelson came to see him again.

'I'm hopeful it will be suspended as before. There's many who'd think of two years in a detention centre in this country as the soft option and would prefer that to going to France.'

Toby wrote:

My beloved Sarah,

My hard labour started immediately, but after only six days I was told my sentence had been suspended and I was to return to my unit to continue training.

I was marched to a hut that housed thirty men but it was dry and there was a stove in the middle and room to move around. I was allotted a bed there; all the best places round the stove had been bagged and so had the corners, but it's better than the bell tent and the guard room.

I was overjoyed to find Clemmo Blake billeted in the same hut, and Chalky White too. They both told me things were much better here. I feel happier about things now, I've left Sergeant Cooper behind in Bebington and it looks as though I've survived again.

Today I went with my unit to the range at Bisley for musketry training – to learn how to use my rifle properly. At last I've found something I'm good at and can enjoy. My instructor thinks I have a natural eye for shooting. I did very well on all the ranges but particularly on the thousand yards. I'm hoping that with practice I might be good enough to be what the army calls a marksman.

I can't say I'm settling in to army life, because we all know we're being trained for the front line and won't be staying here for long. The news from France is bad, and my fellow volunteers are not as enthusiastic as they were.

When Toby left, Sarah couldn't settle to do anything. She had no concentration; her mind kept sliding to him. She was missing him so much it felt as though she'd been torn in two, and she was worried about the trouble he'd be in.

Mam, on the other hand, was very happy with the way things had worked out.

'Fancy you married to a Percival. You've made your fortune and mine as well. Here we are having a much better time at work and more money for doing it. We've landed on our feet this time.

'It's upset Elvira Ferry, though; she's a bit envious. Said she hopes you won't get too big for your boots now you're a Percival.'

Sarah smiled. 'She expected big things from John.'

'Yes, always on about the plans he had. How he was going to make a fortune for her from some sauce recipe. I pointed out you were still doing your best for John. You got him a better job.'

'I didn't really. He was the best person to do the selling. I knew he could do more than load carts.'

'He's grateful if she isn't.'

'He needn't be grateful to me.'

When Toby's letter arrived saying his sentence had been suspended again, she felt much better, but she was still worried for him. She knew that sooner or later he'd be sent to France. She rushed home every dinner time to open the letter she found waiting for her, dreading that it would be the one that would tell her he was on the move again.

At Sarah's suggestion, he started to address his letters to the factory, so that she could have them when the early post was delivered instead of waiting until dinner time. Now that Toby was telling her about his bad moments and his misgivings, he was a good letter-writer. It was a help for him too; a way of letting off steam. He was no longer bottling his troubles up inside him.

My dearest Sarah,

I feel more settled. Now I'm too far away to see you, I can go out and about; sod's law, isn't it? I've been into town several times. I feel I'm back in the swim when I see normal life all round me. We go to the pubs of course, and to the cafés for more to eat.

I've really enjoyed the shooting range and scored well enough to become a marksman. We've just been issued with brand new .303 Lee Enfield rifles. These are a great improvement on the old-fashioned ones we had to start with. Out of five shots on the thousand-yard range I got three bull's-eyes and two inners. I've been given a badge showing crossed guns to sew on my left tunic sleeve. I'm learning signalling too, and hope soon to have another badge showing crossed flags as well.

A week or two later, he wrote that he had his signaller's badge, and that although he didn't know when, rumours kept going round that his unit would soon be on its way to France.

This news niggled in Sarah's mind all day. She'd been dreading it for weeks. It was late in the afternoon when she sought out Trumper to ask after his son Charlie, who'd gone to France two weeks ago.

Trumper was overseeing a first batch of apple chutney. He'd just turned out the heat under the four huge cauldrons and it was still bubbling inside. They were having to try new recipes to take the place of their Madras and mango chutneys because the ingredients were becoming scarce. After pickled onions, they had been their two bestsellers.

'We'll try it as soon as it cools a little.' His face was scarlet and running with perspiration. 'I think we'll be pleased.'

'There you are . . .' John Ferry swept in, brandishing a jar of their Madras chutney. His face was grim. 'We've got trouble.'

'What's the matter?'

'Come to the office. I'll get the others.' John's eyes swept round at their staff in a way that scared Sarah. It seemed to indicate that he didn't want them to hear what he had to say. Five minutes later the six of them were gathered in the office with the door shut.

'Hardman's gave me these.' He waved his hand at the three jars of chutney lined up on the desk. 'It's been returned to them from the shops. Customers have brought it back wanting refunds.'

Trumper's voice was indignant. 'What's the matter with it?'

'Inedible they say. Customers can't bear to put it in their mouths.'

Sarah was shocked. She unscrewed the lid of one jar and sniffed at the contents. 'It seems all right. Very spicy.'

'It looks all right.' Edward was unscrewing another.

'The colour.' Alf Trumper was holding the third jar to the light. 'It isn't quite right.'

Much the same could be said for him. Sarah could see he was very upset. It was his responsibility to measure in the ingredients and to time the cooking. If the finished product was judged to be inedible, he felt he was to blame.

'It's different,' he said. 'Has little green specks in it.'

'We'll have to find what we've done wrong,' Edward said. 'Oh Lord, has this ever happened before?'

'I don't know.' Sarah shook her head. 'But then I wouldn't have been told if it had.'

'No,' Trumper said firmly. 'No, never.'

'It could be a disaster.'

Miss Potts brought a packet of water biscuits from the kitchen which they kept for tastings, together with a plate and a knife. Sarah spread six biscuits with a moderate layer of chutney, and handed the plate round.

Eunice Potts was the first to bite into hers. The next moment she was spitting it into her handkerchief.

'Oh! Oh! My mouth!' She flew to the door. 'Water, I've got to get some water.'

It made the rest of them try their biscuits very warily. Sarah took the smallest possible nibble. She knew immediately what had caused the trouble.

Alf Trumper's shocked eyes met hers. 'Those missing peppers! Them dried green chillies.'

Eunice Potts brought in a glass of water for each of them. She was dabbing her face with a towel.

'My lips are on fire.'

Sarah had a sinking feeling in her stomach. 'We've lost a whole sack of them. How many jars have been ruined?' She couldn't look at Trumper.

Each jar carried a batch number that told them when it had been made. Sarah had the ledger opened on her desk in no time.

'August the sixth. We made twenty cases of Madras chutney that day. Over two hundred jars. Can we recall them, John?'

'I'll do my best.'

'If people pay good money for this, they'll never buy any more. It'll ruin our reputation.'

'All those mangoes wasted too,' Edward lamented. 'So scarce now with the war.'

Maria said slowly: 'The sixth, that was a Wednesday. The day after I had my accident. I was in hospital that day.'

'We can't blame you then,' Edward told her.

'I don't know how this could have happened.' Trumper looked defeated. 'Let me think. That was the day before Mr Percival died. I wish I could remember . . .

'I weigh everything like that out into batches. Where's the book from the stock room? How much chilli did I withdraw on that day?'

Edward ran up to get it. They all pored over Trumper's figures, which were set out neatly down the page. He'd withdrawn a small amount of dried green chillies, a tiny fraction of the amount missing.

'That's what the recipe would need,' he said, stabbing his finger on the page. 'I'm almost sure I can remember putting them in – the right amount, I mean. But I've done it so often. Perhaps I was on automatic. I don't know. I'm sorry. So sorry.'

'I find it hard to believe,' Sarah said slowly, 'that you'd put all those in. Even if you weren't thinking, you'd know it was wrong. You've done it too often.'

Trumper sighed. 'The peppers were ground up. Those specks we can see.'

'You always grind them up, don't you?'

'In chutney, yes. I hope whoever did it washed out the machine, or a lot of other things are going to get more chilli in them than they should.'

243

'We'd better spot-check everything else made around that time.'

Edward said, 'The question now is what are we going to do about this batch?'

'Follow up every case we've sent out,' Sarah said. 'Get back what we can. Replace it or refund what we were paid.'

'I'll go round the wholesalers tomorrow morning,' John said. 'No, I can go to Bellways now, they won't have closed yet. I've already checked my books; they took a lot of it.'

'They might have sent it out to the shops by now,' Sarah pointed out. 'What a mess.'

'I'll do the wholesalers first, get them to look up their records to see where it's gone. Then I'll go round the Liverpool shops we stock direct.'

Sarah shivered. She'd thought of something else. Edward put it into words. 'How do we know it's only this batch number? It could be in other things. We made piccalilli that morning.'

Sarah ran her finger down the page. 'And Madras chutney the next day too. Oh dear.'

'Check the stock room first,' Trumper said. 'It's possible there's still some up there. We've been keeping the Madras for our best customers because we mightn't be able to make more.'

'You go out, John. The rest of us can check the stock room here.'

Edward looked dazed. 'Who has done this?'

'Nobody adds anything,' Trumper said. 'Not without my say-so. I always put the ingredients together. All of them.'

'You might not have done so this time,' Sarah said.

Edward frowned. 'I hope we haven't got a disaster on our hands.'

It was he who located two cases of the same batch in the stock room. It was hot and heavy work moving the wooden cases about. They found other products made around the same date and tasted jars selected at random. They were all all right.

'I must be going mad,' Trumper grunted.

'No, definitely not that.'

'I'm not so sure.'

'We'll get to the bottom of it,' but Sarah knew there was nothing she could say that would soothe his worries.

'Nothing like this has ever happened to me before,' he said woefully.

John Ferry pedalled furiously along the Dock Road to Bellways, one of the wholesalers who regularly ordered their stock in large amounts. He wasn't looking forward to going in with this problem. Being a salesman meant being knowledgeable and friendly to his customers, but above all it meant getting them to trust him. On his previous visits he'd sung the praises of Percival's products. Now customers were pronouncing them uneatable.

As soon as he'd heard that jars of their chutney were being returned, he knew it was a serious problem for Percival's. But the last hour in the office had shown him just how concerned the others were.

All six of them had worked very hard since Toby had left. They were all very involved and keen to make a success of what they were doing. Particularly Sarah, who was a Percival herself now.

It had been only too obvious that Trumper felt he was to blame. He'd been very upset. As for Sarah and Edward, he'd sensed their panic. It was a terrible thing to happen just when they were all gaining a little confidence and thought they'd be able to run the company successfully.

John left his bicycle in the Bellways bike shed; removed his cycle clips from his trousers and slid them on to the crossbar. He felt uncomfortable going in with this problem. In reception he asked to see the manager. He'd been well received up to now. The manager had taken all the new lines and increased their standing order for pickles. John didn't want to upset this account.

'I've just been trying to reach you,' the girl told him. 'Mr Bellway wanted to speak to you.'

His heart sank; he could guess why.

'We've had several irate shopkeepers on the phone who've had to refund the purchase price,' he was told.

It was the same story. Half a dozen jars of chutney had been returned from the shops Bellways supplied. He was shown a letter of complaint.

John apologised and asked if their stock controller could check the warehouse for chutney with the same batch number. They did it together and found one crate left. Only twelve jars. John was disappointed. They'd taken delivery of sixty.

'We'll replace it, of course,' he said, 'and anything else returned to you. I'll come with our cart tomorrow and take these away.'

John knew he could do no more tonight. Other customers would have closed their premises by now. He was later than usual going home. This had been an emotional drain, and he felt tired and despondent.

He was pedalling hard against a blustery wind, afraid he'd be late for the meal his mother always cooked at the end of the working day. The last thing he wanted was to upset her; she'd been touchy since he'd tried to enlist.

She rounded on him as soon as he went in. 'You knew it was liver and onions. I've had to keep it waiting. It gets hard if it isn't eaten as soon as it's cooked.'

'Sorry, Mam. I should have told you I might be late.'

'I saw you come back to the factory. I thought you'd done with visiting for the day.'

'I had to go out again.' He began to tell her why as she dished up. 'A huge amount of chilli pepper has been put into a batch of the Madras. Enough to set your head on fire. Totally ruined it.'

246

With a mound of mashed potato on each plate and the liver still spluttering in the frying pan, his mother backed off to the table, clutching her throat.

'I was afraid that was what it was about,' she whispered.

John took over and finished dishing up. 'What was about?'

'You all shut yourselves in the office. I knew something was up. Edward kept flying out to fetch things.'

'It's very serious. It might be more than one batch; we don't know yet. Nobody could possibly eat it. This could ruin Percival's reputation.'

He put her dinner in front of her and noticed for the first time how white she looked. The frown lines on her forehead seemed deeper than usual.

'What's the matter, Mam? Aren't you well?'

She picked up her knife and fork. 'I'm all right.'

John knew from her voice that she wasn't. He attacked his dinner; he was ravenous. The liver was a little hard. His mother's nervous dark eyes were searching his face.

'What are they going to do about it?'

'I'm trying to trace all that batch. Tomorrow I'll be exchanging it. I'm afraid a lot of it has been sold now. People are taking it back to the shops, demanding their money back.'

He could see his mother's hands trembling. She was pushing the food round her plate, hardly eating anything. He thought she was acting very strangely.

'Are you all right?'

Her knife and fork clattered down on her plate. She pushed it away and stood up.

'What's the matter, Mam?'

'They deserved it.' There was grinding rage in her voice, and her heavy eyebrows were shooting up and down.

John could feel barbs of horror shooting through him. Surely not Mam?

He choked out: 'Who deserved it?'

'The Percivals.'

'What have you got against them?'

'Wasn't the old man as mean as muck with his wages?'

'No worse than anyone else.'

'Didn't Toby lure your girlfriend away? Seduce her upstairs in her own home? Wasn't it driving you mad to know he was up there with her while Maria was in hospital?'

'Mam!' John could feel the heat spreading up to his face. 'Did you have something to do with this?'

'Toby had no shame about doing that. He needed to be taken down a peg. Get his deserts.'

'They're married, Mam. He did the decent thing.'

'But he hadn't when I did this,' she wailed. 'I wanted to get even with them. I did it for you.'

'No! I'd never want this.'

'It was because of what Toby was doing. That was why you were going to enlist, to get away from him. I'd have been left by myself.'

'But they wouldn't have me.'

'I didn't know that, did I? Not when I did it.'

'Oh, God!'

'Everything was going wrong for us. I blamed the Percivals. Nothing ever seemed to go wrong for them.'

John could feel his neck crawl with horror. 'The boss died at his desk! It all changed. Toby had to go away. He didn't bear me any grudge. He gave me a chance, a good job.'

'I didn't know that at the time, did I?'

'Mam! You should have waited. You'd have seen—'

'I was upset,' she cried and burst into tears. 'You were going to leave me.'

John felt as though he'd had the stuffing knocked out of him. 'This could ruin the business. With the chutney already in the shops, they can't keep it quiet. I'll have to explain to Sarah.'

'No!' Elvira jerked to her feet. 'What d'you want to do that for? There's no need to say anything. I don't want Sarah to know what I did. I don't want anybody to know.'

'I'll have to, Mam.'

'It makes me look . . . Well, you know.'

It made her look jealous. Full of revenge and hate. Twisted. He groaned. Perhaps Mam was a little bitter and envious of those who had better fortune. She certainly lived on her nerves, was too ready to leap to her own defence and his.

He said as calmly as he could: 'Sarah is at her wits' end; Edward too. They were going to open jars of stuff made on other days to try to find the extent of the problem.'

'It was only that one batch.'

'I'll have to tell them that, to set their minds at rest. They're worried stiff. Alf Trumper looked ready to slit his own throat and it isn't his fault. How would you feel in his place?'

'They'll find out, all in good time. No need to drop me in it.'

'Mam, I can't sit with them tomorrow while they talk about it and pretend I know no more than they do. Not now you've told me. They trust me; they're desperate to find out how much was spoiled.'

She was staring back at him, her eyes dark with fear.

'Oh God, what have you done? They'd be within their rights to sack you. You've sabotaged their business; it could be a criminal offence. You can't go round damaging people's goods and reputation. You've lost money for the company. And all this while we're struggling to keep it afloat without Mr Percival or Toby.

'What's Sarah going to think of us? She's a Percival now; you've undermined her family business.'

'Please don't tell them. If you were in this trouble, I wouldn't say a word.'

'I've got to. Come upstairs with me now. We'll tell Sarah together.'

'No, I can't.'

'Come on, let's get it over with. Sarah will have her say and that will be that.'

'She'll sack me.'

249

'If Percival's goes under, we'll all be out of work. Have you thought of that?'

John wouldn't let her refuse. It would look better this way and Mam would get it over with. She'd be worse if it stayed hanging over her.

'Show some remorse, say you're sorry. There's no way I can avoid telling them. It would be on my conscience for ever if I didn't speak up now.'

She was persuaded at last. He took her by the arm and led her upstairs.

Maria answered his knock. 'Come and sit down, Elvira.' She removed a newspaper from her basket chair. 'You look worn out.'

John remained standing by the table, watching Sarah, who was washing up their supper dishes in an enamel bowl on the table and setting them to drain on a tin tray.

She said: 'Mam and I've been talking it over . . . can't stop talking it over. We don't think it could be a mistake on Trumper's part. He's meticulous. There's no way he could do such a thing.' She looked tired and dispirited. 'We think it has to be deliberate sabotage.'

'You're right, Sarah. That's what we've come to tell you.'

He looked at his mother. She was crouching in the chair, both hands covering her face. 'Come on, Mam.'

'You?' Maria's mouth had dropped open.

John shivered and said: 'My mother took the green chilli peppers from the store and put them in the chutney. That's what you want to tell them, isn't it, Mam?'

Maria pulled out a chair from the table and sank down on to it. 'Elvira? Why?'

John tried to explain. That had been a terrible time for him too, listening to Toby's footsteps overhead, driving home his loss and Toby's gain.

He knew by the way the colour rushed up Sarah's cheeks that she was angry.

'But that's a dreadful thing to do. I know you were furious

with me that day, Elvira. You were blaming me because John had gone off to enlist. But even so, what you did was vicious.'

'Tell them, Mam, tell them exactly what you did.'

John thought she wasn't going to say anything. She looked a nervous wreck. When at last she started, her voice wasn't much above a whisper.

'Mr Trumper left his pencil in the store room and sent me up to get it. I saw the sack full of green chilli peppers. I'd just finished grinding up a few – to go in the chutney. I got the juice on my fingers, rubbed my eyes. It stung.'

'Go on,' Sarah urged roughly.

'I brought the sack down . . . You know what I did then. It seemed like a good way to get even.'

Sarah's voice rose an octave. 'Did you put them all in? Trumper doesn't think so; he's afraid there's more than we know about. How much chutney did you ruin, Elvira?'

Her whole face was working. 'Only the batch we were working on that day. That's the only time. I put it in two cauldrons.'

'Not in all four?'

'Only two.'

John said: 'Half of that batch number should be all right then.'

Sarah's breath came out in a gusty sigh. 'I suppose we should be thankful for that.'

She turned on Elvira again. 'Were there any chillies left? There must have been.'

'About half the sack.'

'Well, where is it?'

'I couldn't put it back in the store room; Trumper had given me the key but I had to give it back. I put it in the laundry cupboard. Behind the clean laundry.'

'Thank goodness for that. We'll need it. Our suppliers sent us the last they had. I won't be able to get any more for the time being.'

251

'What are you going to do?' John saw his mother's tongue moisten her lips.

Sarah roused herself; she'd been staring into space. 'Carry on with what we've started. John's going to remove any jars of that batch he can find on shop shelves. We'll have to replace every jar that's returned.'

'I meant, what are you going to do about me?' Elvira pressed. 'Because of this.'

'I don't know. I'll have to think about it. Talk to the others. It's going to be a loss for the company. I'd like to make you foot the bill for it. That would be only fair.'

'How much?' John saw his mother's nervous eyes shoot to him. 'About how much would that be?'

'How do I know? How does anybody know? We don't know the extent of the damage yet. We could lose customers . . .'

Sarah swung round on Elvira then, her anger boiling over. 'It's a horrible thing you've done. Spiteful, hateful. A sly way of getting revenge for imagined slights. The rest of us working ourselves silly to do our best, and you spike us like this. I suppose you're proud of what you've done?'

'I'm sorry, Sarah. Sorry.' John saw that his mother could no longer sit still. It wasn't just her eyebrows; her whole body seemed to be twitching. Suddenly she leapt to her feet and rushed to the door. She couldn't get away fast enough.

Maria said: 'You always had a vicious streak, Elvira.'

The door slammed violently, reverberating round the room. John heard Mam clatter down the stairs and into their own room.

Sarah sighed. 'I'd better go back to the office and phone Edward. I'll look up Trumper's address while I'm there, and if it isn't far, I'll walk round and tell him.'

'Jordan Street,' John said. 'Just past the school.'

'It'll be a weight off his mind. He thought he'd done it without realising. He thought he must be going mad or something.'

Sarah left the washing-up to get her coat. 'D'you want to come with me, Mam?'

'No, I've had enough for today. I'd like to sit here quietly by the fire.'

As he went downstairs with Sarah, John said: 'I had to let you know.'

She nodded but said nothing. He hesitated outside the door to his room.

'Shall I come with you? Would it help? I know which is Trumper's house.'

She shook her head. 'No, John, I'll find it. I'd rather go alone. Oh, God! What a mess.'

Chapter Eighteen

By bedtime, John ached with exhaustion. His mother had hardly spoken to him. He'd heated some milk for her, done his best to calm her and make his peace, but she was still shaking. When he got into bed, he couldn't sleep.

He'd thought he was doing his best for everybody by letting Sarah know straight away, but it had done nothing for his peace of mind. He'd never seen Sarah so angry. What must she think of him and Mam now?

He tried to tell himself it didn't matter what Sarah thought of him. She was Toby's wife now; it wouldn't make any difference. But it did matter to him.

He wanted to tell her how much he admired what she was doing. She was more than coping with her new tasks. To him she seemed to have grown physically. In a few short months she'd risen from trimming the shallots to holding the six of them together so that the company could keep running.

The next few days were busy. He had to do his very best to soothe their customers, and persuade them that this one bad batch was not a reason to cancel their orders.

They were fortunate that it had happened at a time when demand was high and shortages were beginning to bite. Shopkeepers needed stock to fill their shelves. John didn't think they would lose business because of this. He was so busy it was several days before he was able to talk to Sarah again.

She said: 'With all the news from France, nobody's paying much attention to this sort of thing. I'm hoping it'll soon blow over.'

'It was a terrible thing Mam did. What are you going to do about her?'

She sighed. 'I've talked to Edward about it. He thinks that when we have our meeting tomorrow, we should have her in, in front of the six of us. Tell her we won't sack her if she promises never to sabotage our efforts again.'

'That's all?'

'She's worked here for years and not blotted her copybook before. Besides, she's your mother.'

'You've lost money because of her. All those jars we've had to throw away. She thinks you'll want some recompense for that.'

She half smiled. 'You can't get blood out of a stone, John.'

He felt he had to offer. It was only fair. 'You know I've been saving for years. I've a bit put by. I could—'

'No.' She put out her hand and held on to his arm. 'No, John. That's yours, not your mother's. Your ambition money, yes?'

Her touch electrified him.

'We can't take that. You still have your ambitions.'

She knew she'd said the wrong thing there. She snatched her hand back and a pink flush ran up her cheeks. His greatest ambition had been to marry her.

She smiled shamefacedly. 'You're a much nicer person than your mother.'

Claudia had been irritable all week. That she might end up with only half of Tides Reach was grim news indeed, and she boiled over with fury every time she thought of it. Maurice really had done her down.

Adam had been very trying these last few days. She hadn't the energy to cope with him now. On top of feeling tired, she was well aware she was putting on weight in all the wrong places.

Earlier in her pregnancy, Gideon had told her he loved

her and that a little bump like hers would not be noticed by a casual observer. As time went on, he found time in his lovemaking to stroke her belly and marvel at the new life within.

But her bump was growing, and now she was afraid it was beyond the size Gideon would find beautiful. She was having to lace her corsets ever tighter to try to disguise it when she went out with him, but it was becoming almost impossible to hide. She saw no other pregnant women in the places where Gideon took her. Society did not approve of women in her condition going out and about. They should be at home resting and preparing for the birth.

Another problem was the full mourning she was supposed to wear. Black was depressing and she couldn't possibly go into fashionable restaurants dressed like a crow. It wouldn't have done at all.

Claudia took the only possible course. She smuggled a selection of her clothes down to Mama's rooms along the terrace and hung them in her wardrobe. Today she was wearing her widow's weeds as she said goodbye to Mama and Bessie at Tides Reach. She strolled down to Mama's rooms and, using her key, popped in there to change.

In the privacy of Mama's bedroom she put on her white blouse and blue skirt. She topped that with a bright blue hat and coat. The coat was straight and did the best possible job of hiding her condition. She added a little face powder and a touch of rouge, then assessed herself from every angle in Mama's looking-glass. She knew she looked her best. It made her feel so much better. Wearing black all the time was making her miserable.

Feeling elegant and fashionable again, she slipped out, avoiding Mama's landlady and hoping that no one who mattered would see her looking like this. She particularly didn't want the Burtons to hear of it. She didn't want her reputation sullied when the time came for her to marry Gideon. She thought it a small risk to take. The occupants of the five big houses on the Esplanade did not meet with those living in the terrace; they were not of the same social strata.

It was a fact that the whole district was not as smart as it had been in 1870 when the first generation of Percivals had built Tides Reach. In 1902, when the terrace was built, New Ferry was already considered to be in decline. It had failed to attract many of the moneyed class; Rock Ferry was equally easy to reach by ferry, perhaps easier since it took the boat less time to get to Liverpool from there.

Her mother still thought highly of the district and was never tired of the wonderful views and the very imposing Liverpool waterfront further down river. She spent hours watching ships going up and down, many still under sail.

Claudia looked forward to her regular meetings with Gideon. They were the only relaxation she had these days. He was always dressed up to the nines and liked to be seen in the smart restaurants in the city. She knew he enjoyed having an attractive woman on his arm. She was spending more on clothes than she'd ever done, but she didn't care. Her new hairstyle did wonders for her face; the big bun on top of her head made her look taller than her five foot five, and her plump face seemed less round and more attractive.

Today she was to meet him in the restaurant of the Adelphi Hotel, which was her favourite. Now that she was a widow, she was more daring about where she went; less careful about who might see her.

It always gave her a thrill to see Gideon waiting for her, as he was today in the foyer. A big, handsome man, almost six feet tall, he looked very sure of himself. He bent to kiss her, and Claudia felt cherished.

As an auditor he worked on the accounts of many important Liverpool firms, and mostly in their offices rather than his own. She knew his father thought he was working when he took a half-day off to see her. He was taking time off so they could both enjoy themselves.

He ushered her into the dining room. Seated now at the table, with its starched white damask and sparkling glass and silverware, she was trying to decide between the halibut and the roast beef when he said:

'You're putting it on a bit, petal dear.' His eyes indicated her abdomen.

'Can't help it. Only twelve weeks to go. I'd have been worried stiff if Maurice were still alive. Now it doesn't matter if the babe does look like you.'

'Hardly likely to. Probably has nothing to do with me.' He smiled, showing off his perfect teeth. His words made her shiver. She thought he'd accepted that as a strong possibility.

She'd told him she thought she was pregnant before she'd told Maurice. Then, he'd spoken of his undying love and his wish to make her his wife. He'd been full of regrets that she was already married to someone else. He'd thought that an insurmountable difficulty, while she'd been obsessed with ways and means by which she might remove the obstacle.

In her own mind she thought Gideon was the father. Gideon was much more dynamic in his lovemaking. Of course, she had no way of knowing for sure which of them it was.

Now that Maurice was dead, she'd expected to hear Gideon say they'd be married quite soon. After all, she was already his wife except in the eyes of the law. Once her child was born, marriage would unite the family. What could be more natural?

Suddenly his hand gripped her wrist.

'Christ! Here's Dad coming in.' His grip tightened. 'Don't turn round! I don't want him to recognise you. It wouldn't do.'

Claudia could feel every muscle in her body stiffening with tension.

'Damn it. He's seen me! Petal darling, just get up slowly and walk out. Don't turn your head, whatever you do. I'll meet you in the foyer in a couple of minutes. We'll have to go somewhere else.'

'But why? Now I'm a widow of nearly three months, what's the harm?'

'Do what I say; go on. I'll have to go over and have a word, or he'll think it strange.'

She couldn't stop herself stabbing at him: 'Not as strange as rushing out just as the waiter's coming to take our order.'

Gideon was getting to his feet, so she had to do the same, but it didn't please her. She didn't see why she needed to be hidden from his family. If she was to be his bride after the baby was born and a year of widowhood, she couldn't see why it should matter if she were introduced as Gideon's friend now. She stood fuming in the foyer until he came out.

Not wanting to upset him further, and determined to put a good face on things, she said mildly: 'Perhaps it is a little soon to come out in the open, but since we were caught like that . . . It could have been kept to your family. It isn't as if they don't already know me.'

'Better not just yet,' he said uneasily, as he took her arm and led her out to the taxi rank.

'It's almost as if you're embarrassed at being seen with me.' Claudia knew her patience was wearing thin. 'I'm a widow; the baby will automatically be attributed to Maurice. I don't understand.'

'I'm supposed to be working.'

'At one o'clock? Everybody breaks off for lunch.'

'Dad wouldn't understand.'

'Rushing me away before we've eaten? He'll understand that all right! You don't want to be seen lunching with me.'

They went straight to the hotel in Crosby and a very good lunch was set before them. But Claudia was no longer hungry, and Gideon spent a good part of the time talking to his friend the manager.

When the time came to pay for the meal, he asked: 'Do you want to go upstairs today?'

'Don't you?'

He was an enthusiastic lover and very good at it. Recently, with the baby coming, she hadn't felt so keen, but Gideon could awaken her in seconds. He'd told her many times it was the best moment of the week for him.

'Not particularly,' he said now.

'Then we won't bother,' she said shortly.

When they went out to the front steps there was no taxi, only an emaciated horse between the shafts of an old-fashioned growler.

Gideon had to wake the driver. 'Take us to the Pier Head.'

The journey was slow. It gave Claudia plenty of time to realise that her afternoon out was to be shorter than usual. If she spoke to Gideon he answered only yes or no. He was staring silently out at the Dock Road.

When the old horse stopped at the entrance to the ferries, he got out to help her down. He was always very polite and attentive in that way.

'Next Thursday as usual?' she asked.

'Could be difficult.' He wouldn't look at her now. His eyes seemed to be watching the circling seagulls. 'I'll be in touch, petal.'

After a brief peck on her cheek, he climbed back into the cab and she heard him name the offices where he was doing an audit.

Claudia held herself very erect as she walked down the ramp to the ferry. She was livid with Gideon; it felt as though he was pushing her away. Her world seemed to be falling apart. She'd had such firm plans for her future, but now they were all disintegrating.

Gideon Burton had felt himself go hot and cold as he recognised his father being shown to a table in the restaurant. He'd always known it could happen and he should have been ready to leap to his feet and pull Claudia out in the few seconds he had. Dad had chosen a chair facing him and had seen him as he sat down.

Dad's companion had attracted his attention for a moment or two, telling him something. Gideon was still wavering about what he should do when his father's icy gaze came up to meet his across the restaurant. He was afraid he could be in trouble.

But Dad might not recognise Claudia; if he didn't, Gideon would say she worked at Peet and Darwin's, whose books he was auditing at the moment. He might still get away with this. He mustn't give the impression he'd been caught out doing something he shouldn't. He crossed the restaurant to his father's table.

'Hello, Dad.'

As he'd drawn closer, he'd seen that his father's face was white with fury. Gideon was introduced to Dad's companion, a business connection, but he knew from his father's pent-up manner that he was in trouble.

He panicked then. 'Just finished,' he'd said. 'An excellent meal. I recommend the beef.'

'Come back to the office this afternoon.' His father's face had been unusually severe. 'There's something I want to talk to you about.'

When Gideon turned round to go out, he couldn't help but see that the cutlery was still in place on the table at which he'd been sitting; the glassware too, and all obviously unused. In fact, it was still early, and none of the tables had been used at that end of the restaurant.

That had been a stupid thing to say. But he'd had to give some explanation. He couldn't have sat on with Claudia and eaten a meal; not with his father's eyes on him, not after what Dad had said about Claudia.

The encounter with his father had soured the rest of the afternoon for him. How could he pretend otherwise with that hanging over him? Claudia couldn't see it.

'But I'm a widow now. What real harm does it do you to be seen lunching with me?'

Gideon had never told her about the row he'd had with his father over her. A glimpse Dad had caught of them getting into a taxi outside the Exchange Hotel had precipitated that.

'Drop any further association with that woman.' Dad had been furious. 'Taking a married woman to lunch in so public a place is bad enough. That she's married to a neighbour we have to meet socially, whom your mother receives into our home makes it impossible. Where were you taking her in that taxi?'

'To the Pier Head. I was just seeing her back to the ferry.'

'You didn't have to escort her there. You should have gone straight back to work. Is lunching with her all you do?'

'Absolutely.'

'She's never struck me as being a particularly scintillating companion. It seems to me she must be offering something in return.'

'No, Dad, nothing like that.'

'With all the young ladies we know, why do you have to choose one who's married? I have to look Maurice Percival in the eye, talk to him. I don't want to think you're bedding his wife.'

'I said I wasn't.'

'I wasn't born yesterday, Gideon. Think of the scandal if it was generally known. Think how it would affect our professional relationships.

'There'd be some companies who would not want you to audit their books. They wouldn't want a man with that sort of reputation working in their offices. We have to be above reproach.

'We can't afford any scandal. What do you think that would do to our partnership? We're professionals, above all that sort of thing. Clearly it's high time you were married. Choose a nice girl and settle down, for God's sake.'

Everything had changed since his father had said those hurtful things. Gideon had promised to stop seeing Claudia, but he hadn't kept his promise. He'd been in love with her; she was wonderful fun.

Now she was free to marry again. Well, in a year or so, when she was out of mourning. If the boot had been on the other foot, if it were he who'd been recently bereaved of his spouse, there would be no objection to his marrying immediately.

Claudia was expecting it to happen. Quite confident that now her husband had died, every obstacle had been swept away. She was always talking of their future together. Discussing her plans for it. Pressing for more commitment on his part.

She was much less fun. Always talking about the coming baby. Always telling him it was his. It couldn't be; he was always very careful about such things. She was beginning to get him down about that. Damn the baby. How did she know it wasn't Maurice's?

Gideon sighed. He hoped his father hadn't noticed she was pregnant. He would be furious if he had. Gideon knew exactly what he was going to say.

'Building up trouble for yourself and your family. Why can't you leave that woman alone?'

Claudia felt depressed. Always before when they parted, Gideon had made firm arrangements about when they'd meet next. It had been the only completely safe way while Maurice was alive.

In case Gideon found he couldn't keep an appointment, they'd fixed up a way in which he could let her know. The garden of Tides Reach rose so steeply from the river that it was possible to enter by the gate from the Esplanade and not be seen from the windows. There were retaining walls and

264

rockeries built up to make flat lawns on three levels. On a few occasions when he'd had to change the day, Gideon had left her a note under the second piece of white stone in the lower rockery. He'd written very careful notes without any names, in case the gardener or Maurice should come across them.

In the days that followed, Claudia looked under the white stone frequently, but there was never a note for her. She told herself she was being silly. Now Maurice was gone, Gideon could put a letter in the post; nobody would question that. Or even send a sealed note up with one of the boys who were to be seen hanging about the pier.

Thursday came and went. She was growing more anxious. She wondered whether she should telephone. There was one she could use in the post office in the parade of shops leading down to the ferry.

Gideon had an office in his father's firm, and there was a switchboard there, so his father needn't know. But it was catching him when he was there that was the problem; he spent so much time working in the offices of his clients.

Claudia kept telling herself all would be well. They hadn't quarrelled, though things had been a little strained between them that last afternoon. She loved Gideon. She wanted to tell him that.

She wished now she'd said yes when he asked her if she wanted the use of the bedroom. It would have meant they parted on good terms as usual. She wanted to explain that now she was six months gone, her appetite for love was not as great as it had been. She felt upset by his silence and totally out of sorts.

By Saturday evening, Claudia was very edgy. She'd been short-tempered with her mother when she'd asked her to send Bessie out to buy chocolate and bonbons. Mama had slammed out of her boudoir and shut herself into the double drawing room. She liked to sit there, and asked for fires to be lit in both fireplaces every day.

When she calmed down, Claudia took a shilling from her purse to pay for Mama's chocolate and went to apologise. She found her mother sitting bolt upright on Maurice's easy chair with the *Evening Echo* spread open across her knees.

'What's the matter?'

'You'd better see this, Claudia.' Mama's aggression had gone; she was frowning sympathetically over the top of her spectacles. Claudia knew from her face that bad news was coming.

She began to read where Mama's finger pointed. The announcement was in the column for forthcoming marriages; it was headed: 'Mr G. R. Burton and Miss S. G. Braithwaite'. It made her draw in her breath with a sharp rasp.

> The engagement is announced between Gideon, only son of Mr and Mrs Benjamin Burton of The Esplanade, New Ferry, and Sophie Grace, younger daughter of Mr and Mrs Arnold Braithwaite of Rock Ferry.

She stared at it in disbelief. He'd spoken so often of marrying her! He'd promised undying love. He'd even talked of moving into Tides Reach when they were married. Or was it she who had suggested that? The room seemed to be eddying round her. Everything was going black. She heard Mama call out in alarm and knew she was falling.

Claudia's head was thumping and she felt sick. Bessie and Ena were half carrying her to her bedroom. They helped her undress and get into bed. She couldn't stop the tears rolling down her cheeks. She'd hurt herself when she'd fallen, all down her left side. Bessie was looking for grazes but there was little to be seen.

'You'll be covered in bruises by tomorrow, I dare say,' she told Claudia. 'You rest now, I'm going to fetch the doctor.'

Oh, God! It was Gideon she wanted. What could a doctor do for a breaking heart?

266

'No need, I'll be all right.'

'For your mother too. She tried to stop you falling and she's in pain; twisted her back. Better if he comes to you both straight away.'

As the door closed behind Bessie, Claudia felt a rush of resentment and anger that left her shaking. Gideon had betrayed her trust. He'd deceived her. She'd loved him and thought him an honourable gentleman, but he'd turned out to be two-faced, a sly and cunning Judas.

She tried to turn over and hide her face in the pillow but found it hurt her too much. She couldn't think of the future. She didn't have a future now. She was totally humiliated.

For three years she'd let Gideon make love to her. She'd wanted this child to be his. They'd both spoken of it as though it was, and yet he'd turned his back on her. Now she was nearly seven months gone, he no longer found her attractive. Claudia didn't feel attractive. Her face was puffy with crying and her body hopelessly misshapen.

Now she hated and loathed the thought of carrying Gideon's child within her. She was willing it to be Maurice's. Gideon wanted to marry someone else. Every time she thought of that it was like a stab in the back. She felt herself bristle with anger that he'd dared to treat her in this fashion. He hadn't even had the guts to tell her to her face. It wasn't love he'd felt for her; it had been lust, he'd just been using her.

He'd wanted what all men wanted: sex. She'd given it regularly and received very little in return. A few lunches, the odd day out. He considered her good enough for that, but not good enough to marry. Disappointment was a physical weight on her shoulders and nothing could stop the tears coming.

Rest in bed was what the doctor ordered, for both her and Mama. He didn't ask what had caused her to faint and she couldn't have told him if he had. He was Gideon's doctor too. He recommended she spend her mornings in bed for the remainder of her pregnancy.

With the door of her bedroom shut, all domestic sounds

were muted. She thought she wanted to be left alone to grieve, but it was a very miserable time.

Gideon made no effort to contact her. She understood now why he didn't. She didn't want to think of him, but it was impossible to get him out of her mind. She'd loved him once, truly loved him, and thought him an attractive and honourable man. Now that love was turning to hate.

For the last two months of her pregnancy, Claudia spent the mornings lying in her bed brooding on the wrong done to her. She'd never felt so cut off from life. She bottled up her fury until it began to ferment within her. Gideon had ruined her life; if it hadn't been for him, she'd have been content with Maurice.

Chapter Nineteen

It was mid November when Sarah received Toby's first letter from France. He'd written:

> We sailed from Southampton to Le Havre on an old paddle steamer, the *Daffodil*. We all whooped for joy when we saw it. It was like seeing an old friend and must be a lucky omen. There was quite an argument as to whether it belonged to Wallasey Ferries or Birkenhead Ferries. I put them all straight about the Wallasey boats having white funnels with black tops, while the Birkenhead boats have red funnels with black tops. I saw *Daffodil* almost daily on the Mersey. It ran between Seacombe, New Brighton and Liverpool Pier Head, until it was replaced by a new boat also called the *Daffodil*. Wallasey Ferries must have sold it on, or perhaps the army commandeered it.
>
> It tossed like a cork in the Channel. I tried to imagine I was back home and crossing the Mersey instead of the Channel, but couldn't. Many of us were sea-sick, though I wasn't. When we arrived at Le Havre, we marched through the town to the railway station where we were packed like sardines into ancient railway carriages.
>
> We expected to be on our way immediately but the train didn't pull out of the station for six more hours. We were all fed up with waiting and of course we all got out again and walked up and down the platform. Those who'd been sea-sick were now starving hungry

and wanted to go back into town to buy something to eat. Corporals were ordered to man every exit from the station to stop them going. It seemed we had to wait for coal before the engine could move, and even when it set off, it kept stopping. A very uncomfortable journey.

We're now billeted in a village behind the lines. It's been shelled to bits, everything's in ruins. Half the roof has been blown off the barn we're in and it's raining hard.

We've each been issued with a mackintosh cape to keep us dry in wet weather. It's wonderfully efficient at that and it doubles as a ground sheet now that we don't have proper beds. Also, it fastens to become a body bag.

We can hear a terrible bombardment going on. The front line isn't far away. We can feel the ground trembling. In this wilderness of mud, wire and rubble, I think of you, Sarah; you bring me a sense of calm.

When Sarah wrote back, she asked him what a body bag was. In a short time she had his reply:

When I wrote that, I was afraid I was saying too much and stopped. Since you ask, a body bag is in lieu of a coffin for those unfortunate enough to need it.

Sarah was gagging when she read that. It was a horrible thought. She wrote back:

France in wartime sounds absolutely horrible but I don't want to be kept in ignorance of what it's really like. Don't hold back, I want to know every single thing.

It brings you closer to me, makes me feel I'm almost there with you. If I don't know exactly what you're doing and thinking, it feels as though a door has been shut in my face, keeping me away from you.

Sarah wrote to Toby daily and regularly received long letters in return.

November 25th, 1914

My beloved Sarah,

Your letters bring you close to me, and the longing to be with you is like a dull ache that never goes away. It comforts me to know you want to feel close to me. I do hope you are keeping well and not becoming too tired. I fear you could be doing too much with the baby on the way. We'll make a pact. You must tell me frankly exactly what you're feeling, how you and the business are faring, what Edward is doing . . . You seem to live in a different world now. Are you keeping well?

In return, I shall do my best to recount every daily incident. I'm afraid you may not like some of it.

We're still in the village behind the lines. It's the rest camp for those serving in the front lines. No proper beds, though; we were sleeping on the hard ground but a load of hay has been delivered. It's feed for the horses but we slept on it last night. Sleeping in hay seemed romantic until I tried it. It's warm and comfortable but full of creeping insects, beetles and flies and things, I could hear them scratching and moving around in it. I do believe the horses are cared for better than we are. Even though there's more motors being used nowadays.

My comrades are all eager to know what the trenches are really like. I told them I had a pretty good idea, having dug a few replicas for training purposes.

'Don't kid yourself,' Clemmo tells me. 'Those you dug in Bebington are as much like the real thing as a doll's house is like a mansion.'

We've just had a talk from our sergeant. His name is Lockyear and I think I can get on with him. He doesn't pick on me like you-know-who. He's taking us into the trenches and up to the front line tomorrow. It's just so we'll see what they're like; we won't be staying to fight just yet. It's to get us acclimatised.

November 26th

We're all feeling very subdued. A terrible thing happened. The sergeant led us through the trenches, all of us paddling knee deep in liquid mud and slithering on loose duck boards; all of us horrified at the awfulness. It was a thousand times worse than anything I'd imagined.

He'd just given us a pep talk about being careful to keep our heads down when Chalky White copped it. A sniper got him. Chalky was a mate, one of the best. He's been with me and Clemmo from the beginning. He was up at the front of the column with the sergeant, standing right next to him at the time. I can't wait to have a go back at the Jerries. With my marksman badge, I can be a sniper. I'm going to apply to do that.

Our tour carried on. We passed poor Chalky lying dead against the side of the trench with his tin hat askew and a bullet hole in his head. He looked in danger of sliding right down into the muddy water.

The men on duty were detailed to see to him. They all looked dreadful; wet, mud-covered, bedraggled and unshaven. Not in proper uniform, all sorts of scarves and coats added in an attempt to keep themselves dry and warm.

The Jerries were shelling our trenches. The noise hurts our ears and if one drops nearby a hail of stones and soil rains down on us. Once we had a tidal wave of muddy water.

It brought home to us with the kick of a mule what serving in the trenches would be like. Chalky is the first in our unit to cop it. It's cast a real blight on everything. Every bad word I've heard about the trenches is true.

Today I've been working in a repair party. It's a never-ending job repairing the sides of the trenches and keeping the duck boards in position. Mostly we can't see them but they provide a firm bottom under several inches of mud. Yesterday we worked on the tangle of barbed wire in no man's land. Putting more and more coils out to prevent the Germans getting close enough to lob Mills bombs into our trenches. These are egg-shaped bombs that weigh about a pound and a half.

Then there's the never-ending supply of food and ammunition needed in the front line, and we in the support trenches have to carry it all up and bring the injured back. We none of us like to be detailed for these jobs, much preferring to stand on the fire step to man the big guns.

On some days, and certainly when we are at the front, we are kept busy all our waking hours. I can't find the time or energy to write to you.

On others, especially on our rest days, I have plenty of time and can indulge my writing habit to the hilt. So I shall in future keep a sort of diary and send it home to you every few days. You will still know what's happening to me but will not receive a letter every day. I'm sorry about this.

Today, having had a good wash and a rest, I shall be playing in a football match this afternoon, and there's a concert party to watch tonight. I suppose I quite enjoy my rest days, being with the lads, but I'd much rather be home with you.

November 30th

I now see that we are working on a rota. We spend four days in the front line, then four days in support trenches two hundred yards behind, followed by four days' rest in our shelled French village. Today we've moved into the support trenches and our orders are to hold them at all costs. We're also told to hold ourselves in readiness to move forward if need be.

While we're in the trenches, we sleep in dug-outs. These are holes dug down in the side of the trench nearest to the enemy. There are steps going down; some are as deep as twenty feet. We all thought the deeper the better, it made it safer, they'd be shellproof, but we've just had to dig out three of our unit because the roof collapsed on them. All three were suffocated by the time we'd dug down to them, and there were a dozen of us all scooping back the muddy earth as fast as we could go. We used anything we could grab; a few had spades, but the rest used their entrenching tools or tin hats, and others were digging with their bare hands.

I'm truly sickened by that. We all are. They were lads we knew and worked with. A bloody awful accident. I'm truly amazed when I remember how we flocked in droves to volunteer for this. We hear they are still doing it but there are fewer of them now. It surprises me that anybody does, because we are all writing home about how awful it is. We are told that conscription may soon be necessary.

Our dug-outs are pitch-black holes and very damp. We have only candles to light them and they blow out in the blast if a shell should burst nearby. Horrible places, but I still feel safer in mine than up in the trench itself.

I haven't mentioned rats before. To be honest, they make me feel a bit squeamish. We found signs of them in the factory a couple of years ago. You might remember, though Father said we must keep it quiet, not admit we'd seen any signs of rat infestation in case it got to the ears of our customers and put them off buying.

We waged what Father described as ALL-OUT WAR on our rats and finally got rid of them. But nothing gets rid of them here in the trenches. They get everywhere. One got in my kit bag when I left it in my dug-out. We all bring extra layers to put on at night when it gets cold. It ate the bone buttons off that camel cardigan I bought in Lewis's when we were on our honeymoon. Would you believe that?

We got it, though. Clemmo threw his boot at it and stunned it. I finished it off. We shoot at them and bayonet them and do our best to rid ourselves of the scourge. They eat the dead if we don't get them out quickly enough. We can hear them turning over the empty bully beef tins after our meals as they look for scraps left inside; scuttling through our newspapers, slithering on duck boards. We're all afraid they'll attack us, the living, if they can find nothing else. My unit has umpteen stories about rats walking over them when they lie down to rest, about being bitten as well.

But even worse are the lice. Yes, body lice. I was disgusted the first time I saw Dan Purdy, one of the men who shares my dug-out, take off his shirt and kill the lice he found between his thumbnails.

'Haven't you seen them yet?' He held one out on his hand to show me, grey and crab-like and an eighth of an inch long.

'Revolting,' he said. 'To think they're sucking your blood and biting you.'

I pulled a face, repulsed.

'Don't you itch?' he asked.

Oh, God! Yes, I did, all the time.

'Bet you've got them yourself,' he grinned.

I couldn't get my tunic and shirt off fast enough, and sure enough, I had. Loads of them, complete with eggs. We were sharing the same dug-out and all huddled together to keep warm. He showed me then how to run a lighted candle down the seams to kill the eggs. We have no chance of taking our clothes off while we're in the trenches and definitely no chance to bath or even have a decent wash. No clean clothes either. Not that there'd be much point when we're covered in so much mud. When we get our four days' rest, we can wash and get a change of underwear and we all spend hours ridding our trousers and tunics of lice.

When I first saw the village where we rest, which is about a mile from our front line, I thought it was just ruins, but here we can catch up on our sleep. We've tried to rig up showers by knocking holes in the bottom of old buckets, but they don't always work as they should. When we recover a little we leg it to the nearest town. The café bars are open for business surprisingly close to the trenches.

December 13th

We are in the support trenches again. I don't have time to write when I'm in the front line. I'm now designated as a marksman, and spend my time on the look-out for something to snipe at. Today, I think I shot a German major while he was inspecting their front line. I don't know whether I should be proud or ashamed of this. The enemy front line is only fifty yards away from our front line; we can hear them talking.

I think of you all the time and hope you're keeping well. I'm not too bad but have a cold; I doubt if you'd find any in the unit who hasn't and many are worse than I am. I'm sure the enemy must hear us coughing. We're all at it, from one end of the line to the other. Diarrhoea is rife too, and trench foot. This is caused when water comes over the top of our boots and having to wear the same wet socks and boots for eight days and nights at a stretch. They give us whale oil to rub into our feet to prevent it, but it doesn't always. Nobby Clark, another friend I've been with all along, has gone off to hospital with a dose of trench foot. Many of us have ringworm and scabies too.

The trenches are not the healthiest place to be, and of course we're being shot at and shelled more or less continuously.

Don't let all this worry you, Sarah. I have to unburden myself somewhere. I'm taking good care of myself. My head is always the lowest, barely an inch above the mud, and I use double whale oil.

Sarah was very anxious about Toby's safety now he was in France. The long lists in the newspapers of those killed and injured terrified her. She lived for his letters. There was one in the post this morning. She relaxed, seeing it as proof that he was still alive.

Another thought hammered in her head. Toby had been alive when he'd written it. In the days it had taken to be delivered, anything could have happened. She dared not let herself think of that. She tore open the envelope.

I must tell you about this. Last night we were in the support trenches, and Nobby Clark and I were detailed to be ration carriers – that means we have to carry the rations up the trenches to the front line.

Yes, Nobby was back. Trench foot only brings a few days out. Each of us is given a huge backpack to carry up. Mine was tinned corned beef, our bully beef. Our menus never vary much; supper was soup followed by bully beef on dog biscuits.

It was Nobby's lot to carry up one of the soup containers. They're huge metal tubs, supposed to be like thermos flasks and keep food hot, but they don't do a good job. Stews and soups are usually lukewarm by the time they get up to the front line.

The ration cart is pulled up from the rest centre in

the village by a tired old horse. We were unloading the food when we realised there was a sniper trying to pick us off. The driver got a bullet in his shoulder.

We could hear more bullets pinging round us and we all rushed to put the lights out, see to the driver and get under cover. In the scrabble, I felt a kick against my back that sent me sprawling.

By then we were all flat on the ground and ripping off the rags we tie round our rifles to keep them free of clogging mud. We let this sniper have it, I can tell you. Blasted him out of the shell hole in which he'd taken cover. I could hear somebody moaning close to me and went cold when I realised it was Nobby.

'I've been hit,' he moaned. 'I'm bleeding badly.'

'Where from?'

He was panic-stricken. 'Dunno, my back somewhere. It's pouring out of an artery or something.'

'Where's the pain?'

'All over, my legs, my bum, everywhere.'

I was trying to release him from the tub of soup. He'd still got his arms through the straps that held it to his back. It was leek and potato, and for once it smelled delicious. It was spreading in pools everywhere. His uniform was soaked in it and it had run thickly down into his boots.

I had his trousers stripped off in no time. There was no sign of blood, just dun-coloured soup. I started to laugh.

'It must be the soup you can feel trickling down your legs. You're not bleeding at all.'

'But it hurts.'

For once it was hot – well, hotter than you'd want poured down your back. We were all of us rolling about laughing by then. Even more when I took off my pack and found a bullet had gone clear through one tin of bully beef and lodged itself in another.

'Blooming lucky, both of you,' the rest guffawed. Nobby bore the brunt of the jokes until it was found he'd been scalded. We were all envious when his scalds earned him twelve days in rest camp.

I got nothing out of it but a good laugh. What a joke, eh?

Those in the front line were not amused. Their supper was much reduced, and what there was was very late that night.

Christmas Day

Happy Christmas to you, darling. I wish I could be with you at this time. I'm on rest behind the lines today. The Jerries have said they'll hold a truce, but those in the front lines have had to stay in case they don't mean it.

I've had my first bath since coming to France. We found a big wine cask that had been cut in half, and filled it with hot water. I wasn't the first to bath in the water, nor the last, and it was a very public occasion, but it was a wonderful Christmas present. We were given fresh underwear too, so I feel really clean for once.

We had turkey for dinner, Christmas pudding and a tot of rum. The food is better when we're on rest in the village. Although all food is prepared here, it's lukewarm or downright cold by the time it's carried up the trenches.

We get bread here too, but in the trenches it's all biscuits. Ship's biscuits. I believe they were designed for use on deep-sea cargo ships. They look like big cream crackers about four inches square and very thick, but they're as hard as nails; the nearest thing to a dog biscuit a human could be asked to eat.

In the trenches, we usually have a slice of bacon on our dog biscuit for breakfast. For dinner, we get bully beef stew with our dog biscuits, and at tea time there's jam to put on them.

There's plenty of tea, but in the trenches it's cold and tastes of chloride of lime with which the water is sterilised. Now that the weather's turned cold, and it's really bitter, they add a tot of rum to our morning tea. It covers the taste of chloride and I think gives us a little false courage for when we're ordered over the top.

Sarah was filled with horror at the accounts Toby was sending home. She didn't tell him so because she was hungry to know every detail of his life, however horrible. It filled her with a raw need to have him safely back with her.

Chapter Twenty

January 1915

Claudia went into the hall at Tides Reach to see if the post had come. Bessie had already picked it up from the mat and put it on the hall table. She paused to run her finger along the edge of the table to check for dust. Bessie was often lazy about dusting.

She could hear Bessie gossiping to Ena in the kitchen, wasting time. Was that the name Burton that she heard? Was Ena discussing Gideon? Claudia moved closer, straining her ears.

'Kate says he has fourteen dressing gowns, a whole wardrobe full, and a most gorgeous pair of slippers.'

'Only one?' she heard Bessie ask sarcastically.

'No, silly, he has lots of slippers too. They aren't like us, Bessie, with only one of everything. There's one lovely pair in scarlet satin with toes that curl right up, like an Arab's slippers.'

Claudia had heard enough. Gideon had everything, and not just material things. How unfair life was. She'd always had to fight for what she wanted. Nothing had ever been handed to her on a plate.

Here she was, about to give birth to Gideon's child. After they'd talked about marriage for three years, after he'd promised it, he'd dropped her like a stone.

While Gideon was amusing himself with a new love and looking forward to an early wedding, Claudia was having the dullest of times. She hadn't felt well for some time. Her health was bound to suffer after such a wounding blow.

Gideon was enjoying himself while she was left to fret on her own, at home.

She wished there was some way in which she could redress the balance. She wanted to make him suffer too. She spent hours thinking of the worst possible fate that could befall him. She dreamed of finding some way to ruin the Burton accountancy practice and make his family penniless; of hurting him as he'd hurt her.

The neighbours who had formed her social circle no longer came near because she and Mama were considered to be in deep mourning. She'd not been close to any of them, but they'd come to her At Homes and she'd gone to theirs. Now, though, society thought it improper for her to visit her neighbours to take tea and talk to them. It would be considered a mark of disrespect to her late husband if she could forget him so easily.

She and Mama had always enjoyed going round the big Liverpool shops and adding to their wardrobe. But now, in the last stages of pregnancy, it wasn't done to be seen in the smart shops. Neither could she buy clothes she'd enjoy wearing, and anyway, she tired very quickly these days. Even Mama didn't want to go far from home; too much walking made her back ache.

Claudia missed her little outings. It made her feel cut off from life itself. Sometimes Mama persuaded her to play the piano, but mostly she sat and brooded, feeling a terrible urge to make Gideon suffer as she was. To think of him tossing her aside in order to marry someone else was more than she could stomach.

Today was her At Home day. The visiting cards came, delivered by servants. Bessie put them on her salver. Occasionally she received a note from one of her acquaintances. Today, there was one from Mrs Burton: 'So sorry to hear you have not been well. I do hope that you soon feel better.' What comfort could she possibly gain from that?

Going to church was almost the only outing thought to

be socially acceptable for the recently bereaved. It had been Claudia's duty to go with Maurice; now she was going just as frequently without him. It was somewhere to take Adam and Mama. She saw her neighbours there; they nodded sympathetically and wished her well. The vicar clasped her hand and tried to say a few uplifting words.

Occasionally Claudia saw Gideon there, following a few steps behind his mother. When Mrs Burton stopped to talk to her, he'd pause too, and give a formal bow before moving on.

Claudia found it took real effort not to turn on him and let everybody know exactly the sort of person he was. She'd have loved to tell the whole congregation that the child she carried was his.

But she also knew that anything like that might rebound on her. She'd be the one ostracised. None of the ladies would come to her At Homes ever again and she wouldn't be welcome at theirs. Gideon would probably move out of the district when he married, where his neighbours would be none the wiser.

Instead Claudia held her head high and looked down her nose at him. She was thankful now that he'd made such a secret of their affair. At least nobody else was aware of the humiliation she was suffering.

This morning she had another shock. The banns of his wedding were read out. She'd known he was going to be married but she hadn't expected it to be this soon. She felt the blood rush into her cheeks and kept her eyes on the polished woodwork of the pew in front. Mama felt for her hand and squeezed it.

Claudia spent much of the service speculating on Sophie Braithwaite, his bride. She couldn't put a face to her, but the name alone conjured up terrible envy in Claudia. It would serve Gideon right if she were to write to her telling her a few facts about her husband-to-be.

Claudia struggled to recover herself before the service was over. To her relief, Gideon wasn't in church this morning, but his mother was. Outside in the morning sunshine, the other local ladies gathered in a group round Mrs Burton. Claudia could not avoid them.

'I'm so pleased to see you looking better, Mrs Digby,' Mrs Burton said. 'You too, Claudia.'

She'd called her Claudia since she was a child and used to visit Beechwood House to play with her daughter Elizabeth.

Claudia asked after Elizabeth now. She'd married a missionary and had gone with him to Africa before the war. Because Germany was blockading British shipping, she was now unable to return. Even her letters were infrequent. Usually Mrs Burton lamented at length about Elizabeth's predicament, but this morning she had other things on her mind.

'So busy with all the wedding arrangements. Such an exciting time for us. What a pity, my dears, that we won't be able to enjoy your company at the event.'

Not wanting to arouse suspicions in his mother about her real feelings, Claudia murmured: 'We send Gideon every good wish for his future.'

'Yes, we wish him every happiness,' Honoria added before Claudia pulled her away.

Claudia's wounded pride made her stalk along the pavement at such a speed that she had Mama pleading with her to slow down.

It was only when they were alone in her boudoir, with the door firmly closed, that Claudia sounded off about Gideon. It wouldn't do for Bessie to hear her; the last thing she wanted was for the servants to know.

Now that the banns had been called in church for the first time, the servants were gossiping. Ena, who was friendly with the Burtons' maid Kate, told Claudia that the bride was eighteen years old and the daughter of one of Mr Burton's partners. That didn't make her feel any better. An eighteen-year-old! Claudia felt heavy, ungainly and old. She didn't want him to compare her to a slim young girl.

She'd spent long hours during sleepless nights trying to

think of some way to hurt him. Something that would let him know how she felt.

'I'd like to send them a bomb as a wedding present,' she stormed to Mama. 'Nothing is too bad for him.'

'No need to send him any present.' Mama poured herself a glass of sherry to fend off the pangs of hunger during the half-hour before her Sunday lunch. 'We haven't been invited.'

Claudia breathed vengefully: 'I just wish conscription would come in so he has to go and fight in the trenches.'

Mama said: 'You'd do better to forget about Gideon Burton and start thinking about the baby. It'll be here soon.'

Claudia clucked with irritation. 'Oh, Mama, I can't be bothered with babies just now.'

'My poor dear, you're very upset. Very lacklustre at the moment. It's a good job I'm here to see to things for you. The last months are always trying. You'll feel better when the baby comes. I'll book the nurse to stay for a month. It's high time that was done.'

Claudia felt exhausted; she decided to leave all the arrangements to her mother. Mama might as well make herself useful since she was here.

At Sunday supper, Edward was ruffled when his stepmother said: 'I want you to bring the accounts home. If you bring them every Saturday, I'll be able to look through them.'

Claudia hadn't been near the factory for months. He'd thought she'd given up the idea of involving herself in the business; that the humiliation Mrs Digby had caused, and the tough line he'd taken over that, had solved the problem for good.

'I need to know what's going on there.'

Edward retorted: 'Nothing's going on that shouldn't.'

'I know that, but I have a right to know exactly what you're making and selling. I depend on it for my living too. Anyway, your father used to bring the books home.'

'Take them,' Sarah advised on Monday morning when he

told her. 'As long as you bring them back so we can work on them. No point in making an enemy of her.'

'For me – and Toby – she has always been that.' He sighed. 'And her mother's a real pain. They both have a go at me at home. I don't like living with them, but it's my home too. I'm not going to move out, though it's what they'd like. Sometimes I feel they're driving me out.'

'No, Edward, she wouldn't do that.'

'I won't let her. Look, Toby wanted you to live with us. Why don't you and your mother come now? It would equal things up a bit if you did. Be better for us all.'

'I don't feel I have a right . . .'

'Nonsense, you have exactly the same right as Stepmother. You both married into the family. We could divide the house, make two separate parts if you want.'

'I'll think about it.'

As Sarah saw it, she was battling with the business and pregnancy and spending a lot of time writing to Toby; she felt she couldn't cope with anything more. Moving to Tides Reach seemed a big and daring step to take.

In January, Edward reported great activity at home.

'One of the spare bedrooms is being turned out. The carpets are being removed, and much of the furniture, to make it hygienic. Stepmother is going to give birth there.'

'How is she?'

'Very near her time and getting more short-tempered by the minute. There's a nurse coming; it'll be like living in a nursing home. I shall be glad when it's over.'

'Then it will be my turn.'

'You won't get short-tempered.'

'I might,' Sarah said. 'Perhaps that's what happens to us all.'

Claudia had spent a lot of time weaving vengeful fantasies during the last months of her pregnancy. Why should Gideon get off scot-free?

Late one afternoon, Bessie came to her boudoir to say that Bert the gardener wanted a word with her. Claudia hauled herself to her feet and went to the scullery to speak to him. His boots were making muddy footprints on the floor.

'We has moles in the garden, missis.'

Claudia didn't take much interest in the garden; that had been Maurices's hobby. 'Do moles matter?'

'Yes, missis. Spoil the lawn, they do, and they're in the rose beds. If you come, I'll show you.'

Claudia looked out across the wet garden and shivered. She didn't want to go out in this downpour.

'Mole hills coming up all over. We got to do something, missis.'

'What do you want to do?'

'Poison will finish them off. We needs to get some.'

Claudia remembered then, and was about to tell him there was arsenic in the garden shed that had been bought for just this purpose.

Suddenly she froze. Arsenic would poison people as well as moles. Hadn't she toyed with the idea of administering it to Maurice? Her heart was thumping loud enough for Bert to hear. Dare she?

He said: 'Arsenic. That's what's needed.'

She couldn't think, not with the gardener's prominent eyes staring into hers.

'Arsenic? But that's terribly poisonous, isn't it? My son . . . and the cat.'

'I puts the poison underground, missis, in the runs that the moles make. The little boy won't be able to get at it. Or the cat.'

Claudia needed time. 'Is there no other way to deal with moles?'

'Traps. Poison and traps. It takes both sometimes. We got the traps, I found them in the shed. I set them up all last week and caught nothing. We needs the poison.'

'Where do we get it?' She knew well enough; the name of

a chemist had been printed on the packet she'd hidden. A chemist's shop in Liverpool.

'We has to order it from the chemist and sign his book. The book for poisons, like.'

'I'll think about it, Bert. I'll have a word with Edward.' She had to get rid of him.

'They's throwing up soil all over the lawn, and in this weather it's turning to mud.'

Bert tightened the sack he wore round his shoulders to keep dry and turned to go.

Claudia went back to her boudoir, feeling dazed. She'd keyed herself up to poison Maurice and it hadn't been necessary. Why hadn't she thought of doing the same to Gideon?

Over afternoon tea, Mama kept up a flow of chatter as relentless as the rain outside. Claudia switched off from it, and thought through what she might do.

The first thing was that there was a vast difference between thinking of ways of taking revenge and actually carrying it out. To fantasise about hurting Gideon had buoyed her up. It had given her a fillip to think of him suffering, but did she really want to go ahead? She'd been relieved when she found she didn't need to poison Maurice.

She helped herself to another biscuit and decided that this time she definitely did want to go ahead. It hadn't bothered Gideon that he was hurting her, even though the child she was carrying could be his. He deserved all he got. She smiled to herself at the thought of getting her own back. After what he'd done to her, poisoning didn't seem too bad a fate for him.

But what if she was caught? She didn't want to swing for him. He wasn't worth that.

Looking at the facts logically, she couldn't see why she should be suspected. Gideon had gone out of his way to keep their affair secret. She'd resented that, but now it was about to rebound on him. Nobody knew she had any but the vaguest contact with him. That fact provided safety for her.

Her mother knew, yes, but she'd keep her mouth shut. Claudia could rely on that. There was the manager of the hotel at Crosby, who'd recognise her as a frequent companion of Gideon's, but she didn't think he knew her name. Gideon always called her 'petal'.

She couldn't sit still. She paced over to the window and back to her chair. She had the arsenic. Or she had if it was still where she'd hidden it. Nobody else in the house knew it was there. Could it be traced from a chemist's poison book after four years? Probably, but she hadn't signed for it then. Maurice must have done that, and both he and the gardener who'd used it were dead.

'You're very restless, Claudia,' Mama complained.

The evening was drawing on. Bert would have gone home long since. It was dark, and everything was dripping outside, but the rain seemed to have eased off for the moment. Claudia paused beside her mother's chair.

'It's time I went in to Adam.'

These days, Bessie saw to his bath; it was no longer easy for Claudia to bend over it. She usually went to read him a story and kiss him good night when he'd been put to bed.

Mama got up from her chair. 'I'll wash my face before dinner,' she said. It was what she usually did. Often she changed her dress too. Claudia watched her until the door of her room clicked shut.

She felt jittery but knew this was a good time to check on the poison. Ena was seeing to the dinner, Bessie was with Adam in the bathroom and Edward wasn't due home for another fifteen minutes at least. She went to her room and looked for her torch. Then, throwing a cape round her shoulders, she went through the double drawing room and let herself out into the garden from the conservatory. She didn't switch her torch on until she was inside the shed, and then she guarded the beam with her hand so it wouldn't show through the window.

She had no difficulty in finding the tin in which the arsenic was hidden. It was still at the back of the shelf. Strands of filmy cobwebs showed up in the beam of light. It didn't look as though it had been disturbed since she'd put it there. Clutching it under her cape, she went back to her bedroom as quickly as she could.

She put away her cape and pushed her damp shoes out of sight under her bed. She found it hard to prise the lid off the tin, which was very rusty now, but the contents looked unchanged. Claudia thought long and hard about a new hiding place and eventually put it in her sewing table. She didn't sew and so never opened it, but neither did anybody else. Bessie polished it but would have no reason to look inside.

There was a deep central compartment lined with pink silk, large enough to store a garment in the making. She wrapped the tin in a scarf and hid it at the bottom under some remnants of cloth left from goodness knows when. Then she went to find Adam. Bessie was getting him into his nightshirt.

Claudia felt quite shaky. She had to tell herself she'd done nothing wrong yet. She read two stories to Adam and played with him for longer than usual. It calmed her down.

Over dinner with Mama and Edward, she mentioned that Bert was asking for arsenic to kill off the garden moles.

'We've had them before,' Edward told her, cutting into his lamb chop. 'There could be some left over from last time in the garden shed.'

Claudia was pleased he'd mentioned that. 'Will you have a look? They're making a mess of the lawns.'

'Right. Tomorrow, when it's light.'

He'd look and find none, and should confirmation ever be needed that the first lot had all been used up, Edward would be able to give it.

Claudia didn't see him until dinner the following night when, as she'd expected, he told her he'd failed to find arsenic in the shed.

'Could you get some more then?' she asked.

'No, I can't. You'll have to sign the poison book; I have to be twenty-one to do that.'

Claudia had expected that and was quite happy to do it herself. It would give her a chance to talk to the chemist. She needed to know exactly how much arsenic it took to kill a man. The chemist would have the knowledge she needed, but she'd have to be very careful how she asked.

She elected to take Adam to school herself the next morning, and afterwards walked up to New Chester Road to find a chemist's shop. She asked to speak to the chemist himself. He looked very professional as he came to the counter in his white coat.

'Yes, madam?'

Claudia told him about moles digging up her lawn and that her gardener had advised arsenic to deal with them.

'It's very dangerous stuff, isn't it? I understand it can kill a human being.'

'It can indeed.'

Was he looking at her queerly? She hurried to explain. 'I'm a bit nervous. I have a little boy.'

'Moles make runs underneath your garden; the arsenic needs to be put into those. Your gardener understands how to use it properly?'

'I think he's used it before.'

'I'll have to ask you to sign the poison book. So it can be traced. In case of accident, you understand.'

Claudia swallowed.

'Do keep this packet under lock and key, out of the reach of children and pets.'

'Yes.'

She made one last effort to find out what she needed to know.

'How much will it take? To kill the moles, I mean. Is there some ratio of weight to body weight?'

'Moles are quite small creatures, but it depends how many you have under your lawn.'

291

'There must be quite a lot, the hillocks they're pushing up.'

'I've given you enough for four applications,' he said gravely. 'Your gardener will know if he's used it before.'

Claudia turned and left the shop. She'd hardly expected concrete advice on the right amount for a deadly dose, but she'd got nowhere.

She went straight to the public library and looked up arsenic in a reference book. She learned that it was a violent metallic poison. A cumulative poison that could result in faintness, nausea and eventually death.

That didn't add much to what she already knew. She found a medical book on poisons and read that arsenic poisoning could be the result of repeated small doses or one large one. That was generally known too. She read on.

The most prominent symptoms were intense abdominal pain, diarrhoea and collapse. Death could occur within a few hours. The book gave clear instructions on how to treat a patient suffering from arsenic poisoning, but that was information she didn't need.

She was still none the wiser about how much constituted a dose large enough to kill. She would give Gideon all she had.

Before she went home, Claudia bought a padlock for the garden shed, and when she handed the arsenic over to Bert she gave him the padlock too, ordering him to keep the shed locked while such a dangerous poison was inside.

She said: 'Adam plays in the garden on fine days, and I don't want him to come to any harm.'

Claudia went to her bedroom to lie down, calling for a tray of tea. She would arrange for Gideon to have one big dose. Repeated small doses would be out of the question now she had so little contact with him.

Her expedition had tired her out and she was scared at what she'd done. She closed her eyes and told herself that as yet she'd committed no crime; she was just getting organised.

She could throw the poison on the fire if she changed her mind, and no one would be any the wiser.

But she wouldn't change her mind. She was not going to let any man treat her like this. She felt the risk of being caught was slight. She didn't think she'd be suspected, even if the doctors found Gideon had been poisoned with arsenic. Nobody would do that without a motive, and nobody but Mama knew she had one. That fact alone should make it safe for her.

She was a respectable widow. Even if the police should make enquiries of her, she'd be able to produce what remained of the arsenic she'd bought. The gardener would confirm he'd used the rest on the moles. She'd be in the clear. She didn't think anything could be proved against her.

Chapter Twenty-one

That night, Claudia lay in bed, thinking. She had already decided how she was going to get Gideon to swallow the poison, but she needed to work out the details and plan carefully. Midnight had long gone before she was satisfied, and then she turned over and went to sleep.

She took Adam to school again the next morning, and then went into New Ferry to buy some gift tags and pretty ribbons; she also bought a small jar of stem ginger in syrup, choosing Gideon's favourite brand, which fortunately was one that came in a screw-top jar.

Gideon had been inordinately fond of stem ginger in syrup. She'd known him buy it often when they'd been out for lunch. He'd take a jar to the hotel with him, and when he tired of lovemaking he'd spear pieces and playfully feed them to her.

He loved anything with ginger: ginger biscuits, gingerbread, marrow and ginger jam. At lunch, if ginger sponge was on the menu he always chose that. But his preference was for the stem ginger. He said he often asked the cook at Beechwood House to add a jar to his mother's weekly order. Sometimes he sent Kate, the housemaid, out to buy him some. He'd told her nobody in his family shared his passion for it. He ate it alone, usually finishing the jar at one sitting. Claudia hoped he'd finish this one.

She took her purchases straight to her own bedroom and called for a recuperative pot of tea before setting to work.

First she removed a pair of Victorian silver wine coasters from the dining room and took them to the kitchen. They'd been in the house when she came to live here. Maurice had told her they'd belonged to his family since they were new, and he much admired them. They were heavily embossed with fruit and flowers and she'd always thought them particularly ugly.

'Bessie,' she said, 'I'd like you to give these a good clean and polish. They'll be just the thing to send Mr Burton for a wedding present.'

'Very nice, ma'am. He'll like them.'

She could see from Bessie's face that she thought it odd to make a gift of something that had been about the house for years.

'They're antique.'

'Yes, ma'am.' Bessie took them to the scullery where Ena was washing up. It gave Claudia the opportunity to take a dinner plate, a knife and a draining spoon from the dresser without them seeing her do it.

She spent the rest of the morning in the privacy of her own bedroom, having turned the key in the lock. She took the packet of arsenic from her sewing table, then opened the jar of ginger and scooped all the pieces out on to the plate.

Next she tried to cut a slit in each piece and insert a few crystals of arsenic. It was a fiddly business and she found she couldn't get enough crystals inside. She jabbed bigger holes using the point of her silver scissors, and cut tiny bits from one piece to plug the holes afterwards. She was heartily sick of the task before she'd finished and was glad to get the ginger back in the jar, but she'd done a neat and careful job.

She studied the contents of the jar, swirling it slowly. Would he notice the difference? She thought the colour of the syrup seemed darker but she was more worried about the taste. Should she have gone to the factory for some root ginger to make the syrup more gingery to cover the taste of the arsenic? It was said to be bitter, but she wasn't going to try it to find out.

She took the jar along to the bathroom then, to wipe and

polish the glass to get rid of any sticky finger marks. Then she washed her hands very carefully indeed.

In her boudoir she burned the wrapper that had contained the arsenic, standing by the fire with a poker to make sure every scrap disintegrated. The tin itself she put out in the dustbin, pushing it down hard amongst the ashes of yesterday's fires.

Then she carefully packed the wine coasters into a dainty box and wrapped it in tissue paper, tying the ribbons in the prettiest bow she could manage.

She addressed a card to Mr G. Burton and Miss Braithwaite, and added the words 'With every good wish for the future. From Mrs Percival and Mrs Digby.'

Claudia was exhausted by then. She put her parcels in a small bag and left it in her bedroom. She was ready.

It was almost lunch time, and Mamma was up and dressed.

'Come and take a glass of sherry with me, Mama. I feel it will do me good.'

She tried to relax. She'd done nothing yet that she shouldn't, and what she planned to do would not be difficult. But she felt jumpy all the same, and she could feel her hands tremble slightly as they gripped her knife and fork. She had no appetite at all.

After lunch she took her bag and strolled along to Beechwood House. It was two o'clock and Mrs Burton's At Home day.

The maid called Kate let her into the hall and went to the drawing room door to announce her. With a shaking hand, Claudia lifted the jar of ginger from her bag and set it down on the ugly chiffonier alongside the silver salver where she dropped her visiting card. She'd seen Gideon take a jar of ginger from exactly that spot.

The maid was holding the drawing room door open for her. Claudia sailed in. As she'd intended, she was the first to arrive.

'Good afternoon, Mrs Burton. My mother and I wanted to give Gideon a little gift to mark his marriage.' She took the prettily wrapped package from her bag and set it on a side table.

'How kind of you. That looks interesting.'

'Just a trifle. A pair of silver wine coasters.'

'Gideon will be delighted with them, I'm sure.'

'We were so pleased to hear the banns being called. You'll be glad to have him settled, I'm sure.'

'Very glad. We've waited some time for this. Nobody could say Gideon had rushed into matrimony. A delightful girl too.'

A trolley set with tea cups and cake was being wheeled in.

'I won't stay, Mrs Burton. I shouldn't have come really, not on your At Home day. Not so soon . . .' She took out her handkerchief and dabbed at her eyes.

'It's so difficult carrying Maurice's baby now when . . . He'd so looked forward to another child, and now . . . Poor Maurice. So sudden.'

'I do hope all goes well when your time comes. It must be close.'

'Tomorrow is the exact date.' Claudia tried to smile. 'That's been a long time coming too. I'll be glad when it's over.'

'Very kind of you to go to this trouble for Gideon at such a time. He and Sophie will be very grateful.'

Claudia went home and lay on her bed again. It was done now; all she had to do was wait. Gideon was about to get his comeuppance.

She'd thought that once everything she'd planned was in place, she'd be able to relax. The opposite was true; she felt really on edge. Had she overlooked anything? Could anything go wrong?

She felt heavy with foreboding and almost sick with worry all afternoon. The time dragged. She spent a lot of it staring out at the river, watching the ferries come and go. Working out which one would bring Gideon home and wondering whether he'd pick up her jar of ginger and eat it straight away. He'd surely eat it after his dinner, if not before.

Claudia was prowling round the house, unable to sit still, when Edward came home from work. He tossed the *Evening Echo* on to the hall table. He often bought one at Pier Head to read on the ferry.

She took it to her boudoir to look at, but after a few moments tossed it aside. She saw Adam into bed and read him a story. The ritual usually soothed her; tonight it did not.

The evening dragged on. Mama came to her boudoir to drink a glass of sherry with her and pulled the newspaper on to her knee.

'I haven't read that yet.' Claudia was peeved because Mama was going to read instead of talking to her. She needed something to keep her mind off Gideon.

'Here you are then.' Mama bundled it over to her. 'I'll get my book.'

Claudia felt she had to concentrate on it after that. As she turned the page, her eye was caught by an account of the first day of a murder trial being held in St George's Hall in Liverpool.

She could feel the hairs on the back of her neck stand up. She remembered reading the preliminaries several months earlier. A young man of twenty-three was accused of murdering his parents by poisoning them. It seemed now that he'd used arsenic. Her stomach seemed to turn over as she read the journalist's comment:

In the past, arsenic was said to be the poison of choice for murderers, but these days, it is possible to isolate traces of arsenic in the body even several years after death. If poisoning is suspected, this can make it difficult for the culprit to evade justice.

Claudia could feel the sweat breaking out on her brow.

She hadn't known that! Oh, God! Even before reading this she'd been worried. Now she felt suffused with panic. She told herself over and over that there was nothing to tie her to Gideon. He'd kept their affair a secret. Nobody would know she had a motive.

Hadn't she gone down to Beechwood House and told his mother she was pleased to hear his banns being called? She got to her feet and paced the room.

'What's the matter?' Mama wanted to know, but she couldn't tell her. Safer not to.

When she sat down to dinner, she couldn't eat. She could feel her heart pounding away in her chest. Her head was swimming.

It was only afterwards, when she felt odd little pains in her back, that she realised there could be a quite different cause for her unease.

She was sure before bedtime that her time had come. She wasn't sorry; it would take her mind off what she'd done to Gideon, and she'd had more than enough of waiting.

Mama panicked when she told her, but she did all the right things. She sent Edward out to telephone for the doctor and the midwife, while Bessie was told to have plenty of boiling water ready for when it was needed.

It unnerved Claudia to see Mama suddenly galvanised into action. She ran a bath for her, then hustled her into bed in the spare room that had been cleared of carpets. A pile of bath towels had been laid out in readiness. Claudia eyed them with trepidation More reassuring were the cradle and baby clothes standing ready.

She resigned herself to the labour that was to come. At least this second time round she knew what to expect. She was relieved when the midwife arrived with her suitcase. She pushed it into the adjoining room, then rolled up her sleeves and took charge. Mama was only too glad to be sent to the drawing room to wait.

The doctor came just after midnight and told Claudia

she was doing well and that everything was proceeding normally.

'Sorry I was a long time coming,' he told her. 'I was called to an emergency close by. I thought you'd be in safe hands with Nurse Dixon. I was there longer than I expected.'

Claudia lay back, sweating. It was on the tip of her tongue to ask if he'd been called to Beechwood House. The timing would be right. Knowing Gideon as she did, she'd have expected him to eat the ginger during the evening, but she must show no sign of anticipating a crisis there. Not to the doctor. Not to anybody. Her own safety depended on it. Be careful, be careful, she warned herself.

'Nothing too worrying, I hope,' she panted.

He smiled reassuringly. 'To some patients, everything is worrying.'

Of course he couldn't tell her Gideon had been poisoned. It would breach confidentiality, wouldn't it? But if he was dead, would he not feel free to tell her that? She was itching to know more but couldn't ask. Another pain gripped her and brought her mind back.

She felt physically racked by birth pains but no less racked in her mind. Birth and death, the beginning and end of life, were the two greatest moments for everyone, and here she was involved in both at once.

It had come as an almighty shock to read that arsenic could now be recovered with ease from the body of the victim, even long after death. She'd read that article a few hours too late. She'd planned and set in motion a murder, deliberately and in cold blood. She could end up on the gallows herself.

Claudia twisted the sheets into ropes, wishing she could undo what she'd done. Yes, she hated Gideon, but she didn't want to swing for him. He could be drawing his last breath at this moment. She was filled with dread about what was going to happen next.

'Relax,' the midwife said. 'Nothing to be scared of. Everything's going well.'

Claudia truly felt she was suffering more in her mind than in her body. At two in the morning, her baby was born.

'A girl,' Nurse Dixon said enthusiastically. 'A lovely little girl.'

Claudia felt drained. She turned her face to the pillow and sighed. She'd have preferred a boy, if only to keep more of the business on her side of the family. It was just one disappointment after another. Nothing was going right for her.

'There now, you've got a little boy already, what could be nicer than to have a girl? She's very pretty. Got quite a lot of ginger hair.'

Claudia recoiled and felt every joint in her body stiffen as her new daughter was placed in her arms. She stared down at her in awe. Her hair was just the colour of Gideon's!

Thank God Maurice wasn't here to see this! He'd have been very suspicious as to whether this was his child. Even if she had got him to change his will in her favour, he might well have changed it back on the strength of this child's red hair. Perhaps it was just as well he'd died when he had. Mr Masters was going to see she wouldn't lose out entirely.

At breakfast time, Honoria came in to see her, wearing curlers in the front of her hair and a dressing gown over her nightdress.

'Such a pretty baby,' she enthused. 'Lovely.' She was joined five minutes later by Edward.

'A stepsister. Father would be pleased, a daughter at last.'

'A fine healthy baby.' The nurse held her up for Edward to see.

'She's got ginger hair,' he said in amazement. 'Not much like Father. Or any of us Percivals. Must take after your side of the family, Stepmother.'

'Indeed not,' Mrs Digby said. 'No red hair in our family.'

'Must be a throwback from somewhere,' Claudia said uneasily.

'She's lovely anyway,' Mrs Digby pronounced. 'She's to

be named Rosemary. Maurice would like that. He loved his roses.'

'Rosemary is a herb,' Claudia corrected irritably. 'Quite a different plant to the rose.'

Edward went to work and reported to Sarah that Claudia had given birth to a baby girl during the night.

'She wanted another boy,' he said. 'Then half the business would have gone to her sons. Toby and I should be pleased; we'll get a third each instead of a quarter.'

Sarah smiled. 'You should let Mr Masters know.'

'I shall,' Edward said, 'the moment he opens his office. He'll be able to settle Father's estate now.'

At mid morning Claudia was still agonising about the jar of poisoned ginger she'd delivered to Beechwood House. She told herself she might have to wait a long time before she found out what the consequences were. Nobody from Beechwood was likely to rush round to Tides Reach to let her know Gideon was dead. The nurse fussed over her, trying to cheer her up.

'It's all over now. You have a lovely new daughter. You're just tired; you had to work hard last night. Let me settle you down for a nice sleep.'

Claudia dutifully allowed her pillows to be plumped up. It was torture, not knowing what had happened. Should she send Bessie round with cards announcing Rosemary's birth?

No! Do nothing, don't mention it, not even to Mama. This was too terrible a secret to entrust even to her. Keep quiet, that was what she must do now. Sooner or later the news would come.

For goodness' sake! News like that would surely spread like wildfire. She'd no idea how long it would take from eating the ginger until Gideon began to feel ill. She'd thought of it as instantaneous, but maybe she was wrong. Perhaps for once he hadn't eaten the ginger immediately. The doctor had not said definitely that it was Gideon he'd visited. To wait and see was her only course of action.

She studied her new daughter as she slept in her arms. Hair of such an unusual colour would not go unnoticed. She was worried the Burtons might see a family resemblance in the baby's features and suspect that Claudia and Gideon had been closer than they'd first thought. Rosemary could turn out to be a danger to her.

Mama was being more helpful than usual. She offered to collect Adam from school at lunch time. Claudia would have liked to say no, let Bessie go as usual. Bessie was more likely to hear some gossip from the other maids waiting outside. But she let Mama go; nothing must be altered because of that poisoned ginger. And anyway, there were no small children at Beechwood House. Bessie would not meet their maid outside the school.

She wondered whether Edward would have heard anything by the time he came home, but she wouldn't dare ask.

Claudia managed to doze off after lunch. She was just waking up when she heard Bessie rattle the tea trolley up the passage to the drawing room to serve her mother. She pulled herself up the bed; her own tea would be coming in a moment or two. She lay listening for the tinkle of tea cups and heard the tea trolley come out to the passage again.

Then the back door slammed and she heard Ena talking to Bessie. She strained her ears to catch what she said.

'. . . poisoning at Beechwood House . . . Taken ill in the night . . . Kate . . .'

Claudia went rigid. Her heart was hammering in her chest. Ena must have been down to see Kate, the Burtons' housemaid, during the hour or so she had off after lunch.

Nurse Dixon knocked on her door. It had been ajar and now swung wide.

'Good, you've woken up, Mrs Percival. You'll feel better now you've had a nice sleep.' She was helping Bessie wheel the tea trolley to the side of Claudia's bed.

Claudia could hardly get the words out. 'What was that I heard about Beechwood House?'

Ena came to her door then, still wearing her outdoor hat and coat.

'Food poisoning, ma'am. The housemaid has been taken ill. Mr Gideon too. They had to call the doctor out in the night to them. Not far off midnight it was. He was very rude to their cook about kitchen hygiene.'

'Food poisoning?' Already Claudia felt better. 'Just the two of them?'

The nurse was pouring out her tea. 'Didn't Doctor say he'd been called out to an emergency?' Claudia waved away the plate of assorted cakes she was being offered.

Ena said: 'Yes, just the two. Apparently they both ate liver pâté last night. Finished off what had been made for lunch days earlier.'

'How are they?'

'Mr Gideon was very bad in the night, but he's a bit better now.'

Claudia took a deep breath. She was in the clear. Gideon hadn't had enough arsenic to kill him. But Kate? She could only assume Kate had helped herself to some of the ginger, and by that means had prevented Gideon having enough to do him much harm. The maid had a sly look about her; serve her right.

Claudia pulled herself together. 'I hope Gideon will be well again by his wedding day. How far off is that now?'

'Next Saturday, ma'am.' She knew well enough, but had got into the habit of letting them assume she took only a minor interest in him.

She lay back against her pillows when they'd gone and thought about it. Food poisoning! It didn't give her much confidence in the doctor, but it meant nobody would be looking for arsenic poisoning. And they were not dead. If she'd killed Gideon she'd have been scared stiff of being caught. She felt waves of relief wash over her like a tide. She had nothing to fear now. Never, ever would she do anything like that again.

But she hoped she'd made Gideon feel truly ill. She hoped he'd felt he was dying. He deserved that much for what he'd done to her.

Chapter Twenty-two

February–April 1915

John Ferry was cycling into the city. Percival's Pickles had provided him with an excellent bike with a pannier on the front to hold his briefcase and a carrier on the back to which he could strap his wooden case of samples. He found it hard to equate bowling up St James Road on a sunny day with work. This part was pure fun.

He had learned now how to sell the pickles and was thoroughly enjoying that part too. With each new order, he was gaining confidence.

He'd lost Sarah. He'd had to accept that. It helped that Toby had gone away, and time was easing his hurt. He was still seeing a good deal of her at work and was trying to think of her as a friend. But when she tossed her blonde curls back from her face and her amber eyes looked directly into his, he felt such a shaft of desire it left him breathless. Sometimes, at the meetings, it took him an age to get his answer out. They must all think him an absolute nitwit.

There had been no major dip in sales following the sabotaging of the Madras chutney. John thought they had the war to thank for that.

He would have liked to think the breach between his mother and those managing Percival's had healed, but it hadn't yet. He could feel Trumper's antagonism, and Maria was still keeping her distance. He wasn't even sure he'd got over it himself, though he'd tried hard with that too.

Elvira herself was less content than she had been with her

lot in life. She was more anxious, more nerve-racked. She'd found it difficult to hold her head up in Percival's factory after that, even though the full story had not been allowed to leak out to the work force. She was always finding fault with what John did, or even more frequently, with what he'd failed to do. She spoke frequently of finding another job, but did nothing about it. Instead, she tried to galvanise him into action.

'Look what Sarah Hoxton's done for herself,' she kept saying. 'And for her mother.'

'Good luck to them. It's no good being envious.'

'I thought you had more go about you, John. I thought you had big plans for giving us a better life.'

'Life is better,' he said. It was, if he counted the the greater satisfaction from his job.

'Not much. We're still jammed together in this one room. Eating and sleeping and everything. You do nothing with your extra wages but save them. When are you going to start?'

John had heard that a hundred times. His mother was always going on about it. There was really no reason why he couldn't set his plans in motion. His new job had taught him what he needed to know about marketing his own sauce. But somehow the inclination had left him.

'One day I'll do it,' he promised.

'One day,' she scoffed with an angry toss of her dark head.

Ever since Toby had gone, Sarah had felt she was taking care of his inheritance for him. She'd thrown herself into the work of the factory.

To start with, they'd all crowded into the office for a twice-weekly meeting to discuss what they should do next. Recently, since everything seemed to be progressing on an even keel, the meetings had been cut down to one a week, on a Wednesday afternoon. Today John Ferry had been exultant.

'I've got a huge order, from Captain Meadows, quarter-master of the King's Own Regiment. I've been working on him for a while, but I can't believe the size of it. I just hope we can fulfil it. He wants pickled onions in seven-pound jars. Can we manage that?'

They'd always packed them in one- and two-pound jars up to now.

'In theory, no reason why not,' Sarah said. 'It depends when he wants them delivered and how soon I can find suitable jars. I'll get on to it right away.'

They were steadily increasing their profit. Vegetables were becoming more expensive, but shallots not alarmingly so. So far they'd managed to increase their prices to cover higher costs. Sarah was pleased with the progress they were making and Edward was over the moon with it.

'Toby kept saying how Father needed to loosen up and try new methods. He was right, wasn't he?'

When the meeting broke up, Sarah rang the firm in St Helen's from whom they bought their jars. They told her they didn't make glass jars of that size but that they could to special order. Sarah knew that meant there'd be a delay before they'd get them.

It was Mam who suggested stone jars. Sarah rang round and discovered a local firm making them. She could have a gross delivered the next morning. She then tried to put in a bigger order for dried shallots.

The order was too big for their normal suppliers and she had to find more onions elsewhere. It took a long time on the telephone and was very wearing. Sarah had reached the stage in her pregnancy when she was beginning to feel ungainly and tire more easily.

She was also beginning to feel anxious. The days were passing without any word from Toby. More days than had passed ever before. Even Mam had commented on it.

Sarah was sitting at Maurice Percival's desk because that was the one near the telephone. She was tired but well pleased with what she and John had achieved this afternoon. She sat with her head propped on her hands.

When Mam came in, Sarah knew from her face that

something terrible had happened. Then she saw the yellow envelope in her hand. Everybody knew a telegram meant bad news these days. They all scoured the long black-bordered lists in the newspaper for the names of men they knew. Four of their ex-employees had already been killed.

Sarah froze as she stared at her name printed on the envelope. It couldn't mean . . . ? But she knew it could and lost her nerve. She leapt up from the chair and backed away from the desk. She couldn't even touch the telegram. Mam's arms went round her.

'You poor love.'

Sarah put her head down on her mother's shoulder and wept.

Mam murmured: 'Do you want me to open it? We ought to see what it says. Perhaps it's not as bad as . . .'

It was another minute before Sarah could choke out: 'Open it, Mam.' She closed her eyes and clung on harder to her mother.

She heard a little gurgle which sounded joyous. 'It's all right. Toby's been injured. Shrapnel wound to the calf of his leg.'

Sarah felt the black weight lift from her shoulders. 'He's coming home?'

'No. He's in hospital. A flesh wound, not bad enough to bring him home.'

Sarah couldn't stop the tears flowing down her cheeks then. Tears of emotional turmoil, but also tears of relief. Even if Toby wasn't coming home, it meant he'd be safe in hospital for a while.

She had a letter from Toby a few days later.

I'm in hospital, tucked up safely in bed, and you're not to worry. I'm sorry my injury isn't worse. Nothing I'd like better than to be wounded badly enough to be invalided out. It's what all of us pray for.

They expect to keep me in hospital for a few weeks, and then I'll have another week or so in a rest centre here before being sent back to my unit. I've had bits of shrapnel removed from my calf, but it's a flesh wound only and hasn't damaged the bone.

It's not even bad enough for me to be sent home to Blighty. I'd have loved a hospital in Liverpool where you could come to see me. This time I've lost out on both those and it proves I'll be all right. Nothing for you to get upset about.

Before it happened, I'd written several pages ready to send to you but I don't know what happened to them. Blasted to bits in the shelling, perhaps. Anyway, they're lost, so I have to start again from scratch.

I know I wrote about the coming baby. I want you to have it at Tides Reach. You say Stepmother had one of the spare bedrooms cleared for when she had hers. What could be better than for you to move in and have yours in the same room?

Book the same doctor and midwife for the delivery. I'd feel much happier if I could think of you there, rather than our baby being born in your rooms where there's no running water. Do not try to economise by having just a nurse. I want you to book both. I want you and our child to have the best attention.

Do say you will, Sarah. Take your mother with you, so you can be looked after. I'm sure it's what Edward would like. I had a letter from him not so long ago and he spoke of wanting you to move in there permanently.

Incidentally, I've also had a letter from Jeffrey Masters, who tells me he's distributed Father's estate. In addition to a third share of the business, I've been left Tides Reach with the proviso that it is to be considered a family home. Edward and Claudia are to have the right to live there too for the rest of their lives – should they want to.

When I finally get home from here, I shall certainly have the house divided so that we can all live there in peace. It's big enough and would quite lend itself to that. You and Edward could do it straight away if you have the time and energy.

Can't write any more now. I feel quite woozy with the painkillers they've given me and can't keep awake.

Sarah felt better now she'd heard from Toby. That he expected to make a full recovery in a few weeks was exactly what she wanted to hear. She wrote to him and asked how he'd got his wound. His reply came within a few days.

We were in the front line. The routine is that we have raiding parties. These are to keep us on our toes and stop us getting bored in between major offensives when we try to gain ground, and defending ourselves against the Jerries when they're having a big push.

We start by shelling the enemy trenches and blowing gaps in the barbed-wire tangles that cover no man's land between us. Then, just before dawn, a couple of officers, second lieutenants usually, lead a raiding party over. Everybody blackens his face with mud and puts a scarf round his head and is given a tablespoon of rum before setting out. They hurl Mills bombs into the enemy trenches. There's usually savage hand-to-hand fighting with bayonets and daggers.

The object is to bring back prisoners to be interrogated and any intelligence material such as identity discs from those slain, maps and papers. Usually the party holds the trench for the best part of an hour before falling back. Then they have to bring back our own dead and injured as well as the prisoners.

Don't let this frighten you; I'm rarely required to go over the top and do that. When I got my badge for marksmanship I didn't realise how glad I'd be of it.

As you know, I've been a designated sniper for the last few months. We crawl out an hour or so before the raid while it's still dark, and find cover at a point from where we can see into the Hun trenches. We provide cover for our own men whilst picking off any of the enemy that show themselves. The rubble of what used to be a building is good, but failing all else we use shell holes. We lie patiently in wait then, and hope to get back with the raiding party, or we might have to wait for darkness again.

On the night I was hurt, I was already back in our own trenches before all the raiding party had returned. I stood covering them from the firestep as they came. I could see Clemmo half dragging Lieutenant Copeland, who'd been injured, and getting both of them tangled up in the barbed wire. I went to give him a hand; took wire-cutters with me. We all got back safely, and guess what? For once I pleased my commanding officer. He said he was putting my name forward for the Military Medal. Clemmo's going to get one too.

Edward came into the office and perched on the corner of Sarah's desk.

'I've had a letter from Toby. He says I must persuade you to come over to Tides Reach to have your baby. How about it?'

'He's on at me too.'

'Why not? He says your rooms are up three flights of stairs and have no running water.'

'Four flights,' Sarah smiled. 'But your stepmother won't want me there.'

'She doesn't want me there either, but I'm staying. I'd like you to come, and your mother too.'

'I keep telling her.' Mam had come in from the adjoining office. 'It's the Percival family home; it'll belong to your husband one day. What better place is there to have your baby?'

'It'll be safer,' Edward pressed. 'Come over and see the place. I'll tell Stepmother you're coming to see her new baby.'

'How is she?'

'Rosemary's thriving. She's nearly six weeks old now; quite a little pudding already.'

The following night, Edward took Sarah and Maria to Tides Reach. It was a fine evening. Sarah couldn't believe how attractive the house looked from the rail of the ferry boat. Her mother exclaimed with delight when Edward pointed it out to her; long and low, nestling on the bank between high trees.

When she saw the elegance inside, Mam wouldn't hear of anything else.

'You'd be a fool not to come here. Two maids in the house to wait on you. To lie in here will give you a lovely rest.'

'Leave it to me,' Edward said.

Sarah sat in the double drawing room with Rosemary kicking in her arms. The baby was smiling up at her, looking so robust and healthy, Sarah couldn't help but look forward to the time when she'd be holding her own child like this.

Claudia's face was white and strained. Ignoring Sarah and her mother, she barked at Edward:

'Bring Sarah here? What for?'

'For the birth of her baby. Toby wants her to come. Where she lives now isn't suitable.'

'There are nursing homes and hospitals.'

'The guest room you used would be just right for Sarah. Toby's set his mind on having his child born here.'

Claudia paced to the window. 'Afterwards she'll go home?' Sarah cringed; they were talking about her as though she were not here.

'No, I don't think so. Toby thinks we should divide the house in two. Build on another bathroom.'

'Certainly not. I'll not have that. Tides Reach is my home.'

'Mine too,' Edward said. 'And Toby's. He says he talked to you about this. He wants his family to live here.'

'Well I don't. I don't want to lose half my home.'

'But you wouldn't want to live with Sarah?'

'Of course not! Why does she want to push herself in here where she's not wanted?'

'She has the same right as you, Stepmother. She's a Percival by marriage.'

Sarah could feel Claudia's glare of loathing. She cuddled Rosemary closer. The next instant, the baby was snatched from her arms.

'Come and look round,' Edward said, leading them down the hall.

Sarah said: 'Claudia's furious. I don't know whether . . .'

'Take no notice of her,' Edward said. 'She thinks of Tides Reach as her personal empire, but it belongs to us all.

'Just say the word, Sarah, and we'll find a builder to start work here right away.'

'What do we need a builder for?'

'I'm only guessing, but I reckon Stepmother will want the double drawing room, the music room and the conservatory. That's when she accepts the house will have to be split. That end would not then have a kitchen or a bathroom. They'd have to be built on.'

'We won't be sharing the bathroom? I saw two lavatories . . .'

'No. You would end up with the kitchen and dining room. The only sitting room would be the room Claudia now uses as her boudoir, which isn't very big. And Father's study, of course.'

Edward led them round the premises and pointed out the bedrooms. 'Adam would have to move to another room, but it wouldn't hurt him. We'd have four bedrooms on each side. Is it all right, if I live on your side?'

'Of course. We'll have a vast amount of space between us. The rooms seem big and airy, very gracious.'

'Let's go back and talk to Stepmother again. Get it fixed up.'

When they went back to the drawing room, Claudia looked forbidding. Mrs Digby threw herself on a chair and called for her smelling salts when Edward broached the subject of dividing the house.

'It's going to happen,' he told them firmly. 'You're out-voted on this. The rest of the family have rights too.'

'A dream house,' Mam said as she and Sarah walked back to the ferry; there were stars in her eyes. 'I can't believe it. A life of luxury for us from now on.'

Sarah's arrangements for the birth had only been in place for ten days when she woke early one morning feeling rather strange. She remembered the dull backache she'd had the night before and wondered if it had any significance. She'd thought not, because she still had six weeks to go before the baby was due.

Now she had her first pain. It was too early to get up for work, and Mam was still asleep. Sarah woke her up to tell her.

'A pain?' Mam was scrambling out of bed in an instant. 'Just one mightn't mean anything. I'll make a cup of tea and put a few things together just in case.'

Before she'd drunk her tea, Sarah had another pain. 'And I've got awful backache.'

'We ought to get up and go over to Tides Reach straight away.'

'But it's not due for another six weeks.'

'All the more reason to go. The midwife and the doctor are organised over there. We don't want your baby born here. It wouldn't do, not now.'

Mam packed a bag, worrying all the time. 'We should have gone over there before now.'

'I'm all right. I think I can get there. It's not likely to be instantaneous.' Sarah was scared but didn't want to let Mam see that she was; it would only make her worse.

'The overhead railway?' Mam suggested. 'Or shall we walk?'

Sarah decided to walk to the Pier Head. She didn't know whether they'd have to wait for a train. As it happened, it was just before the rush hour, and one passed them. They only had to stop once, when Sarah was convulsed with a pain.

It was a fine spring morning and she felt better on the ferry with the wind in her face. There were few other passengers so early, but a group of workmen were waiting at the end of New Ferry Pier to be taken back to Liverpool.

'It's no distance from here,' Mam assured her several times, which made Sarah think her mother was afraid it would prove too far. They went along the Esplanade to the front door. Sarah heard Bessie's footsteps coming to answer their knock. She looked startled to see them.

Edward came to the door of the dining room with a piece of toast in his hand.

'Our Sarah's time has come,' Mam announced. She saw the consternation that brought.

'Oh, ma'am! Shall I fetch the midwife?' Bessie wanted to know.

'No,' Edward said. 'I will. You make Sarah comfortable. There's nothing I can do here.'

'Where's Mrs Percival?' Mam asked. 'Or Mrs Digby. Had we better . . .'

'No, they're still in bed. The baby wakes in the night. She has breakfast in her room now.'

'The monthly nurse left only last week. She was kept on for two months,' Bessie lamented. 'Oh, and the room's not made up yet. I'll do that first. Oh deary me. We didn't expect you here for a few weeks.'

'I didn't expect to come just yet,' Sarah said as she doubled over in another pain.

How she wished Toby were here. It seemed so strange to be in this house without him.

Toby had been discharged from hospital, together with six other patients who were strangers to him and not from his unit. They were dispatched by ambulance to a rest centre just outside Le Havre.

They were all delighted when they saw it. It was an old French château with blue-slated turrets like those pictured in books of fairy tales. Toby was allotted a place in what had once been the stables, but he had a real bed with sheets and blankets, and he could roam freely in the grounds. He could walk on his injured leg, but not for any distance. It ached a lot and became painful if he overdid things.

He wandered round and found a little knoll from which it was possible to look out across the Channel. The weather was fine but chilly and he sat down to rest on a wooden bench, straining his eyes into the distance in search of the English coast. It was lost in mist, but he could see a ferry boat coming into the port, and even from this distance he could tell that its decks were crowded with troops and equipment.

The mail had been delayed again, four of Sarah's letters had caught up with him just before he'd been sent here. He read them in date order. The last one was dated the third of April.

Dearest Toby,

This will come as a shock to you, it was very much a shock to me. You're the father of a baby daughter. She was born at three o'clock in the afternoon of April 2nd at Tides Reach. I only went there in the morning, just in time.

It's such a thrill to be able to hold her in my arms. She weighed in at a little less than five pounds and looks a minute doll alongside Rosemary, who is so strong and big now and still gaining weight hand over fist.

Our babe has hardly any hair but what there is is fair. It's more like down than hair. Her eyes are bright blue, when they're open.

As we agreed, I've told everybody her name's to be Dinah Helen Maria Percival.

It's not all good news, I'm afraid. Because Dinah has come six and a half weeks early, she isn't very strong. She's losing weight and is already four ounces down on her birth weight, though the nurse says not to worry too much, they all lose weight after birth.

The monthly nurse who looked after Claudia and Rosemary has come back to look after us. She says I'm to feed Dinah as much and as often as she'll take it. In fact she isn't feeding well yet and she looks quite frail. She's quiet and hardly cries at all.

Nurse Dixon says it would be better if Dinah cried more. I'm so glad I've got a proper midwife. I'd be terrified looking after so tiny a baby without help. She seems a little chesty today, but she's being well looked after.

Mam's very taken with her grandchild. She says she's like you, but I can't see it. Dinah has a red crumpled face and is so very tiny. I'm almost scared to pick her up in case I hurt her.

Her birth was so sudden I left lots of jobs half done in the office. I had to explain to Edward what needed doing. He says I mustn't think I'm indispensable.

I'm very comfortable here. Unbelievably comfortable. Everything I need, and waited on hand and foot by Bessie and Ena. Edward is doing his best to persuade us not to go back to St James Street.

Mam is all for staying here and talks of giving up our rooms. She's even talked to John Ferry about it. It seems he and his mother want them if we don't. They are better than the room they have at present.

Edward thinks I'd be able to go back to work much

sooner if I stayed here where Bessie could look after Dinah as she looked after you and Edward. And I wouldn't have housework to do when I came home. It's what he wants, even if it's only for a few hours each week. I feel a bit lost without work, so it must be what I want too.

Claudia is very frosty and withdrawn. She doesn't want me to stay and Mrs Digby keeps asking when we intend to return to our rooms. She's set our date of departure for the day the monthly nurse leaves.

I've told her that if Dinah isn't strong and thriving, I shall keep the nurse on longer. I don't think I'd feel so confident about Dinah if I went back to our rooms.

Toby let Sarah's letter drift down to his knee. His need for more news was whetted. He desperately wanted to know how his baby was getting on. Because his mail would have to be redirected again, it was likely to be several days before he received any more.

He felt lonely, for although there were people all round him, he knew none of them. What he wanted was to be at home with Sarah, and he wanted more than anything else to see his new daughter. The baby had been born a little too soon and her hold on life sounded precarious. How could he rest knowing that?

He'd been sitting still for so long, the cold had made him stiff. It was on his conscience that Sarah had had to work long hours during her pregnancy. She'd said she felt fit and well, but he couldn't help but wonder if she'd worked too hard and that was why the baby had been born early.

He eased forward, and saw the ferry boat nosing out of the harbour on its way back to Southampton, its decks bare now. He craned further forward and smiled. It was the *Daffodil*, the old Wallasey ferry that had plied the River Mersey before being replaced by a new and larger boat.

Toby drifted off in a daydream. He was aboard the *Daffodil* again and it was heading not for Southampton but straight round the coast up to the Mersey estuary and then up river to the pier at New Ferry. How easy it would be to get home that way.

And what difference would it make to the army if he took his convalescence at home where his heart was, instead of here near Le Havre?

Chapter Twenty-three

May 1915

Sarah felt tightly knitted to baby Dinah. She nursed her and fussed over her, wanting to do everything she could for her instead of letting the midwife do it. She fed her herself, more often than Nurse Dixon advised, in an effort to stop the ounces falling off.

Dinah was being weighed every morning, and at last the day came when she'd gained half an ounce. Thereafter she began to put on weight slowly but steadily.

'She's beautiful,' Mam told her. She demanded a turn at nursing her. 'She's just like you were. You came early, only five weeks though. You were like a tiny doll, and now look at you.'

Sarah was pleased to see the crumpled look go as Dinah's cheeks filled out; the redness faded too.

'She's going to be spoilt with all this fussing,' Edward said, but he cooed over her as much as any of them.

'Here I am an uncle, and not yet sixteen.'

'And Rosemary is an aunt at two months of age.'

'Step-aunt,' Edward laughed. 'I wonder how they'll get on.'

To Sarah, who was giving so much of her attention to the baby, everything seemed to be happening at once. Toby had written to say that funds to alter Tides Reach should come from the business. Edward had found a builder. He'd talked of the shortage of building materials, but bricks and slates were piling up in the garden. A kitchen was being fashioned within the conservatory, thus reducing it to half its size. Claudia said it was the only convenient place for it. Two new bedrooms and a bathroom could be built in the steep roof over the music room. Claudia's half would no longer be a bungalow.

'We'll just lock some of these doors from the hall and shut that half of the house off,' Edward said.

He and Mam brought their problems home from the factory. Sarah studied the figures coming in and made up the books. Edward arranged for a telephone to be installed in their half of the house so he could talk to her without delay when he had a problem.

After a few weeks, Sarah started going over to the factory again. She never spent more than an hour or two there, but she needed to go to check their stocks. She brought work home, and found she could do quite a lot this way.

Even with such a change in her life, she still found time to write to Toby every day, but her mind dwelt on him less. His letters didn't come daily any more; she would go for a few days without one and then several would come together. She was pleased he was in hospital with a minor wound; he was much safer there. It gave her a welcome break while the death toll on the front seemed more ferocious than ever.

Today, she'd had a letter.

Dearest Sarah,

I'm hungry for news of you and the baby. I ache to be with you both. I feel so frustrated sitting about in this rest centre with so many strangers. I'd love to hop on one of the ferries I see leaving for Blighty and come home to you.

Today, I saw the doctors. My leg is healing well. They've given me two more weeks to convalesce and then I'll be well enough to go back to my unit.

I asked for permission to go home. I'm sure two weeks

with you would set me up much better for my return to the front line. They told me I hadn't served here long enough to earn home leave. I even offered to pay my own fare, but that isn't allowed. What possible difference could it make to the army?

I'm very tempted to come anyway. I could be back before my fortnight is up. I've got away with it before, haven't I? And I'm very glad I came home to marry you; it was the right thing to do. I'd have been tortured with remorse and guilt if I hadn't. Especially now baby Dinah is born.

This afternoon I shall go down to the quay and see if it's possible to get on board. Just a scout round. I'd like to say I'll see you in a day or two, but it depends on how things look.

Look after yourself and Dinah.

Lots of love from Toby.

Sarah had read the letter through three times already. Now she laid it down slowly. It was a week since he'd written that, so she supposed he hadn't found it possible. Slipping away from his unit at Bebington station was one thing; getting himself home from Le Havre quite another.

Besides, he'd been in big trouble for coming home to marry her. She'd been grateful ever after that he'd dared to do it, but now she feared for him. If he were to do it again, the army might not go on suspending his sentences.

She had a sense of waiting; of half expecting to hear from him that he was on his way home. He could telephone from any post office once he reached England. Every time somebody came to the door, she tensed and listened. If he could get home it would be absolutely wonderful. She'd love to show Dinah off to him. Love to feel his arms go round her.

All the same, she'd written back straight away and advised him against it. Each time he'd been court-martialled she'd lived in dread. Surely it must be ten times worse for him? Would it be worth that? She didn't think so.

Sarah heard the ratatat as the lunch-time mail slithered through the front door. She shot up the hall, but there wasn't a letter from Toby.

For John it had been a tiring day. This morning he'd helped Sarah and her mother move out of the two attic rooms they'd rented above his own. They'd not lived there since Sarah's baby had been born, but it had taken them some time to decide whether to return or not.

That had kept his mother on a knife edge. Elvira very much wanted to move upstairs if the Hoxtons were not coming back. And why should they? Maria was letting it be known they had splendid accommodation in the Percival house. John had already agreed that they'd move upstairs if they could.

'No point in taking this furniture,' Maria had said as she took a last look round. 'We have everything we need already there.'

His mother would be very excited when she saw how much stuff the Hoxtons had left behind. Sarah and her mother had packed up a few of their clothes and ornaments to take with them, and John had helped to carry great bundles of stuff out to the yard to be taken away by the bin men. Their neighbours had the bundles undone and were going through them within fifteen minutes.

After that, he had caught the train to Warrington to visit customers there. That had given him time to think things through.

He knew it had taken him a while to sort himself out after Sarah had turned him down, but he was now feeling better about it. His mother had kept on at him about there being more fish in the sea than ever came out. He'd tried; he'd asked a girl called Lorna who'd recently come to work at Percival's to go the pictures with him. After two evenings spent together, she found she had other things to do when he asked her again. But he knew by then that Lorna would never be able to take Sarah's place.

Sarah had brains and guts as well as looks. He could hardly believe what she'd achieved. From the beginning, everybody at Percival's had been amazed at how she'd kept the team together and the factory working. They all knew it was making more profit than it had ever done under Maurice Percival.

Sarah had told the others at one of their weekly meetings that it was largely because of the new orders John was bringing in. She always gave credit where it was due, and that had been a great pat on the back for him. It had given him new confidence, but he said:

'It's not all due to my efforts. The war has helped. Industry is booming and the forces have to be fed.'

Sarah had smiled her slow smile. 'The army's ordering vast amounts. There's another big order in today. That's definitely due to your efforts.'

'Pickles are just the thing to help tinned bully beef down. For the fighting forces, that's said to be a staple part of their diet.'

John didn't know what it was that had brought him back on track, but now suddenly his ambition was flaring up again. He was enjoying his selling job, but there were other things he wanted to do more.

He began turning things round in his mind and realised that everything he needed to make his own sauce had fallen into place. He could start up now.

If they kept on their present room, as well as renting the two rooms the Hoxtons had occupied, they'd just about have enough space to start.

He'd saved money to get married, which could now be used to set up the business. He'd learned how to sell Percival's pickles and knew he could do the same for his own sauce. He could work up a market for it. With that, the last block had fallen in place.

It was closing time when he returned to the factory. The workers were streaming out on their way home. He'd told his mother he'd be late, so he spent half an hour getting his paperwork up to date.

Sarah had told him to do that at home if he preferred, but at this time of day his mother would be preparing a meal for them, and in only one room it was difficult for him to concentrate.

When he'd put his books away, he walked slowly round the deserted factory, looking closely at everything. This was the sort of place he aimed to have himself one day. It could almost be a pattern for him. Percival's had started small, just as he and Mam were about to. Would they succeed to this extent? He felt a sudden burning determination to do even better.

His mother was frying sausages when he got home.

'The Hoxtons have moved out,' he told her.

'Sarah told me. Have you been to see the landlord?'

'Haven't had time yet. Tomorrow morning, first thing. I've got the keys. Sarah left them with me.'

'I'll go up and look round. After we've eaten.'

'How d'you feel about keeping this room on too? I've been thinking; it would give us space to start making up that sauce.'

'What a good idea,' she said, and he was left to dish up the sausage and mash while she looked out the recipe for it. He could feel a tingle of excitement as she read out the ingredients:

'Molasses, dates, onions, tomatoes, horseradish, malt vinegar, sugar and mustard.'

'Are dates really needed? We won't be able to get those now.'

'They add to the taste and colour. I suppose it could be made without. What about molasses? Is that still obtainable?'

'Occasionally. Sarah bought a new supply last month. She managed to get ten drums – how many gallons is that?'

'Sometimes we've had to use a mixture of syrup and treacle. I remember doing it.'

'We'll try our sauce made with black treacle, see how it tastes,' John smiled. 'What a help Percival's is going to be to us.'

The next day John tried to buy what he needed. Dates were unobtainable and so was molasses. His mother had suggested adding carrots, and after work they set about making up a small batch of the sauce. It had just the right colour and consistency, darker and thinner than the average brown sauce. But he was disappointed with the taste. It was rather sharp on his tongue.

'We'll need to fiddle a little with these ingredients, Mam. We have to be able to get them or we won't be able to make it in any quantity.'

They tried another batch, using parsnip instead of carrots. Another with beetroot; yet another using a mixture of vegetables. None pleased John.

'The sauce has to mature,' Elvira insisted. 'We've always kept it for a few weeks. Never eaten it straight away.'

'How long exactly?' John wanted to know. Elvira shook her head; she wasn't sure.

He made a note of the dates on which the different varieties had been made, and tasted them on dry bread every week. He thought they all mellowed with time and the flavour improved.

When his mother decided it should be ready, she made scouse with best end of neck for their Saturday dinner, and brought out a little of each of the varieties they'd made.

The carrot tasted best. It was just as piquant as John remembered the original. Quite different to anything at present on the market.

'What d'you think, Mam?'

'Definitely the carrots. Tastes like Mother's sauce. Wouldn't know the difference.' She helped herself to more.

John thought his mother seemed better since she'd had the

sauce to think about. Not so anxious and nervy. Her eyebrows still went up and down when she spoke, but not so rapidly as they had. It was a habit she had. She said:

'We'll start up, then? We'll make Mother's sauce?'

'We can't call it that. Sounds too much like Daddy's. It's not a copy of that.'

'Nothing like it.'

'Much darker, and the flavour is all its own.'

'Ferry's Sauce? Does that sound better?'

John frowned. 'I've been thinking and thinking. We need a name with more kick. Something that won't be forgotten. The best I can come up with . . . What d'you think of Scouser's Relish?'

'Scouser's Relish. Ye-es. Nobody could forget that.'

'We'll need to get some labels printed. I thought a picture of the Liverpool waterfront with a ferry tied up alongside. Mainly in blues.'

'That sounds wonderful.' He could see enthusiasm in his mother's eyes.

'I'll order some bottles and make up a few samples. Take them round my customers and see if they'll buy.'

'I'll help you. Haven't we always dreamed of doing this?'

'We'll need bigger pans once we get going. And a proper stove.'

'One day we'll be like Percival's. Copy what they've done, that's all we have to do. They've taught us the trade.'

'Even down to keeping the books,' John laughed. 'I'll buy a few cheap exercise books to start. Better keep account of what we spend on this venture from the word go.'

Claudia had assumed Bessie and Ena would automatically move to her side of the house and continue to work for her, but she hadn't exactly asked them. Sarah heard them talking it over in the kitchen as the work progressed, and sensed their reluctance.

They had their bedrooms down in the cellar. There were

330

other rooms down there that weren't being used. Claudia wanted the garden divided too, and didn't seem to think it mattered that her servants could only reach their rooms by walking through the other half of the garden.

One Saturday afternoon, Sarah went into the kitchen to get some boiled water for Dinah and found Edward sitting at the table demolishing a plate of Ena's fresh fairy cakes.

'We want a word,' Bessie said. She and Ena were standing side by side as stiff as pokers, looking very serious.

Edward bit into another cake. 'What is it?'

'We want to work for you, Mr Edward. And you and Mrs Hoxton,' she said to Sarah. 'We don't want to move over with her.'

'I've been trying to persuade Claudia to let us keep one of you. That way—'

'We don't want to be split up,' said Bessie. 'We've always been together.'

'This is my kitchen,' Ena said. 'I don't want a new stove and all that. I wouldn't be used to it.'

'She was talking of getting a nursemaid anyway,' Bessie said indignantly. 'We don't need any nursemaid here. We can do everything that's needed. Just the two of us.'

Sarah found Edward's eyes were on her. 'What d'you reckon?'

'Nothing I'd like better.' She smiled at Bessie and Ena. 'Nothing Edward would like better, if the truth was known. You're both too popular. The problem is, Claudia wants you too.'

'Can't we choose?' Ena asked. 'We've always worked for your side of the family, ever since you were a baby, Mr Edward.'

'You'd better have a word with Claudia,' Sarah told him. 'You can manage her better than I can. She takes no notice of me. I'm just a newcomer.'

'Right.' Edward pushed his chair back. 'I'll go and talk to her now.'

★   ★   ★

The alterations to Tides Reach were finished. Sarah was delighted with her new quarters. The rooms were large and comfortable and seemed very grand. Claudia was seen to be in tears. A new door had to be made into her bedroom. She had the large wardrobe moved so it hid the old one.

'I don't know what you've got to complain about,' Edward told her. 'Our only sitting room is your ex-boudoir.'

'I shall miss it very much,' she retorted. 'You have your father's study too. You aren't short of space.'

Edward made no secret of the fact that he was pleased she was now in an entirely separate part of the house.

'No need to double up here,' Sarah told her mother. 'You can have a bedroom to yourself. I'll have Dinah in with me; she'd only disturb you. Anyway, Toby will be home one day and we might as well start as we mean to go on.'

She was pleased with the progress baby Dinah was making now. At seven weeks she no longer looked frail, and she had a wavering smile for Sarah when she looked over her cot. Sarah had decided to return to more regular work. Not full time straight away; she'd give Dinah her ten o'clock feed in the morning before catching the boat over. Bessie was to give her a bottle at two, and she'd try to be home early in the afternoon.

Every day she wrote to Toby with news of Dinah. One thing that did worry her was that she had no further letters from him. There had never been such a long break before. She told herself not to worry. He'd been nowhere near the front line when he'd last written and he was expecting to be on light duties when he did return to his unit. It was just a hiccup with the post. It had to be.

The letter fell on to the doormat with the rest of the post one Monday morning when Mam and Edward had already left for work. Sarah heard it come as she was undressing Dinah to give her a bath. The house was quiet except for the occasional clatter of crocks from the kitchen.

Half an hour later, with Dinah in her arms, she picked up the post from the hall stand where Bessie had put it before taking Adam to school and sat down to read it.

Dinah was in a playful mood. Sarah laughed down at her, tore open the envelope and held the letter at arm's-length to read.

May 12th 1915

Dear Mrs Percival,
    It is my painful duty to inform you that your husband Private Tobias Percival died on service at Armentières on May 9th 1915. He was buried in Chapelle d'Armentières Old Military Cemetery on the same day.

It fluttered through her fingers to the floor. Her head felt as though it was spinning with the shock. She couldn't believe it. Didn't want to believe it. Could there be some mistake?

She picked it up and read it again. The tears came then. Hugging Dinah to her, she ran to the kitchen, where Ena was rolling out pastry.

Sarah put the letter down on top of it and collapsed on a chair. Moments later floury arms went round her.

'Such dreadful news! Master Toby gone! I've feared for him since he went to France. Whatever shall we do now?'

Ena took Dinah from Sarah's arms and guided her towards the new telephone.

'Tell your mother what's happened,' she said. 'She'll want to be here with you. I can't use those new-fangled things.'

She ran to fetch Claudia, who was white-faced but kind. Sarah had a cup of tea put into her hands. She felt numb and couldn't stop shaking. It was not until Dinah started to cry that she realised she'd forgotten all about her ten o'clock feed. Bessie came back from taking Adam to school, followed soon after by Mam and Edward.

'It happened on the ninth,' Edward said, outraged. 'And they didn't bother to write until the twelfth. I thought they sent telegrams when this happened?'

'I thought he was safe, well behind the lines in some big rest centre,' Mam said. 'How could it have happened?'

Sarah shook her head in misery. 'He'd have been there only until the seventeenth of last month. I haven't heard from him since.'

She was guilt-ridden too. Her mind had been on Dinah rather than Toby. Even on the daily minutiae of the work at the factory and of altering the house. She'd told herself that no news was good news. But if he was back with his unit, why hadn't she heard from him in all that time? Postal delays were only of a few days' duration, and Toby wrote something every day and posted his pages whenever possible.

Mam was angry. 'They pushed him back in the line too soon. They must have done. He should have been allowed to get over his injury first. Poor Toby. What a dreadful thing to happen. Everything to live for, a new daughter . . . And not yet twenty-one himself.'

Although Edward and her mother did their best to comfort her, Sarah went to lie on her bed in tears. The one tiny scrap of comfort she could find was holding Dinah's tiny fragile body against her own. She felt screwed tight inside with grief. Her loss blotted out everything.

By evening, she was looking after Dinah again and going about other duties, but doing it mechanically and without joy. Toby was filling her mind. He'd died in a foreign country, miles away from those who loved him. It seemed he'd been hastily buried. For her and the rest of his family, there was to be no funeral service and no grave she could tend. Nothing to mark his passing but that brief, awful letter.

The best thing for her, the only thing now, was to get back to work and fill her life as best she could with that. And she had Dinah.

Everybody was kind when she went back to work. Many

of the workers came to tell her how sorry they were to hear about Toby. Each time it brought a prickle of tears behind her eyes that was difficult to control. They clubbed together to buy her flowers.

John Ferry was white-faced and serious. He held her hands in his.

'I can't believe what's happened. Such dreadful news. He and I, well, we didn't always see eye to eye. But I'm sickened that he's lost his life. He was very popular with everybody. So full of life and fun. How did he die?'

Sarah shook her head in misery. 'The letter was just a bare notification. It just said he'd died on service. No details at all.'

'A letter, not a telegram?'

'Yes, that's why it was such a shock. I didn't expect such news in a letter.'

'I thought he'd been injured and was recovering in some château? That he was in a safe place.'

'He was the last time I heard from him, but that was weeks ago. I can't understand it; he must have recovered and been sent back to the front. I've no idea how it happened.'

'Perhaps one of his friends will write to you. Tell you more. Toby always made friends.'

'I can't understand why I didn't hear from him.'

She saw John's lip quiver. Then he pulled her closer and put his arms round her in a gesture of comfort. She laid her head on his shoulder for a moment and he pushed his handkerchief into her hand. Sarah blew her nose hard.

'At least he died for his country,' he said. 'You must think of that.'

'I do, and there must be thousands like me mourning their loved ones. To know they died heroes brings a tiny grain of comfort.'

As John Ferry left the office, he could feel himself shaking. He'd left Sarah sitting at Toby's desk with her tears not quite under control. He had to get out in the fresh air. Right away from her.

Toby's death had come as a shock, but of the young men who'd volunteered from Percival's factory he was the sixth to be killed in France. John wondered if he was becoming hardened by the continual death toll. It was Sarah's distress that had upset him more than anything else.

John strapped his case of samples on to his bike and set off. There was half a gale blowing off the Irish Sea and gusting up river. It was not the best morning for cycling; the strong wind was making his strength seem puny, and he felt very insecure.

He'd held Sarah in his arms for the first time in many months, the first time since she'd rejected him. He'd wanted to many times, but now he'd done it, the experience had proved bittersweet.

While he was feeling aroused by the scent of her hair and the feel of her cheek against his, she'd been experiencing very different emotions. Her mind had not been on him. His desire hadn't reached her. He'd kissed her forehead and he doubted she'd even noticed. It had been like kissing an empty shell and it had left him feeling shaken. He hoped she'd felt comforted.

Within a fortnight, Maria was taking a more down-to-earth view of Toby.

'Thank goodness he made a will. He had his head screwed on the right way when he did that. Claudia would hound us out if he hadn't. He's left you everything he owned. I can't believe you'll now own a third of Percival's pickle factory.'

'Is it that important?' Sarah's voice was flat.

'Sarah! You know it is. Look at the difference it's made to our lives. To mine as well as yours. Think of the money.'

She could hear the irritation in her daughter's voice. 'I don't care about the money. I want Toby back here with me.'

'Nothing will bring him back, love.'

'He was so young, he had everything in front of him. Too young to die.'

'He laid down his life for his country. His was an honourable death. You should be proud of him.'

'I am.'

'He did the right thing by you. He'd want you and Dinah to have a good life.'

Maria read through the long lists in the newspapers of those who'd given their lives for their country. She failed to find Toby's name in any of them.

'I should have known Toby would be killed. I should have expected it,' Sarah said listlessly. 'It's happening to thousands of others. Why should he be any different?'

Chapter Twenty-four

May–June 1915

It was Sarah's nineteenth birthday. When the postman delivered a small parcel addressed to her, she assumed it was a gift. It didn't lift her low spirits, but she opened it with pleasurable expectations. At the first glimpse of the contents she was reeling back against the sitting room wall, gasping with dismay.

These were Toby's personal belongings, the things he'd had with him in France. She stared at them from a distance of ten feet but couldn't bring herself to touch them. They were pathetically meagre and shabby: a few battered-looking books, his fountain pen and some envelopes, a pair of leather gloves and their wedding photograph. When she felt steadier, she bundled them back into their wrappings and put them out of sight at the back of a cupboard in her bedroom.

She missed Toby terribly, but she'd told herself she was over the first awful shock; that she was beginning to push that horror to the back of her mind. The parcel reawakened all her feelings of loss. Like thousands of other young men, Toby had died in battle. She wished she knew more about how it had happened.

A week later she received a letter. She saw it on the hall stand and recognised it for what it was before she opened it. It had come through the army postal service.

She left it where it was for over an hour while she got on with bathing and feeding Dinah. When she'd put the baby down to sleep, she got herself ready to leave for the factory. It was a fat envelope and she didn't recognise the writing. She didn't want to open it. For her own peace of mind, Sarah thought it better to forget what might have been. Toby was dead, and nothing could bring him back, but at the same time she hungered for details about how it had happened.

The house was quiet and peaceful; she had a few moments in hand before she had to leave for the ferry. She'd just glance at the letter before she went. She took it to the sitting room. It was a very long letter in small, cramped writing. She looked at the end first. It was signed 'Clement Blake'; she remembered Toby writing about his friend Clemmo. She sat down and started to read.

Dear Mrs Percival,
    Toby was my greatest pal. He saved my life once. He was a great marksman and one of the best. We all feel terrible about what they did to him.

Sarah paused and drew in a great jagged breath. When she felt steadier, she went on.

We heard from those on guard duty that Toby had been brought back early and was under close arrest. The news spread through the brigade in moments. We all knew Toby, we all knew how he'd been injured. If it had been one large piece of shrapnel instead of small fragments; if it had torn a jagged hole in his leg, it could have been a Blighty One and got him home for good. He was hoping for that, we all do, but he didn't get it. We all expected him to be away for at least six weeks. Nobody has ever been returned to the front in less.
    For us, the news came out of the blue. It was announced to us all on parade that he was to be court-martialled for desertion, for trying to evade capture and striking a senior officer.

Knowing Toby as we did, we guessed he'd tried to spend his convalescence back in Blighty and been caught. I was very fearful for him, knowing he was already serving under two suspended sentences.

We don't really know what happened at the court martial, the likes of us ordinary soldiers are never told. While it was going on, I had to do my turn of four days in the front line and four days in support. So did Nobby Clark, his other mate.

When we came back for our four days' rest, it was posted that he'd been found guilty on all three counts and had been sentenced to death. That really shook the whole battalion, I can tell you, but we knew his sentence would have to be reviewed by the commander of our unit, then by Brigade Headquarters, and up through Divisional Headquarters, by the Adjutant-General and finally by Sir Douglas Haig, the Commander-in-Chief. His sentence could either be confirmed or suspended by each of these.

We all waited with our hearts in our throats for the outcome of that. There was a terrible feeling of foreboding in camp. We all knew Toby. He was the sort you couldn't help but like. The sort you'd want watching your back when you had to go over the top. God only knows how he felt while he waited, but he was always optimistic. He'd have believed all would be well in the end. He always did.

The sentry turned his back when we wanted to see Toby. We were all his friends. Toby wasn't well, he had a dreadful cold and cough and he was sitting with his injured leg up, but he seemed calm. He grinned at me just as he always did.

'It'll probably be commuted to imprisonment and hard labour and then suspended. I've been through all this before. No point in worrying till we have to.

'If it isn't,' he said. 'If the worst comes to the worst, I

want you to write to my wife. Tell her everything. She's the sort who wants to know what's going on, even the worst things. I've heard that the top brass fudges this sort of thing over and pushes it under the carpet. I want her to know what happens to me.'

So that's what I'm doing now. It's because Toby asked me. The awful thing I have to tell you is that this time his luck ran out. We heard about it at parade. Major Lutterworth, our unit commander, told us Toby's sentence of death had been confirmed, and that it would be carried out at 5.30 a.m. on the 9th, two days later.

We were all in a state of shock. He gave out that Toby had deserted twice before; that he'd struck a senior officer before and had two suspended sentences for hard labour, and that the death sentence had to be mandatory this time. That Toby lacked a sense of responsibility.

He stood there on the parade ground, saying in the sort of voice that carries half a mile:

'You all know these offences have to be treated with the utmost severity. Let this be an example to the rest of you. We can't have you all boarding a ferry when you feel like a few days at home.'

As if any of us would *dare*. Only Toby had the nerve for that. There was nothing about his exemplary behaviour when he saw me and Lieutenant Copeland caught in the barbed wire in no man's land. Nothing about him coming back with wire-cutters to cut us free. Nothing about the Military Medal they were going to recommend him for at the time.

We couldn't believe what we were hearing. We all felt so angry; there was no braver soldier than Toby. He didn't seem to care about danger, he laughed it all off. It was a joke to him. The only thing he took seriously was his responsibilities to us, his friends. He was always quite sure that things would come out right for him. In the past they usually had.

There was a lot of unrest and mutinous talk when we were dismissed. The whole unit was upset.

The next thing we heard was that Sergeant Halkin was mustering a firing party. He picked out six men. Nobby Clark and Danny Purdy were two of them, and they counted themselves as Toby's friends. They were horrified.

After talking it over, they went back to see this sergeant and said they couldn't do it; he couldn't ask them to shoot Private Percival. He was turning them into murderers. He said it was an order and they'd have to do it; that they should be used to shooting to kill by now.

When we first came to France, a lot of us found it hard to kill another human being. It was seeing our comrades being killed that hardened us to that. But there's a huge difference between firing at the enemy and firing deliberately at a person you regard as a friend. In the line, Toby would have done anything to protect us. We couldn't kill him like that, in cold blood.

Nobby and Danny came back to the billet in a very angry mood. They were determined not to do it. They said they were going to refuse and they talked the other four into doing the same.

One reported sick and was allowed three days' rest, so he got out of it that way. The others all refused point blank to kill somebody they knew and liked. Nobby and Danny were put under close arrest and told they'd be court-martialled for disobedience and could find themselves in Toby's position.

The other three were given the option of changing their minds or being arrested too, so they changed their minds. We could all see that they were being forced into it and now three more would have to be picked to make up the number. I thanked my lucky stars I would be in the front line on the morning of the 9th so they couldn't ask me.

Nobody knew who the other three were to be until the the night before. Instead of setting off under cover of darkness for the front line, I and two others were ordered to join the firing party at dawn. This was one time when we'd have preferred the front. I bet the Germans aren't treated like this by their own. It makes you wonder who the enemy really is.

Nobody in our billet slept that night. We were talking half the night and I felt terrible. We were being forced to shoot our friend. The six of us in the firing party were determined we wouldn't do it. And we sent a note to Toby to tell him that we all planned to fire wide. We none of us were prepared to have his death on our conscience. Of course, it wouldn't save Toby. The sergeant in charge would fire at point-blank range if the firing party failed to kill him outright, but at least Sergeant Halkin would have to do his own dirty work.

It was still dark when we had to muster as the firing party. Sergeant Halkin marched us to the execution site. We had no idea where it would be, it was kept secret from us. There was a medical officer and the chaplain, who said prayers, and an escort of military police.

We waited and waited for them to bring Toby. It was awful for us and must have been a thousand times worse for him. It was 6.30 when I saw him walking out to the stake between the medical officer and the chaplain.

'So long, Clemmo,' he called to me. 'Don't let it bother you, I know you were forced to come and see me off. So long, lads.'

We were ordered then to line up with our backs to him and with our rifles on the ground in front of us. Sergeant Halkin collected them and took them all away, saying he'd load two of them with blanks so none of us would know whether we'd been the one who killed Toby or not.

But of course we would! Blanks make a different sound and the kick into your shoulder is less. He must think we're stupid if we don't know that. We all start our musketry training with blanks before moving on to the real thing. Our rifles came back in front of us and we waited until we got the order to pick them up and turn round. It was explained to us that after that, all our signals would be silent.

Another terrible wait. I was shaking. At last the order was barked out at us. We six bobbed down for our rifles in unison and did a right about-turn.

They'd tied Toby to the post with his hands fastened behind him and pinned a folded white handkerchief to his shirt over his heart. We'd been told to aim for that, it was our target. The doctor was blindfolding him.

I heard Toby say: 'I don't need that,' but he was persuaded to have it anyway.

The chaplain had gone. The medical officer backed off to one side, and the sergeant to the other with his revolver at the ready. He kept us waiting again while every muscle in my body cringed. Then came the silent signal to take aim. I was horribly conscious of six rifles pointing at Toby's heart.

Finally the sergeant's arm came down. It was the signal for us to fire. We all did what we had been ordered to do, and the noise reverberated round. I knew I had been given blanks. Toby was still standing up unharmed. We'd all fired wide as agreed.

Of course it did Toby no good. Perhaps it eased our consciences but it must have drawn out the agony for him, even though we'd told him of our intentions. How could he be sure we'd all do it when the time came?

How awful to go through all that and still be standing there unharmed. The doctor ran over to Toby and signalled to the sergeant. He barely gave him time to leap clear before he fired at point-blank range. Toby's head fell forward, though his body could not because he was tied to the stake. It slumped down as far as it could. He was gushing blood.

We were marched off then, leaving the escort of military police to do what was required after that.

We wept when we'd done it and were totally distraught. Others went on the rampage and broke up the kitchen as a breakfast of eggs and bacon was being prepared for the officers. That was truly terrible to see, shots being fired over their heads by our own officers. It did nobody any good. There was no food sent up for those in the trenches that day, and twenty-two men were locked up and charged with mutiny.

It didn't get as far as a court martial for them. When they'd all calmed down, our commanding officer sentenced them all to one year's penal servitude with hard labour, then suspended their sentences and dispatched them to the front line. But the unit hasn't been the same since.

I found the whole thing humiliating and shocking, but I'm writing to tell you what happened as Toby asked me to. My own instincts are that I should censor this account to the woman he loved but I'm not going to do it because he asked me to tell you the full story.

Sarah could feel bitter bile rising in her throat. She rammed the letter back in its envelope, feeling sick. She found it hard to believe the British Army could do that to one of its own. But it explained several things that hadn't added up.

He'd been trying to come home to see her and the baby. What harm was there in that? He'd been injured; he wasn't fit to fight. He'd have gone back when his time was up. Like him, she'd thought it hard that he wasn't sent home as soon as he was discharged from hospital.

They'd caught him coming home and shot him for that, doing it with indecent haste. She was filled with revulsion and instead of going to the factory went to lie down on her bed. She cried for Toby then; he hadn't deserved such a shocking end.

It was almost lunch time when she heard the new telephone bell ring through the house, and Bessie coming to knock on her door.

'It's Edward,' she said. 'He wants to know if you're all right because you haven't gone to work.'

Sarah got up and went to speak to him. She felt she couldn't say a word about Toby. What he'd gone through was all too vivid in her mind, a horrible experience. And Edward was his brother.

'I felt a bit sick, Edward. I went to lie down for a while, but I'm better now. I'll be in soon.'

'Are you sure? You don't have to if you don't feel up to it. I just wondered if something had happened. Usually we can set the clocks by the time you arrive.'

Sarah had to choke the words out. 'No, I'm all right. I'll come now.'

'Better have your lunch first.'

The thought of food made her stomach churn. She drank a cup of tea before setting out. She knew she was acting strangely; even Bessie asked her if she was all right.

She had told Toby she wanted to know everything that was going on, but this time it had really caught in her throat. She couldn't talk about it. Couldn't even think of it. It didn't seem possible that Toby had been shot by his own brigade. She knew now that the phrase 'died on service' had been used to conceal the true cause of death from his relatives, who would assume he'd been killed in battle.

She hung over the rail on the ferry, feeling sick again. Edward had put a notice of Toby's death in the *Liverpool Echo* and had copied that phrase from the letter. Everybody in the know would realise Toby had been shot at dawn. That was horrible. She wanted people to go on thinking of Toby as a hero.

Sarah lifted her face into the breeze until the wave of nausea had passed. She didn't know how much use she would be at the factory that day. She sat at her desk pretending nothing had changed, pretending to work. She stared at ledgers but saw only Toby. The only thing she achieved was to get through the afternoon. Her colleagues came to talk to her from time to time. Her opinion was asked on various matters, she couldn't say exactly what. She answered without thought. She couldn't think of anything but Toby's utterly dreadful, needless death.

She stayed a little later than usual and travelled home with Mam. She wanted to tell her, had every intention of doing so, but Mam was talking about some problem in the accounts and the words wouldn't come. They were walking up the Esplanade and she still hadn't got round to it.

Once they reached home, she sat quietly for a time cuddling the baby. She knew she'd never be able to tell Dinah what had happened to her father. It would alter how she'd think about him. Sarah couldn't bear to think of Dinah being ashamed of him. Toby would have made a good father, she was sure.

When she measured how much he meant to her and his family, and how little he'd been valued by the army, she wept again.

She went to the dining room and made an effort to eat dinner, but it stuck in her throat. Mam and Edward were being extra kind and showing sympathy. They knew she was thinking about Toby, but they didn't realise how much more she now knew about his death.

She looked up and found Mam's eyes were searching her face. 'You look tired, Sarah.'

'I am.'

'It's all the broken nights you're having. Give Dinah her

ten o'clock feed early and go to bed. She can spend the night in my room; I'll see to her if she wakes up.'

Though it was an hour early, Dinah was awake, so Sarah started to feed her. She was taking her feeds eagerly now and was soon ready to be put down for the night.

Mam carried the empty crib to her room. 'I'll play with her for a bit,' she said, 'and put her down when she seems sleepy.'

Back in her own bedroom, Sarah felt a pang of guilt. It wasn't right to push Dinah away, but she felt in a terrible state. She got herself ready for bed and slid between the sheets, but sleep wouldn't come. She tossed and turned until her bed was a rumpled mess.

The numbness she'd felt had passed, and she was now burning with anger. She felt gripped by a terrible rage that the army had put Toby to death. They could have got rid of him just as easily by sending him home. She wanted him. His family wanted him, and the business needed him.

What they'd done was unjust, inhuman. Sarah wanted to shout about it from the rooftops. She wanted the whole country to know how badly the army treated its volunteers. Men who had offered to fight for their country, who were prepared to give all. She wanted to let everybody know how disgusted and revolted she was by the treatment Toby had received, and to stop the army doing it to any other soldier.

But she knew she couldn't make the slightest protest. Her hands were tied. Everybody would then know that Toby wasn't a hero who had given his life for his country. They'd know he'd been put to death like a common criminal. She didn't want to tell anybody, not even Edward.

He was still two weeks off his sixteenth birthday. She prayed the war would be over before he had his eighteenth and had to follow in his brother's footsteps. With conscription now in force, he wouldn't have a choice.

She didn't want to talk about Toby's death to anybody, not ever, didn't even want to think about it, but she couldn't get his horrible end out of her mind. He'd deserved so much better.

She heard Dinah wake up and cry. She heard Mam get up to comfort her. Sarah couldn't bring herself to get out of bed. She wanted to die too.

Chapter Twenty-five

1915–1917

Sarah felt Toby's death ended an era in her life. She didn't know how she got through the months that followed. It was impossible to cut him out of her thoughts; he was there beside her day and night. She lost weight and no longer looked well. Her sparkle faded.

Having Toby's daughter helped. Dinah was a great comfort to her; so was Mam. She didn't know how she'd have got through those first months without her mother. Maria oversaw the housekeeping and encouraged Sarah to spend as much time as possible with Dinah. She kept saying things like:

'Toby was a lovely boy. None better.' She seemed to have forgotten that last August she'd been very much against Sarah having anything to do with him. Now she couldn't praise him enough. 'He died a hero. For King and country.'

Sarah couldn't tell her mother the truth. She wished she hadn't found out herself. She'd have liked to think of Toby in those terms. As far as she was concerned, he deserved the best. Nobody spoke ill of the dead; she certainly wasn't going to.

She found having Edward's company helped too. They seemed to have knitted into a tight family unit. Adam often came round to their side of the house, wanting to play with Edward and have stories read to him by Maria. Sarah had seen him in the kitchen with Bessie and Ena several times. Partly for Adam's sake, Sarah did her best to be on friendly terms with Claudia and Mrs Digby. She hoped that Dinah would play with Rosemary when they were older.

But Sarah knew that it was having to go to work in those first difficult months that helped her more than anything else. It kept her in contact with other people, made her feel in the thick of things. Kept her mind busy in the present.

When Toby had had to go away, they'd all thought of Percival's Pickles as being rudderless. The effort she'd put into the company then had been to help Toby. The work force had rallied round. They'd all pulled in the same direction and become a team. Month by month the profits were increasing. They all prided themselves on achieving that. Now, unbelievably, one third of the business belonged to her.

Sarah drew strength from the fact that she and Mam were no longer poor. Dinah would not have a father, but she'd not lack material goods during her childhood. Sarah vowed to bring her up to work in the business. She would eventually inherit a share; she must be capable of running it.

Sarah also learned to love Tides Reach. She'd inherited Toby's interest in the house and felt she had a right to live here now. To divide it in half had been the right thing to do.

The future was not as she'd have wished it, and Sarah found it impossible to shake off her loss. But she worked hard and involved herself with Dinah and the rest of her family, though she felt cut off from everything else. By losing Toby she'd lost too much. She'd lost direction.

Sarah knew John Ferry and his mother had taken over the rooms she and Mam had rented. It was some months later, and only when she asked Elvira how she was getting on with her new neighbours, that she realised they'd kept on the single room on the floor below too.

'I expect John wants a bedroom to himself,' Mam said. 'Sharing with a daughter is one thing; sharing with a son quite another. They were very cramped in that one room.'

'There was a family of five in one room on the ground floor,' Sarah retorted, 'and it was a smaller room than theirs.'

'But that woman's husband drank; he was always in the boozer.'

It pleased Sarah that John could afford the rent of three rooms now. She felt she'd helped him achieve it. He'd always been so full of plans to go up in the world and enjoy a better life. She wasn't proud of the way she'd deserted him in favour of Toby, but they'd put all that behind them and were on good terms again.

He'd come into the office one afternoon when she was alone there and said:

'How about coming to the pictures with me tonight?' His dark eyes were shining with enthusiasm. '*The Birth of a Nation* is showing at the Picture House in Lord Street.'

Sarah didn't want to. She felt that with the business and the baby and the rest of the family, she had as much as she could cope with in her day. She hadn't the energy for anything more. If she couldn't have Toby she didn't want anybody else.

'No, John, thank you.'

She saw hope fade from John's face. He pursed his lips, making the cleft in his chin more marked.

'Come on, it would do you good. A change for you.'

She couldn't look at him. She had to offer some explanation. She didn't want to hurt him more than she already had.

'I'm not over Toby. Not yet.'

'I know, but we're friends now. Just friends. I've heard it's a very good film. Everybody's talking about it.'

On Saturday night, John went on his own to see the film. He couldn't persuade his mother to go with him either.

'Too tired,' she said. 'I'd rather sit by the fire and rest.' They'd both been making sauce since Percival's closed at one o'clock. It made him feel guilty that she had to work so hard.

It was a good film and John enjoyed it, but surrounded by couples and family groups he felt very much alone. He'd never been to the cinema on his own before.

On Monday, in the office, Miss Potts was holding forth about the film to Maria.

'It's about Lillian Gish being separated from her lover. She was wonderful.'

'It's an account of American history,' John said. 'And it's rousing a lot of bad feelings there. They say it isn't true.'

Edward came in at that point. Eunice Potts turned to him and said:

'You shouldn't miss it. It's a great picture.'

'I'm not going to,' Edward smiled. 'I'm taking Sarah to see it tonight.'

John snatched up his paperwork and hurried out. He wanted to get away. It was hard to swallow that Sarah was willing to go with Edward after refusing to go with him. He felt very low. It seemed Sarah didn't want him to have a bigger part in her life.

It was over two years since Maurice Percival had died, and Sarah was sitting at his desk working out what supplies she needed to order for the coming month. Many of the exotic fruits and spices were now unobtainable or in short supply because the German navy was blockading British ports.

They were getting countless requests for their Madras chutney and their hot lime chutney but couldn't fulfil them because they couldn't get mangoes or limes. Before the war they'd used a lot of lemons, which had also become scarce, and they were now having to use an artificial flavouring which they all thought detracted from the taste.

They'd discussed the shortages over and over in their meetings. It was Edward who said they needed to find a new popular product to replace most of their chutneys. They'd tried out all sorts of recipes and were now making apple and plum chutneys in season, and pickling more beetroot and red cabbage. They could sell everything they made.

They were still in need of another product, though. Something they could make all the year round, from ingredients grown in Britain. Sarah was turning over in her mind the feasibility of mint sauce when the telephone on the wall behind her rang.

It was the owner of a chain of grocery shops with outlets in most of the Liverpool suburbs, a long-term customer who regularly phoned in substantial orders. He asked for Madras chutney, but when Sarah told him they were unable to supply that, he requested a good selection of other chutneys as well as putting in an excellent order for pickled onions. Sarah was writing it all down carefully. Then he said:

'Oh, and another three cases of Scouser's Relish.'

'Scouser's Relish?' She sucked the end of her pencil. She'd never heard of that!

'Yes, the new brown sauce. It's going very well. Proving very popular.'

'Brown sauce?' Her mind whirled. 'You ordered it from our representative?'

She could guess what Scouser's Relish was now!

'Yes – ordered from John Ferry. It's always billed separately through. It's all right for me to do it through you?'

Anger made the blood pound in her head. 'I'll let him know,' she choked.

She managed to read the order back to check it, including the request for Scouser's Relish, but she was furious with John. He was taking orders and selling his sauce to the customers of Percival's Pickles, elbowing in on their market.

She was seething as she made the usual copy of the order for Trumper and another for John. She looked for John in the next office, then in the factory, taking the copies instead of leaving them for the office boy to deliver. She failed to find him but left messages that she wanted a word as soon as he returned. She hadn't calmed down when he came to the office half an hour later.

'You're mad at me,' he said. 'I know why; I've seen the new order.'

'John, I've a right to be mad. All of us have. You're working up your own business while we're paying you to work at ours.'

'Yes, I'm sorry.' He was composed, unruffled. 'I have no excuse. Except that with the war, there's not much in the shops and we can all sell everything we make.'

'I know that. I know the problem now is getting the raw materials, not selling the finished product. But that's not the point . . .'

He was calmer than she was. 'Don't let's have a fight.'

'I don't want to fight with you. But you took advantage. You went behind our backs, said nothing about it.'

'I used to talk about it a lot. You knew it was always my intention.'

'Years ago.' Sarah didn't like being reminded of that time. It put the boot on the other foot, made her feel she'd done him down instead of the other way round.

'I have to take my chance where I can.' He was still showing restraint. It irritated her further that she couldn't discuss it calmly herself.

'But to sell your sauce when you're paid to sell our pickles? It isn't right.'

'But I'm selling more of Percival's products than Toby ever did. I've brought in two big orders this month. I can't see you've much to complain about.'

Sarah wished he wouldn't bring Toby into it. She made herself take a deep, steadying breath.

'You're doing very well for us. I don't complain about that.'

'I'll always do my best for Percival's. You can trust me; I wouldn't let you down. I work overtime to make the time up. Honest, Sarah.'

356

'I know you work overtime, but what you're doing . . . It looks bad.'

'I know it does.'

'Any other company would give you the sack.'

'You aren't thinking of that?' He looked aghast. 'I'm not yet ready.'

'No, it's the last thing I want. You know we need you.'

His dark eyes glistened down at her. 'You know how keen I've always been to set up on my own. You helped by getting me this selling job. It taught me what I needed to know. I'm very grateful.'

'You're copying us. Copying what Percival's did.' She wanted to stamp with impatience.

'So what? I'm two generations behind. Anybody working here could do the same – if they had a good recipe for a sauce.'

John stopped to take a breath. 'Anyway, we won't be in direct competition. Mine's a sauce, yours is pickles.'

That made her fume again. 'We will! If you sit down to a plate of scouse, or sausage or whatever, you'll have pickles or sauce with it. Never both.'

'Speak for yourself. I do.' He laughed.

She wanted to scream at him.

'Look,' he went on mildly. 'It's easier for a woman to make her way in the world. You can marry up.'

Sarah felt the heat run up her cheeks. 'What's that got to do with it?'

'I don't begrudge that you chose to do it. Toby was right for you and I wasn't. You've done well for yourself.'

She saw that as hitting below the belt. 'So have you. You've got a much better job now.'

'Perhaps I'm big-headed, but I think I can do better still. This is my chance. I have to try.'

She knew why she was so cross with him now. Yes, Percival's were paying for his time, but it wasn't entirely that. He'd done this without saying a word about it to her. Without a word to anyone. She'd thought they were friends, that they could talk openly to each other. In the old days he'd never stopped talking about how he'd make their fortune with his sauce. That he didn't feel he could talk to her now was hurtful. She'd been as open with him as she'd been with anyone.

Sarah calmed down a little. 'When you took over our old rooms, I wondered why you kept on your old one too. It was to have space to do this?'

'Yes,' he admitted. 'We hoped to be able to.'

'How long have you been making this sauce?'

'For over a year.'

'And you've said nothing in all that time?'

His voice was resigned. 'No. I'm sorry.'

'And your mother?' Sarah felt another rush of indignation. 'She gave up her job with us, how long ago? Six months? Was that so she could make your sauce?'

He was nodding. 'You've got it. I'm afraid it was.' He was trying to smile at her.

'She said her job was too much for her.'

'It was, when she was making pint after pint of our sauce at home. Come on, Sarah. I didn't make things hard for you when you wanted to throw me over and go your own way.'

She smiled uneasily. He hadn't. 'You'd better bring me a sample of this sauce. I'd like to try it.'

'All right.'

Sarah frowned in concentration. 'Make it four samples. We'll all try it.'

On Wednesday, before their weekly meeting, Sarah lined up the four bottles of Scouser's Relish on her desk. When John had brought them in this morning, she'd warned him that she was going to tell the rest of them what he was doing. He'd elected not to be present.

'I'm a bit ashamed,' he told her. 'Perhaps I have been taking advantage.'

Maria came in with Trumper and Miss Potts, and Edward opened the meeting. Sarah told her colleagues about John's sauce. She'd been giving it a lot of thought since she'd first heard he was making it commercially, and had discussed it with Edward. She turned the bottle round to show off the handsome label.

'John has learned his lessons well. A good-quality bottle with a strong screw cap. It looks like a top-of-the-market product.'

She pushed one bottle towards Trumper and another towards Eunice Potts.

'Will you try it? Edward and I would like to know what you think of it.'

They were only too keen, very curious about it now they realised it had been made by John. Each had the cap unscrewed in moments to sniff at the contents.

'Smells very appetising,' was Miss Potts' opinion.

'I'm taking these two bottles home,' Sarah told Edward. 'I'll give one to Claudia, see if she likes it.

'John's a bit cagey about the exact recipe, but I gather he isn't finding the ingredients hard to get even now. He's given me this breakdown of his costs.

'I've been wondering whether we should try to do a deal with him. Make his sauce here. He doesn't have the facilities to expand; he'd have to rent new premises. It might prove a profitable new line for Percival's Pickles. Taste it and give it some thought.'

That evening, Sarah took one of the bottles round to Claudia. A few days later she asked what Claudia had thought of it.

Claudia said in her superior way: 'Pickles, chutney, brown sauce, I'm not fond of any of them. You know that, Sarah, but I have tasted it.'

'I thought you'd want to. If only to keep up with what we're doing.'

'I see that as my duty.'

'So what did you think?'

Grudgingly she said: 'I suppose it's as good as any brown sauce.'

'It's not any brown sauce. It's very different in flavour.'

Mrs Digby said: 'Now I've seen where and how all those things are made, it's put me off. I really couldn't enjoy any of them. Not now. But the servants will like it, I'm sure.'

Adam piped up: 'I had a double helping. Mama said it would make me sick, but it didn't. I think it's lovely.'

The months were passing quickly. Sarah would hardly have noticed except that the passage of time was evident in the way Dinah was growing and developing. She was now a boisterous toddler of fifteen months, running more often than she walked. She was talking well for her age, too.

One morning, Sarah ate breakfast with Mam and Edward as usual, but there were things she wanted to sort out at work, so she caught an earlier boat. She was surprised to see Edward looking quite upset when he came into the office half an hour after her.

'I was handed a white feather on the ferry,' he told her. 'It was embarrassing; everybody was staring at me.'

'Don't take it to heart. Handing out white feathers these days is a load of nonsense. Out of date. There's conscription now; no one can avoid going to fight.'

It had been heavy on her mind for some time that in nine more months Edward would be called up. 'I hope you told them that.'

'I said I wasn't old enough, and let the feather flutter off in the breeze.'

'It's the people who do that who should be embarrassed, not you. Don't worry about it.'

Circumstances had made Edward grow up in a hurry. In both looks and character he was very different from Toby. He took everything extremely seriously and was becoming more like his father. He looked older than his years rather than younger.

Sarah feared for him and hated to be reminded that he'd have to go. These were very different times from when Toby had volunteered. The heady nationalistic fervour was gone. The war was dragging on, killing and maiming thousands each day. She'd hoped it would all be over before Edward had to go, but it was looking increasingly unlikely now. She'd more or less accepted that he'd have to go and fight in the trenches. She was terrified he'd be killed like so many others.

It made it all the more painful that Edward was beginning to be of real use in the business. He'd shown great interest and had learned fast. The company was still being democratically run, and he'd taken on his share of responsibility, chairing the staff meetings and doing many other jobs. Sarah found him supportive and reliable.

Edward had been much happier since Sarah and her mother had come to live at Tides Reach and the house had been divided. The atmosphere was friendly. They included him in everything they did, and asked and seemed to value his opinion. The tiffs and prickles he had experienced with Claudia and her mother were no more.

Being of much the same age as Sarah and working closely together in the office, Edward began to seek out her company at home. Occasionally he suggested they go to the cinema, or straight from work to the Playhouse Theatre. On summer evenings when Dinah had been put to bed, she'd join him out on the Esplanade when he went out for a breath of air.

'I want you to know I'm very grateful,' he told her one evening as they strolled in the last of the sun. 'For all you've done for me.'

'It doesn't seem much. I'm afraid my mind is more often on Dinah – or other things.'

'You arranged for Trumper and Miss Potts to teach me. You eased me into the business.'

'You had to be eased in. You own part of it.'

'Stepmother was trying to keep me out.'

'I did what Toby wanted done. What seemed fair. No more.'

'You go out of your way to be as much help as you can. To persuade the others to give unstinting help too. If you'd been like Stepmother, goodness knows what I'd have done.'

'You'd have hung on and picked things up just the same.'

'I hope I would. You made it easy for me, that's what I'm trying to say. Toby picked himself a great wife.'

She said sadly, 'I was never any sort of a wife to Toby. Never had the chance.'

He felt so sorry for her. He wanted to put his arms round her to comfort her. He was feeling increasingly drawn to Sarah.

As he dressed each morning, he looked forward to seeing her at the breakfast table. When the morning sun came through the dining room windows to glint in her hair, he thought her very beautiful. She wore her blonde hair up in a curly top-knot now. Always as the day wore on, corkscrew curls escaped to hang over her forehead.

He found her very easy to love. As for baby Dinah, from the first moment he'd held her in his arms, he'd vowed he'd take the place of her dead father.

That night, as he was going to bed, he opened his prayer book and checked through the table of kindred and affinity to see if marriage was allowed to his brother's wife.

It was; he breathed a sigh of satisfaction. That was what he wanted above all else.

Chapter Twenty-six

October 1917

Edward knew he wouldn't have much more time at home with Sarah. By unspoken consent they didn't mention conscription or the relentless approach of his eighteenth birthday, but he knew she was as conscious of the deadline as he was.

Sarah was filling his thoughts night and day. He was proud to have her on his arm when they went out, but he enjoyed their evenings at home just as much. They'd sit on over the dinner table long after Bessie had removed most of the dishes. They talked over details of work that had filled the day. Maria always got up first and left them to it.

Edward wanted to let Sarah know how much she meant to him. It needed to be said; he'd put it off for too long, and he wanted to know where he stood before he went away. He'd made up his mind he'd do it tonight when Maria left them. All through dinner his eyes wouldn't leave Sarah's face.

It was a jolly meal tonight; Sarah and Maria laughed a lot and were more animated than usual. Maria sat on with them longer than she normally did. Edward found he was willing her to go. At last she pushed her chair back.

'I'm tired, I think I'll have an early night.'

Maria had been in the office all day. She had to work very hard on Fridays when there were the wages to pay. The dining room door clicked shut behind her. Into the silence she left, Edward said in a little rush:

'I thought she'd never go. There's something I want to say to you.'

With her amber eyes on his face, he found it hard to go on. She'd shown him real affection, was always kind. She always asked if he felt he could manage some extra job; it was never pushed on to him.

He swallowed hard. 'I think . . . I think I'm in love with you, Sarah.'

Her hand came up as though to fend him off. 'No, Edward.'

'How could I not be? Living here with you, sharing everything. I want us to be married.'

She put her hand down on top of his. 'No, Edward.'

His eyes looked into hers then. 'All right, you're three years older than me, but what does that matter?'

'It doesn't.' She was choking the words out.

'I love you, Sarah. It's been creeping up on me for ages. I thought you . . . Well, you seem to care about me.'

'Of course I care. You're Toby's brother.'

This wasn't what he wanted to hear. His voice was harsher. 'His little brother?'

'Toby thought a lot of you, and so do I. I'm very fond of you, but that isn't the right sort of love. Not for getting married. It's sisterly . . .'

'I feel so much at home here with you and Dinah. Maria too. So happy. We make a real family. What could be better than we get married?'

'You're only just eighteen . . .'

He drew back. 'That's it, you think I'm too young. I was afraid you would.'

'It's too young for you. You'll meet somebody of your own. Give yourself time. You don't have to rescue me from widowhood.'

'That's not why . . . I love you.'

'Ed, I'm not ready to marry again.'

'It's over two years since Toby . . .'

'I know, but I still feel raw about it.'

'You need somebody to look after you.'

He saw her pull herself up. Straighten her shoulders. 'I've learned to do that for myself.'

'Perhaps you have. Anyway, it would be very good for the business. We'd bring two thirds of it together.'

'We can't get married for the sake of the business.' She smiled. 'We don't need to; it's doing all right without that. I'll take good care of it while you're away.'

'I know you will. Without you it might have foundered. I'm very grateful. For all you've done for me, apprenticing me to everybody in turn. I feel I could run the company now.'

'Come back and do it.'

He nodded. 'I wanted to feel fixed up with you before I went.'

'You've always been fixed up with me, Ed. Nothing will change that.'

Two or three days later Sarah was alone in the office when John put his head round the door.

'Have you tried it yet? My sauce?' His eyes were eager. 'What did you think of it?'

'I've tasted it before. Years ago. Your mother must have made up the recipe.'

'You remembered! It wasn't exactly the same. Anyway, what's the verdict now?'

'I loved it, and so did Edward.' She saw his smile of satisfaction. 'We found two other brands of brown sauce in the larder and compared the taste. Yours was much the best. The flavour's great. Bessie and Ena liked it too.'

John was beaming by now. 'Thank you.'

'I mean it. Trumper and Miss Potts, they're both impressed. Come and sit down for a minute.'

He scraped back the chair.

'We've talked it over. Would you like to come to some sort of arrangement with us?'

He was staring at her, his expression giving nothing away. She had to go on.

'How d'you feel about letting Percival's make your sauce and marketing it under our own label?'

Sarah could see that came as something of a surprise. His eyes wouldn't meet hers now.

He sighed. 'Years ago I brought a bottle here to Maurice Percival and asked him if he'd do exactly that. He turned me down flat.'

'Oh! Why?'

'He said it would need bottles, and everything else he made needed jars. It would be too much trouble. He wouldn't even taste it.'

For the first time Sarah wondered if they'd be taking on too much. 'We've worked out some figures. What it would cost us to make, what the likely profit would be. I've put them down on paper for you. We'd pay you a small percentage.'

She took a sheet of foolscap from the drawer of the desk and gave it to him. Still he said nothing. He was turning the paper round and round in his hands.

She said: 'You'll want to study those figures. The attraction for us is that it would keep the lines running at the back end of winter. It would be like our pickled onions; we could make it all the year round. We used to get a lot of vegetables from the Canaries before the war, not to mention the tropical fruit. What I mean is, the ingredients aren't impossible to come by.'

'I know what the attractions are, Sarah. They're the same for me, don't forget. You'd call it Scouser's Relish?'

Sarah's heart leapt. He seemed to be giving it consideration; after all, there were benefits for him too.

'Yes, it's a good name. Just the thing to go with scouse. We all thought so.'

'My grandmother used to make it. It's a family recipe.'

'I know.'

'I ought to think this over. Talk it over with Mam.'

'Of course.'

She could see him hesitating. 'I don't think Mam will want . . . She thinks we'll be able to grow as big as Percival's on our own. She won't want to give it up until we've had a good try. Not now we're making it pay.'

That caught her unawares. It wasn't what she wanted to hear.

'You'll never be able to make much in that one room. Up all those stairs. Sooner or later you'll need to move. If you want to expand.'

'Yes.' He paused, frowning. Sarah waited.

'We could find bigger premises,' he said quietly. His eyes came back to search her face.

'Are you saying that's what you want to do? Don't you want time to think about it?'

'No, I'd prefer to do it with Mam. Take my chance.'

'Have it your own way,' Sarah said roughly, turning away.

'Don't be like that,' John pleaded. 'You followed your dream. This is mine and I want to see it through. See what I can make of it.'

She shrugged. 'If you've made up your mind . . .'

'Yes.' He got up and went to the door. 'I have.'

As the door closed behind him, Sarah said under her breath: 'Damn John Ferry.'

John strode through the factory with burning cheeks. He had to get out by himself. He strapped his sample box on to the carrier of his bicycle and pedalled furiously into the city.

He was afraid he'd cut off his nose to spite his face. He understood only too well the huge step between making his sauce on a domestic stove and renting factory space. It meant taking on employees, for one thing.

It was a chill, damp morning. At the Pier Head he dismounted, propped his bike against a seat and took out the figures Sarah had given him. The wooden slats of the bench were wet; the strong breeze was fluttering the paper. His mind was racing and it took him an age to assimilate the information.

He certainly had his hang-ups. He should not have refused Sarah's offer outright. What harm could there be in thinking about it first? The figures were fair. He could rely on Percival's being fair with him.

To turn down the offer straight off had been almost an automatic action. He wanted to reject any suggestion from Sarah outright, the same way she'd rejected him.

He told himself he'd been petty. He couldn't believe he'd been that small-minded. He had to ask himself if he was letting his past ties to Sarah interfere with the way he would develop his sauce. He was a fool. She probably thought him a fool too.

He couldn't put his mind on his work all day. He made a few calls but achieved little. He went home that evening and found his mother exhausted. She'd been on her feet all day tending pots on the stove and bottling the result.

He told her of Sarah's suggestion; gave her the figures to study. She pushed a damp strand of hair off her hot face and tried to focus on them.

'I've told her no, we won't go in with them.'

From the weary look she gave him, John was afraid she wished he'd decided otherwise. Elvira had had her fifty-eighth birthday, and he wondered if he'd left it too late to start up like this. He was giving her a lot of work to do; he could see the future would bring more. He hoped she'd still have the energy to do it.

She sighed. Her forehead tightened into deep furrows. 'I suppose you're right.'

He wasn't at all sure about that.

'You know what your trouble is?' Mam's exhausted eyes searched his face. 'You've never got over Sarah Hoxton.'

He didn't need Mam to tell him that. Perhaps it was just that he was doing his best not to get hurt again.

Having turned down Sarah's offer, John knew he must expand on his own, and the sooner he did it the better.

He hired Ethel, a strong fifteen-year-old girl, to help his mother, and took orders for more sauce. Within a few weeks, he realised the sauce still wasn't being made quickly enough to fulfil the orders. He took on a second girl, called Winnie – a twenty-year-old this time, because his mother said she needed someone with more sense than the first – but they still weren't filling many more bottles. Elvira blamed the conditions under which they worked. John knew they fell far short of being ideal.

He'd not yet moved his bed upstairs. At first it had been bliss to have the room to himself, a real luxury. He'd moved his bed behind the curtain that had hidden Mam's bed and continued to sleep there, glorying in the privacy when Mam went to bed in Sarah and Maria's old room.

But once he'd hired the two girls, he'd had to carry his bed and the curtain upstairs. They needed the space it took up. They had to stack the crates of empty bottles on one side of the room and the full ones on the other. There was the further problem that the sauce had to mature for a few weeks before he could dispatch it to the shops.

Within a very short time, the one room became too cramped. Everything, including water, had to be carried up three flights of stairs, and they had no electricity. To deliver the sauce, he had to hire a cart and driver, which then had to park in the road while the finished goods were carried down. The only logical step forward was to find more suitable premises.

John found he was working all day for Percival's and half the night for himself. His sauce was taking up every minute of his available time. Even worse, he knew Mam was working at the same pace. She looked absolutely worn out and was growing anxious and irritable again.

John felt utterly weary. His double work load was beginning

to tell on him. It was Wednesday afternoon; he'd been busy all morning and only just managed to get in to Percival's before the regular weekly meeting started. Sarah and Edward both looked very low. He understood why when Edward announced:

'I've received my call-up papers. They came yesterday. It seems I'll have to go and fight.'

'When?'

'My medical's next week. Straight in, unless I'm found unfit.'

'No reason to suppose that,' Sarah said gloomily. 'You haven't had a day off sick since you started here.'

Edward looked a prime specimen, strong and agile. Even though they'd been expecting it, his call-up cast a blight.

'I'm glad Sarah has you four to help her,' Edward said, looking round at them. 'You'll all have more to do when I'm gone, but I know we can rely on you. We count ourselves lucky to have you.'

John had been going to tell Sarah he'd have to leave soon, but after that he decided to put it off.

'You could ask for deferment,' he told Edward. 'On the grounds that you're needed to run the family business.'

'I can't!' Edward was aghast.

'Of course you can. Percival's are producing food for the armed forces.'

'No, John.' He told the story of how he was given a white feather. 'It's my duty to go. I don't want to be thought a dodger.'

'We wouldn't think that. We know you're needed here.'

'I'd feel I was dodging. My brother volunteered; I can't fight against being conscripted.'

John saw Sarah's face twist at the mention of Toby. He wished he knew how to inspire affection like that.

Trumper stirred in his seat. 'Those trenches, absolutely terrible; our Charlie says he'd do anything to get out. But once you're in, there's no way back.'

Edward said: 'I've been thinking about it. I'll try for a commission.'

Sarah sighed. 'We'll manage somehow. Keep things going until you get back.'

She had the knack of being able to delegate work to others. She didn't stay at the factory throughout the day; often by mid afternoon she was gone. Sometimes she left at lunch time.

'I want to spend more time with Dinah,' she'd said a few months ago. 'I want her to know she has a mother.'

To ease the pressure of work, Sarah bought a typewriter and hired a typist to use it, a young lady straight from commercial school. Louise Corbishley was another blonde, not unlike Sarah to look at.

'A pretty girl,' Edward told Sarah. 'She'll fit in well.'

Sarah also promoted the office boy to clerk, but his help could only be short term because he would be called up in another twelve months.

John thought the work at Percival's ran very smoothly, though they were all going to miss Edward's input. Maria and Miss Potts volunteered to take over some of the jobs he'd been doing.

John wished he was able to delegate in the same way. His mother was stretched beyond her capacity as it was; the girls would take no responsibility at all. He knew that if his business was to grow, he needed to leave Percival's so he could devote all his energy to his sauce-making. He had to manage things better than he was.

Even with that decision made, he put off doing anything for several more months. It was the right thing to do for his own enterprise, really the only thing to do, but if he stopped working at Percival's, he'd not see Sarah again. She'd be gone out of his life, and he couldn't bring himself to do that.

Sarah lived in dread of Edward being sent to the front. She couldn't bear to think of him being killed. The casualty figures were appalling. Edward's application for a commission had brought delays, and Sarah welcomed them all. Even a few extra weeks spent training in England might save his life. With a little luck, getting a commission could mean extra months in this country.

The war was dragging on. Everybody was heartily tired of the rationing, the high prices and the shortages it had brought. Most people were exhausted by the effort needed to keep going.

Sarah knew her mother would like to spend more time at home. Maria enjoyed the peace of the garden in fine weather and the fireside when it was cold, but like Sarah, she had to keep working for the sake of the business.

With Edward away and Adam still at school, Sarah had no choice but to take over the entire responsibility of running the company.

She found herself unexpectedly lonely without Edward. She was missing his company both at home and in the factory. They'd been in the habit of discussing every move they made and working out future plans. She hadn't realised how much support Edward had provided until he'd gone.

Tides Reach seemed empty without him. Without realising it, she'd come to rely on Edward for her social life. He'd always been the one to suggest outings to places of interest, and usually the two of them had gone alone.

Edward had grown into a man and she'd hardly noticed it happening. Sarah hoped she hadn't hurt him too much by resisting his advances. She was sorry she'd taken Edward so much for granted.

Chapter Twenty-seven

1917–1919

John sat on at his desk, his work for the day completed and put away. Tonight he was a little later than usual; the building had emptied of workers ten minutes ago. He leaned back in his chair and stretched out his legs, enjoying the peace and quiet after a busy day.

He knew he was dragging his feet over his own sauce-making business. It was making little headway, though he and his mother were working round the clock. He needed to find bigger premises and he had to give up working for Percival's.

Long ago he'd acknowledged to himself that he couldn't bring himself to turn his back on Sarah. In moments like this, the longing for her brought an ache to his chest. He'd thought he was cured of it when she married Toby. He'd had to think that; her marriage had put her out of his reach for ever.

Everybody had been very upset when Toby was killed. John had been upset too, but all the time, underneath, he'd had this warm feeling he couldn't mention to anybody, that Sarah was free again. He'd done his best to be sympathetic to her; he'd done his best to be patient, knowing he couldn't expect her to return to him straight away. Yet he'd been quietly confident that she would.

His eyes sought the calendar hanging on the wall. Toby had died in May 1915; it was now November 1917. He had been patient. Very patient. Always he'd been on hand, friendly and supportive, ready to drop everything for Sarah at a moment's notice. Always he'd wanted to take her into his arms.

In return she was friendly too, and kind, yet he knew she treated him as she treated everybody else here. He'd thought at first that she just needed time to get over Toby. Now he was beginning to fear she never would.

Yet he still couldn't bring himself to precipitate any change that would put him where he wouldn't see her every day. But he was afraid Mam would not be able to go on much longer with things as they were.

He leapt to his feet. Daydreaming like this wasn't likely to get him anywhere. As he was charging past Sarah's office, she came out. It made him gasp; he'd thought she'd gone home long ago.

She asked about the orders he was taking for their new beetroot chutney. He walked with her through the factory and stood watching while she locked up. Then, without making any conscious decision, he fell in step with her as she turned towards the Pier Head.

'Lovely to get out in the fresh air,' she said. She was carrying her hat, and her topknot of golden curls bounced as she walked.

He couldn't take his eyes from her. Maturity had improved her looks. She held her head high now, and her wide-set amber eyes looked at him with greater confidence. He wanted, more than ever, to be part of her life. He wanted to see where she lived, what she'd done to the old Percival house. Maria gave out more information about that than she did. Sarah sometimes spoke of her daughter, but he'd never seen her, and he wanted to very much. Maria was always talking about Dinah's exploits: the nursery rhymes she could recite, the speed with which she learned things.

'Aren't you going home?' Sarah was looking up at him, smiling.

He ought to. Mam would be cooking. Instead he said:

'Have a cup of tea with me in that place on the landing stage before you catch your ferry.'

'Simpson's Café?' Her smile widened. 'Why not? Though I can't stay long. I have to read Dinah a story before she'll go to sleep.'

John couldn't imagine the sort of life she led at home, though he'd tried to many times.

He sat opposite her at a small table in Simpson's and watched her pour out their tea. She was talking about their new beetroot chutney again. It was the sort of conversation they usually had in the office, but it was lovely to be with her all the same.

John made himself say: 'I'd like to take you to the pictures. I know you used to go with Edward sometimes . . .'

'Yes.' She was watching seagulls soar over the stern of a boat sailing up river.

'You must want some company.'

'I do miss Edward.'

'Now he's gone, couldn't I take his place?' She didn't answer immediately. 'Come out with me once in a while,' he urged.

Sarah sighed. 'There are times when I feel quite lonely. No, not lonely exactly; I'm always surrounded with people. More alone.' She smiled again. 'I don't suppose that makes sense to you.'

'It does. That's how I feel all the time.'

John felt pleased with the way things were going. If he could persuade Sarah to take up with him again, he could still see her and work for himself. It seemed the only way round his problem.

He was thrilled when she agreed to go out with him on Friday night straight from work. He'd take her to Radley's Refreshment Rooms first to have something to eat, and then to a cinema or theatre in town.

Mam was furious with him when he got home because she'd had to keep the meal waiting for him. And worse, because he'd shared a tea cake with Sarah he wasn't hungry. Mam had boiled a piece of ham for them as a special treat.

John felt triumphant all the same. What he wanted more than anything was to get back with Sarah. And why not? She'd been a widow for over two years.

Elvira wasn't pleased when John told her of the arrangements he'd made for Friday. Normally, every evening, as soon as he'd eaten, he'd stick the labels on the bottles of sauce Mam had made that day and pack them into crates.

'What about the labels? When are you going to stick those on?'

'I'll do them over the weekend.'

'We'll be making more on Saturday.'

'That's all right, just keep the two lots separate.'

She spat out angrily: 'I don't know why you want to bother with that girl again.'

John had been telling himself his mother was over her problems, but the truth was she'd been having these fits of sudden savage rage ever since she'd sabotaged Percival's chutney at the beginning of the war. That was one of the reasons she'd been so keen to stop working for them.

'She won't look at you now she's gone up in the world. Neither will Maria. A bit snooty, that one.'

He found that hurtful. 'No, Mam, she isn't.'

'You're wasting your time on Sarah. She turned you down once; what makes you think she won't do it again? Don't forget she's your boss now.'

On the day she'd agreed to go out with him, John found Sarah had come to work in a smart coat and hat he hadn't seen before. He was pleased; it showed she was treating their outing as an occasion. He'd had to dress much more smartly since he'd been selling for Percival's. He'd bought himself two suits and a bowler hat. He changed into the newer of the suits in his dinner hour. He wanted to look his best for her.

He'd asked Sarah to choose where they would go. She

settled on a Charlie Chaplin film called *The Rink* which was showing at the Picture House on Lime Street, where they used to go all those years ago. That rather surprised him. He'd expected her to prefer somewhere different.

He took her to Radley's Refreshment Rooms for a meal first. He wasn't too sure he'd chosen the right place. Sarah and her mother sometimes came here for a meal in their dinner break as a change from bringing sandwiches. But the Refreshment Rooms were affordable for him and provided hot meals throughout the day, while the high-class places in town would not be serving dinners so early in the evening. He was used to having his main meal at that time and didn't want to be hungry.

He enjoyed the boiled beef and carrots; she said the dumplings were fine. It was never hard to talk to her, but he couldn't get her off company affairs. He didn't want to talk about chutneys. He wanted to hear what was happening in the part of her life he couldn't see.

Charlie Chaplin was very funny, and they both laughed until they had stitches in their sides. Afterwards he walked her to the Pier Head.

'I'll see you to the other side,' he told her, deciding to have a rare blow on the river.

'You don't need to, John. I'll be quite all right.'

He wanted to take her to her door. Perhaps be asked in. He insisted on getting on the ferry with her.

She pointed out where Tides Reach was, but as it was dark he saw nothing but lights sparkling against the night sky.

She thanked him prettily as the ferry was tying up, and said he ought not to come any further because if he did he'd have to wait for the next ferry back, and they didn't run very often at this time of night. She put up her face and kissed him on the cheek before turning to hurry down the pier.

He sailed back on the same ferry, feeling quite exhilarated by the evening. It had been a wonderful change to go out with Sarah after spending all his free time working on his sauce. And best of all, Sarah had agreed to do it again next week.

Sarah told him she'd have to pay her share if they were going to do this regularly. That really gave him hope, and they went out together every Friday for the next five weeks.

John had been so sure this would bring them closer, but he felt she wasn't relaxing in his company. Not in the way she used to. It was almost as though she wanted to keep him at a distance.

Eventually, he'd managed to escort her along the pier as far as the ferry house, and even kiss her on the lips before they parted, but he knew by then that she felt no passion for him.

'Next Friday?' he asked as they were parting.

Sarah shook her head and said sadly: 'We can't go back, John. I know that's what you want. We're both different people now; too much has happened to us.'

'I don't see why not,' he told her. 'I'm not different. I still feel the same way about you, you know that.'

'Then too much has happened to me. I'm sorry, John. I do wish things could be different, but they can't.' She kissed him on the cheek, and as she moved away he saw a tear glistening on her lashes. He felt heartbroken as he watched her turn along the Esplanade and be swallowed up in the dark.

As the ferry took him back across the black waters of the Mersey, John felt disheartened. He kept his eyes on the lights at the far end of the Esplanade; the lights showing from the house he'd never entered, never even seen in daylight. Sarah would be inside it by now.

He'd tried his best to win her over and he didn't understand now why it couldn't work out. But if Sarah didn't want it, he'd have to accept that.

He asked himself if he could leave Percival's Pickles to expand his own business. He would be in competition with Sarah, however much he'd tried to talk that aspect down.

Could he cut the ties that bound him to her? He couldn't make up his mind. It was impasse yet again.

'I told you she wouldn't want the likes of you. Not now,' Elvira told him when the following Friday came round and John had to explain why he wasn't going out.

'A good-looking girl like her? A young widow with a share of a prosperous business? She's got money now, she could marry anyone she likes. She turned you down years ago; why would she change her mind now?'

John continued to drag his feet. Somehow they muddled on until Winnie, one of the girls who was helping his mother, went down with flu. Within days Elvira had caught it too and took to her bed.

Ethel, the younger girl, was useless on her own. John took the week's holiday that was owing to him so that sauce would continue to be made. He had orders that needed to be filled. He found out for himself what hard work it was to carry all the water they needed up from the yard.

That gave him the push he needed. He set about finding better premises for his business. He wanted them nearby. He wanted a ground floor with running water and electricity; gas too would be useful. Within two days he found what he was looking for and started to negotiate about the rent.

His week off was flying past. It was no holiday. He worked longer hours than usual. He had to look after his mother too, up another flight of stairs, and shop and cook for them both.

His week's holiday was over and Mam was not much better. Certainly not well enough to take over the sauce-making. Neither was there any sign of Winnie coming back to work.

On Monday morning, John went in to the factory early. He expected to find Sarah alone at this time. For once he hadn't slept well. It had been another night of indecision.

Sarah smiled up at him. 'You look tired. I won't ask if

you've had a good holiday. It's been a working holiday for you?'

'It has that. Look, Sarah, I want you to train up somebody to do my job.' He saw her face fall.

'Heavens! You're not thinking of leaving us?'

'Not immediately. I don't want to walk out on you. Not until you've found someone else. I could take them round, break them in . . .'

'John! It's almost impossible to get a man of any sort. The young are conscripted at eighteen and the old . . . Every employer is chasing them, and most are too set in their ways.'

'Don't I know it? I've tried to get someone myself. I really need to stop working here if I'm to give my sauce its best chance.

'I have to do it, Sarah. I think I've found better premises. I've got to get on with things now.'

He saw the sympathy on her face. 'How's your mother? Better, I hope.'

'Not much. Still aches all over. She got up yesterday for the first time, but was back in bed after a few hours.'

'Do you want a bit more time off?'

'That would be a real help, thank you.'

'Take another week, see how she is then.'

'Very generous of you.'

She said: 'I hate the thought of you leaving for good.'

On Wednesday Winnie came back to work, but his mother was still a long way off being fit enough to work all day.

John had a great cauldron simmering over both burners of the oil stove he'd bought. He and Winnie were restacking the crates to make more room when he heard quick footsteps coming upstairs. Ethel was down in the yard, scrubbing out the utensils they'd used, and these feet were moving more quickly than hers ever did. He looked up and found Sarah had come to the door.

'I thought I'd call round and see how you're getting on.'

She looked so well groomed, so neatly dressed. It made John very conscious that his torn shirt was stained with sweat.

'Making headway. Can't complain.'

Wooden crates filled with bottles were stacked six high and six deep across one end of the room. They could barely move in the remaining space, even though they were now storing many of the ingredients up in their living quarters.

'No shortage of orders, by the look of things,' Sarah said.

'No shortage of orders, no shortage of work to be done. No shortage of anything but the time and energy to do it.' He pushed his thick straight hair off his forehead in a gesture of defeat.

'Oh dear. Is your mother feeling better?'

'She says yes, but she looks dreadful. It'll be another few days before she can start working again. But by Monday with a bit of luck.'

'I've brought her a jar of calf's-foot jelly. Ena, our cook, made it; she swears by it for invalids.'

'That's kind of you, thank you.' He couldn't drag his eyes from her face.

'I've been mulling things over,' she told him. 'I hate the idea of you leaving for good. I'll never get anybody to take your place, not while this war goes on. Why don't you think again about letting Percival's make your sauce? You wouldn't have to leave then. You wouldn't have to take on bigger premises.'

'And Mam wouldn't have to go on working,' John sighed.

'Think about it,' Sarah said quickly. 'Don't say anything just yet. You can be a bit hasty about things like this.'

He saw her eyes go to Winnie, who'd slumped down on a stool. 'Your girls can come and work for us; no need to worry about that angle.'

John took a deep breath. She didn't want him to leave! She

was offering him a second chance. He'd learned his lesson; he'd take it this time.

'Come upstairs to talk to Mam. I'll make a cup of tea.'

She smiled. 'No, John, thanks. I need to get back, and I want you to talk it over with Elvira.'

Two weeks later, Sarah breathed a sigh of satisfaction as she saw John add his signature to the agreement she'd asked Mr Masters to draw up for them. From now on Percival's would be making Scouser's Relish on a legal contract. John had tried out the market and made a good start; she hoped he'd feel they'd been fair with him.

She'd got what she wanted: John would stay on as their salesman. She'd tried to find a replacement for him, but no one had answered her advertisement. Percival's needed a good salesman to keep their customers happy. Their products wouldn't be as easy to sell once the war was over and supplies were back to normal.

'You're happy with this?' Sarah was folding the document back into its creases.

He sighed. 'Mixed feelings, I suppose.'

'Oh . . . Why?'

'All my big plans . . . I used to hold forth about them, didn't I? All my ideas for the future, they've come to naught.'

'I wouldn't put it like that . . .'

'How would you put it, Sarah? I've failed in what I set out to do.'

'Some of my plans have come to naught too.'

She didn't know what had possessed her to say such a thing; it almost guaranteed he'd bring up . . .

'You had no control over what happened to Toby.'

'No.'

There was a painful pause. Why couldn't she talk about Toby? She should be able to after all this time.

'Everything else has gone well for you. You've made a great success of the business. You must be pleased about that?'

'Yes. The sauce – it's going to be profitable for you this way. You've not failed.'

'Well, I'm glad to be rid of all the work it gave me. I left it too late to get much help from Mam. She can't work all day like that now. And I was delighted I didn't have to move everything to that building I was going to rent. That would have been a mammoth task.'

'It was a big job moving it to the factory,' Sarah smiled.

'There's still crates and crates of the finished sauce. The stuff that still has to mature.'

'I'll send a cart round again tomorrow. Your mother's there; she can show the men what they're to bring.'

'Yes.'

'You'll give up your old room once it's empty?'

'No. I'm going to spend the weekend white-washing it. Really cleaning it out. Then I'm going to move my bed down again. I liked having a room to myself.'

For Sarah, the last year of the war dragged on. It became clear that it was finally nearing its end. Everywhere people were weary of it, and totally sickened by the appalling number of those being killed and injured.

When the armistice was declared on the eleventh of November, Sarah rejoiced with the rest of the staff of Percival's Pickles. Soon the era of shortages would be over and hopefully they'd be able to go back to making genuine mango chutney.

Sarah had found the shortage of manpower the most difficult thing to cope with. She was very much looking forward to the return from the forces of the men who'd worked in the company.

Charlie Trumper had survived the whole four years with only minor injuries. Edward had served in France for only two months and would be coming home unscathed. That filled her with relief. She couldn't have borne it if he'd been killed too.

It was well into 1919 before Edward had a date for his discharge from the army. *The twenty-seventh of June*, he wrote. *I can't wait for it to come.*

Sarah was very much looking forward to having him back home. They all were.

From his window seat in the train, Edward watched the sun-drenched landscape flying past. He felt exultant; he was going home at last. Behind him was duty done, ahead lay what was to be his real life.

He felt hot and drowsy and half closed his eyes against the brilliance of the sun. The fields were baked brown; sheep were crowding into whatever shade they could find, cows were standing knee deep in streams and ponds. England was enjoying a heat wave.

Suddenly he noticed the railway lines had multiplied and now snaked in all directions; the open country had been left behind. The heat of the day was bouncing off slate roofs, brick and concrete. There were dusty streets of shops and houses, warehouses and factories. They were running through the outskirts of Liverpool.

Edward roused himself and looked at his watch. The train was on time. It was due into Lime Street at half past five.

Very convenient, Sarah had written. *I'll be able to meet you on my way home from the factory.*

He shivered with pleasure as he pulled his case down from the luggage rack and joined the hustle to leave the train.

It seemed a long trek up the platform and then he had to stand in line in front of the barrier. He could see Sarah behind the ticket collector watching the passengers as they streamed through. She caught sight of him and waved; her lips lifted into a welcoming smile. More mature now, she looked even more beautiful than he remembered. The next moment he was lifting her off her feet in a great bear hug.

'Welcome home, Edward. Lovely to have you back. I've really missed you, we all have.'

He sighed contentedly. 'It's lovely to be back, but isn't it hot?'

Sarah looked cool and bandbox fresh in a blue summer dress and straw hat. It was impossible to believe she'd worked all day in a stifling pickle factory.

'Unbearably hot at work today. It'll be better on the ferry.'

First they had to take a taxi down to the Pier Head. It felt no cooler there, heavy cloud was building up and the sun had gone. Edward mopped his brow. 'I think there's going to be a storm.'

From the top deck of the ferry, he leaned against the rail and took out his field glasses. 'Seems ages since I left home.'

'You won't need those when we get a little closer.'

'I can see your mother sitting out in the front garden.'

'She loves that. Says it revives her after a day in the factory. On hot evenings like this, we make a habit of putting the chairs out on the top lawn. Usually we can feel a bit of breeze from the river there.'

He could see garden chairs and sunshades out in several of the gardens along the Esplanade. The tide was full in and lapping gently on the narrow fringe of yellow sand.

'It's getting darker,' Sarah said as they strolled up the pier and turned on to the Esplanade. 'Definitely a storm coming.'

As they drew nearer, Edward saw Sarah's mother coming to meet them, her face all smiles. She swept him into a hug.

'So glad to have you back. So much easier for Sarah when there's two of you. We'll be handing back all your old jobs.'

'I hope I remember how to do them.'

'You will once you get back to the factory. It'll all come back to you.'

'You've done wonders, Sarah. I hated leaving everything to you.'

'Mam's been a great help. Couldn't have managed without her.'

'Now you're back, I'm hoping to work fewer hours,' said Maria.

'Mam, I've told you. Once Edward's settled you can stay home all the time if that's what you want.'

'I'd love that. A life of leisure. I'll queen it round the house and look after Dinah.'

All the doors and windows at Tides Reach were propped open. Edward shed his jacket and dropped his bags in the hall before striding to the kitchen to see Bessie and Ena. Sarah and her mother followed.

'We've decided to have a special supper to welcome you home,' Sarah told him. Ena was decorating a whole cold salmon. Soup simmered on the stove.

He sniffed. 'Nothing like the smell of good food,' and all the other familiar scents of home. He felt he belonged here.

Through the open window Edward could hear the children shouting to each other as they played in the back garden.

Sarah said: 'Come and say hello to Dinah. You'll hardly know her she's grown so much. She's four now and has started at nursery school.'

As he followed her out into the back garden, he heard the children shrieking with laughter but he couldn't see them. There had always been hedges of climbing roses dividing up the back garden. They were in full flower at the moment and provided a magnificent display of pink blooms. Their scent was heavy in the still air.

He heard another laugh and a small scream and two small bodies came hurtling round the hedge. A flying ball of red curls and pink cotton cannoned into his legs. He held on to the sturdy shoulders, keeping the child on her feet. She lifted her face and laughed up at him.

'Good gracious,' he gasped, and said to Sarah before he could stop himself: 'Isn't she like Gideon Burton? Spitting image.'

386

Rosemary had grown a lot in the time he'd been away. The baby roundness had left her cheeks leaving the unmistakable Burton likeness stamped on her face.

The three children were circling round him, noisy with excitement, but he clearly heard the snort of indignation from the other side of the rose hedge. He was saying hello to Rosemary when seconds later, Stepmother stormed round to confront him. He knew she'd heard his unguarded comment.

'Hello Stepmother.' She was disconcerted, he could see. Sarah was trying to cover the uncomfortable moment by lifting Dinah to show her off. Adam was clamouring for attention.

'Rosemary!' Claudia scolded loudly. 'Where is your sun hat? How many times must I tell you to keep it on?'

The child giggled. 'Too hot, Mama.' The sky was black now and thunder could be heard grumbling in the distance.

'What have you been saying to him, Sarah? You're always stirring up trouble for me.'

'Nothing. Nothing at all, we haven't mentioned you or Rosemary.'

Edward stepped forward to plant a kiss on his stepmother's soft plump cheek. She stood still and stiff, keeping well away from him. 'I'm sorry, Stepmother,' he said.

She gulped with distress. 'How dare you? How dare you goad me with that name?' He saw her lip quiver before she turned and hurried towards the conservatory door.

Sarah bit her lip. She whispered, 'Hadn't you better make your peace?' As she gathered the children and led them all back to her half of the house Edward felt the first large drops of rain.

'Stepmother.' He followed her. The temperature was oven hot under the glass but Claudia had gone into the music room which was now her sitting room. 'I didn't mean to upset you.'

'Why does everybody have to hound me? That name! You never miss a chance to have a dig at me.' Claudia had her hands over her ears. 'You've always been like this. It's a hateful thing to do, casting aspersions on me.'

'I'm sorry. I wasn't thinking. It was a shock to see Rosemary after all this time. She's grown so much more like her father.'

'She has not! Maurice was Rosemary's father – your father too. The auburn colouring is from my side of the family. Many of my forebears had hair like hers. What's so strange about that?'

Edward took a deep breath and said gently. 'The fact that you lose your temper over it. It shows an uneasy conscience. If what you say is true, it wouldn't bother you like this.'

'It is true.' Sudden lightning jagged across the sky, followed by a crack of thunder loud enough to make them both jump.

Claudia's hand clutched at her heart and her breathing rasped. She'd aged; put on a lot of weight and was now stout like her mother. She was no longer attractive. The over-ripe bloom Edward remembered so well had faded, leaving her face podgy and her discontent obvious.

'No, Stepmother. I know Rosemary is not my father's child. I watched you and Gideon Burton . . .'

'Stop it. I hate that name.'

'As a boy, I didn't like him either. Neither did Willie Lowther and Charlie Dowling. We waged war on him. You must remember that? We followed and watched you both, I hoped we'd catch you together. I wanted to disgrace you both in Father's eyes.'

'How dare you? I hardly knew him. My acquaintance was of the slightest.'

'Come now, Stepmother. I've apologised for what you overheard, but there's no point in denying the truth. I know you had an affair with Gideon Burton that lasted for years. I knew the moment I saw your daughter that Burton was the father. Rosemary is not my stepsister.'

'In the eyes of the law, she is.'

Edward sighed. 'Since my father's estate pays for her maintenance, perhaps yes, in the eyes of the law. But not in my eyes.

'You've been very lucky, Stepmother. Once Father died, everything changed. I had to put away my boyhood concerns and grow up in a hurry. I doubt if you'd have got away with this if Father had lived. Count your blessings.'

'What blessings?' Her face crumpled with anger. 'And I haven't got away with anything.'

'You've succeeded in keeping a comfortable home and a good income.'

'I want to get away from this dreadful half house. That's all it is, half a house and it isn't comfortable. I feel like a prisoner here. I want to get away from all of you. I hate your knowing looks, censoring me, blaming me, pointing accusing fingers at me. I loath the neighbours who cut me dead when we meet in the street. They won't speak to me. I hate everything about this place.'

Claudia collapsed on a sofa burying her face in a cushion. Edward retreated to the door telling himself he didn't really feel sorry for her. In his boyhood, Stepmother had exacted instant obedience from both Toby and him. She'd had power over them and she'd wielded it ruthlessly. He'd rebelled but it had got him nowhere.

But time and fate had stripped Stepmother of her power. He no longer needed to fight her.

The rain was drumming on the conservatory roof and washing down like a curtain across the door. Edward ducked through it and sprinted across the garden. His shirt was soaked when he reached the hall. He snatched up his bags which were still there and took them to his bedroom to change.

He found the children in the sitting room, quiet now as they listened to Mrs Hoxton reading them a story. When Sarah saw him in the doorway she got up and led him to what had been his father's study. 'Is Claudia all right?' she said.

389

'She's furious with me.'

'I was afraid she would be. She's very touchy, can't bear any mention of Gideon Burton.'

He was still curious. 'Does she ever see him now?'

'No, I don't think so. He hasn't lived at Beechwood House since he married, so we don't see him on the ferry any more. I've heard he's living in Rock Ferry.'

'Does Stepmother cause you any trouble? Come to the factory like she used to?'

'No, never, she's almost a recluse. She has a nursemaid who takes the children to school; she and Mrs Digby rarely go out.'

'Why not?'

'The neighbours don't want to know her. When she came out of mourning for your father, nobody came to her At Homes and it seemed she wasn't welcome at theirs. She doesn't have them any more.'

'Does anybody?'

'Not so much these days. Claudia can be very strange. She makes Rosemary wear a hat all the time. Always every strand of that lovely red hair is tucked under it out of sight. It's as though she can't bear to have it seen by anyone.'

'Poor Rosemary.'

'I have her here with Dinah as often as I can. Adam too. He's a lovely little boy, full of energy and bounce.'

The rain had eased. Edward could hear the children scampering up the hall.

'Mam's sending them back to Claudia. It's time for supper, come on, you must be hungry.'

'Are we being too hard on Stepmother?' Edward had come home in such high spirits, he mustn't let her upset him.

Sarah smiled broadly. 'I've schooled myself not to be too sympathetic. Remember that saying? "Be sure your sins will find you out". It's what I'd call true justice.'

He chuckled. 'Stepmother hasn't been able to hide her sins.'

★　　★　　★

390

As Sarah had expected, her relationship with Edward was very different from what it had been before he was called up. He played with Adam and took an interest in Dinah and Rosemary. They went for brisk walks on Sunday afternoons in the cold of February, and they travelled together to the factory every day, but his intense feelings for her and the close bonds they'd forged were gone.

Eighteen months in the army had broadened Edward's shoulders and given him confidence and maturity. He'd always looked older than his years. Now at nearly twenty he looked more like his father than ever. Except that there was a more kindly look about Edward that his father had never had, and Sarah thought she could see a likeness to Toby too.

He was settling back into the work of the company very quickly. Sarah pushed him to take over responsibility for Scousers's Relish. It was proving profitable both for them and for John. Despite the shortages, she'd always managed to buy the ingredients it needed.

It came as something of a surprise to Sarah to find Edward taking an interest in Louise Corbishley, the typist she'd hired to take over some of the office work when he was called up.

He was soon taking her to cinemas and theatres, and before long he said he'd like to ask her over to Tides Reach for Sunday lunch.

'She's a lovely girl,' Mam told him. 'You could do a lot worse. And isn't she like our Sarah to look at?'

Within six months he was talking of marrying Louise. Sarah was pleased, and expected him to bring her to live at Tides Reach too.

'No,' Edward said. 'We'll be married next spring when Louise will be twenty-one. That'll give us plenty of time to find a small house of our own.'

'I don't like to think of you living anywhere else,' Sarah said. 'You're a Percival by birth.'

'There's a limit to the number of times a house can be split.'

'Edward, Claudia wants to get away. Why not let her find the small house? Then you can live in her part.'

He felt a surge of pleasure. 'What a wonderful idea! Stepmother would surely see that as a favour.'

'Of course.'

'And she'd feel better and perhaps be more normal if she could live further away where no one knows about Gideon Burton.'

Sarah was smiling up at him. 'Yes, and I'd much rather have you and Louise living here with us.'

It made Sarah feel old, though she was still only twenty-three. She could see herself going on working at the pickle factory for many decades yet, a widow bringing up her daughter. She was beginning to feel she wasn't getting enough from life.

Chapter Twenty-eight

Armistice Day 1919

As the first anniversary of the end of the war drew close, the newspapers were filled with articles recalling the horrors. Talk of it was on everybody's lips. Several men now back working in the pickle factory had personal memories of the trenches, many more had lost relatives and friends.

Sarah had told herself many times that she was over the trauma of Toby's death, but for her, the approach of Armistice Day was bringing it all back into focus.

She was thinking of Toby as she went home with Edward one cold, dark evening. From the landing stage, she could see they'd have to wait a while for their boat; it was just leaving New Ferry Pier. Much nearer was a brightly lit ferry, churning up a creamy bow wave as it came across the river from Seacombe.

Edward was watching it too. 'It's the *Royal Daffodil*.'

Sarah had seen it many times as she'd waited here. It never failed to remind her that Toby had crossed the Channel to fight in France on a Wallasey ferry called the *Daffodil*. It hadn't been this boat, for which she was thankful. She couldn't bear anything that reminded her of Toby's last days. The *Daffodil* had been this boat's predecessor, sold off before the war had started.

The *Royal Daffodil* and her sister ship the *Iris* had been requisitioned by the Government half-way through the war and had served in operations with the navy at Zeebrugge. They'd come back to the Mersey showing the scars of battle, but these were quickly made good and the vessels were rechristened the *Royal Daffodil* and the *Royal Iris* to honour them for the part they'd played in winning the war.

Edward started to tell her the story. He'd heard it while stationed in Aldershot and was proud of the role of the Mersey ferries. Sarah couldn't tell him it had been emblazoned with pride on the front pages of the local newspapers. For years she'd wanted to turn her back on anything that had the remotest connection with Toby's death. Even now it brought back all the feelings of loss and anger, frustration and grief that she'd felt at the time.

There was no peace when she reached home. Dinah, now four years old, was romping round the house with Rosemary and Adam, playing some noisy game. Edward joined in straight away. Sarah went to her bedroom. She was not in the mood for boisterous games.

She sat on her bed; really she wasn't in the mood for anything. Dinah's excited voice became more distant and Sarah got to her feet to put away the coat she'd been wearing. She needed a warmer one; winter was beginning to bite. She reached into her wardrobe to pull out a navy blue melton she hadn't worn since last year and dislodged a package. It fell out on the floor.

The sight of it made her cringe. It was the parcel of Toby's belongings that she'd received on her nineteenth birthday. She hadn't been able to look at the contents then, but she hadn't retied the string and now they were all spread out across her floor.

She laid her heavy winter coat across her bed and told herself she was stronger now; it was silly to feel revulsion. These were the things Toby had had with him at the time. She'd thought them pathetically few and shabby then; now they looked worse. She sank down on her bed and let her eyes travel over the three well-thumbed novels, their wedding photograph inside a leather folder, the large packet of unused envelopes. Her eyes came to rest on a loose-leaf notebook.

When she'd first opened the parcel, it had been such a shock to see his pen and his gloves and his brush and comb that she hadn't been able to think.

She'd forgotten that for months he'd been using a loose-leaf notebook as a sort of diary, and sending her the pages as and when he'd written them. She hadn't looked for anything like that at the time. Now she snatched the book up eagerly and found several pages covered with his handwriting. Feeling slightly sick, she lay down on her bed to read them.

April 31st, 1915

Last night I took a trip down to the quay at Le Havre. Just to get the layout of the place. The *Daffodil* was still tied up unloading stores and equipment with military personnel milling all round it. I didn't want to be seen watching them, so I went across the road to a café bar and sat outside at a table on the pavement. The road is busy and quite wide here and I could watch the boat in comfort.

I came to the conclusion that getting on wouldn't be too difficult if I timed it right. I know the layout of the boat like the back of my hand – well, the public part anyway. I'd have to keep out of sight, but there aren't many places to hide. Only the ordinary saloon and the smoking saloon which both have open-slatted seats fixed round the walls. I decided the best place would be on the top deck out in the open. I could dodge round the funnel and the seats if I had to, especially if it were dark.

I was drinking a cup of coffee when I had what I thought was a stroke of luck. Seven fusiliers from the Green Howards came to the next table and ordered beer. They were going on leave and had been given warrants for the ferry but had an hour or so to kill. I was totally envious, I can tell you. I got talking to them and decided my best chance would be to tag on to them and board straight away even though I had nothing with me.

I didn't say anything about going with them; they were all well sozzled by then and in soaring spirits. When they got up to go, I just followed on behind and getting on board couldn't have been easier; nobody was checking. They shared their sandwiches with me, bully beef of course, and I even managed to kip down for a few hours. I knew getting off at Southampton might not be so easy, so I hung back to see what would happen. There were military police at the bottom of the gangway and I thought I could see more at the dock gates. I lost my cool then, I can tell you.

The only other way off was over the side of the boat and then to swim for it. I'd have had to swim a long way to get out of the dock, and I've never been much good at it. Without my gammy leg I might have stripped off and tried, but as it was I decided to tag on behind the Green Howards again. They had their leave passes and travel warrants checked, and of course I didn't have the paperwork. I tried to bluff my way through. I thought my hospital blues would help, but it didn't work. The military police kept me back, took me to their guardhouse. Eventually I was placed under arrest. It was all very low key and quietly done and I found myself going back on the *Daffodil* under escort.

I expected to be taken back to the château to continue my convalescence – after all, I still had two more weeks of rest – but the corporal escorting me said he'd been ordered to take me straight back to my unit at Armentières. I thought that very unfair and was angry.

I did the wrong thing again, Sarah. I cracked my fist into my escort's face and ran for it. The leg wasn't up to it; I was recaptured two hours later.

I expect you know what's going to happen now as well as I do. I'm heading for another court martial.

May 3rd, 1915

Oh God, Sarah, I've done it this time. I've been charged with striking a senior officer and two counts of desertion. I need Lieutenant Nelson to speak for me, I could trust him to do his best, but he was badly wounded last month, a chest wound, and I've heard he's since died of his wounds. I don't much like Captain Morris who has been given the job instead, and worse, I don't think he likes me.

I can't hide it from you that I'm very worried this time. Two suspended sentences, for desertion and a whole load of other sins.

May 6th

Found guilty and sentenced to death. That was yesterday but nobody told me until this morning. It's a bit worrying but there's a good chance it'll be commuted to something like penal servitude for life. Then that can be suspended so I can do my turn in the front line again. It's happened before, hasn't it? There are mitigating circumstances; I was on sick leave. It's not as though I was deserting from the trenches. I wasn't well enough to fight anyway. I believe the CO has recommended me for mercy; that will help too.

May 8th

I've just been told that my sentence has been confirmed. It's not easy to take in. No mercy after all for me. There's nothing more I can hope for. I'm to be shot before dawn tomorrow. At half past five precisely. It's all going to happen very quickly, I want to stop time moving on. I'm so sorry, Sarah. So much better for you if I could have died a hero. Don't think badly

397

of me. I wanted so much to see you again, and our new baby. Even now I can't see what's so very wrong about what I did. I know this must upset you and I wouldn't hurt you for the world. I love you very much. There's nothing I want more than to be a real husband to you and have years and years to spend with you. Instead I've done this, to make you ashamed of me.

I'm glad Father isn't alive to see it. He'd definitely be very ashamed of me now. He always said I was hot-headed and never made the right decisions. It seems he was right.

I do very much regret that I'll not see you again, not hear your voice or see your wide smile. And most of all, I regret dying before I even see my daughter. If only I'd been caught coming back . . . It all seems very cruel, but I'll think of you and Dinah when the time comes, and do my best to die with dignity.

Try not to think ill of me. Goodbye, my beloved.

The tears were flooding down Sarah's face. Toby's letters brought him so vividly before her eyes. His innocent child's face was smiling at her. It was as though he'd been speaking to her. At last she knew the full story and he'd said goodbye.

She would have liked to tell him she wasn't ashamed of him. What he'd done, he'd done because he loved her and wanted to see her. He'd died bravely, and she was proud of that.

It took immense courage to think of others when he was facing death. To think of the effect his actions would have on her. That he wanted to die with dignity made her tears fall again.

Should she tell Edward? He had a right to know, but she couldn't bring herself to do it. She wanted him to think of his brother as a hero. It might tarnish Toby's image for him if he knew.

On Remembrance Sunday, Edward took Maria, Sarah and Dinah to the church he and Toby had attended throughout their childhood. Sarah sat feeling the hard pew pressing against her shoulders, thinking of Toby.

She felt there were two difficult days in the year to get through: May the ninth, the day of Toby's death; and the eleventh of November, Remembrance Day. Two anniversaries she couldn't put behind her.

Today she was full of emotion. Her tears had not been far away even before the sermon. The vicar told them that Remembrance Day was a time for the nation to mourn their soldiers killed in battle. He reminded them of what they owed to the young men who had laid down their lives for King and country. Slowly and solemnly, he read out the list of those from the parish who had laid down their lives. Toby's name was amongst them.

'A day to remember them with pride,' he said.

He went on to extol their courage at making the supreme sacrifice. The thought of Toby being killed by his own comrades stuck in Sarah's throat. Perhaps if they hadn't shot him at dawn he would have gone on to lay down his life for his country. He hadn't been given the chance.

Together they observed the two minutes' silence. Sarah thought of the early months of the war; enchanting, terrible months, full of shocks and anxieties, delights and ecstasies, and then the appalling end. The best months of her life, and also the worst. Toby was gone, but it seemed on days like this that he was here beside her.

During their usual large Sunday lunch, Edward said:

'Remembrance Day will always make me think of Toby. Make me think his death was worthwhile after all.'

Sarah had to choke back her distress, but she knew she was doing the right thing keeping the truth from him. When they got up from the table, she asked her mother to take care of Dinah. She wanted to be alone for a little while; she wanted to go to the factory. She made the excuse that she had an urgent job to do.

Although Tides Reach had been Toby's home, somehow his presence seemed to linger more in the factory. Perhaps that was because she'd seen him there more often than she had at home.

The factory was still and cold on this dark November afternoon. She walked slowly through the silent dark caverns, saying her own final goodbye to Toby. His presence was almost tangible today in this deserted place.

She was in the bottling room when the slam of the outside door made her jump. Had she left it open? She didn't think so. She thought she could hear footsteps. She went to see who it was.

She gasped with relief when she found John Ferry blinking in the gloom. He had a key of his own so that he might come and go.

He said: 'The door was unlocked. I wondered if Trumper had forgotten to lock it.'

'No.' They were staring at each other.

'I came to get some samples.' He was carrying his case. 'I'm off to Manchester in the morning and I want to catch an early train.'

Sarah couldn't tell him why she was here; it would be too difficult to explain. Outside she could hear the Boys' Brigade band playing 'It's a Long Way to Tipperary' as they marched through the streets.

'You must be very proud of Toby,' John said. His dark eyes glistened with intensity. 'He died a hero.'

She gasped audibly and felt the tears welling in her eyes.

'No,' she choked, and she knew she sounded anguished.

'Poor Sarah.' His voice was soft with sympathy. 'You're feeling a bit low today; that's understandable.'

'Very low.' She shook her head. 'But you don't understand.'

His arms came round her, pulling her against him in a comforting hug. John had always known how to make her feel safe.

'All this makes you remember Toby. It's bound to.'

The tears were coming now, and nothing could stop them. He was pressing his handkerchief into her hand.

'I'm sorry,' she whispered. His tweed coat was rough against her face.

'No need to be.' She felt his lips brush against her temple. For months she'd been feeling lonely and isolated and miserable.

He was smiling down at her. 'Toby would be flattered to find you grieving for him like this. Years after . . . Anybody would be, but he'd rather see you smile. He wouldn't want you to be unhappy.'

'I know.' She blew her nose. 'He was that sort.'

'Shook his own problems off like a dog shakes off raindrops. Remembrance Day brings it all back?'

She nodded. 'And all the talk of heroes. And how proud we should be of them.'

'We're all proud of Toby. Aren't you?'

His end was there in her mind, harsh beyond words. Hauntingly horrible. 'Yes. In a funny sort of way.'

She could feel John's affection, his warmth. A sudden impulse made her add: 'He was shot, John.'

She stepped back to see how he was taking it, and his eyes met hers. She saw the question there. He knew she was trying to tell him something important, but of course millions of young men had been shot.

She added in a little rush: 'Killed by our own side. Shot at dawn. It was all so awful, I couldn't tell anyone.'

His mouth was open. She could see from his face, by the way it was working, that he could hardly take it in.

'You mean . . . ?'

She'd had to say it. Had to share the terrible secret with somebody. 'Such a terrible way to die. Such a dreadful waste.'

401

He understood now. 'My God! Why? What did he do?'

'Toby came home to marry me . . . Well, you know.' Her voice was a whisper. 'He tried to come again to see Dinah when she was born. He was on sick leave but they called him a deserter. He was court-martialled; they gave him the death sentence.'

'Christ!' His arms were reaching for her again. Sarah went into them with a sob.

'I'm always doing this,' she choked. 'Crying on your shoulder.'

She felt his arms tighten round her. 'We all have to have someone.'

His mouth touched hers gently, so she could feel the softness of his lips. His breath was hot against her cheek. She could feel the warmth of his body spreading through her, drying her tears.

He moved his head back. At a distance of three inches, she could see his eyes searching her face.

'I love you, Sarah. I've always loved you. I've never been able to think of anybody else.'

The rush of emotion she felt took her by surprise, making her cling tighter. She'd loved him once. She'd hated fighting with him. She should never have cut herself off from him as she had.

An hour later, they were still in the office. Sarah had spilled out all she knew about Toby's last days. It was an emotional purge, and already she was beginning to feel steadier.

'I've bottled it up inside me all this time. Never breathed a word to anybody. The army tried to keep it from me, hush it all up, but Toby wouldn't have that. He wanted me to know the truth.'

'A burden for you to carry.'

She gulped. 'I used to write to him every day.'

'I know.'

'I told him I wanted to know everything that happened to him. I didn't want him to brush bad things away and pretend all was well if it wasn't. But I didn't expect anything like this.'

He said gently: 'What about Edward? You didn't tell him?'

'He was only sixteen at the time. I knew that unless the war ended first, he'd be conscripted when he was eighteen. How would he have felt then, knowing what the army had done to his brother?'

'Those days are long since over.'

'I didn't want anybody to think ill of Toby. Still don't. He did everything right for me.'

'They won't. We all know what he was like. But Edward's a grown man now. What was right then isn't necessarily right now.'

Sarah shook her head. 'He thinks the world of his brother. I want him to go on doing that.'

'If no one else, you should have told your mother. Talked about it.'

'How could I? I'd have felt I was letting him down. Nobody speaks ill of the dead. I felt locked in with a dreadful secret.'

It had made her feel she couldn't get on with her life. When Toby had enlisted, she'd thrown herself heart and soul into the business for his sake. It had become automatic; she'd gone on attending to the duties she'd taken over even after Toby had been shot.

'You won't say anything here, will you? I don't want this to go round the factory.'

'Of course not.'

'And I don't want Dinah to know. I often talk to her about her father. She thinks he's wonderful and is so proud of him. I couldn't tell her, not ever. Or Edward. I don't want to change the way any of them think of Toby.'

She could see tears glistening in John's eyes, though he didn't let them fall.

'I'm glad you've told me.' He gave her another hug. 'You needed to talk about it, get it off your chest.'

'Poor Toby, you didn't like him much. Not like everybody else.'

John sighed. 'I envied him. No, it was more than that. I was downright jealous of him. If my father had owned a business like his, I'd have done anything to make it grow. Toby never seemed serious; I thought he played at it. Then he took you from me. I thought he'd had the life of Riley. Everything he ever wanted, handed to him on a plate.'

Sarah swallowed hard. 'At the end, everything was taken from him. Very cruelly. I thought the secret would be safe if I told no one at all.'

Her tears had dried up now that she'd talked it through. 'But now I've told you.'

'Toby's secret is safe with me,' he said, and she knew that was true. She'd always been able to trust John.

For the first time she wanted to put the years she'd spent with Toby behind her. She felt that at last she could. She'd said goodbye to him now.

He'd stayed in her mind, drawn her away from everybody else. When she'd found out how he'd died, something in her had died too. Killed by the brutality of the army that had turned against him.

She hadn't allowed herself to feel love again. Hadn't wanted it. And she'd bottled up inside her the awful details of Toby's death. To get them out and talk about them to John had brought her such a sense of release.

'I'll make us some tea,' she said now, but when it was ready she found that what little milk remained in the office had gone sour.

'Come home with me,' John said. 'I'll make you some tea there.'

She began to drink hers black. 'Better not. Mam will be wondering where I am. I'd rather you came home with me.'

'I've wanted to for ages.'

'Have you? Come and have supper with us.'

'Will there be enough? I mean, I'm not expected.'

'Bessie and Ena have a half-day off on Sundays and leave a cold supper out on the sideboard for us. Since the war ended, there's always been more than enough.'

'I'd love to. I've always wanted to see where you live. See where you spend your time when you aren't at work. Meet your daughter.'

'Dinah's four; she's growing up.'

'I've never seen her.'

'Really?' She hadn't realised she'd shut John out to that degree. She'd shut everyone out, except her family.

It was getting dark when they left the factory. They had to call in to see Elvira on the way. John wanted to let her know he wouldn't be back for supper.

'Hello, Sarah.' There was total surprise on Elvira's face to see them together again. 'Come and sit by the fire and get warm.'

Sarah looked round what had been her old home. How her life had changed. How they'd all changed. John took her arm.

'We've a lot of time to make up, Mam. We'll be on our way.'

It was a raw evening and the wind was icy against Sarah's face. It made them step out briskly as they went down to the Pier Head. It was even colder out on the river. The few passengers on the ferry made straight for the saloon, but Sarah and John stayed up on the deserted deck. John drew her back into the shadows and pulled her close to the vents that gushed hot air from the engine room.

'You know how I feel about you,' he said. 'You've always known what I want.' His voice was being snatched away by the icy wind, and she moved closer to hear him.

'We always talked of getting married. Now I don't know how I dare ask you.'

'What d'you mean? You've always dared to go after what you want.'

'You're better placed than I am. You're my boss.'

Sarah smiled. 'There's Scouser's Relish.'

'Nothing compared with what you own.'

'You needn't worry about that. With all my worldly goods I thee endow. Toby took that literally and so shall I. When we're married, it'll be share and share alike. With everything.'

He kissed her, gentle, comforting kisses that made her feel better.

'It's such a long time since you last did this.' Sarah looked back to those far-off days; a time, it seemed, without worry.

Mam had always thought John was right for her. He was, even if she hadn't realised it then. Now their love would light the path through the years ahead.

Merseyside Girls

Anne Baker

Nancy, Amy and Katie Siddons are three of the prettiest nurses south of the Mersey. They've been brought up to respect their elders and uphold family honour at all times. Then sweet, naïve Katie falls pregnant, bringing shame upon the family's name.

Alec Siddons, a local police constable, cannot and will not forgive his daughter for her immoral behaviour. But Katie isn't the only one with troubles ahead. Amy is in love with her cousin Paul, but owing to a family feud the mere mention of his name is forbidden in her father's presence; and Nancy is eager to wed her fiancé Stan before the Second World War takes him away.

With the outbreak of war, the three sisters offer each other comfort and support. Their mother, meanwhile, is battling with painful memories of the past, and their father lives in dread that his own dark secrets will be revealed. As the war takes its toll on the Merseyside girls they learn that few things in life are more precious than honesty, love and forgiveness.

0 7472 5040 5

HEADLINE

A Mersey Duet

Anne Baker

When Elsa Gripper dies in childbirth on Christmas Eve, 1912, her grief-stricken husband is unable to cope with his two newborn daughters, Lucy and Patsy, so the twins are separated.

Elsa's parents, who run a highly successful business, Mersey Antiques, take Lucy home and she grows up spoiled and pampered with no interest in the family firm. Patsy has a more down-to-earth upbringing, living with their father and other grandmother above the Railway Hotel. And through further tragedy she learns to be responsible from an early age. Then Patsy is invited to work at Mersey Antiques, which she hopes will bring her closer to Lucy. But it is to take a series of dramatic events before they are drawn together . . .

'A stirring tale of romance and passion, poverty and ambition . . . everything from seduction to murder, from forbidden love to revenge' *Liverpool Echo*

'Highly observant writing style . . . a compelling book that you just don't want to put down' *Southport Visitor*

0 7472 5320 X

HEADLINE

Now you can buy any of these other bestselling books by **Anne Baker** from your bookshop or *direct from her publisher*.

FREE P&P AND UK DELIVERY
(Overseas and Ireland £3.50 per book)

Nobody's Child	£5.99
Legacy of Sins	£5.99
Liverpool Lies	£5.99
The Price of Love	£5.99
With a Little Luck	£5.99
A Liverpool Lullaby	£6.99
Mersey Maids	£5.99
A Mersey Duet	£6.99
Moonlight on the Mersey	£6.99
Merseyside Girls	£5.99
Paradise Parade	£5.99
Like Father Like Daughter	£5.99

TO ORDER SIMPLY CALL THIS NUMBER

01235 400 414

or e-mail orders@bookpoint.co.uk

Prices and availability subject to change without notice.